Everyone loves Paige Toon!
Have you read them all?

If You Could Go Anywhere
'Heart-warming, wistful and full of joy' **Lindsey Kelk**

'Warm, inspiring, like a holiday mood in
book form' **Mhairi McFarlane**

One Perfect Christmas and Other Stories
'Paige introduces us to characters old and new in this witty,
heartfelt and romantic collection of short stories' *My Weekly*

'Like a delectable Boxing Day buffet, this tasty collection
reunites some much-loved characters from Toon's fifteen
novels in nine never-before-printed short stories' *Heat*

Five Years From Now
'Filled with warmth and poignancy, *Five Years From
Now* is a page turner and a delight' **Catherine Isaac**

'Full of living-in-the-moment and what-might-have-been
contrasts, this tender read pulls at the heartstrings' *Fabulous*

The Last Piece of My Heart
'Wonderfully heartfelt... her best book yet!' *Heat*

'A gorgeous, warm novel' **Adele Parks**

Also by Paige Toon

Lucy in the Sky
Johnny Be Good
Chasing Daisy
Pictures of Lily
Baby Be Mine
One Perfect Summer
One Perfect Christmas (eBook short story)
The Longest Holiday
Johnny's Girl (eBook short story)
Thirteen Weddings
The Sun in Her Eyes
The One We Fell in Love With
The Last Piece of My Heart
A Christmas Wedding (eBook short story)
Five Years From Now
One Perfect Christmas and Other Stories
If You Could Go Anywhere

Young Adult

The Accidental Life of Jessie Jefferson
I Knew You Were Trouble
All About the Hype

paige toon

the minute I saw you

**SIMON &
SCHUSTER**

London · New York · Sydney · Toronto · New Delhi

First published in Great Britain by Simon & Schuster UK Ltd, 2020

Copyright © Paige Toon, 2020

The right of Paige Toon to be identified as author
of this work has been asserted in accordance with the
Copyright, Designs and Patents Act, 1988.

1 3 5 7 9 10 8 6 4 2

Simon & Schuster UK Ltd
1st Floor
222 Gray's Inn Road
London WC1X 8HB

Simon & Schuster Australia, Sydney
Simon & Schuster India, New Delhi

www.simonandschuster.co.uk
www.simonandschuster.com.au
www.simonandschuster.co.in

A CIP catalogue record for this book
is available from the British Library

Paperback ISBN: 978-1-4711-7948-8
eBook ISBN: 978-1-4711-7949-5
Audio ISBN: 978-1-4711-8496-3

This book is a work of fiction. Names, characters, places and
incidents are either a product of the author's imagination or are
used fictitiously. Any resemblance to actual people living
or dead, events or locales is entirely coincidental.

Typeset in Bembo by M Rules
Printed and bound by CPI Group (UK) Ltd, Croydon, CR0 4YY

MIX
Paper from
responsible sources
FSC® C020471
www.fsc.org

For our lovely friends, Georgie and Lewis Barnes.
When's our next Grantchester pub crawl and can we
continue to pretend it's research?

Chapter 1

Hello, hello…

There's a good-looking man standing on the pavement outside the window. He's talking on his mobile and his eyes are hidden behind sunglasses, but a slight frown is detectable on his brow.

When he turns toward the window, I see that his short dark hair is longer on top and sun-lightened to more of a caramel shade. It's swept back from his forehead in a retro almost-fifties style.

He ends the call, shoves his phone into his pocket and disappears from view, only to reappear a second later when he pushes open the door to the shop.

'Good morning!' Abbey chirps, and we both sit up straighter as he takes off his sunglasses. 'How can we help you?'

'I have an appointment at eleven forty-five.'

While Abbey checks her desktop screen, he looks my way, a polite smile fixed in place.

'Hello,' I say, tucking a stray lock of hair behind my ear.

'Hi,' he replies, his folded sunglasses swinging from between the tips of his thumb and forefinger.

Blue eyes…

'Sonny Denton?' Abbey asks, snapping his attention back to her.

'Yes,' he confirms.

Sonny? His name is retro too.

'It's been over two years since your last eye test?'

'Must be.'

'Can I get you to fill out this form and check your details?' She hands over a clipboard with paperwork attached, before adding, with a nod in my direction: 'Hannah, our dispensing optician, will be with you shortly.'

I indicate the black leather seat inside the bay window opposite my desk. In the time it takes for him to walk the few metres across the room and sit down, Abbey and I have furtively cast each other cheeky grins.

That's the last time I'll dare to look at her for a while. A similarly hot client came in earlier this week and she enthusiastically licked her lips the moment his back was turned. Unfortunately, he spun around to ask her something, catching her in the act. I nearly choked on my tea.

Thankfully, this all went over the boss's head. Umeko, the optometrist, owns this place. She's kind and clever and has high standards that, quite understandably, she expects us to maintain. I've only been here for a few weeks so I'd rather not lose my job just yet, thanks.

It's not uncommon for young people to come in here – Umeko's is a small independent practice with a stylish (albeit slightly on-the-pricey side) range of eyewear that tends to appeal to a more designery crowd. We're based in Newnham, a suburb of Cambridge and only a short walk south-west of the city centre. Our road and the ones nearby are lined with neat Victorian terraced houses, but this is a semi-detached red-brick corner building that we share with the pharmacy next door. There's a lovely little delicatessen across the road and a hairdresser a few doors down. It's a nice part of town and only a twenty-five-minute walk from the village of Grantchester, where I'm currently living.

Abbey and I spend most of our working days in the bright and airy front room. Abbey's desk is up against the back wall. My desk is to the right, separated from Abbey by a central corridor and facing the bay window. Glasses displays are dotted all around.

Along the corridor are two consultation rooms, one occupied by Umeko. It's my job to carry out pre-screening tests in the second room before handing clients over to Umeko for their main consultation. It's where we'll be headed as soon as Sonny has finished filling out his form.

'All set?' I ask as he gets to his feet.

'Yep.'

I take the clipboard, giving it a quick once-over before glancing up at him. 'You're a photographer?'

'Yes.'

He's tall, but not toweringly so – six foot? A good head-height higher than me, and he's wearing a denim shirt layered over a white T-shirt with slim-fitting charcoal-grey chinos.

'That's cool,' I comment, noting two other important pieces of information: one, he lives in Barton, which is a ten-minute drive away, tops; and two, his date of birth places him at thirty-two. 'We've got a couple of tests to do before you go through to Umeko. I'm sure you remember how it goes from the last time you were here.'

Avoiding Abbey's gaze – I'm not taking any chances – I lead him down the corridor and into the first room on our right, inhaling a hint of spicy aftershave as he passes by.

'Are you wearing contacts today?'

'Yes, monthlies. I brought solution with me.'

'Great. Can you take them out?'

His eyes are *so* blue. Azure blue, I'd call them. They're startling against his dark lashes.

'Have a seat and pop your chin on the rest,' I say when he's ready.

After taking pictures of the back of each eye, we switch to a second multifunctional machine so I can do a quick reading of his prescription.

'Have you worked here long?' he asks.

'Only a few weeks.'

'What happened to Mr Grumpy?'

He's leaning back in his chair, smirking and gently swivelling from left to right.

'If you're talking about Bernard – and I wouldn't like to presume – then he's moved up to Scotland to be closer to his ailing parents.'

He grins. 'Can't say I'll miss his halitosis.'

'You haven't got up close and personal with me yet.'

No, no.

No, no, no, no, no.

Those words did not just leave my lips.

Except, from the look on his face, it appears that they did. His eyes have widened, not to mention his grin.

'I did *not* mean that the way it sounded.'

He laughs with delight, and despite my embarrassment, the sound makes me feel jittery.

'One last test,' I say through gritted teeth.

'Is this the videogame one?' he asks hopefully, sitting up straighter.

'You're thinking of the visual fields test.'

'Yeah, you press a button every time a wiggly line appears around the edges.'

'All the boys like that one,' I say with a smile. 'But no, I'm afraid it's the pressure test.' It assesses for risk of developing glaucoma. I lower the machine into its tonometer setting. 'We'll start with your right eye. Keep looking straight ahead with your eyes wide open.'

He flinches as three puffs of air are blasted into each eye. The procedure doesn't hurt, but it's not particularly pleasant either.

'That's me done for a bit.' I gather together the printouts with the retinal images and test results. 'I'll go and see if Umeko is ready for you. Are you okay to wait here for a moment?'

'Yep.'

Umeko is sitting at her desk, tapping away at her keyboard.

'Sonny Denton is here to see you,' I tell her.

'Aah, Sonny,' she says with a smile, taking the paperwork from me.

'Has he been a client for long?' I try not to sound too interested.

'Since he was a teenager,' she replies, scanning the information before her. 'His father does our accounts,' she adds.

Umeko has been living in the UK for going on forty years now, but her Japanese accent has not faded much with time. Though she's in her early sixties, she looks a good ten years younger with smooth, unlined skin and barely a grey strand to be found amongst her jet-black locks. She always wears her hair in a sleek topknot at work, but I've seen her socially on many occasions and when it's loose it comes halfway down her back.

It's like mine in that respect, except where her hair is as straight as a pin, mine is wavy: light-brown and streaked with natural highlights. I also wear it up for work, but it's a messy bun at the best of times. Sleek topknot it ain't.

After listening to Sonny and Umeko greet each other like old friends, I head back to my desk and flash Abbey a grin. She picks up a magazine and fans her face, making the wispy strawberry-blond strands that have fallen out of her high ponytail fly away from her round cherub face.

'*How* hot?' she whispers.

'Shh,' I reply, but I'm grinning. 'Apparently he's been coming here for years. You've not seen him before?'

'No.'

She's only been here for twelve months so that figures.

Umeko's previous practice manager was a bossy matronly type who took retirement at the age of fifty-three. She trained Abbey up before she left. Abbey worked alongside Bernard and wasn't sad to see the back of him. She thinks it's no coincidence that Umeko went on to hire me, a second younger, livelier member of staff – Abbey's twenty-six and I'm twenty-seven.

I continue filing NHS forms, but it's hard to get stuck into it when I know Sonny won't be with Umeko for long.

Sure enough, he's done in fifteen minutes.

Umeko sees him to the front room. 'Have a wander, see what you like the look of,' she encourages.

'Can I get you a tea or coffee?' I ask him. 'Latte? Cappuccino?'

We have a fancy coffee machine in the kitchen.

'A latte would be great,' he replies.

Umeko and I have a quick handover chat while I make his drink. It's all very straightforward – he mostly wears contact lenses but prefers to use glasses when he's photo editing at his computer, sometimes late into the night.

When I return, Sonny is trying on a pair of metal-framed glasses in front of the mirror.

'I like those,' Abbey says as I place his coffee on my desk.

'They're a bit light in colour, I think,' he replies. 'A bit too bling.'

'Are you after metal frames?' I ask.

'Yeah, but I'd prefer more of a mid–gunmetal shade.'

'Have a look at the Kilsgaards,' I suggest, directing him towards a stand hosting several of the Danish brand.

'This is exactly the colour I was talking about.' He picks up a pair and puts them on, checking his reflection.

'They look great,' Abbey remarks admiringly.

'They do,' I agree. 'You should try these too.' I pass him a pair, not wanting him to feel pressured into deciding too quickly.

We encourage him to peruse the other stands, but he ends up going back to the Kilsgaards, settling on the first pair he tried on.

'I've got to nip to my sister's.' Abbey reminds me. Her sister is having work done on her house nearby and Abbey promised to let one of the tradesmen in. 'Can I get you another coffee before I go?' she offers as Sonny and I head over to my desk together.

'No thanks, this one is still warm,' he replies, taking a sip.

'Do you want to put those on again,' I suggest when Abbey has left, turning the small mirror on my desk towards him. 'They really suit you,' I reiterate. Most of what he tried on did, to be fair. 'Can I check the fit?'

'Sure.'

He leans closer to me across the narrow desk space. He smells *amazing*.

There's the slightest trace of abrasion under my thumbs as they rest on his cheeks and give the frames a wiggle.

The corner of his mouth tilts up, but he hastily presses his lips together, trying to suppress a smile.

I bite my lip, trying to straighten my own face. His humour is having a contagious effect.

'Sorry,' he apologises.

'It's okay,' I murmur, running my fingers along the length of the arms of the glasses to make sure they're long enough to sit properly on his ears.

Once again, his lips twitch.

'Sorry, sorry,' he mutters adorably as we full-on grin at each other.

'Lots of people get the giggles,' I reassure him as I complete my checks.

'I didn't get the giggles with Bernard,' he comments drily and a thrill darts through me.

'Right, now I need to take some measurements.' I pick up a marker pen. 'Look at me again.'

He stares straight into my eyes as I mark the spot where the centre of his pupil aligns with the lenses. I am far more aware than usual of this particular client's close proximity, but I'm focused on the task – it's important that the strongest part of the prescription marries up with his eyeline.

'You have very unusual eyes,' he says in a low voice as I finish with his second eye.

'Do I?' I reel back slightly as I reply, but in truth, I know I do. They're a strange, almost-golden colour, flecked and circled with green.

'Yeah, you do.' His gaze is unwavering.

I raise one eyebrow at him. 'You can take them off now.'

I am pulse-racingly aware of him watching me as I measure the dimensions on his glasses with a ruler and input the relevant information into the computer. By the time we're ready to discuss lens options, my heart rate has thankfully been restored to normal.

'Who makes the lenses?' he asks.

'Zeiss,' I reply. It's an astute question for a photographer. 'Do they do your camera lenses?'

He nods. 'I've got a few by them.'

'What sort of photography do you do?' I ask conversationally.

'Fashion, mostly.'

'Where? Here?'

'No, all over. Amsterdam, London, New York. I live in Amsterdam,' he explains, then, noting my look of confusion, adds: 'I used my parents' address on my form.'

'Aah, okay.' So he's *not* local. *Interesting.* 'One of my friends moved to Amsterdam a few months ago. I need to get over there this summer.'

'You should. It's an easy weekend break.'

'When do you go back?'

'Two weeks tomorrow. Hopefully these will be ready in time.'

'You leave Saturday the twenty-fifth?' I check my online calendar.

'Yep.'

'That should be fine. Shall we make you an appointment to come in the day before you go?'

I'll need to fit his new glasses and make any adjustments, so it's not simply a case of him dropping by to pick them up.

'Sure.'

'Same sort of time?'

'Perfect.'

'Not that I'm suggesting you should go anywhere other than this excellent establishment, but why don't you get your glasses in Amsterdam?'

'I like Umeko. I've been coming here for years. Even Bernie Bad Breath couldn't keep me away,' he adds with a smirk.

I laugh and turn the computer screen towards him. 'Okay, so we're looking at a total of...'

He doesn't balk at the price.

'What are you up to while you're here?' I ask casually as he gives me a credit card. 'On holiday or working?'

'Catching up with my family for Easter, then back to work.'

'Do you come home often?' I ring up the amount.

'Not as much as I should.'

I wonder if he has a girlfriend in Amsterdam. He's not wearing a wedding ring.

'That's us all done,' I say with a smile, handing him his card. His fingers brush mine as he takes it, causing a strange heat to prickle up my arm.

'Thanks. Guess I'll see you in two weeks.'

'I guess you will.'

We're both still grinning as he walks out the door, and then he casts one last look over his shoulder at me before disappearing from view.

I bring my hands up to my face and find that his aftershave has lingered from where I touched him. I'm strangely reluctant to wash my hands, but the next client will be here at any minute and I'll have to go through that entire process all over again.

I have a feeling it won't be as memorable.

Chapter 2

'Today's the day,' I say out loud with a grin at the reflections staring back at me from the mirrored cabinets mounted on the wall. Snatching up my toothbrush, I proceed to brush my teeth, but it's hard to keep the smile from my face.

It's Friday, 24 April. Sonny is due to come in and collect his glasses at midday.

'I wish I'd booked him an appointment for this morning.' I twirl my hair up into a bun and secure it with bobby pins, then pick up my silver bracelet from the edge of the basin and fasten it around my wrist.

My smile falls when I walk into the bedroom and see Bertie sprawled out on the bed. 'Oi! Naughty!'

My uncle's black Labrador stares up at me with doleful brown eyes as I click my fingers.

'Come on, down you get.'

Bertie eases her weary bones into a reluctant standing position and slumps onto the rug. I scratch behind her ears and her tail wags appreciatively. She knows we're headed from here to the kitchen for breakfast, so she doesn't bother to lie down again.

My uncle, Charles, is on a round-the-world cruise until the end of September. I'm housesitting his cottage and, happily, Bertie comes with it. At twelve years old, she's a bit long in the tooth, while Charles is eighty and not getting any younger himself. He'd always wanted to travel, but his wife couldn't think of anything worse than being stuck on a boat with hundreds of strangers. June suffered with seasickness, general antisocialness and also, sadly, heart disease, as it turned out. She passed away a few years ago, but Charles only recently agreed to fulfil his lifelong ambition on the condition that I return to the UK to take care of things for him. I didn't mind too much – I was in India when he called, but I've been floating around for a while now. I didn't know how ready I was to come home until Charles asked me to.

Bertie's claws click and scratch against the red floor tiles as she follows me into the cosy kitchen and drops to her haunches in front of the always-warm Aga.

Only one small window looks out onto the nearby street, with a vista that reaches straight past June's roses lining the white picket fence. The green bushes are already bright with pops of colour, from pastel pinks and yellows to luminescent oranges and cherry reds. The month of June is when they really come into their own, though – *our* June used to fill this place with vases full of them.

Pouring kibble into Bertie's bowl and switching on the kettle, I set about making myself tea and toast before taking a seat at the kitchen table. Outside it's sunny with only a few clouds drifting across the pale-blue sky.

'Perfect weather for walking to work,' I muse, and Bertie's tail thumps in response.

She knows she's coming with me. Robert, Umeko's retired husband, takes care of her during the day. He and Charles are good friends, having met at university many, *many* moons ago. Robert likes Bertie's company, Bertie likes his, and Charles can relax knowing his old girl isn't going to be lonely. It's a win-win situation.

As I pull on my old frayed denim jacket over my navy staff uniform, Bertie dances around my legs, almost knocking me over in her excitement to leave the house. She reminds me of the puppy she once was, panting and delirious as I grab her red lead from the coat hook and attach it to her matching collar. Opening the door, we step out from under the thatched porch into the cool spring air. The lawn is cast in shade and laden with dew so I'm careful to stick to the garden path as Bertie tugs me towards the gate.

A car turns into the drive. It's Evelyn, arriving for work. She's the therapist who rents the room attached to Charles's home. I say attached, but it's actually set within the original cottage layout and used to form part of the living room, which is substantially smaller now. It has its own private access at the side of the building, granted by the council before they listed the place.

I give her a wave and she responds in kind, as warm and approachable as ever. She's in her late fifties now and her bob is tinged with grey, but when I first met her it was platinum blond.

She disappears down the side of the cottage to the back where she parks each day.

Bertie and I pass two pubs on our way to the rural footpath that leads into town – Grantchester has four within a hop, skip and a jump from each other. Right now, the windows look onto dark, empty rooms and the outdoor tables are damp and unwelcoming, but it'll be a different story if this weather holds through the weekend as it's supposed to.

The grass is too long and wet to walk down by the river, but I catch glimpses of the water occasionally, glinting in the early morning sunlight.

Eventually we break out of the green fields onto the residential roads. I look left and, sure enough, there she is again: the girl from the next-door pharmacy.

Laughing, I come to a stop and wait for her.

'Right, that's it,' she calls as she approaches. 'If we're going to keep meeting like this, we need to be properly introduced.'

This week has been so strange. Not only have we continually crossed paths on our ways into work, we've also found ourselves leaving at the same time. It hasn't made a difference if I've been five minutes early or five minutes late – we have been on *exactly* the same timetable. It was getting so ridiculous that yesterday I waited inside the doorway of Umeko's for a few seconds before daring to step out onto the pavement. I almost jumped out of my skin to see her doing the same thing at the same moment. We stood there, facing each other with dumbstruck expressions on our faces, and then we both cracked up laughing like a couple of nutcases.

'I'm going to the supermarket,' she said at last, tears of

laughter making her green eyes sparkle as she pointed in the opposite direction.

'Okay, see you in the morning!' I called after her as we went our separate ways.

'I'm Hannah,' I tell her now. 'And this is Bertie.'

'Hello, Bertie,' she says warmly, bending down to give her a proper pat. 'And hello, Hannah,' she adds, grinning up at me. 'I'm Matilda.'

'Nice to finally meet you.'

She's in her early thirties, at a guess, with dark hair that comes to her shoulders. Her features are slightly pixie-like, with high cheekbones and a sprinkle of freckles dusting her small, upturned nose. She's pretty.

'Where do you live?' I ask.

'Selwyn Avenue,' she replies, straightening up and jabbing her thumb over her shoulder. 'You?'

'Grantchester.'

'Nice. Have you been there for long?' We walk on together.

'About six weeks. I'm looking after this cheeky monkey while my uncle's away.'

'She's gorgeous,' she says affectionately, stroking Bertie's head again. 'I've always wanted a black Lab.'

'You can't get one?'

'My boyfriend and I work during the day so it wouldn't be fair. What do you do with Bertie?'

We carry on chatting until we reach our building. I learn that Matilda and her boyfriend were on holiday in Sri Lanka over Easter, which explains why we haven't crossed paths until recently.

'See you at five o'clock,' I tease, coming to a stop outside

Robert and Umeko's front door. They live in the apartment directly above the practice and their entrance is on the right of the building.

'Or maybe even at lunchtime!' she replies with a comedy wink.

I laugh and knock on the door. By the time Robert has made his way down the stairs to answer it, my thoughts have become once more preoccupied by what else is happening at lunchtime...

Abbey heads out for her break, leaving me alone in the shop to wait for Sonny. His appointment is minutes away and my stomach is overrun with idiotic butterflies.

It was that comment about my eyes that did it, and the last look he gave me over his shoulder. I'm not imagining it; he was attracted to me too.

Yes, I know he's leaving for Amsterdam tomorrow.

But there's always tonight.

I smile to myself then quickly rearrange my features, aware that insanity is not a typically appealing personality trait.

It's been a while since I've felt any sort of chemistry with a man so it's easy to get caught up in this minor distraction. After today, I'll be back to my humdrum reality and there will be no more cause to daydream.

I sigh, drumming my fingertips on the table. I bet he does have a girlfriend in the Netherlands. She's probably a tall, stunning model that he met at a photo shoot.

Okay, now he's late. But he *is* coming. Abbey called him yesterday to confirm the appointment.

The door opens and a jolt ricochets through me.

It's him. He's dressed in black jeans and an army green T-shirt.

The next thing I notice is that his head is down.

'Hi!' I welcome him brightly.

'Hey,' he mumbles.

His eyes remain fixed on the floor, but I can see that he's wearing glasses.

'Take a seat. I have your new glasses here for you,' I say genially, pressing on.

He walks over and pulls up a chair, but continues to avoid my eyes. His whole demeanour is totally different. This is not a man who's interested in me at all, I realise, with a stab of disappointment. I've misjudged the situation entirely.

I pass him his stylish new glasses case, hoping for a sign that he might be pleased, but his face is impassive.

Maybe he's embarrassed. I mean, his behaviour before – all that smiling and staring into my eyes – was a little intense. Perhaps he felt disloyal to his girlfriend and is trying to make amends.

That's probably it, I realise with a sinking heart as he takes off his old glasses. Now I feel like a fool too.

I had planned to launch into chatty small talk, intending to ask how his Easter was and what he's been getting up to in Cambridge, but the circumstances have tied my tongue.

He opens the case and extracts the Kilsgaards.

Wait. *Are his hands shaking?*

'Can you try them on?' Perplexed, I push the mirror towards him.

Something is definitely off. His hands *are* shaking. In fact, *he* seems shaken. Is he ill?

He turns his face towards me without looking at his reflection. His eyes remain lowered. It's clear that there will be no smiling today.

'I need to check the fit,' I prompt, and he obediently and perfunctorily leans towards me across the desk.

There's such a strange atmosphere in the room. I'm full of tension as I reach out to touch the frames.

He hasn't shaved for a couple of days, judging by the length of his stubble. My thumbs brush against his cheekbones as I check the fit of the glasses, confirming that the arms sit comfortably over his ears. I give the frames a wiggle to ensure they're steady and won't slip off his nose.

'I'd like to make a small adjustment to one of the nose pads,' I say, and he takes off the glasses and hands them to me.

This time, he doesn't watch me as I work.

'Are they pinching your nose?' I ask when he puts them on again.

'No.'

'How's your vision?'

'Fine.'

'Can you have a look around the room,' I prompt. 'Is everything clear? Can you read what that poster says?'

He swallows and nods.

'Do you want to check the mirror?'

He shakes his head and takes them off. I stare at him and he swallows again as he returns the glasses to their case.

'Sonny?' I ask worriedly. 'Are you okay?'

Suddenly he looks straight into my eyes, and what I see chills my blood. He stands up abruptly, shoving his chair back in his attempt to get to his feet.

I'm in front of him before I even realise. 'Sonny?'

'They're fine,' he mumbles, his gaze once more averted.

'What's wrong?'

Another shake of the head. He picks up his old glasses and puts them on. 'Nothing. Are we done?'

He looks at me directly then and another jolt goes through me. His eyes have filled with tears.

I'm shocked, but my overriding emotion is concern. However, before I can say another word, he sidesteps me and stalks out through the door.

Chapter 3

If I thought I was going to be able to stop thinking about him, I was wrong.

As April melded pleasantly into May, Sonny continued to be a distraction. And not a pleasant distraction, not in the way it was at first.

That look in his eyes was *so* stark, *so* bleak. He seemed broken. I couldn't forget it.

I confided in Umeko that he seemed upset when he came in to collect his glasses. She replied that she didn't know his father well enough to call him about personal issues, but promised to ask after Sonny the next time she spoke to his dad about something accounts related. To my knowledge, that hasn't yet happened.

One late afternoon in mid-May when I'm out at the front deadheading the roses, I hear the side door to Evelyn's clinic open. I can't decipher specific words, but I can hear Evelyn's serene, musical voice and the low, deep tone of a man's reply. A minute later, this same man, I'm presuming, appears from the side of the building, wheeling his bicycle down the gravel driveway towards the road. I straighten up with a start. It's Sonny.

My sudden movement catches his eye and he glances my way, giving me a cursory nod. Then he does a double take, puzzlement creasing his brow.

'Sonny,' I say.

'Oh, hi,' he replies vacantly, coming to a slow stop.

'Hannah. I work with Umeko,' I remind him awkwardly as his gaze sweeps over my appearance.

'I didn't recognise you,' he admits.

It's a fair comment. My casual clothes couldn't be more different from the strait-laced uniform I'm required to wear for work.

My long wavy hair is down and I'm wearing a grass-skimming sky-blue skirt with an apricot-and-white floral pattern. Several teeny-tiny plaits secured with colourful beads break up the monotony of my sun-lightened hair while the rest of it falls free, and my top is lacy and white, contrasting with my nut-brown skin tone.

He nods at the whitewashed thatched cottage behind me. 'You live here?'

'It's my uncle's house. He's away at the moment.'

'Oh.'

'Glasses okay?' it occurs to me to ask.

He's wearing them and they look good on him, even if he himself seems troubled. His blue eyes are rimmed with red, he looks as if he hasn't shaved for a week or so and his face is gaunt beneath his stubble.

'Yeah, fine.'

It doesn't matter that I'm out of words because he's in no mood to chat. I can't ask if he's well, because he's clearly not if he's seeing Evelyn.

'Nice to see you.' I try to fashion my expression into something that he won't mistake as pitying.

'You too,' he replies, swinging his leg over his bike saddle and cycling out into the road.

He disappears from view and I return to deadheading roses, the cogs inside my head whirring.

Why didn't he go home to Amsterdam?

Or if he did, why has he come back so soon?

And why is he seeing a counsellor?

Evelyn took over my uncle's practice when he retired. Once upon a time, Charles used to kiss June goodbye and walk out of his back door, then make his way around the side of the building. He could have accessed his clinic via the now-locked interconnecting door in the living room, but he never did. He always said he preferred to keep his work life separate from his home life, but the claim was laughable – Charles was forever bringing his work home with him. To say he's retired now is also stretching the truth.

Having spent most of my teenage years living here, I'm speaking from experience.

Charles is like a father to me, and June was like a mother. I *do* have a mother and father, but they're not what you'd call conventional. They raised me on a small farm miles away from anything closely resembling civilisation and home-schooled me in my early years. It was only Charles and June's intervention that brought me to Cambridge when I was

23

thirteen. They persuaded my parents that a traditional education would be in my best interests and my parents conceded.

Charles is my mother's older brother, but they're as different as chalk and cheese. Charles is… well, I guess he's what most people would call normal. My mother, on the other hand, is a free-spirited hippie who rarely does things by the book.

Sometimes I feel torn between my bohemian youth and my current situation, but right now I know I'm where I need to be.

After everything Charles has done for me over the years, I owe him the peace of mind to go travelling, safe in the knowledge that things at home will be taken care of.

The sound of Evelyn's car starting up returns me to the present. A moment later she cruises down the driveway, giving me a friendly wave as she pulls out onto the road.

I go back to wondering what it was that brought her last client of the day to her doorstep.

Chapter 4

'What time are you heading there?' I ask Matilda.

It's a couple of weeks later and we're on our way home after what turned out to be a difficult day. I need a drink. And I'm pleased to say that a drink will soon be forthcoming.

'Archie won't be back for a bit so shall we say seven thirty?'

'Yep, great. That gives me plenty of time to feed this little madam and get myself changed.'

'I hope you're bringing her,' Matilda says affectionately, patting Bertie's head.

'She'd probably be as happy in front of the Aga, but yes, I'll drag her along.'

'Good,' she states definitively.

It's been over a month since Matilda and I first started chatting on our way to and from work. Soon after, we bumped into each other in the queue at a coffee shop and, after slightly self-conscious 'hello agains', ended up sitting together.

We've bonded over many a lunch in the last few weeks

and this evening she's invited me out for drinks at the pub with her boyfriend and some pals. I'm looking forward to a night out. My only friend from school who still lives around here has recently had a baby and hasn't been up for much socialising.

'I'll see you later,' Matilda says as she crosses the road.

'See you,' I call back and soon I'm in the grassy field walking on the high footpath that will lead me to home.

It's Friday night and the route is busier than usual with cyclists. Everyone's keen to get home to start the weekend and I'm constantly stepping off the footpath onto the grass to make way. This is made trickier by the fact that there's a herd of cows about and several have taken more than a passing interest in Bertie.

It's all I can do to get us home in one piece.

'I want to look nice. I'm meeting new people,' I say as I redo my plaits in front of the mirror. 'What do you reckon, black off-the-shoulder top tonight?'

Deciding on a black and ochre patterned long flowing skirt to go with it, I head downstairs to survey my choice of footwear.

Bertie clips her way into the tiny hallway behind me.

'I know I should wear those.' I stare downheartedly at my comfortable but dull black work shoes. 'But I really want to wear these.' I pick up the emerald-green sandals that I bought on a whim earlier this week. 'I know they're not good for walking in, but it's not far.'

Bertie stares at me as I put them on, her ears pricked fully up.

'You heard me say "walk", didn't you?'

She wags her tail in response. She's not going completely

bonkers though, so she must be tired. Maybe I should leave her here. She's already been to work and back today.

'Are you coming or staying?' I'm still undecided as I open the door.

She wags her tail harder and pants, beginning to resemble the grinning lunatic I'm familiar with.

'Come on then.' I reach inside and grab her lead from the coat hook. 'We'll take it easy, I promise. I'm a bit weary myself.'

I pull the door closed and come to a startled stop. Sonny is outside the gate. He looks hesitant as he waits for me.

'Hello again,' I say.

'Hi.' He smiles awkwardly.

I feel sorry for him. The last thing you want when you're visiting your therapist is to keep bumping into people you know.

'I heard you talking,' he says, and I'm instantly on edge. 'Thought your uncle must be home.'

'No, he's away until the end of September. This is his dog. We're keeping each other company.'

'What's her name?' He crouches down to pat her.

'Bertie.' She's a helpful little icebreaker. 'Not on your bike today?'

'No, I drove and parked at the pub. I'm meeting a mate there.' He gazes up at me as he speaks. It's not the steady eye contact of our first meeting, but it's not complete avoidance either. He seems better. A far cry from his earlier confident self, but certainly improved from the last couple of times I've seen him, with more colour in his cheeks and clear blue eyes. He's had a shave too.

'Which pub are you going to?' I ask.

'The Blue Ball.'

'Me too!'

'Oh, right.' He lets out a self-conscious laugh and straightens up.

'Feel free to walk on ahead, though,' I say. 'We'll be taking it slowly.'

'Slowly works for me.'

We set off in silence. I'm racking my brain to think of something to say, but he gets there first.

'I'm glad I've seen you again, actually,' he confesses. 'I wanted to apologise for how I behaved when I came to collect my glasses.'

'No! There's no need for that.'

'I'd had some bad news. I was reeling, to be honest.'

'I'm sorry to hear that.' I don't ask what the news was and he doesn't elaborate, but naturally I'm curious.

'Have you been at work today?' he asks.

'Yep. Back in tomorrow.'

'You work Saturdays?'

I nod. 'Sundays and Mondays are our days off.'

'Not a big one for you tonight, then?'

'I don't know,' I reply dejectedly. 'It's been a rough day.'

He casts me a sideways look. 'How so?'

I hesitate, then decide to cut through the small talk. 'A child came in for an eye test and I think she might have a brain tumour.'

'Shit,' he says. 'How old?'

'Not quite three.'

'Oh God.' He's shocked.

28

Her parents brought her in because one of her pupils was dilated. I took her straight through to Umeko, who ended up calling the hospital to make an emergency referral. The little girl, Ella, was showing classic signs of a rare tumour.

'Will she be okay?' Sonny asks.

My eyes prick with tears. 'I hope so.'

He sighs heavily. 'That puts my problems into perspective.'

'We all have our crosses to bear,' I reply quietly.

We cross the road and continue along the footpath. After a while he shoots my left leg a look.

'Are you all right?' he asks. 'Have you done yourself in?'

'Old injury,' I explain.

'What happened?'

'Accident. Car crash. Years ago.' I wave off his concern. 'Normally I wear shoes that compensate, but figured I didn't have far to walk tonight.' It's why he wouldn't have noticed me limping at work.

'You should've insisted on meeting at the Green Man,' he says. 'Or the Red Lion.'

'Or the Rupert Brooke,' I add with a smile, nodding up ahead.

We're about to pass our third pub.

The Blue Ball Inn is the furthest from me, but it's the nearest to town, where Archie and Matilda live. It'll be an easy enough walk home for them, but the cottage is closer still so I'm not complaining. Anyway, the Blue Ball is my favourite.

'I need to grab something from the car,' Sonny says as we approach our destination. 'It's a bit further on.' He points down the road. 'But I'll no doubt see you inside.'

This is likely true. It's not a big venue.

'If not, I'm sure we'll cross paths again.'

He smiles and lifts his hand in a wave, then carries on his way, leaving Bertie and me to head up the steps alone.

I check my feelings and realise I'm not attracted to him anymore. He's unquestionably good-looking, but it was his confidence that reeled me in. Without it, he's more ordinary. It's a strange relief.

The Blue Ball Inn is on a stretch of road lined with small terraced houses. There are a few tables outside on the patio in the sunshine, but they're full and there's no sign of Matilda, so I lead Bertie inside to scope out the joint. My new friend is not in either of the two cosy front rooms so we bypass the bar and head out the back to the beer garden.

'Hannah!' Matilda leaps to her feet at the sight of me.

She's at a table, surrounded by three men, one of whom also gets up.

'This is Archie,' she introduces her boyfriend.

He's tall and broad with delightfully dishevelled dark-blond hair and warm brown eyes.

'Hey,' he says, giving me a friendly kiss on my cheek. 'This is Kev and Warren.' He nods at his mates.

Kev is tall, blond and in his early thirties, and Warren looks a few years older with short black hair, olive skin and the sort of heavy stubble that laughs in the face of a razor.

'I'll go to the bar,' Archie says, still on his feet. 'What are you having?'

'I'll go!'

'No, sit down,' he insists. 'It's my round. Guys? Same again?'

We place our orders and Archie disappears inside.

Matilda pats the seat he vacated, moving it out from the table so there's room for Bertie too. 'Sit next to me. I'm desperate for female company. These guys have been talking cricket.' She casts her eyes to the heavens. 'They play for the local team.'

'Awesome.' I smile at them.

'No, *not* awesome,' she states adamantly. 'That's my summer wasted sitting on cricket greens.'

Kev and Warren laugh. 'It's a hard life,' Warren says, leaning back in his chair and stretching his legs out.

'At least men in cricket whites look quite hot,' she says. 'I'm talking about *the opposition*,' she adds loudly, making them chuckle again.

'Have you been here long?' I ask as Kev and Warren chat to each other. Her glass of rosé is almost empty.

'About twenty minutes. Archie finished work early and was out the door like a shot. I barely had time to touch up my make-up.'

'You look amazing,' I say. 'I love your dress.' It's knee-length, black and covered in tiny violet flowers.

She leans in conspiratorially. '*You* look amazing! I love your hair. I haven't seen it down before.' She reaches out and fingers one of my plaits. 'I had no idea you were a super-cool hippie chick.'

I laugh out loud. 'I'll take that description, thank you very much. I'm glad to be out of that awful uniform.'

'Yours is better than mine,' she says good-naturedly. 'Navy beats royal blue. Not that I'm complaining. My job is a darn sight more fun than it used to be.'

Matilda was a bookkeeper, but a few years ago she went back to university to retrain as a pharmacist. She's currently doing a working gap year.

31

'Why did you decide to become a pharmacist?' I ask.

'I wanted to be a doctor when I was younger, but went off the idea as a teenager. Anyway, I didn't quite get the grades. After my dad passed away, Archie encouraged me to go back to university. I was always good at science and maths, and pharmacy seemed like a valid option. My dad left me his house so I could afford to take the time off work to study.'

'Wow,' I say. 'Although I'm sorry about your dad.'

'Thanks.' The corners of her lips turn down. 'He would have liked that something positive came out of me losing him. I met Archie, for a start.'

'How did you meet?'

She smiles. 'I was living in London, but I'd come up to Cambridge for the weekend. I needed to clear out Dad's house.' Her smile fades a little. 'I was on my own because my parents split up years ago and I'm an only child. I decided to take a break to go punting as it was something Dad and I always used to do together and it was his birthday. Archie was on the river with his sister and some friends, and he got his pole stuck in the mud. I stepped in to help him out. He was bloody awful at punting. He's *still* bloody awful at punting!' She raises her voice, grinning past me at her boyfriend returning, I presume.

I smile and turn to see Archie carrying a pint of beer, a half-pint of what I'm presuming is my cider and Matilda's glass of rosé.

'I don't need to know how to punt when you do it so well.' He grins as he distributes our drinks and then jerks his head over his shoulder. 'Sonny arrived in time to help me at the bar.'

I don't believe it. Yet there he is. Again. Appearing from behind Archie with three pints of beer in his hands.

He clocks me instantly.

'Hi!' he exclaims, his eyebrows jumping up.

'Hi,' I reply with equal surprise.

'You know these guys?' he asks as he places their drinks on the table.

'No, I just thought I'd sit down at their table and drink their alcohol.'

He wrinkles his nose at me. I laugh as he kisses Matilda hello and greets Kev and Warren.

Matilda leans towards me and whispers in my ear: 'How do you know Sonny?'

'He came in for an eye test last month,' I whisper back.

'Aah. So you and he haven't…'

'What? No!'

Her look of relief doesn't escape my notice.

Sonny drags a couple of chairs over from the next table and sits down beside me, leaning down to give Bertie a rigorous pat.

'You can't seem to get rid of me,' he murmurs, flashing me a crooked smile.

'Nor you me.'

He picks up his drink. 'Cheers.'

'Cheers.' We chink glasses and then feel compelled to do the same with everyone else around the table.

'So why did you choose optometry?' Matilda asks, continuing with the theme of our earlier conversation as Sonny and Archie strike up a conversation between themselves. 'Hang on, it's not optometry, is it?'

'No, I'm a dispensing optician, which is a step down from optometrist and a step up from optical assistant. I didn't get the grades either. I might go back to studying one day, but right now I'm content doing what I'm doing.'

'And what inspired this career choice?' she asks in a mock reporter-style voice.

Apart from the fact that Charles and June practically railroaded me into a respectable career path?

'Um… It was something that happened to a friend of mine, actually.'

Her face falls at the change in my tone. 'What?'

'One of my best friends from school had a brain tumour. She's okay now, but it was caught during an eye test. It saved her life.'

'Jeez.'

Sonny pauses in what he was saying, his ear cocked towards us. He'd be right in thinking that today brought back some bad memories.

'I spent a lot of time with her at the hospital that year, keeping her company.'

'When was this?' Matilda asks.

'We were doing our GCSEs.'

'That must've impacted on your exam results,' she says with a frown.

'I don't like attributing my grades to that,' I admit.

'I know what you mean. I feel the same about my parents' divorce. It got so messy around the time I was doing my GCSEs, but I hate allocating blame. Anyway, I'm doing okay. It all worked out well in the end.'

'What are you two talking about?' Archie interrupts, intrigued.

As Matilda fills him in, Bertie gets to her feet and squeezes in between Sonny's legs.

'Sorry,' I apologise, reaching for her collar and trying to tug her away.

I get a whiff of his aftershave and feel a little dizzy. He still *smells* attractive.

'How are the kids?' Matilda asks.

'They're good,' Sonny replies.

'Have you persuaded Rochelle to get one yet?' Archie asks, nodding at Bertie.

'She's having none of it,' Sonny replies.

Hang on, what? He's married with kids?

'You have children?' I ask.

'Two daughters. Imogen and Natalie. Imogen would settle for a cat, but for Natalie, nothing less than a dog will do. She wants to be a vet when she's older.'

'I wanted to be a vet when I was that age too,' Matilda chips in nostalgically. 'I think all nine-year-olds do.'

'I thought you wanted to be a doctor?' Archie asks her with a frown.

'Doctor, vet, I would have been satisfied with either.'

Sonny has a nine-year-old? He's only thirty-two.

'How *is* Rochelle?' Archie asks.

'She's all right,' Sonny replies noncommittally.

'Is this your wife?' Curiosity has got the better of me.

Archie snorts and Sonny raises his eyebrows at him.

'*Really?*' Sonny asks his mate in a dry, pointed voice.

'Sorry,' Archie mutters, trying to suppress a smirk and failing. 'But "wife" would imply marriage and that's too much of a leap for my imagination.'

Sonny rolls his eyes and turns back to me. 'We're not together,' he says.

I have no idea what that interaction was about.

'How did you guys all meet?' I change the subject.

'University,' Archie replies, indicating Sonny and himself. 'We went to Anglia Ruskin, here in Cambridge. Warren's on the cricket team and Kev and I work together.'

'What do you do?' I ask Archie. Matilda hasn't told me.

'I'm a graphic designer.' He nods at Sonny. 'We studied graphic design together, but Sonny ended up becoming a photographer. We actually spent a semester in the Netherlands as part of our course. Sonny liked it so much he decided to move there after we graduated.' He gives his friend a cheeky grin.

'How long are you in the UK for?' Matilda asks Sonny.

He shrugs. 'I'm not sure yet. Maybe for the summer.'

'Just taking a break?'

He shrugs again, and he seems uncomfortable. 'Yeah. And I wanted to spend some time with the girls.'

'We'll have to drag you onto the team,' Warren interjects, and as the conversation returns to cricket, my mind wanders.

His children live here and he lives in Amsterdam? How does that work?

Does anyone else around the table know that he's seeing a counsellor?

And if so, do they know why?

I bite my tongue to stop myself from asking any more too-personal questions.

Chapter 5

I bump into Sonny again on Monday as I'm heading out with Bertie for an afternoon walk. As before, he's just finished up at Evelyn's.

'Hey,' he says warmly, not in the slightest bit put out to see me. 'Talking to yourself again?'

'What? Oh, er...' I laugh awkwardly and look over my shoulder at the cottage, realising he overheard us leaving the house again.

'At least you're in the right place for madness.' He opens the garden gate to allow us to pass through.

'Evelyn's a counsellor, not a psychiatrist,' I correct him, keeping my tone light.

'You know her?'

'She took over from my uncle. That was his practice once.'

'Where *is* your uncle?' he asks.

'Currently somewhere in the Atlantic Ocean. He's on a round-the-world cruise.'

Charles called me yesterday from the Falkland Islands and he was very perky. He's been emailing with updates, but it was heartwarming to hear his voice. He's made a whole host of friends and is now on his way to South America.

'Where are you off to?' Sonny asks.

'We're going for a walk down by the river.'

'Mind if I join you? I've got some time to kill.'

'Sure,' I reply, pleased, if a little surprised.

But then, we did get on well on Friday night. Despite the initial weirdness of the situation, it was a really fun evening with lots of banter being batted around. It was good to see how relaxed Sonny was with his friends. Whatever's going on with him, I'm glad he has decent people around him.

'Have you heard anything more about that little girl?' he asks as we walk side by side on the narrow pavement.

I'm touched he thought to ask after her. 'Yes, Umeko called this morning to fill me in. Scans showed that it *was* a tumour, which is what she suspected. It's a rare one – only about one in twenty million are affected. The doctor said she would have died if they'd left it another one or two weeks.'

'Jesus.'

'By the time she went in for surgery yesterday, she'd lost all vision in her left eye. They were going to try to save her right eye. We don't know yet if they were successful.'

He shakes his head. 'Poor thing.'

'I know.'

'Thankfully you guys spotted it.'

'Thankfully her parents brought her in. I hope your kids go for regular eye tests.'

'I'm not sure,' he reluctantly admits. 'They don't have anything wrong with their eyesight, as far as I know.'

'It's not only about that.' I'm unable to stop myself from dishing out a small lecture. 'They should be tested every year or two anyway, once they're at school. There's more to eye tests than needing glasses. The optometrist might pick up on other problems. And it's free for children, so there's no reason not to take them.'

'I'll speak to Rochelle,' he assures me.

We pass St Andrew and St Mary, Grantchester's beautiful centuries-old church. Charles and June used to regularly attend services there, and I'd allow myself to be dragged along at Christmas and Easter. Now the most I see of the inside of the church is when it appears on ITV's *Grantchester*. I'm about to ask Sonny if he's watched the 1950s-set detective drama series, but he speaks first.

'I *should* know.' He sounds deflated. 'About my daughters' eye tests. I haven't been around much, but I'm trying to change that.'

'Is that why you didn't go back to Amsterdam?' I ask gently.

He nods. 'Partly.' He sighs. 'But my life is generally a bit of a wreck at the moment.'

My mind whirls as we veer off to our left on the footpath that leads down to Grantchester Meadows. On our right is the Orchard tea garden and through the breaks in the trees, dozens of sea-green deckchairs and wooden tables are visible, spread out on the grass beneath the apple trees.

'I haven't been to the Orchard in years,' Sonny says.

'Me neither. Oh, their *scones*…'

'Shall we?' He halts in his steps, his face breaking into a grin. 'Or does Bertie need a walk?'

'No, she's already been out once today. This was all about getting a sunshine hit.'

'Let's do it,' he urges, and his boyish excitement is infectious.

'Okay!' I reply with a laugh, taken aback at this turn of events.

Are we becoming friends?

The thought makes me feel surprisingly warm.

We opt to sit in the sun. Sonny, who carried the tray from the café, places it on the table.

After pouring with rain for much of the weekend, the weather is a welcome change, but I check my chair for dampness before daring to sit down.

On the weekend in summer, it can be hard to find an empty table, but today it's perfectly tranquil. There are a few people dotted around at the tables surrounding us and we can hear their low chatter and the gentle sounds of cutlery clinking against crockery as people stir sugar into their tea. The air is warm and smells of cow parsley – the tall wildflowers are crowded together under the shaded bushes and fruit trees, the scent of the white umbrella-shaped blooms bringing back memories of summer.

I pour my tea and sigh with contentment. Sonny leans in and picks up his own teapot.

'So the friend you were talking about to Matilda on Friday night… I heard you saying—'

'Nina,' I interject. 'She was sixteen when Umeko suspected a tumour.'

'*Umeko* spotted it?' he asks with surprise, his milk jug paused in mid-air.

'Yes.' That's two rare brain tumours my boss has had to contend with in eleven years, and they're just the ones I'm aware of.

'You've known her for a while?'

I nod. 'Years. Her husband and Charles, my uncle, are old friends.'

'But you only started working with her recently?'

'Yep.' Not for my uncle's want of trying. I slice my currant scone in half and proceed to smother it with strawberry jam and clotted cream. 'Before that, I was in India.'

'What were you doing there?'

'Travelling at first, but I ended up settling in Mumbai for a few months and helping out at an eye clinic.'

'That must've been interesting.'

'It was a lot of things. Interesting was one of them. Challenging, traumatic and frustrating are other words I'd use to describe the experience, but above all it was rewarding.'

After finishing my degree, I landed a work placement in Bradford, but within a year, I got cold feet. Perhaps it was my cranky boss, perhaps it was because I never really felt at home in my university city for various reasons, but I decided to take a break to re-evaluate what I wanted from life. I was unconvinced that a career as a dispensing optician was for me, and I didn't see anything on my travels that persuaded me otherwise, but in India I crossed paths with an American girl at a youth hostel who was complaining of headaches. When she lost vision in one of her eyes, I suspected she was suffering from ocular migraines. The poor girl was completely and understandably freaked out, but I took her to a charitable eye hospital and was so blown away by the help she received there that I was inspired to ask if they needed volunteers.

It was definitely a baptism of fire kind of situation because it was the first place I'd worked practically unsupervised, and to say I was thrown in at the deep end is an understatement. I learned a lot in a short space of time and came across a wide variety of eye problems, from cataracts to corneal ulcers, inflammations and infections.

Later, when Charles told me that Umeko had a position opening up, I found the prospect of returning to a permanent position in the UK far less daunting than I otherwise would have.

Day-to-day life at Umeko's is a whole lot easier and less stressful, but I do sometimes miss the madness and unpredictability of Mumbai.

'So is your friend, Nina, okay now?' Sonny asks.

'Yes, she made a full recovery, thankfully.' I bat away a wasp. 'She's the one who lives in Amsterdam.'

'What does she do there?' He leans back in his deckchair, taking his teacup with him. He's wearing a white shirt, rolled up at the elbows, and grey shorts with light-coloured canvas Vans on his feet.

'She runs a design shop with her boyfriend. He's Dutch.'

'Do you know where their shop is?' The wasp bobs up and down over the remnants of his scone. He frowns at it.

'I think it's near the Anne Frank House. I can't recall the street name.'

'That's a nice area.'

'I *will* make it over soon to see her,' I vow, batting away the same pesky wasp.

There are wasp catchers hanging from the tree branches

all around. We're lucky to only be bothered by one. Later in summer, when the ground is scattered with sweet-smelling rotting apples, they're everywhere, lazy and drunk on fruit juice.

'What about you?' I ask. 'You're not planning on going back for a while?'

His expression becomes instantly strained and I regret asking.

'Sorry, I don't mean to pry.'

'It's okay.' He stares into his teacup and something about his manner – the way he glances at me, slightly thoughtfully, before looking away again and taking a sip of his tea – makes me act on an impulse.

'Do you want to talk about it?'

It's odd. We barely know each other, but it doesn't feel like that. It's as though something between us has clicked into place. I think it's the same for him.

Sure enough, he begins to speak.

'A mate of mine died recently,' he confides.

'I'm so sorry.' I put my last piece of scone back down on my plate.

'He'd been on a downward spiral for a while.' He meets my eyes, but only momentarily. 'He overdosed. We don't know if it was accidental or deliberate.'

'Oh no, that's awful.'

'Yeah,' he agrees heavily. 'It hit me pretty hard.'

'That's why you're seeing Evelyn?'

He shrugs. 'It's part of it.'

He falls silent and looks across the orchard. A small boy is climbing one of the apple trees nearby.

An elderly, eccentrically dressed lady calls out to him.

'Please don't! Some of these trees are over a hundred years old! They're very frail.'

The child's mother looks mortified as she rushes over and urges the boy to get down. He jumps off the branch, narrowly missing some stinging nettles.

Sonny smiles at me. 'I remember coming here as a kid. I'd love to bring the girls. I don't know if Rochelle ever has.'

'How long were you and she together?'

'Not long,' he replies glibly, placing his teacup down on the saucer with a clatter. 'If Matilda hasn't already told you, she soon will: I'm a fuckwit when it comes to women.'

My stomach inadvertently does a somersault.

'But you can relax because I'm currently sworn off them,' he adds with a rueful smile.

'You're sworn off women?' Now I'm intrigued.

He nods. 'Sex too.'

'You're not serious.'

'I am, at least for the next year.'

'Shut the front door!'

He lets out a low sardonic laugh and shakes his head. 'Well, maybe six months. I haven't decided yet.'

'But *why*?'

'I can't form lasting relationships. It's something I'm working on with Evelyn.'

Oh God, he *is* serious. There's absolutely no humour in his tone as he continues:

'She suggested a period of abstinence and I've agreed. I don't remember the last time I felt this determined to stick with something.' He gives me a candid look. 'So you can tell Matilda that no warning is necessary.'

44

'What makes you think she'd warn me off you anyway?' I ask, feeling surreal about the fact that we're having such a straightforward conversation about something like this.

'She's done it before with other friends.'

'Was she right to?' I ask.

He grimaces. 'Yes, unfortunately.'

Hmm.

Chapter 6

The warning comes the very next day.

'He's a nightmare, that one,' Matilda says on our way out to lunch.

We're walking across Lammas Land – a stretch of green parkland – on our way into town.

We've been talking about Friday night, saying how we both want to do it again soon. Matilda hadn't expected Sonny to turn up, even though she'd known that Archie had invited him. She revealed that he'd been going through a bit of a rough patch, but didn't go into detail before launching into the 'nightmare' comment.

I knew it was coming, but curiosity ensures that I take the bait regardless. 'Why?'

'He's such a dickhead to women. I don't even know if you're interested, but please don't go there.'

I laugh. 'I wasn't intending to. He did say you'd warn me off him though,' I drop in casually.

She's taken aback. 'When did he say that? At the pub?'

'No, yesterday. We bumped into each other when I was out for a walk. Ended up going for tea at the Orchard.'

Afterwards, Sonny and I wandered along the river together for a while before parting company. Rochelle had given him permission to take the girls to a local café. She has full custody, so any contact he has with his daughters has to be on her terms.

'And he said I'd warn you off him?' Matilda asks dubiously. 'What did he say exactly?'

'He said that he was "a complete and utter fuckwit when it comes to women" and then claimed to be sworn off them entirely.'

'Bullshit!' she shouts, and a couple of joggers take a wide berth as they go round us.

'He's taken a vow of abstinence,' I add.

'Oh my God!' she says slowly. 'What a load of crap! What will that guy do to get into your knickers?'

I laugh while at the same time feeling bad that we're laying into Sonny like this. But he must've expected this reaction when he asked me to tell Matilda that there was no need to warn me.

'He really said that to you? That he's abstinent?'

I nod.

'I'll get the lowdown from Archie,' she states.

We go to Hot Numbers coffee shop, a cool little indie on Trumpington Street, not far from the Fitzwilliam Museum. I hunt out a table while Matilda places our order at the counter. We don't have long so there's no time to waste.

'I liked Archie,' I say when she returns with our drinks.

I managed to nab a sunny table in the courtyard.

'Yep, I'm a lucky girl,' she says flippantly.

'He's lucky too,' I point out, sipping my raspberry lemonade through a paper straw.

'I am so glad you and I are friends,' she states.

'Me too.'

We grin at each other and then she shakes her head with bewilderment. 'I can't believe Sonny said that crap about abstinence.'

'Go on then, spill the beans,' I command. 'If you're going to warn me off him, do it properly. Why's he so awful?'

She screws up her nose. 'He's a perpetual one-night-stand man. In the time I've known him, I don't think he's had a relationship that's lasted more than a day. Plenty of women have fallen at *his* feet, though. He crushes hearts with every footstep.'

I snigger at her melodrama.

'Archie says he often sleeps with the models he photographs.'

This comment sobers me up. I try not to show that this, of all things, bothers me, but it's hard not to feel threatened by perfect female specimens when I feel like I'm lacking. I cross my feet at the ankles, glad to see a server arriving with our lunch.

I've gone for avocado on sourdough toast with feta, chilli and mint. Matilda has opted for a bacon sandwich.

'Has Sonny slept with any of your friends?' I ask as we tuck in.

She looks fed up. 'At least two that I know of. Nessa was planning on coming out on Friday night, but changed her mind when she heard that Sonny was invited. Faith is over it, I think. She's seeing Cameron now, one of the other guys who plays cricket with them.'

'Do you know Rochelle?'

'No, but Archie does. She went to the same university. I think they did some work on the student magazine together. He said she had a crush on Sonny well before he slept with her. I didn't know him back then, but from what I've heard, he's barely had anything to do with his kids' upbringing since he buggered off to Amsterdam.'

'What a shit.'

'That's putting it aptly.' She polishes off her sandwich. 'So did I do a good job?'

'Good job of what?' I ask.

'Warning you off him?'

'Yeah, but there was no need. Even if I was interested, he's sworn off women.'

'I'll believe it when I see it,' she comments wryly.

Chapter 7

On Friday evening, there's a jaunty knock on the cottage door. I've changed out of my work clothes and am on my way downstairs, trying to decide what to cook for dinner.

Bertie rushes past me and lets out her requisite five-bark warning, her tail going so far sideways that her whole backside moves with it.

'Come here,' I mutter, pulling her back by her collar.

Sonny is standing on the doorstep.

'Hi!' I say with surprise, looking up at him.

'Hi!' he replies buoyantly.

He's wearing shorts and a light-blue T-shirt and, if his sun-kissed skin is anything to go by, he's been spending most of his time outdoors this week.

Bertie strains at her collar, panting, so I release her and straighten up while Sonny crouches down to give her a proper greeting. She licks his face a couple of times, but he doesn't recoil.

'Have you come from Evelyn's?' I cock my head towards the southern end of the building.

'Yes. Thought I'd say hi.' He grins at me, his blue eyes made even bluer by the colour of his shirt. He's clearly in high spirits.

'Hi,' I say again, with amusement. 'Do you want to come in?' I open the door wider.

'Sure.' He stands and follows Bertie inside, while I back up against the hallway wall to make room. Two steps later, he hesitates.

'Go right,' I prompt, closing the front door.

He rounds the corner to the kitchen, looking around at the cosy space with its old-fashioned copper saucepans hanging on the whitewashed walls.

'You seem well,' I can't help but say.

'I feel great,' he replies with a heartening grin. 'I always feel better when I walk out that door.'

'That's awesome to hear,' I say warmly, glad to know these sessions are making a difference. It appears he's going twice a week. 'Would you like a drink?'

'I'd kill for a beer.'

I go to the fridge and peer inside, chewing on my lip. 'Sorry, don't have any beer. I have wine? I'm a bit low on supplies.'

'How about a drink at the pub?' he asks hopefully.

I slam the fridge door shut again. 'Why not?'

'*I'll tell you why not,*' a voice in my head says, and in my mind's eye I see Matilda, looking furious, with her hands on her hips and her foot tapping.

Inwardly laughing at the image, I sit on the stairs and

put on my sandals – sorry, Matilda, but I'm going for the pretty ones.

June's roses are in full swing. The evening air is perfumed with them and I'm suddenly very glad of an excuse to get out of the house for the evening. I was supposed to be seeing my old school friend, Danielle, but she asked to postpone, claiming exhaustion. I'll meet her newborn baby on Sunday instead.

Sonny, who took it upon himself to attach Bertie's lead while I was getting ready to leave the cottage, doesn't relinquish her to me as he sets off at a keen pace. I can't keep up with them and I'm not about to break into a run. He soon notices, looking over his shoulder at me.

'Sorry.' He seems chastened as he slows down.

'It's fine. Green Man?' It's the closest pub.

'Sounds good. Does it hurt?' he asks after a moment, glancing at my left leg.

'Er… Sometimes. Usually it's fine.' I change the subject. 'I meant to tell you! The little girl!'

'Yes?' he asks expectantly.

'Her sight came back after the surgery. Not only the one they were trying to save, but the eye she'd lost vision in.'

'That's incredible!'

'She's not completely out of the woods: she has to have chemotherapy to reduce the size of the tumour. It's benign but in a malignant place. The chemo will give her time to grow so she should be able to have less invasive surgery at some point. The doctors think she'll make a full recovery.'

'That is such good news.'

'I know. I'm so relieved.'

We walk past the busy tables out at the front, under the canopy of wisteria heavy with cascading purple flowers, and straight inside to the bar.

After grabbing some drinks, we make our way to the beer garden, a long, narrow stretch of grass lined with bench tables. At the end is a footpath that leads directly to the Meadows. It's the perfect pub for a post-dog-walk drink, as I know, having been here with Charles on countless occasions.

'Would it be all right if I leave my car parked at your place overnight?' Sonny asks. 'Evelyn said it was okay to park there if I couldn't find a space on the road,' he adds.

'Of course. You thinking of catching a taxi home?'

'Yeah. I could easily sink a couple of beers. I'll ride my bike over and collect it first thing.'

'I'll be at work, so you're welcome to grab it whenever.'

'Thanks. It belongs to my dad so I'd better get it back to him. Whose is the old Morris Minor?'

'Charles's. I learned to drive in that car.' He re-insured me before he went away so I have a set of wheels if I need them.

He's intrigued. 'Who taught you? Charles?'

I nod, then seeing his mind ticking over, explain, 'I lived with him and my aunt June when I was a teenager.' Realising this explanation is raising more questions than answers, I continue, telling him about my homeschooled upbringing and unconventional hippie parents.

'So this is not just a look for you.' He nods at my general appearance. 'It's not a fashion statement.'

'Me? Fashionable? Ha!'

'I've met plenty of women who couldn't pull this look off nearly as well as you,' he comments casually.

'Now you're making me laugh.'

'I'm not joking.'

I'm not laughing.

'You're more interesting-looking than half of the models I've worked with,' he insists. 'Models can all seem a bit bland after a while. You, on the other hand.' He leans forward and studies my face. 'Your eyes are out of this world.'

I regard him suspiciously, trying to ignore the butterflies that are stretching their wings in my stomach.

'I'm not coming on to you, by the way,' he says with a grin, knocking back a mouthful of beer.

'That's good to know,' I remark, mock-indignantly.

'Only because I'm sworn off sex, though.' He plonks his pint glass down on the wooden table and gives me a cheeky look. 'Was I right about Matilda warning you off me?'

'Yep.' I'm trying to adopt a flippancy I don't entirely feel. 'You've been a very bad boy, Sonny Denton.'

He snorts at the description, rubbing away some of the condensation on his glass.

'You're going to have a job convincing her you've changed,' I add.

'I'm not entirely sure I have changed yet. But the intent is there.'

'Do Archie and Matilda know you're going to Evelyn?' I ask curiously.

'No. It's not a secret, but it's not something I wanted to get into in front of everyone. I'll bring Archie up to date soon. Man, I fancy a burger,' he says abruptly. 'Shall we eat?'

'Sure. I've got nothing else on tonight.'

'I'll go get some menus.' He slides out from his bench seat.

'I'll have the vegetarian option if you want to order while you're up there?' I grab my purse from my bag.

'You're a vegetarian?'

'Pescatarian. I eat fish.' I offer up a twenty-pound note.

He waves me away. 'You can get it next time.'

I'm warmed by his assumption that we'll be doing this again.

He returns with another round of drinks. 'I got you fish and chips. No way was I ordering you a vegan potato, pea and seaweed burger.'

'I quite like the sound of that,' I complain jovially.

'Sorry, you're having fish and chips. Deal with it.'

I grin, picking up my fresh glass of cider. 'That sounds good too. And thanks for this.'

'Thanks for coming out and keeping me company,' he replies, raising his glass.

'I wonder what Matilda and Archie are up to tonight,' I muse.

'I thought about giving Archie a call, but decided I'd try you first.'

'I'm flattered. Or was it simply a case of you being lazy and me being right next door?'

He laughs. 'Something like that. No.' He shakes his head. 'I like you. It's admittedly quite a novel concept for me, but I think we could be friends.'

I grin at him. 'What's novel about our being friends?'

'I don't really do girl *friends*.'

'Why not?'

'Evelyn and I are in the process of working that out,' he replies humourlessly.

I consider him for a moment as he reaches down to pat Bertie – for want of something to do that doesn't involve eye contact, I think.

'What are your parents like?' I ask after a while.

'Ordinary. Dad's an accountant, Mum's a librarian. I have two older sisters: Harriet's a hairdresser, and Jackie's a secondary school teacher. They're all very normal.'

'How much older are Harriet and Jackie?' I ask.

'Harriet is twelve years older than me and Jackie is nine. I know what you're thinking – I've been through this with Evelyn – and you're right. I was spoiled as a child. Given practically anything I wanted. The baby of the family. The prodigal son,' he finishes deprecatingly. 'It would make sense for my fuckwittery to stem from there, but I had good role models growing up: my dad's never been anything other than decent to my mum – as far as I know, anyway – and my sisters are happily married with five kids between them. They're all very *normal*,' he repeats, stressing the last word. 'I think I'm just flawed.'

'And this – your flaw, as you call it – was making you unhappy?'

'It was making me *empty*,' he reveals. 'I felt hollow. Vacuous. I still feel a bit like that, to be honest. Not right at this moment,' he clarifies. 'I always feel better after seeing Evelyn.' He hesitates, his blue eyes sincere. 'And you're easy to talk to too.'

'I did learn from the best. I grew up with Charles, remember? I was forever being psychoanalysed.'

'Why did you need to be psychoanalysed?'

'I was a *teenager*,' I reply emphatically. I don't want to elaborate. 'How did you come across Evelyn?' I steer the conversation back to him.

'My sister, Harriet, recommended her to me. Her husband went through a low point a couple of years ago. Crisis of confidence, lost his job. She said Evelyn really helped him. She *made* me make an appointment. Literally pressed dial and put the phone in my hand.' He averts his gaze, but his bleak look is hard to miss. He must've been in properly dire straits after his friend died. What I've seen can't have been the half of it.

One of the bar staff is walking towards us, carrying two plates of food in his hands.

'Sonny?' he asks on his approach.

'That's me,' he replies. 'Thanks.'

I thank him too as he places my fish and chips in front of me and leaves us to it.

'If your parents are so ordinary and middle-of-the-road, why did they name you Sonny?' I ask.

'What's wrong with Sonny?' he replies with a frown, picking up a chip and biting it in half.

'Nothing. But it's a bit cool for school.'

'Am I not cool?' he asks.

I laugh. 'You're all right.' I don't want him to get a big head by telling him otherwise. 'But your parents aren't cool, are they?'

He grins and picks up his burger. 'My real name is James. When I was a baby everyone called me Jimmy. Then my grandad started calling me Sonny Jim and it stuck. At least, the Sonny bit did. I've been Sonny ever since I can remember.'

I can't say it doesn't suit him.

Later, we find ourselves sitting in two battered old leather armchairs in a cosy nook by the window. The midges came out and the light began to fade so we moved inside to the centuries-old building, where its dim lighting and predominantly wooden interior – low beams, bar, wall panels, floorboards, bookshelves – makes everything seem darker and more intimate.

For the first time this evening, our conversation has run dry. Sonny is looking at me steadily and the alcohol swimming in my veins is enabling me to stare back at him without feeling self-conscious.

'I think I'd better call a taxi,' he murmurs in a low, reluctant tone.

'Really? Already?' I ask with dismay, snapping out of the moment and checking my watch. It's only ten thirty.

'Yep,' he replies firmly but unenthusiastically, digging into his pocket to retrieve his mobile phone.

'What's the rush?' I ask as he searches through his contacts.

'You've got work tomorrow,' he mutters, his attention on his phone screen.

'I'm a big girl—'

'And if I have another drink I'll try to sleep with you,' he interrupts, meeting my eyes directly and pointedly.

'Oh.'

'Yeah.' He holds the phone to his ear.

My stomach is cartwheeling. Thankfully I have time to pull myself together while he talks to the taxi company.

'They'll be here in ten.' He puts his phone away, his expression pensive. 'I'm sorry,' he says, running his hand through his hair. 'I really want to see this through, this promise that I've made to myself.'

'If it makes you feel any better, I wouldn't have let you sleep with me anyway.'

His lips quirk up. 'Okay, then!'

I laugh at his cheerful tone.

'You know, I was planning to ask you out for a drink that day I came in to pick up my glasses,' he confesses.

'I would've gone,' I admit.

'Really?'

'Yep. You were going to Amsterdam the next day so it would've been easy: no strings attached.'

'And you would have been okay with that?' He's surprised.

'Yes. You're not the only one who has a problem with lasting relationships,' I enlighten him. It's why I haven't given him any stick about his behaviour towards women – he and I have this in common. 'The only long-term boyfriend I've ever had was when I was sixteen, but I broke up with him after it got physical.'

'Don't you like sex?' he asks with almost comical confusion.

'Of course I like sex. It wasn't about that. He got too close, too clingy.' He wanted to know all of me, inside and out, and I wasn't comfortable laying myself bare – I never have been. 'I prefer shorter flings. It's simpler that way.'

It was easier when I was abroad. Everything feels temporary when you're travelling, and people are more willing to go with the flow than muddy experiences with serious relationships. But now that I'm back here for months on end – thank you very much, Charles – I'll probably go stir crazy. I don't want to complicate my life by starting something up with someone who lives locally. One night with Sonny before he left for Amsterdam would have been perfect, but there's fat chance of that happening now.

'So you don't have to worry,' I conclude. 'I'm not going to

let you sleep with me. Not now that I'm getting to know you. In fact, I *promise* I won't let you sleep with me,' I say firmly.

'I promise not to try to sleep with you either,' he replies weakly, and I detect regret mingled in with his relief, which my ego finds mildly gratifying.

'Great. Let's get back to being friends.'

Chapter 8

'He is so beautiful,' I say with affection, staring down at the tiny bundle cradled in my arms. He's looking right at me, directly into my eyes.

A few years ago, I read an article about some research that had been conducted on babies. It claimed that infants of between two and five days old preferred to look at faces that were gazing back at them. Recordings of the brain activity of four-month-olds also showed that they processed gazing faces more deeply than faces that were averted.

Calvin is less than two weeks old and he certainly seems to like looking at me. It's hard to tear my eyes away from him to talk to his mother.

'How are you finding everything?' I ask Danielle.

She's tired but elated, her feet tucked up beneath her on the sofa and her head resting against a cushion as she cradles a mug of hot tea in her hands.

'I'm loving it,' she replies softly. 'It's hard, but mind-blowing, you know?'

I don't know. But I nod and smile empathetically.

Danielle's husband, Brett, has gone to the supermarket, so we've got the house to ourselves.

We talk about her for a bit, about her sleepless nights and breastfeeding trials and tribulations, about how her body is recovering after giving birth for the first time, about the friends she's met through her antenatal classes and how *they're* coping with all of the above.

Eventually she wants to know about me.

'What have you been up to since you've been back?'

This is the first time we've caught up, though not from my lack of trying. Danielle had so much on in the later stages of her pregnancy that she was busy every time I attempted to see her.

'Working. Looking after Bertie. Keeping Charles's house and garden in order. And I've made a couple of new friends.'

She sits up straighter. 'Who are they? What are they like?'

'Matilda works in the pharmacy next door to Umeko's.' I tell her about how we kept bumping into each other and started chatting, which makes her smile. 'And then there's Sonny.'

'Ooh.' She perks up at my change of tone, sensing a bit of juicy gossip coming her way.

'Like I say, he's a friend. But he's a good-looking one.'

Her eyes widen with glee. In my arms, Calvin starts to cry.

Danielle's face scrunches up and she checks her watch. 'He can't be due a feed yet,' she mutters, reluctantly putting her mug of tea on the table and getting to her feet. 'I'll take him,' she says with a sigh, but as soon as he's in her arms she's smiling again. She stands in the middle of the room, bouncing and cooing and he immediately stops making noises and fixates on her face.

'Good-looking?' she prompts, willing me to go on. She doesn't sit back down, doesn't want to risk setting Calvin off again.

I launch into the story of how we met, but her gaze keeps drifting to her beautiful baby boy and I'm not sure how much she's taking in.

I don't hold it against her.

She seems so different from the girl I went to school with. So grown-up. She's a *mother* now and that is *massive*.

Her cornrows need redoing and I keep thinking about how *I* used to braid her hair and she would do mine in turn. We lived in each other's pockets, once upon a time, dressed in each other's clothes, squeezed into single armchairs, feasting on popcorn and TV. We were like two peas in a pod, but that time is long gone and it's hard not to feel nostalgic for it.

Danielle and Brett have known each other even longer than she and I have. They went to the same primary school, started going out at the age of sixteen and have barely spent a day apart since. She's twenty-six – I started secondary school a year late so she's younger than me – and she's so settled already, so sure of what she wants from her life.

'Are you guys still in touch with Joshua?' I ask.

Joshua was my first boyfriend, the one I was telling Sonny about. He and Brett were best friends at school. Danielle was all about us being a foursome and I succumbed to her plans. Our friend Nina was going through treatment and I felt left out at school – it was easier to fall in.

'Yeah, we see him all the time. He's engaged. You'd know that if you were on Facebook,' she teases.

'That's great. I'm happy for him.' I hope I sound it, even if it is hard to escape the niggling fact that everyone else is moving on and growing up. Everyone except for me.

Chapter 9

My phone beeps to announce an incoming text as I'm getting into Charles's old car. Every time I drive it I experience a feeling of déjà vu that takes me right back to my teenage years: the smell of the worn maroon leather interior that matches the external paintwork colour and the distinctive ash wood frame that's scratched, inside and out. A couple of those scratches on the inside rear doors were made with my fingernails, I remember guiltily, having lost my virginity to Joshua in this very car.

Shaking my head to expel the memory of him and the other insignificant boyfriends who followed in uncomfortably quick succession, I reach into my bag for my phone.

The message is from Matilda: *The boys are playing cricket on the meadow from 1.30pm if you fancy it?*

My spirits instantly lift. *Sounds great*, I reply, starting the ignition and wondering who 'the boys' are.

My phone beeps again.

And bring your swimming costume! she messages.

I've been feeling surreal about my conversation with Sonny on Friday night. Friends don't generally talk about how they want to have sex with each other. Alcohol had loosened us up, but will it be awkward when we next see each other?

I may be about to find out.

The match is already in full swing by the time I go via home to collect Bertie, and it's such a quintessentially English scene – men in cricket whites dotted across the large green space with the River Cam in the background – that I feel compelled to simply stand for a while and watch the action.

Archie is bowling and Kev and Warren are in the field, but there's no sign of Sonny, and the realisation that he's not here makes me feel frustratingly flat.

Scanning the spectators, I spy Matilda all the way down by the river. Bertie and I go through the adjacent field to avoid getting clocked on the head by a cricket ball.

'I'm so glad you made it!' Matilda cries at the sight of us, getting up from her picnic rug to give me a hug. 'This is Faith.' She turns around to introduce her friend and my stomach churns as I realise I recognise the name: I think this is one of the women Sonny has slept with.

'Hi!' Faith says with a friendly, welcoming smile.

She's about my age and pretty: tall and thin with shoulder-length blond hair and a heart-shaped face.

'Hello!' I try to sound upbeat in turn as I pull Bertie back from the rug.

She's excited to be out because I didn't take her with

me earlier – Danielle has never been a big fan of dogs and she wouldn't have wanted one to come into contact with her newborn.

'Pimm's?' Faith offers, lifting up a jug.

'Now you're talking.'

As Matilda holds up an empty glass for Faith to fill, I settle on the side of the rug that's closest to the nearby hedge, patting the shaded grass to encourage Bertie to lie out of the sun.

Now that I think about it, didn't Matilda say it was her friend *Nessa* who refused to come out when she heard there was a chance Sonny would be there? Wasn't Faith with one of the cricketers?

'Are you a cricket fan?' I ask, hoping to clarify matters.

Matilda answers. 'About as much of a fan as I am. Faith is seeing Cameron, over there, behind the stick thingies.'

'Stumps,' Faith corrects. 'And I think he's called the wicketkeeper.'

'Don't start getting all technical with me.' Matilda gives her a withering look.

'Sorry,' Faith replies, chastised.

I laugh and take a sip of my first Pimm's of the summer. The combination of lemonade, ginger ale, fresh strawberries and mint is ridiculously drinkable.

Faith and Matilda have both kicked off their sandals, so I do the same.

The sun is beating down on my arms and legs – I've hitched up my long skirt and I'm glad I remembered to apply sunscreen and pick up my floppy straw hat before I came out.

When England feels so inclined, it does summer very well. Maybe it's the Pimm's, maybe it's the company, maybe it's the view – Matilda is right: men in cricket whites are hot – but I'm soon feeling very chilled.

'Where do you live?' Faith asks me when we're well into our second jug.

'Grantchester.' I point up the hill. 'Near the Green Man. You?'

'I'm in Barton, but Cameron's in Grantchester. He lives on Coton Road.'

Barton is where Sonny's parents live.

'I meant to ask you,' Faith says, turning towards Matilda. 'I saw Sonny coming out of the farm shop the other day. What's he doing still around?'

Our thoughts have clearly travelled in the same direction.

'Yeah, for the summer,' Matilda replies, digging into her glass and plucking out a strawberry.

'Oh, right.' She doesn't seem particularly fazed by the news. 'I'll probably bump into him at some point then.'

'I don't think he'll be staying in Barton for much longer,' Matilda reveals. 'He wants to rent a room somewhere. Keen to get out of his parents' house.'

He told me on Friday night that he was craving his own space.

'I've got a spare room,' Faith says. 'But I don't think Cameron would be too happy about it. Do you know Sonny?' she asks me.

I nod.

'Not like that,' Matilda interjects helpfully. 'Hannah's an optician. She met Sonny when he was having an eye test. We work next door to each other.' She waggles her thumb between us. 'I've warned her what he's like,' she adds ominously.

Faith grins. 'If you're after boyfriend material, steer clear, but a bit of fun never hurt anyone.'

'On the contrary,' Matilda says indignantly. 'What about poor Nessa?'

'Nessa?' Faith barks out a laugh. 'She should've known better. She *did* know better.' She glances at me and explains: 'Sonny and I shared a taxi home a couple of years ago and ended up back at mine. He returned to Amsterdam the next day and that was it. No hard feelings.' She turns to Matilda. 'Nessa seemed to think their shag on New Year's Eve was going to be the start of a beautiful relationship or something. She practically threw herself at him.'

'Ahem!' Matilda interrupts loudly.

Faith laughs. 'Yeah, yeah, pot calling the kettle black, I know. I was determined to share that taxi,' she admits with a grin. 'But at least I wasn't deluded. I don't know Nessa that well – she's more Matilda's friend – but apparently she had a crush on Sonny and was devastated when he didn't fall at her feet and declare his undying love.'

'*Slight* exaggeration,' Matilda chips in, but she doesn't correct her.

The sound of applause makes us look over at the boys.

'Have they finished?' Faith asks with surprise.

'Looks like it,' Matilda replies, getting to her feet and clapping.

Archie looks our way and jogs towards us, a grin on his face. Faith, meanwhile, sets off across the grass towards Cameron. She and Archie high five as they pass.

'Did you win?' Matilda calls as Archie approaches.

'Weren't you watching? Of course we won.'

'Ooh, you're all sweaty,' she complains with a grin as he reaches her and bends down to give her a hug.

'I'm so hot,' he says.

No one around here is denying it.

He catches sight of me over her shoulder. 'Hey, Hannah,' he says in warm greeting. 'I won't kiss you.'

'Thanks,' I reply with a smile.

Sweat is running down his face.

'We're heading to the Blue Ball,' he says. 'But a few of us are going for a swim first.'

'Just as well I packed your swimming trunks.' Matilda turns to me. 'Did you remember yours?'

'No, but it's fine. I'll be happy sticking my feet in over the side.'

'Are you sure? You could nip home?'

'I'm sure.' I'm not getting into a swimming costume in front of anyone.

I soon find myself standing next to Matilda in the shallow water of the river a bit further on towards Cambridge. She decided that she couldn't be arsed to get changed, so we've hiked up our skirts. Well, *I* have. She's wearing a thigh-length dress.

The mud is oozing between our toes, but the water is blissfully cool and it's worth the effort it's going to be to get clean later.

Faith and Cameron have left – they've got a late Sunday lunch with Cameron's parents this afternoon – and a few of the team members have already set off to the pub.

The river is heaving and barely a moment goes by without

the sound of children squealing and laughing. There are families everywhere – picnic rugs have been set up all along the banks and kids are dive-bombing in from the sides and swinging from a rope hanging from the tree opposite. Canoes, punts and paddle-boarders are going past at regular intervals and a fair few noisy ducks are loitering in the hope that there might be some spare picnic morsels coming their way. There's also a certain black Labrador joining the shenanigans. Bertie has been playing fetch and her slick solid body has been darting between the delighted children who have been taking turns to throw a stick to her. She loves swimming in the river.

Archie is floating on his back near the opposite bank and staring up at the sky, but suddenly he sinks into the water and swims over to us, looking around to check the whereabouts of his friends, I think.

'Have you heard from Sonny today?' he asks me, pushing his wet dark-blond hair off his face.

'No.' Why is he asking me?

He looks apprehensive. 'I tried ringing him earlier, but he diverted the call and then texted to say he couldn't speak. I thought he would've rung back by now. He came over last night,' he reveals. 'Told us he was seeing a counsellor. The woman who lives next door to you, right? Apparently you guys keep bumping into each other.'

I nod awkwardly and move out of the way of a child who is trying to get past me to the bank. 'He said he wanted to catch up with you properly. I didn't want to get ahead of myself by bringing it up.'

'No, of course not,' Archie says, dismissing my need to excuse myself.

'Are you worried about him?' I ask as Bertie paddles towards us, her busy feet coming to a standstill as they sink into the mud. She whines, but I'm trying to focus on what Archie is saying.

His brow furrows. 'Yeah, a bit. He didn't seem himself last night. What was he like on Friday night?'

So he and Matilda know we went out for drinks together. Matilda must be wondering why I've kept so quiet about it, especially since Sonny was a topic of conversation earlier with Faith.

'He seemed well, to be honest.'

'Hmm,' Archie says thoughtfully as Bertie quits whining and dolefully dredges through the mud towards the bank. She looks at me and I can tell she's moments away from shaking river water all over us. Luckily a child distracts her by throwing the stick again and she can't resist going after it.

Archie turns to Matilda as Bertie bounds past her, into deeper water. 'Maybe we can have him over for dinner in the next few days? Try to be supportive?'

'Yeah, sure,' she replies half-heartedly.

'He could really do with good old friends around him at the moment.' It sounds as though he needs to convince her.

'I know,' she replies. 'Yeah, of course we can invite him over.' She turns to me. 'Maybe Hannah can come too?'

I nod. I'm listening out for judgement in her tone, and I'm relieved that there seems to be none.

Then again, maybe I'm hearing what I want to hear.

Chapter 10

It's Monday afternoon and I'm in the garden at the back of the cottage when Sonny pulls up in his father's light-blue Volvo.

Archie tried calling him yesterday after his swim, but again there was no answer, so he texted to say we were heading to the pub.

I kept expecting him to turn up, but he never did.

'Hey,' I say warmly as he gets out of the car, my concern for him erasing any embarrassment I feared we might feel after Friday night's conversation.

'Hi,' he replies faintly, closing the car door behind him.

'You okay?' I ask as I walk towards him.

He shrugs listlessly. 'I'm here, aren't I?'

I stop abruptly, his dark tone catching me off guard.

'Sorry,' he mutters, his gaze fixing on the canoe I've dragged onto the grass.

'Archie isn't a fan of punting, I hear.'

'No,' he concurs.

'Canoe paddles are a lot easier to handle than punting poles. I remembered Charles had this so I thought I'd clean it up in case we want to go out in it sometime.'

He doesn't say anything, his expression blank. A moment later, he turns towards Evelyn's. 'I'd better go.'

'Okay, see you in a bit.'

'Yep,' he replies, sounding bleak.

He walks away with his head hanging down.

I carry on working on the canoe for an hour or so, and I'm still there when Sonny finishes up. I'm doing my best not to eavesdrop on what Evelyn is saying to him, but her voice carries on the breeze. She'll see him Friday, apparently.

He appears around the corner of the building, his blue eyes finding mine.

'Hey.' His lips tilt up at the corners into a small smile as he makes his way over to me.

I'm relieved to note that he seems a bit better, but I avoid asking him if he's okay, figuring that such a question asked repeatedly might become annoying.

Instead I smile and gesticulate grandly at my handiwork.

'That's an improvement.' He nods, impressed.

I've scrubbed off the grime and the green, beige and brown camouflage paintwork is gleaming.

'I still need to rinse out the inside, as you can see.' It's a quarter full of muddy water.

I notice his eyes grazing over my lower half. I changed into my old denim shorts because my skirt was getting in the way of cleaning.

'Bit grubby,' I say self-consciously, futilely brushing my hands over my dirt-smeared thighs. I wouldn't normally have my imperfect legs on show.

His expression is unreadable as he meets my eyes again.

'How was your weekend?' I'm fighting the urge to go inside and put my skirt back on.

He shrugs. 'All right. I caught up with Archie and Matilda on Saturday night.'

'They said.'

'You've seen them?'

'Yesterday, at the cricket match.'

He raises an eyebrow. 'You went to that, did you?'

'Yeah. You were missed.'

He returns his attention to the canoe. 'How will you get it to the river?'

'Charles has a set of wheels, but it's very heavy.'

'You want some help emptying it?'

'That'd be great,' I reply gratefully.

As he goes around to the other side of the canoe and prepares to tip it onto its side, I turn on the hose.

'It's okay, I've got this,' he says when I try to help him. 'You rinse it out.'

He's wearing a white T-shirt and the muscles on his biceps pop as he holds the heavy boat in place. He's still on the slim side, but he looks healthier, his skin glowing with a honey-coloured tan.

'Thank you so much,' I say when we've finished.

'Glad to be of service. My girls would love to have a turn in this.'

'Borrow it at any time,' I offer.

His expression darkens. 'The trick is persuading Rochelle to let me take them out of the village.'

'Won't she let you go anywhere with them?' I ask with surprise.

'Nope. Everything is on her terms.' He sighs. 'I don't really blame her. How was your weekend?' he asks conversationally, backing up to the bench seat wrapping around the trunk of the old apple tree and sitting down.

'Well, Saturday was a work day,' I remind him as he pats the space next to him. I wander over and sit down. The grass beneath my bare feet is squelchy and foamy with soapsuds.

'Were you hung-over?' he asks.

'No, but I'm glad you called it a night when you did. As it was, I still had to play it safe and hold my breath while dealing with clients.'

He smiles. The sunshine is filtering through the leaves, casting a patchwork of light and shade on his face. He hasn't shaved in days.

'I think I've been experiencing a bit of an alcohol low,' he admits in a subdued voice. 'I never really noticed before that drinking affects my mood, but then I used to drink more than I do now.' He hesitates before asking: 'Are you up to anything for the rest of the day?'

'No.'

'Want to take a run out to Gog Magog Hills with me?'

'What do you need to go there for?' There's a great café and farm shop, but there are closer cafés and farm shops. In fact, Burwash Larder, which is right in Barton where he lives, is one of the best in the area.

'I fancy a coffee and a drive. And I'm sick of bumping into

people I know at Burwash. My parents live in the cul-de-sac opposite the entrance,' he explains. 'I'm always seeing their friends around.'

I bet he's constantly being asked how he's doing.

'Okay, but let me nip inside and get changed first.' I realise that his previously pristine white T-shirt is now smudged with dirt. 'Sorry about your shirt. Don't suppose you have a spare?'

'It's fine,' he brushes me off. 'At least I'll be able to claim I've done something productive today,' he adds drily.

I take Bertie inside and leave her in the kitchen. I don't want her shedding black hair all over Sonny's dad's car.

The café is a twenty-minute drive away. Sonny plugs his iPhone into the stereo and sets an indie rock playlist going at top volume. We wind down our windows instead of turning on the air conditioning and opt for singing instead of talking. He seems relatively happy by the time we turn into the farm entrance. Then I point out two adorable Shetland ponies in a paddock and his mood takes a nosedive.

'The girls would love them too,' he mutters, sighing heavily as he cuts the engine and gets out of the car.

'Why won't Rochelle let you leave the village?' I ask as we walk towards the coffee shop.

'She doesn't trust me. Thinks I'm useless. Doesn't believe I'm capable of keeping them safe. I might've been useless in the past, but I *am* trying, and I'm not going to hurt them, for God's sake. I want to be able to go out for the day with them, maybe even have them overnight. I'd love to take them camping, but I can't see that *ever* happening.'

'She might come around. The worst thing you can do is give up.'

'That's what she's expecting me to do,' he agrees, opening the café door for me.

We order at the counter and then go outside to sit at a square table in the sunshine. Sonny takes the seat to my left so we're side by side, facing the courtyard, rather than opposite each other. While we're waiting for our coffees to be delivered, he picks up where he left off.

'I was hoping to see the girls yesterday, but Rochelle cancelled in the morning.'

'Do you know why?'

'Told me her new boyfriend wanted a family day.'

'Ouch.'

'Yeah.'

'You should've come out with us. We would've cheered you up.'

'I wasn't in any fit state for socialising.' He throws me an apologetic look. 'I don't mean to moan.'

'You can moan to me, I don't mind.'

'All I seem to be doing at the moment is moaning.'

'You're having a bit of a tough time, but it'll get better.'

The waitress appears with our coffees so we fall silent, thanking her as she walks away. Sonny picks up a sugar cube and drops it into his latte. He stirs it in slowly.

'Has Rochelle had a lot of boyfriends, do you know?'

He shrugs. 'I have no idea. When I've asked in the past if she's seeing anyone, she's made it clear that her personal life is none of my business.'

'Hopefully this new guy will be good for her. He must be fairly decent if he wants to have a family day with the girls, don't you think?'

'Guess so,' he replies unhappily.

'Perhaps you could offer to babysit more so she can go out with him?'

He nods. 'I suggested that on Saturday, actually. We spoke on the phone.'

'How did she take it?'

He shrugs again. 'Hard to tell with her. I'll keep offering and see where it gets me.'

Poor guy. He seems so despondent. On impulse I reach over and squeeze his arm. He glances at my hand.

'Sorry you're down at the moment,' I say sympathetically, letting him go. 'You seemed so up on Friday night. Is it only Rochelle and the kids or...?'

He sighs heavily and picks up his coffee cup.

'You don't have to talk about it if you don't want to,' I add as he's taking a sip.

He returns his cup to the table. 'It's going to sound wanky.'

'I grew up with Charles,' I remind him. 'I've heard all the therapy mumbo jumbo there is to hear.'

His lips lift up into a half-smile and he throws me a side-ways look. He makes very little eye contact when he's low, I've noticed, so when it does come, it sparks a small jolt inside my ribcage.

'My life isn't very *meaningful* at the moment,' he says sardonically.

I wait for him to go on.

'My work... My *relationships*...' His voice drips with sarcasm at that last word. 'Everything about my life right now... *No*, everything about my life for *years*... It's felt meaningless.'

I regard him patiently and my expression must compel him to continue.

'I used to love taking photographs,' he confides. 'But fashion photography… It makes me feel so empty. It's been making me feel like that for a long time.' He exhales heavily and reclines in his chair, casting me a look. 'I've got to go to Amsterdam in a couple of weeks for a job. It's the last thing I want to do, but I committed to it months ago and I can't get out of it. I don't feel at all ready to go back there again.'

'Have you been home since Easter?' I ask.

'No. I feel so guilty that I didn't go to Scott's funeral.'

'Is he your friend who passed away?'

He nods. 'I just *couldn't*. I couldn't even get out of bed.'

'Oh, Sonny,' I murmur. 'Were you very close?'

'That's the thing. We weren't. We were mainly social friends.' He sighs heavily. 'But I could see myself in him. When he died, it hit me, all at once, that I was headed the same way.'

Jesus.

'I had a choice,' he continues as my mind races. 'Stay on a downward spiral like Scott or make some changes.'

I reach across and squeeze his arm again. 'And you *are* making changes. You haven't given up. You're still here, trying to create something meaningful by spending more time with your daughters. It *will* get better. I really believe that.'

He nods. I don't think he's able to speak.

'And this job in Amsterdam…' I add. 'Maybe it'll be good for you to go home for a bit, see what you're capable of. Test this *vow* you've made to yourself.'

He looks up at me and raises an eyebrow. That last sentence was *impossible* to say completely seriously.

'You were starting to give Evelyn a run for her money until you said that.'

'I'm sorry, I'm sorry!'

He chuckles and I can't help following suit as he knocks back the last of his coffee.

Chapter 11

We're back in the car, pulling out onto the main road, when Sonny's phone rings.

'Rochelle,' he notes aloud, sounding taken aback. He gives me the universal 'pipe down' gesture with his flattened hand before pressing a button to answer the call. 'Hi,' he says.

'Where are you?' she demands.

Her snappy tone instantly puts me on edge.

'In the car. Why?'

'Where in the car? Are you far from mine?'

She sounds very impatient.

'I'm about ten, fifteen minutes away. Why?' he asks again.

'Can you pick up the kids from school and take them home for an hour or so until I can leave work? The childminder has come down with a stomach bug and my mum's at the gym.'

'Sure! But I've got a friend with—'

'Male or female?'

'Female.'

'I don't want you introducing my girls to any of your hussies!'

'She's not a...' He sounds exasperated. 'She's just a friend,' he states firmly, flashing me a look of apology as I slide down in my seat in a useless attempt to escape the onslaught.

'Well, excuse me for remembering you've slept with half of Cambridgeshire,' she snipes.

'Rochelle, you're on speakerphone,' he says calmly, while I give him a look of absolute 'are-you-kidding-me?' astonishment. Is he *trying* to wind her up?

'Forget it!' she barks. 'I'll call a friend.'

'Wait!' he shouts. 'Don't! I'll be there in ten. *Don't* call anyone else,' he adds hastily. 'I *want* to be there. I'll *be* there,' he insists.

'Fine,' she snaps, ending the call.

He hangs up and looks at me. 'Sorry. Do you mind?'

Still squirming, I tell him, not entirely truthfully, that I don't.

Rochelle lives with Sonny's children in Hauxton, a small village south of Cambridge. We drive along winding roads that take us past thatched cottages and seventies developments alike before arriving at our destination.

'I hope she called ahead,' Sonny says as he pulls up outside the village school. 'The only other time I've picked them up, their teacher wouldn't release them to me because she didn't know who I was.'

'Good luck,' I say feebly as he gets out of the car.

His life – this entire situation, in fact – sounds complicated.

It occurs to me far too belatedly that I should've asked him to drop me somewhere. I could've caught a taxi home, or even waited inside that nice delicatessen that we passed. But it's too late now.

It's a good five minutes before children start to emerge from the school gates and another five before Sonny appears. For a moment or two I'm confused. His daughters look identical: they're the same height, wearing the same school uniform and their light-blond hair is tied up into matching high ponytails. And then it hits me that they *are* identical. They're twins.

I feel as though someone has upended a bucket of ice water all over me.

Matilda made some comment about remembering what it was like to be nine and I assumed she was referring to the age of only one of his daughters. She also told me that Sonny was a perpetual one-night-stand man, and Sonny himself revealed that he hadn't been with Rochelle for long. I assumed he meant a couple of years, but knowing what I now know about him, I realise it was probably days, if that. I feel stupid for not questioning all of this sooner.

All around me, car doors are opening, with Sonny climbing into the front and his daughters piling into the back.

I force myself to turn around and smile.

Sonny twists in his seat. 'Girls, this is Hannah. Hannah, this is Imogen and Natalie.'

'Hello, Natalie!' I chirp, my insides clenching as I wave at the child Sonny indicated was Imogen. 'Hello, Imogen!'

'No, *I'm* Natalie,' Natalie says.

'No, you're *Imogen*. Wait, no, *you're* Imogen.' I point and pretend to be confused and stupid and they begin to giggle.

The sound of their identical laughter causes my heart to contract.

The Minute I Saw You

They have their father's eyes: bright, almost violet, blue, and there's something about their smiles that reminds me of him too.

'Everyone got seat belts on?' Sonny asks.

Two yeses come from the back seat.

'Hannah?' he asks me in a stern-sounding voice.

'Yes, Dad!' I yell, and they giggle again.

We go to the playground in the village, which is set within a large, green, well-kept space. I push Natalie on the swing while Sonny, next to me, pushes Imogen. Higher and higher they go until their squeals of delight verge on squeals of fear and then we slow down until they complain and we're forced to go through it all again.

Eventually Imogen says she's hungry, which sets Natalie off, and Sonny, who didn't have time to pick up any after-school snacks, says we'll have to head home. I'm not at all comfortable about the idea of entering Rochelle's territory, but it would seem very odd to the girls if I stayed in the car. Who knows how much longer their mum is going to be.

Rochelle and her daughters live in a square-fronted eighties detached house on a road full of other square-fronted eighties detached houses. The front garden is neat, but characterless: a patch of recently mown grass with a pot of pink geraniums under one of the windows.

The spare key is in a key safe by the front door and the girls know the code so we let ourselves in, Sonny and I freezing comically when the alarm begins to go off.

Natalie calmly steps up to the keypad and punches in four digits and the house falls silent.

'Phew,' Sonny murmurs, giving me a look of what

seems to be terror, and it's only then that I realise he's as on edge as I am.

'You haven't done this before?' I ask as the girls run on ahead to the kitchen.

He shakes his head with trepidation. 'Last time, Rochelle told me to wait at the playground until she got there.'

'It's a good sign!' I whisper. 'She's trusting you.'

'Mm,' he replies shortly.

There's a lot weighing on this. I can't say I'm not feeling the pressure.

Sonny walks into the kitchen and claps his hands. 'Right, what do you usually have as an after-school snack? And don't tell me it's ice cream and sweets because I won't believe you.'

'We do sometimes have ice creams and sweets!' Imogen protests.

'Yeah, we do!' Natalie gets in on the act, her little face hopeful and pleading as she stares up at her father.

'Are you trying to get me into trouble with your mum?' Sonny asks with a frown. 'What else?'

'Toast?' Natalie suggests slightly less enthusiastically.

'Toast, I can do.' He looks around, spies the breadbin and gets out a loaf of supermarket sliced wholemeal. 'How many slices?'

'Two!' come the simultaneous replies.

He puts four slices into the toaster. 'Drinks?' he asks, going to the fridge and peering inside. 'Apple juice?'

'Yes please!' Again, simultaneous.

I offer to take over the drinks, needing something to do.

All four of us are sitting at the table when we hear a key turn in the lock. Sonny gets up, but indicates that I should stay where I am. I listen to him talking to Rochelle in a low voice in the hall and her responding curt replies. She appears in the doorway.

'Hello, my darlings!' she says sunnily, her eyes darting from her daughters to me and back again.

She's not at all how I expected her to look. She's very petite with curly, almost frizzy, brown hair tied in a low ponytail. Her face is narrow, her jawline sharp, and she's wearing a light-blue uniform that is not unlike the one I have to wear to work.

'Hi,' I say, getting up from the table and holding out my hand as she approaches. 'I'm Hannah.'

I'm not sure I've ever felt this ill at ease.

'Hi.' She shakes my hand briefly, her blue eyes appraising me.

'It's been lovely meeting your girls. They're a delight.'

'They're trouble, is what they are,' she says in a joke cross voice, her eyes on her daughters.

Imogen and Natalie look over at us and giggle.

I grin at them.

When Rochelle next meets my eyes, her expression has softened slightly. 'Sorry about the late notice,' she apologises. 'But thanks for helping out. I hope I didn't disrupt your plans.'

'Oh no, not at all. It was a pleasure. I don't work Mondays so it was nice to have something to do. We'd only gone for a coffee.' I nod at Sonny, who's been hanging back behind her, watching this exchange.

'What do you do?' Rochelle asks me.

'I'm an optician.' I don't bother to say the 'dispensing' part.

Most people don't differentiate between the different roles in any case. 'My uniform is very similar to yours, actually. What do you do?'

'I'm a dental nurse.'

'Awesome.'

She smiles tightly. 'Well, thanks again.'

'As I say, it's been a pleasure.' I get to my feet, sensing the approaching expiry date on our welcome. 'Great to meet you both. Bye, Natalie! Bye, Imogen!' I wave in a ridiculously over-the-top fashion and they start to protest that I've got them mixed up again. 'I'm joking,' I say with a laugh. '*You're* Natalie and *you're* Imogen.' I'm still jesting with them and they know it now, giggling like a couple of nutcases as I back out of the room, taking my clown act with me.

'Bye,' I call to Rochelle with a grin.

'Bye,' she calls, and her smile, at last, seems genuine.

'I'll wait outside,' I tell Sonny as I pass.

He gives me a brusque nod in return, but his eyes are full of warmth.

He exits the house a few minutes later. The car was locked so I've been leaning against it with my face turned up to the cloudless sky, trying to still my frazzled heart with a few steady breaths.

'Sorry,' he apologises, hurriedly unlocking the car.

'No worries,' I brush him off, pushing off from the side and turning around.

He flashes me a look of unbridled relief, but doesn't look my way again until he's reversed out onto the road and driven out of sight.

'Thank you for that,' he says, exhaling loudly. 'She said

maybe I can pick them up from school more often, cut down on the hours the childminder does.'

'That would be cool.'

I'm amazed and slightly awed by how such a tiny person can wield so much control over a man. And I mean Rochelle, not the kids, but them too.

He nods. 'Yes, it would.'

Bless him, he really does sound utterly blown away.

Chapter 12

Sonny's phone rings again as we're driving into Grantchester.

'Archie,' he says aloud, answering on speakerphone. 'Hey.'

'All right, mate, how's it going?' Archie's deep voice fills the car.

Inside my bag, my phone begins to vibrate. I pull it out and, smiling, flash the display in front of Sonny before answering it – it's Matilda.

'Hi, you!' she says.

'Hello!'

'Quick one as I'm at work, but are you free tonight? It's supposed to rain tomorrow so Archie and I thought we'd make the most of the weather and have a barbecue.'

'That's a great idea!'

'Archie's going to invite Sonny too, if that's okay.'

'…but she's vegetarian,' I hear Sonny say, giving me a sidelong look that implies he's referring to me.

'Pescatarian,' I correct him.

'Pardon?' Matilda says in my ear, then, with surprise: 'Is that Archie I can hear?'

'Yes, he called Sonny. I'm in Sonny's car.'

'Put me on speakerphone,' she urges, so I do. 'Archie! Sonny!' she shouts.

'Wait, where did you come from?' Archie's disembodied voice asks with confusion.

'Hannah's *with* Sonny!' she tells him. 'Can he come?'

'Yes, but he says Hannah's a vegetarian.'

'Pescatarian,' Sonny chips in.

'I'll bring something for myself!' I say quickly.

'Would a halloumi burger work?' Matilda asks. 'We've got some.'

'That sounds perfect.'

'So you can both come?' Archie asks.

'Yes!' we reply.

'What can we bring?' I ask.

'Booze,' Archie replies while, at the same time, Matilda says, 'Just yourselves!'

'What time?' Sonny checks with a grin.

'Six thirty?' Archie suggests.

'Sounds good! See you later!' I say, and then we all shout bye.

Sonny and I laugh at each other.

'I don't know why they're not married already, do you?' he asks me.

'No. They make a great couple.'

'They do,' he agrees affectionately.

Sonny drops me home so I can take Bertie out for a walk while he heads back to his parents' house to get showered and changed.

He returns for me an hour or so later. The sound of his jaunty little knock makes me smile as I fight back an eager Bertie to open the door to him.

He's wearing a fresh T-shirt – navy this time – and as he greets Bertie and straightens up, I see that he's also stubble-free, and *oh wow…*

I close my eyes briefly. 'Man, you smell good.'

It's out of my mouth before I can stop it.

His lips quirk up in amusement and I laugh. 'Honestly, I think I'm addicted to your aftershave. I might have to steal some from you.'

He chuckles. 'I might've overdone it a bit. It was the end of the bottle.'

'You need to get some more.'

He steps closer to me, tilting his chin up and away to reveal his clean-shaven neck. Without thinking, I stand on tiptoe and press my nose against his neck, just below his jawline, and inhale deeply.

I'm instantly light-headed. My heels sink back onto the floor and I stare up at him.

Momentarily he seems alarmed, and then his nostrils flare and his irises are flooded with black.

His gaze drops to my lips…

And then he snaps out of it, shaking his head and taking a step backwards.

'Yeah, maybe don't do that again,' he warns, and even though his mouth is smiling, I know he's not joking.

'Okay,' I reply weakly, backing up into the hall and trying to avoid being knocked over by Bertie as I swoop down to pick up my sandals.

Shit, shit, shit, I'm thinking as I sit on the bottom step and put them on.

Sonny lets out a laugh and I regard him apprehensively, but then he doubles over. His humour sets me off and soon my hand is clutched to my chest and I'm lost to hysterics as Bertie barks madly at us both.

'Shall we go?' he asks when the three of us have calmed down. Tears of laughter have caught in his eyes, making them sparkle like sunshine on an ocean.

I nod determinedly and get to my feet, clicking my fingers to move Bertie out of the way. 'See you later,' I say to her, giving her head a pat before remembering to grab the bottle of Prosecco from the fridge and the roses I picked earlier for Matilda.

Following Sonny out the door, I pull it shut behind me.

Sonny is driving tonight – he didn't want to drink – and he's managed to park on the road right outside. When we're shut up together in the confined space of his dad's car, I realise that our laughter hasn't dispelled the nervy feeling in my stomach. In fact, my butterflies have whipped themselves up into a whirlwind.

I can't think of *anything* to say. I'm glad he's driving because I need a drink. I should have bloody well walked.

'Oh, I got a text from Rochelle earlier,' he says when we're out of Grantchester and are on the hedge-lined country road leading towards town.

I'm relieved that he's broken the silence, but his voice is artificially nonchalant.

'Did you? What did it say?'

'Thanks for helping out earlier. She says I can do something with the girls on Saturday.'

'That's great!'

'Yeah. And she said to say thanks to you too.'

'That's nice.'

'Yeah.'

Seconds tick by. I frown and stare out of the window as we pass a couple of college sports fields.

'What will you do with them?' I think to ask, turning back to him.

'I don't know yet. Depends on whether she'll let me take them out of Hauxton.'

'Why don't you suggest canoeing?'

'Have you got life jackets?'

'Only adult ones.'

'I could buy some,' he muses as the green spaces on either side of the road give way to semi-detached houses.

He flicks on his indicator and turns right.

'I've never been to Archie and Matilda's house,' I say, looking out of Sonny's side window at the small double-storey tawny-brick Victorian houses lining the entire length of the road. They're accessed directly from the pavement and have no front gardens, so they're only distinguishable from each other by their painted doors and the numbers hanging outside.

'It's cool. Archie's got a good eye for design.'

Our friends live behind a teal-coloured door – Matilda answers it when we knock.

'Hello!' she says, beaming and embracing me before backing up into the hallway.

'Hey, guys!' Archie calls from behind her, lifting his hand in a merry wave.

I squeeze past Matilda to exchange a cheek kiss with Archie while Sonny and Matilda greet each other behind me, but Archie waits until we're in the kitchen with more room to move before giving Sonny a friendly hug. The sight of their easy affection fills me with warmth.

Sonny is right: behind the uniform outward appearance of the house is a stylishly designed interior.

The kitchen has light-grey walls on one side and a slightly darker grey central island, but the rest of it is decorated in a palette of greens and blues, from the pale-green wall tiles to the teal-coloured cabinets and the emerald pendant lights hanging over the island. To the front of the house is the living room, and I can see through the open double doors that the colour scheme is predominantly greens and yellows. To the back of the house is a new extension opening up onto the garden and containing a dining table that seats six.

'Your place is amazing!' I exclaim, distractedly handing Matilda the roses, a selection of June's brightest – the colours scream summer.

'These are *beautiful*,' she enthuses, going to a low kitchen cupboard and bringing out an opaque white vase. 'Archie's the designer around here. I fell in line.'

I stop nosing around and proffer the bottle of Prosecco. 'I brought this too.'

'There was no need,' she says, filling the vase with water. 'But thank you. Archie, can you…?'

'Sure.' He drags his attention away from Sonny's collection of fancy-looking beer bottles – Sonny brought them along, even though he's not drinking – and gets a couple of flutes out of the cupboard.

When our drinks have been poured, we head outside to the garden. It's long and narrow and looks straight out onto one of the college playing fields – Downing College, as I discover when I ask.

'How long have you lived here?'

'About two years,' Matilda replies as we all sit down at a sleek bench table made out of weathered silvery-looking wood.

There's an array of snacks set out: nuts, olives, crisps and dip served in jewel-coloured bowls.

'Archie used to live on the other side of town, but agreed to come this way,' she adds with a smile.

Matilda's dad lived on one of the roads close to where we work in a two-storey Victorian detached. She pointed it out to me once when we were going for a walk at lunchtime. Selling it enabled her to buy this place outright, leave her boring job in London and finance a new life and career up here with Archie, but I sense her current happiness is bitter-sweet. She and her dad were close.

'This is a much nicer area,' Archie acknowledges. 'But my place was handy for your degree.'

'It was. *And* your work. I'm sorry.'

He grins at her and reaches across to brush his knuckle across her cheek. I think he'd agree to live in the arse end of nowhere if that's what she wanted.

'Oh, guess what!' I chirp. 'I found Charles's canoe earlier and cleaned it up. Sonny helped.' I feel compelled to give him credit.

'I hardly did anything.' He bats it back to me.

'Anyway, it's ready to go if we want to use it sometime.'

'Definitely!' Archie exclaims. 'How about this weekend, if the weather comes good again?'

'We could canoe into Cambridge and have a few drinks?' Matilda suggests excitedly. 'Are you free Saturday night?'

'I am, tragically,' I reply and we all look at Sonny.

He nods. 'I've got the girls Saturday daytime, but Rochelle will probably want them back in time for dinner.'

'What are you going to do with them?' Matilda asks.

'Funnily enough, Hannah has offered us the canoe. I've only got to persuade Rochelle to let me take them out in it.'

'How could she have a problem with that?' Archie asks with a frown.

'She's still keeping me on a tight leash,' Sonny replies.

We come up with a plan in the event that Rochelle agrees: Archie will help Sonny take the canoe down to the Cam while Matilda and I are at work on Saturday. Sonny can go out with his daughters in the afternoon, and then Archie will man the boat while Sonny drops the girls home. Matilda and I will head to the river straight from work.

I'm already looking forward to it. I feel lucky to have made such lovely new friends. And we've still got a whole evening ahead of us.

Chapter 13

Over dinner we get into a conversation about TV. Neither Charles nor Sonny's parents have Netflix or Sky, and Sonny in particular has been going a bit stir crazy of an evening. His parents are addicted to soap operas and, with only one TV in the house, it's been a challenge for them to find something they all want to watch together.

As for me, I've been working my way through a couple of DVD box sets that I picked up from a charity shop, but it's been kind of lonely. Charles was never one for watching television – he preferred to talk, read or play cards and board games – so I used to go to Danielle and Nina's houses to get my telly fixes. There was something so lovely about watching TV with a friend, sharing the experience at the same time and talking about it afterwards – I'm nostalgic for it.

When Archie brings up *Stranger Things*, a TV series that he and Matilda are yet to start watching but which is set in the eighties and references everything from *The Goonies* to

E.T. The Extra-Terrestrial, Sonny and I get excited. We share a mutual love for eighties films, it turns out.

'Shall we watch the first episode now?' Matilda asks eagerly. 'We could make it our thing!'

I love this idea and so do the boys, so we enthusiastically file inside, collecting empty plates and bottles as we go.

There are photo frames on the mantelpiece in the living room and while I'm waiting, I take a closer look. There's one photo of a man, aged about sixty, with his arm around Matilda, captured at Christmas I think, from the presence of fairy lights in the background. He has a wide, open face with thinning brown hair falling down slightly across his forehead.

'Is this your dad?' I ask Matilda as she joins me.

'Yeah,' she replies.

'You have the same smile.'

In the photograph they're beaming, but her expression is miserable now.

'I'm sorry you lost him too soon,' I murmur.

'Thanks.' She arm-bumps her gratitude before going to the coffee table to put down two large bowls of popcorn.

She returns to the kitchen, shooing off my help, so I sit cross-legged on the floor next to the oversized armchair, leaving the two-seater sofa free for Archie and Matilda. Sonny comes through and offers to sit on the floor instead.

'I'm happy,' I reply. 'If my bum gets numb, I'll squeeze onto that with you.'

I'm not wholly serious, but he says, 'All right,' and seems to be sincere.

Matilda and Archie join us and start up their own protests about seating arrangements.

'We can take the snuggler seat,' Matilda offers.

Is that what it's called?

By the time I've convinced her I'm content, I've had to get a bit stroppy.

'Fine, we'll sit there next time,' she decides.

The show is properly creepy. I love it.

About half an hour in, I shift and rest my back against the right-hand side of the armchair, stretching my legs out in front of me and crossing them at the ankles. As I sweep my long hair over my right shoulder, Sonny's knee becomes visible out of the corner of my left eye, so I'm aware when his leg begins to jiggle.

I glance over my shoulder at him. 'Are you scared?' I whisper teasingly.

He plays along and nods, wide-eyed, before edging across to the left-hand side of the chair. He pats the empty space he's created.

I act without thinking.

Now we're actively pressed up against each other, the entire left-hand side of my body firmly connecting with his right. I can feel his chest expanding with every breath and it's making my heart feel all skippy and skittery.

The tension is building on the TV, which adds to the tension I'm already feeling. I know there's a jump-out-of-my-skin moment coming, but I still act accordingly when it arrives.

Sonny chuckles. Then he murmurs, 'Excuse me,' and slowly and deliberately leans across me to place his empty bottle on the side table. In doing so, I'm exposed to a direct hit of my new favourite drug.

'What the hell?' I mutter as he retreats, and the look he casts me tells me he knew exactly what he was doing.

His eyes – navy in this light – are glittering with amusement.

'Are you trying to drive me crazy?' I ask in the same barely there voice.

'I don't know what you mean,' he replies innocently.

I'm certain the warning he gave me earlier was genuine, so this feels a whole lot like playing with fire. If we get burnt, the blame is squarely in his corner.

I lose whatever control I had and lean towards him, pressing my nose against his warm skin and inhaling deeply. I feel him shudder beneath me and the blood coursing through my veins picks up speed, making me giddy with something that feels dangerously like lust.

'What was *that*?' Matilda's perturbed voice breaks us apart. 'She just sniffed his neck!' she exclaims as Sonny throws his head back and laughs.

Matilda lets out a groan and buries her face in her hands.

'What's wrong?' Archie asks her with amusement.

She lifts her head and stares at me forlornly. 'You.' She looks at Sonny. 'And you. You're into each other, aren't you?'

'It's all under control,' Sonny states, trying to keep a straight face and failing massively.

I notice he didn't deny it.

'I have promised Hannah that I won't try to sleep with her,' he continues facetiously. 'And Hannah has promised me that she won't *let* me try to sleep with her, so we're all good.'

'Oh. That's awesome to hear,' Matilda says sarcastically as a thrill zips through me.

'Does this agreement have an expiry date?' Archie asks with a grin.

'Oh, once my six months are up, I'm making no promises,' Sonny replies flippantly, giving me a cocky grin that reminds me of how he was on the day we met.

'Six months, now, is it? Not a year?' I ask.

'Six months is plenty.'

I stare at him for a long moment. 'I'll be gone by then anyway,' I say flatly, twirling a lock of hair around my finger.

'What do you mean?'

'I'm only here until Charles comes back.'

'When's that? The end of September?'

I nod.

'Where will you go?' Matilda asks, and she sounds put out now too.

I shrug. 'I don't know yet. I might pop down to Australia for a while to catch up with my parents.'

'Where do they live?'

'South Australia,' I reply. 'On a houseboat.'

'Cool!' Matilda says.

'They like it.'

My dad's Australian, but he met my mum when they were travelling around Europe. After they were married, they settled in the UK, but when I was in my final year of school, my dad's mother – my only remaining grandparent – fell ill so they decided to go back to Australia to take care of her. It was supposed to be a temporary arrangement, but they made it permanent, selling everything they owned on land and reinvesting in a home on water.

'You're only going on holiday though, right?' Sonny is frowning at me.

'I'm not sure. Anyway, aren't you returning to Amsterdam at the end of the summer?'

He shrugs. 'I've been thinking about moving back here permanently.'

'Really?' Archie interjects.

Sonny nods.

This information makes me feel oddly unsettled.

Chapter 14

It's Saturday and I'm at work, polishing lenses and willing the hours to pass quicker. They're not complying.

'Any plans for tonight?' Abbey asks me casually, leaning so far back in her chair that it wouldn't surprise me if she put her feet on her desk.

Our next client is not due for another twenty minutes and it has been deathly quiet in the shop today. After four days straight of rain, we woke up this morning to glorious blue skies, so everyone seems to be out in the sun, enjoying themselves.

It's a perfect day for messing around on the river. I'm so pleased for Sonny that Rochelle agreed to let him take the girls out.

'I'm heading into town on a canoe,' I jubilantly reply to Abbey's question. 'Can't wait. What about you?' I reach for the Kilsgaards – the same ones Sonny ended up buying. I hardly ever see him wearing them.

'Dale and I are going to Cecily and Ricky Dick's.' Dale's her boyfriend, Cecily is her sister and 'Ricky Dick' is Cecily's husband Richard. I'm not sure he's aware of his nickname. 'All the work is done now, so we're toasting the opening.'

I flash her a quizzical look, while continuing with my polishing. 'Opening?'

'Their Airbnb,' she says. 'That's what Cessy's been doing: converting their garage into a studio flat that they can rent out.'

'Oh, right! I had no idea that's what she was up to. Has it gone live online yet?'

'Nah, she didn't want to risk putting it up on the web-site until the work was done, but she reckons it'll get booked up fast. It's a great location and very reasonable price-wise.'

I pause what I'm doing. 'Do you think she might be inter-ested in a short-term rental?'

As if the day weren't already passing slowly. Now I have to contend with the added anticipation of telling Sonny that I might've found him somewhere to live. Abbey called Cecily to ask about it and she jumped at the idea, even going so far as to say she'd agree to a vastly reduced price if Sonny could move in straight away. I'm gutted I don't have his number because I'd text him if I could – he keeps turning up on my doorstep unannounced so it hasn't occurred to me to exchange contact details.

Yesterday evening was the first time I regretted that we hadn't. I knew he was supposed to be seeing Evelyn and I'd assumed he'd have the last appointment of the day like he had previously, so I found myself twiddling my thumbs, waiting for him. When I heard Evelyn leaving, I impulsively ran outside and flagged her down.

'Did Sonny come to see you earlier today?' I asked.

The look on her face mortified me. 'I can't discuss my clients, Hannah,' she said with regret.

'Of course! Sorry!' I blurted. 'I was only worried about him, but I'm sure he's fine!'

Properly cringe-inducing. I went straight indoors and gave myself a stern talking to.

Matilda later texted me to say that we were all set for today's plan, with Archie and Sonny coming to collect the boat at midday.

I left the canoe in the garden with the paddles inside. Sonny would no doubt have sorted kids' life jackets.

It bothers me how much I wanted to see him last night, and it alarms me how much I'm looking forward to seeing him this evening. I don't like being sidetracked by a man – nothing positive can come from it. I'll need to think of something else to consume my headspace.

When five o'clock finally comes around, I nip into the staff bathroom to get changed before saying goodbye to Umeko and collecting Bertie from Robert.

Bertie used to love going out in the canoe with Charles, but it's been years since he took her, so I hope she'll be okay in it tonight.

Matilda exits the pharmacy as I'm saying goodbye to Robert.

'I was coming to call for you next,' I tell her. 'You look nice.'

She's wearing a red capped-sleeve knee-length dress covered with tiny white flowers.

'So do you!' she replies. 'I love your hair.'

I woke up early this morning so took the time to braid the front section into a plait, leaving the rest of my hair down in its usual loose waves.

'Thanks! Shall we go?'

'I need to pop to the supermarket first to get chilled Prosecco. Archie texted to say he forgot ice.'

'We can get some of that too.'

I hover outside on the pavement with Bertie while she does the honours, then we head to the river together.

We spy Archie before he spies us – possibly because he looks like he's fast asleep.

He's moored the canoe to a tree and is lying on the grass, his arms folded behind his head and his long legs crossed at the ankles. He's wearing sunglasses, so I can't be certain his eyes are shut, but I'm guessing they are because he doesn't look up until Bertie is almost upon him.

'It's all right for some!' Matilda calls out as he bolts upright with alarm and then grins, giving Bertie a rigorous pat. 'Nice day?'

'Great,' he replies, getting to his feet and wandering over to greet us. We exchange kisses and he takes the bag of ice from me. 'How was yours?' he asks as he carries it back to the boat over his shoulder.

We talk for a bit and he tells us that everything went well

earlier with Sonny, Imogen and Natalie – Sonny only left an hour ago to drop them home.

'Did he seem okay?' I'm still wondering if he went to see Evelyn yesterday.

Archie nods. 'Yeah, but who knows if he was putting on a front for his kids. I guess we'll find out later. He said he'd meet us in town at six thirty near Garret Hostel Bridge.'

With much clambering and wobbling, we manage to get the four of us – Bertie included – into the boat without it capsizing. Bertie's claws scritch and scratch on the bottom and she doesn't seem as though she wants to settle, so I stay sitting in the middle with her while Matilda and Archie paddle. Archie, the heaviest, sits at the back, while Matilda takes to the front.

The river is already busy with water traffic, but Archie and Matilda quickly get the hang of paddling and soon we're bypassing people in punts on our way into Cambridge.

'You guys are good at this,' I comment, enjoying the journey. I've been watching brilliantly blue damselflies darting in and out of the nearby rushes, and sometimes the water is so clear that small fish are visible swimming between the reeds below.

'Yep, she's a natural,' Archie replies, his paddle sluicing through the water on our left, as Matilda propels us forward with hers on the right-hand side of the boat. They're in perfect sync with each other. 'You should see her punting.'

From the front, Matilda laughs. 'This is even easier.'

'I can take over whenever you like,' I offer. 'Bertie seems to have settled at last.' She's lain down across my feet.

'I'm happy,' she replies. 'But let me know if you want a turn. Or you can swap with Archie.'

'Oi!' he snaps. 'This is the one thing I can do!'

'*The one thing…*' Matilda says with a snort. 'The only thing you *can't* do is punt.'

He laughs. 'That's not true, but very kind of you to pretend that I'm excellent.'

'You *are* excellent,' she says.

I make a show of act-vomiting over the side. They laugh.

'How are we doing for time?' I ask. 'Shall I crack open this bottle?'

'Go for it!' Matilda enthuses. 'As long as you can hold my glass for me while I'm doing this extremely important job.'

'Yep. Archie?'

'Can you grab me a beer?'

I sort out Archie first, passing a can to him. He brings his paddle up and over his knees, allowing the boat to coast for a bit, while Matilda steers. Then I pop the cork on the Prosecco.

'Woohoo!' Matilda cheers obligingly.

I pour out two glasses and she takes one, chinking mine before taking a sip.

As we continue to drift, I turn my face up to the sun. The sound of the Prosecco fizzing mingles with the noise of the water moving through the rushes and a duck incessantly quacking nearby.

Archie breaks the silence. 'Ooh, shit!' he gasps, and we jolt as the boat hits the bank.

Bertie gets to her feet in alarm, causing me to spill some of my drink as her backside shoves against my legs.

'It's all right, it's all right,' I soothe, but to my horror she puts her feet on the side of the boat and looks as though she's about to make an exit. I try to grab her collar at the risk of my drink going everywhere. But she's too strong and when she wants something…

Too late. She's in.

'Oh, Bertie, no!' I cry with dismay as Matilda starts laughing.

Now what do I do?

It's hard not to see the funny side, but I know I'm going to be wet through when she gets back in the boat. And how exactly am I going to haul her in? Please do not tell me that I'll need to jump in after her… I look around wildly for access to the bank, but it's dense with stinging nettles.

Archie stands up, causing the boat to quiver precariously.

'Shall I lift her in?' He swoops down to try to grab Bertie's bright red collar as she swims past. She's effusively oblivious to the trouble she's causing. A duck dashes out from between some low-hanging tree branches, quacking in fright, and Bertie swerves out of Archie's reach.

'There!' I shout, spying an exposed section of the bank where I should be able to disembark.

Archie and Matilda manoeuvre us into position – I have no idea how they're managing to paddle with drinks to contend with – and I clamber out, turning around to call for Bertie.

Of course, she's having far too much fun to quit swimming anytime soon, but Archie guides her in my direction with his paddle, and I manage to snag her collar. Getting her out of the water is another matter entirely, but one very wet and muddy Hannah later, the dog is on the bank.

I collapse onto my back and laugh my head off, not even

bothering to push Bertie away when she tries to lick my face, dripping water all over my lacy white top.

'I'll give us some time to dry off before we attempt to get aboard,' I say finally, standing up. The path runs alongside the river so I can walk while they paddle along beside me.

'At the very least, take this.' Matilda dispenses a fresh glass of Prosecco.

'If you insist.'

The path occasionally veers away from the river, but when we're in eye and earshot of each other, we talk as we make our way into town. It's clear, however, that the pace of the boat is much faster than the speed I'm capable of on foot so I soon tell my friends to go on ahead and moor up somewhere where they can enjoy their drinks. They're happy to oblige.

Meanwhile, I revel in the peace and quiet and the light-headedness that the bubbles are bringing on.

It's a beautifully warm evening, but Bertie soaked my top and part of my skirt right through so it'll be a while before it dries.

There's male laughter up ahead and around a bend I see two guys swimming, their long lean torsos glimmering in the early evening sunshine. Further along the river, I catch sight of Archie and Matilda. It looks like they've found some-where to wait.

'Hallo!' one of the men calls to me in what sounds like a German accent.

'Hi.' I throw him a smile.

'Wait!' this same man says.

I come to a stop and stare at him. He looks familiar and,

even partly submerged underwater, the breadth of his shoulders implies what I already know: that he's very tall. His hair is blond and his eyes are denim-blue. I know this too, even though he's too far away to truly tell. I know, because I *know him*, although I still don't know *how* I know him.

'Spain,' he tells me with a wide, attractive smile. 'Granada. You don't remember, Hannah?'

And then it all comes flooding back. 'Johann!'

We met when I was twenty after I'd spent time travelling through Europe. I was delaying my return to the UK, nowhere near ready to take up studying again. I had been accepted onto an Ophthalmic Dispensing course in Bradford, but had postponed it a year and was thinking about putting it off again. I was torn between what I wanted for myself and the high expectations that June and especially Charles had for me. It was a case of heart versus head. Head won, in the end. But those months before I came home were some of the wildest and most carefree I'd ever had.

A fellow traveller had told me about a hippie commune in the Sierra Nevada mountains in Southern Spain and I'd decided to try to find it. My parents had fallen in love at a similar commune – it might have even been the same one – and I was curious to see what it was like.

As it turned out, it was just a bunch of very ordinary people living a basic, no-thrills lifestyle. I spent a few chilled, albeit unexciting, weeks there.

Anyway, Johann was Interrailing through Europe and we met on the train en route to Granada. There was an instant attraction between us so I decided to hang in the city with him for a few days before going my own way.

He swims towards me now, taking in my appearance. 'It's incredible to see you again.'

'What are you doing here?'

He nods at his friend. 'Giles is getting married next weekend. I'm here for the wedding.'

Giles waves at me. 'Hello!'

He's British.

'Hi,' I reply with a smile.

'Where are you off to now?' Johann asks.

'I'm heading into Cambridge with some friends.'

'You live around here? Perhaps we could meet up later?'

'Oh, I'm not sure what we're doing yet. Also we're going to be on a canoe that only fits four at a push. Well, five.' I indicate Bertie.

He seems disappointed and something occurs to me... Could this be the distraction I need?

'But maybe we could catch up while you're here?' I run with that thought.

'Great! Let me get your number.'

Before I can suggest taking his instead, he's pushing himself out of the water on muscled arms. As he gracefully gets to his feet, rivulets of water stream down the entire length of his super-ripped body. I pull my eyes away from his abs as he grabs a towel to dry his hands.

'What's your number?' he prompts, having retrieved his mobile phone from a pocket of his discarded jeans.

I come to with a start, reeling it off for him.

'I'll text you,' he promises with a significant look. 'It's really good to see you again,' he repeats with a grin.

'It's good to see you too,' I reply, heat collecting on my cheeks.

At that moment I'm hit with a flashback of our last night together.

Yes, this is *exactly* the distraction I need.

We say our goodbyes and I walk on.

Chapter 15

By the time we reach the weir, I'm extremely tipsy.
Unbeknownst to me, Matilda and Archie witnessed my entire
exchange with Johann, so Matilda has spent the last part of the
journey plying me for details about him. The more I've drunk,
the looser my tongue has become. I think she worked this out
because she kept pausing in her paddling to top up our glasses.

Now we have to concentrate on lifting the canoe out of
the water and carrying it across the footpath to the ramps that
will ease it into the lower part of the river. It would be hard
enough doing this sober, but drunk is another matter. We
have to avoid cyclists, pedestrians and, bizarrely, a single cow
that has wandered here from the nearby meadow. Luckily
Archie can hold his liquor better than Matilda and I can.
She and I are in fits of giggles, and when she asks the cow to
'please mooooooove', I almost wet myself.

God knows how we manage to get back into the boat
without falling in.

The section of the Cam up near Grantchester felt busy, but that river traffic was inconsequential compared to what's in town. It's a sunny Saturday evening and the punters are out in force. There are dozens and dozens of vessels to contend with. Many of them are larger tour boats seating twelve passengers, but there are plenty of smaller six-seater boats containing novices who have no idea how to steer themselves away from danger.

'You guys are amazing!' I exclaim, awed at how my friends keep managing to avoid collision. 'Even drunk, you can paddle straight.'

Matilda laughs.

This is Cambridge at its most picturesque, with bridges arching over the glittering water and historic buildings butting right up to the river in places. And then there's the grand sight of the towering King's College Chapel, set back behind a huge, perfectly mown lawn.

'I need a wee,' I say loudly, aware that this crude statement is not really in keeping with our glorious surroundings.

'We're almost there,' Archie tells me, and I think he's trying not to laugh, even though he's behind me and I can't see his face.

The need to go intensifies to such an extent that by the time we're approaching Garret Hostel Bridge, my thoughts are almost entirely consumed by how quickly I'll be able to run to McDonald's to sneakily use the bathroom. I do look up at the bridge to see if Sonny is here yet, but I'm too preoccupied to mind when there's no sign of him. Then we turn into the small waterway where I plan to disembark and he's right there, sitting on the edge of the platform with the safety railings behind him, dangling his bare feet in the water.

'Hi!' he says, grinning.

'Hi!' I reply with surprise, already standing up and attempting to keep my balance while holding Bertie back.

'Hannah's desperate for the loo!' Matilda helpfully interjects.

Sensing the urgency, Sonny jumps to his feet and climbs through the railings to assist me. I jolt at the touch of his strong hands closing around mine as he helps me onto solid ground. He places his hands on my waist, steadying me.

'Um, do you know your top is currently see-through?' he asks with raised eyebrows.

'Is it?' I glance down at myself with alarm and see the coral colour of my lacy bra emanating through the fabric of my still-damp white top.

'Is it?' Matilda asks with equal alarm, turning to stare at me. Her eyes boggle. 'Archie, why didn't you tell her?' She sounds accusatory.

'I didn't notice! She had her back to me! Why didn't *you* tell her?' he barks in return.

'Right now, I wouldn't care if I was running through the streets naked!' I yell as they continue to bicker, but before I can reach the road, Sonny has whipped off his white shirt and held it out for me to put on.

'Much as I'd love to see that,' he murmurs in a low voice that only I can hear as I slip my arms in – the sleeves are rolled up.

I flash him a cheeky grin and set off at a run across the uneven cobblestones, resisting the urge to look over my shoulder.

Five minutes later, I exit a cubicle feeling a *lot* happier. Tying Sonny's shirt into a knot at my waist, I come out onto Rose Crescent and see him leaning up against the sandstone walls of the building opposite, waiting for me.

'It's as well you were wearing that underneath,' I say with a grin, nodding at his white T-shirt.

Not that *I* would have minded seeing *him* run through the streets naked... Well, *half*-naked.

He's looking very cool and summery in sunglasses, light-grey shorts and cream-coloured Vans.

He pushes off from the wall and comes towards me, bending his head down to casually kiss my cheek.

'You really have run out of aftershave, haven't you?' I say sadly.

'I'm afraid so,' he replies.

'I've already sniffed your shirt.' Pause. 'Not saying that's not weird.'

He laughs and nods at the restaurant spilling out onto the pavement up ahead. 'Archie and Matilda suggested pizza for dinner. I volunteered to come and get them. Thought you might wait with me?'

'Of course.'

A table comes available outside so one of the servers lets us sit down and order a couple of drinks to pass the time.

'I need to slow down,' I say, opting for an apple juice.

'I need to catch up,' he replies, going for a beer.

'You're drinking tonight?'

He nods. 'My mum gave me a lift in. What?' he asks, seeing the spark of excitement on my face.

I completely forgot I had something to tell him.

He loves the sound of Abbey's sister Cecily's place and right then and there sends her a text, telling her he's definitely interested. She replies within minutes and makes arrangements for him to visit tomorrow. While this is going on, we find time to chat about today and how much Imogen and Natalie enjoyed canoeing. They took a picnic with them, moored up and even went swimming.

'They were still chattering ten to the dozen when I dropped them home,' he says fondly. 'Asking when we can go out in it again.'

'As I've already said, you're welcome to borrow it anytime.'

'Maybe next time you can come with us?'

'Oh, I wouldn't want to intrude,' I brush him off.

'You wouldn't be. You could bring Bertie.'

'Bertie! Ha! You saw the state of me – the little madam jumped over the side!'

'Is *that* what happened?'

'Yes, it was a total nightmare trying to get her out onto dry land.'

He seems entertained by the thought of it.

'Rochelle asked me to look after the girls next Saturday night,' he reveals. 'She's got a date.'

'Ooh.'

'Yeah.' His smile is half-hearted. 'Unfortunately, I can't. I have to go to Amsterdam for that job.'

'Oh.'

He sighs. 'I asked if I could do Friday night instead. She said she'd get back to me. I'd really love to have them for a sleepover. Maybe if Cecily's place works out.'

'That'd be good. How are you feeling about going home?'

119

He shrugs. 'Same. Not looking forward to it, but it's something I've got to do.' He gives me a small smile. 'Want to come with me? See your friend?'

'When are you going?' I don't immediately dismiss the idea.

'Saturday. But we could go Saturday evening after you finish work? Back Monday night?' He looks hopeful.

'That might work.' It actually sounds incredibly appealing. 'I'd have to check Nina is free.'

'Text her now.'

'Shall I?'

'Yeah, go on,' he urges.

I hesitate, but then get out my phone, trying to sort through my jumbled thoughts. Is this a good idea? It *feels* like a good idea. But *is* it? I can't think why it wouldn't be. We'd be able to share travel costs to and from the airport, for a start.

I text Nina, not expecting her to reply anytime soon, but before I can put my phone back into my bag, it buzzes.

Her reply is one word: *YES!*

'She's keen,' I tell Sonny.

'Really?' He's delighted.

'Yeah.' I show him the text. But then my phone buzzes again. I check the display.

'Oh,' I say aloud.

'What?'

'She's remembered her boyfriend's sister is staying next weekend.'

'Crash at mine,' he offers.

'Have you got a spare room?'

'No, but I'll sleep on the sofa.'

We stare at each other for a few seconds before I return

my attention to my phone. 'Shall I suggest it?' I don't sound as casual as I'd like to.

'Yes.'

That would be brilliant! Nina texts. *She's leaving Sunday anyway, so you could always stay that night!*

I fill Sonny in.

'Great!' He seems glad to have the company. 'I'll look into flights tomorrow.'

'Okay.'

I text Nina to say I'll keep her posted and try to push aside the niggling feeling that I've jumped into this too quickly. There's time to back out, if I want to.

I take a sip of my drink and peer through the window into the restaurant, wondering how much longer we'll have to wait for these pizzas. When I look at Sonny, he's gazing past me at the market place, and then his expression abruptly changes from relaxed to horrified. He scrapes his chair out from the table and I register the simultaneous sound of gasps of alarm from people nearby, but before I can ask Sonny what's wrong, he's bolted towards the market place. I twist in my seat in time to see him reach the road and crouch down over a figure.

Has someone been hit?

I get to my feet and run towards him. A small crowd of people has gathered, but they're keeping their distance, and when I reach Sonny, I see a girl in her early twenties, with matted auburn hair and baggy, misshapen clothes sitting on the kerb. A cyclist nearby has dismounted.

'She walked straight out in front of me,' the cyclist is saying.

He's only young – probably a student. He seems stunned.

Others are attending to him, but Sonny is focused on the girl on the ground – I think she might be homeless.

'Are you hurt?' Sonny asks her, his hands on her shoulders.

'I didn't see him,' she mumbles, dazed.

'Can someone get her a sweet tea?' Sonny asks the crowd.

'I'll go,' a middle-aged woman volunteers.

I kneel down beside them. 'Are you okay?' I ask her.

She nods. 'I didn't see him,' she repeats.

Sonny turns to me. 'She literally stepped onto the road and he hit her.'

'What's your name?' I ask.

'Mel.'

It occurs to me that there might be something wrong with her peripheral vision. This could be caused by several things: glaucoma, head trauma, detached retina or even eye stroke. When I was in India, we treated a middle-aged man with the latter, but he came in so late to us that there was little we could do to save the sight in his right eye. This meant that he could no longer work, which was incredibly traumatic for him and his family. It's something I still think about to this day.

'Can you look at me for a moment, Mel?' I ask. 'Keep looking at me.' I hold my finger up between us and move it around to the left-hand side of her face. 'Can you see my finger out of the corner of your eye?'

She nods.

I move it round to the other side. 'Can you see it now?'

Again, she nods.

I do the same thing, moving my finger up and down. To my relief, she passes this basic test, but she's not out of the woods yet.

I repeat the same test, this time asking her to follow my finger, and then ask her to read a poster in the market.

She squints and concentrates, but to no avail.

'When was the last time you had an eye test?' I ask, thinking she almost certainly needs glasses.

She shrugs. 'Can't afford it.'

'You can get one free on the NHS,' I point out with a frown.

'You need to be registered for benefits,' she replies, and now there's an edge of sardonic impatience creeping into her tone. 'I don't have an address, let alone a bank account.'

'I'm an optician,' I explain as she continues to stare at me defiantly. 'I'll give you a free eye test, but do you think you can get to my practice? It's in Newnham, so it's not too far to walk.' I describe where we are, hoping Umeko won't mind. 'Come in this week if you can. You might have to wait for a bit, but we'll definitely sort something out. Okay?'

She nods, her expression softening. She makes to get to her feet so Sonny helps her to stand up.

'Are you sure you're okay?' he asks.

'A bit bruised, but I'll be fine.' She gives him a small smile of gratitude.

'Want something to eat? We have pizza coming?' he offers affably.

'No, I've got to go.'

'Here's your tea!' the volunteer from earlier calls out, hurrying across the road from the market place with a takeaway cup.

I hear Mel mumble a thank you as she takes it, and then she makes her way slowly along the footpath.

Sonny watches her leave with a frown. He meets my eyes

and sighs, resigned, before nodding towards the restaurant. At that moment, our server exits the building with a stack of takeaway boxes. She comes to a stop at our empty table and looks confused before catching sight of us and smiling with relief.

We wander back to the canoe without saying much, but I can't stop thinking about the way Sonny was with Mel – the gentle human kindness radiating from him.

Whatever he's done, however much he currently struggles to like himself, he's a good man at heart. I truly believe that.

Chapter 16

'I can't believe you almost gave these away,' Matilda jokes, polishing off her third slice of pizza.

We filled them in on what happened.

'Is that true?' Sonny asks me. 'That you can't get free eye care if you're not getting benefits? What about all the other homeless people out there? What do they do?'

'I don't know,' I admit, feeling bad that I'm so clueless.

'Maybe there's a charity that deals with that sort of thing,' Matilda conjectures.

'If there's not, there should be,' Sonny says. 'But it does seem crazy that they can't walk into an optician and make an appointment.'

'I wonder if she'll come and see you,' Matilda muses.

'I'm not hopeful,' I reply, glancing at Sonny. 'Are you?'

'I don't know,' he replies thoughtfully.

A few moments pass without anyone speaking and then Sonny crumples his empty can in his hands.

'Are we out of beer?' he asks Archie.

'Yeah, sorry, mate,' Archie replies.

'I completely forgot to bring some. I might nip to the offie. Anyone else want anything?'

'I'll come with you,' Archie offers.

'Actually, I could do with a bathroom break,' Matilda says. 'Hannah?'

'I'm fine. I'll look after the boat.'

We've moored up outside the Wren Library and have been eating our pizzas on the grassy bank. I'm not sure dogs are allowed here, or even if *we're* allowed here, but no one has told us off yet. It's an idyllic spot – St John's gleaming white 'wedding cake' building can be seen through the trees on the other side of the river and, behind me, the uniform windows of the Wren Library are reflecting the evening sun.

When the others leave, I lie down and gaze up at the cloudless blue sky. It's after eight o'clock but there's still so much daylight. The longest day of the year is fast approaching.

Summer solstice…

From out of nowhere I'm hit with a memory from my childhood. I'm lying on my back in a field full of grass and the sky is everywhere, a wide expanse of twilight blue taking up almost all of my peripheral vision. From somewhere off in the distance, I can hear my name being called, but I don't answer. I'm totally alone, and I feel empty.

The memory is still playing on my mind when Sonny, Archie and Matilda return. I'm sitting upright again, absentmindedly twirling my silver bracelet around my wrist.

'We're all set!' Matilda calls, lifting up another bottle of Prosecco.

'I'm going to be off my face,' I warn, forcing my hands apart.

'Who has to work tomorrow?' she replies with a giggle. 'Come on, back in the boat. Let's paddle up towards Silver Street. Sonny has been telling us about this book he's been reading,' she adds as I clutch the bank, trying to keep the boat steady so everyone can climb in. 'Can I sit next to you? The boys want to look macho.'

Archie and Sonny exchange long-suffering looks.

'Sure.' I edge across to make room for her. 'So what's this about a book?' I ask when everyone is seated except for Bertie. I have one hand firmly on her collar so she'd better not be thinking about going anywhere.

'It's a book about eye contact,' Matilda says as the boys use their paddles to push us off from the side.

'It's not a book about eye contact,' Sonny corrects her patiently. 'It's a book about stress. Evelyn recommended it,' he explains to me over his shoulder.

He's at the front, facing forward, and Archie's at the back, behind Matilda and me as we sit side by side on the central bench seat.

'Do you want to tell her?' Matilda asks as they begin to propel us forward.

'No, go on,' he insists.

'It's a book about stress and depression and anxiety and part of it talks about the importance of doing something meaningful with your life. Right?' she checks with Sonny.

'Spot on,' he replies, continuing to paddle.

'What's it called?' I ask.

Matilda stares at the back of Sonny's head.

'*The Stress Solution,*' he answers.

'There's this bit in it about eye contact,' Matilda continues, removing the foil around the neck of the bottle. 'An exercise this guy— Dr who?'

'Rangan Chatterjee,' Sonny chips in.

'An exercise he was asked to do that involved him staring into a stranger's eyes.'

'I'm always staring into strangers' eyes,' I point out, letting Bertie's collar slip through my fingers as she settles at my feet.

'This you have to do for five minutes,' Matilda says, handing me our glasses to hold so she can fill them up.

'Five minutes straight?' I ask.

'Yes,' she confirms.

'I'd get the giggles,' I say, then, because I can't resist, add: 'Wouldn't *you*, Sonny?'

He chuckles. 'Yep. I probably would.'

'Is this an insider joke?' Matilda asks, but doesn't wait for an answer before excitedly saying, 'Let's try it!'

'You want to stare into a stranger's eyes for five minutes?' Archie asks, baffled.

'No, you dimwit, I want to stare into *your* eyes for five minutes. Apparently, you experience a strange connection with the other person or something. I don't know. It sounds interesting.'

'What, and I'm supposed to stare into Sonny's eyes?' I ask, alarmed.

'Yeah! Come on, it'll be fun,' Matilda urges. 'Guys, pull up under the Bridge of Sighs.'

'You can't simply pull up under the Bridge of Sighs,' Sonny mutters as we glide towards the beautiful stone covered bridge. 'We might be able to find somewhere to stop a bit further on though.'

'Wait, are we doing this?' I'm surprised that he's up for it.

'Why not? Dr Rangan Chatterjee says everyone should try it,' he adds glibly.

Really? All right then.

We find somewhere to moor up. Bertie is snoozing, but I attach her lead to the bench seat to be on the safe side.

Matilda giggles as she stands up and steps over our central bench, settling down on the other side so she's facing Archie.

'This is so weird,' I hear him mutter as Sonny checks that Matilda is seated before turning around himself.

We laugh at each other when we're face to face.

'I agree with Archie,' I say. 'But I *am* intrigued. You wouldn't normally make eye contact for more than a few seconds.'

'Unless you're having sex,' Matilda points out.

'I keep my eyes closed,' I reply.

'Me too,' Sonny admits.

'You haven't shared meaningful eye contact during sex?' Matilda asks us with astonishment.

'I haven't had meaningful sex,' Sonny retorts.

Matilda turns around to look at us both so purposefully that the boat violently rocks.

'Steady on,' Sonny chides, placing his hands on either side of the canoe to maintain his balance.

'You've seriously never stared into anyone's eyes when you've had sex?'

'No!' I exclaim.

She's oddly flummoxed. I'm not sure what the big deal is.

'Are we doing this or what?' I'm growing impatient with the Spanish Inquisition.

'You have to sit with your knees touching the other person's,' Sonny directs.

The boat rocks as we get into position.

'How will we know when our five minutes are up?' Archie asks.

'Ah,' Sonny remembers. 'I need to set a timer.'

He taps away at his watch.

I've pushed the fabric of my skirt off to the side and I'm hyper aware of the point where our bare skin is connecting. There's warmth seeping from him and the soft, curly hairs on his legs are tickling my knees.

He looks at me and butterflies come to life in my stomach.

'Okay?' he asks.

I nod.

'Close your eyes.'

Why are we doing this again? Oh, that's right, because I'm drunk.

'Now open them,' he says.

A jolt goes through me at the sight of his brilliant blues. He was wearing his sunglasses earlier and I hadn't noticed that he'd taken them off.

Only a few seconds pass before we both get the giggles, but this time it's even more uncomfortable because we're not supposed to look away.

Matilda tells us to shoosh – she's taking it more seriously.

I try to suppress my smile and a short while later, Sonny's lips stop tilting upwards at the corners and his mouth relaxes.

Whoa. This is quite full on. I've never been locked in a stare like this before.

His eyes are beautiful. There's a navy ring around the rim of his irises and wavy lines extend outwards from his pupil, made up of different shades of blue. They remind me of water rippling in sunlight.

His pupils are neither fully dilated nor constricted but somewhere in between.

What are you thinking? I wonder and at that moment, his pupils dilate a little more. My butterflies pick up speed, my breathing becoming shallower. The urge to avert my gaze becomes unbearable, agonising even. My eyes widen with the effort of continuing this prolonged contact and his pupils constrict again.

He blinks and looks down, and I feel a surge of relief, but then he gently reinstates eye contact and I find it hard to breathe.

He purses his lips and the tension eases slightly, then he leans towards me a couple of inches and I retreat. His mouth curves up and I realise he's teasing me. I smile and raise an eyebrow, leaning towards him. If we're playing this game, I intend to win.

We're less than a foot away from each other. I could count his lashes if I wanted to.

His eyes dart between mine and then his gaze settles and his stare suddenly feels very intense.

I'm profoundly aware of our knees touching and the craving for more contact is like an itch I can't scratch. His gaze drifts downwards to my lips, but he sharply reinstates our eye connection. His pupils are fully dilated. My butterflies whip themselves from a whirlwind into downright dangerous hurricane territory.

Holy shit, I want to kiss him.

My eyes widen and his do too. He retreats slightly to put more distance between us, but it only makes me want to close the gap. It takes an immense amount of willpower to hold back.

I try to focus on thinking about his eyes, the colour of them, the way his pupils have pushed out some of the waves of blue. I think about how no one else has ever stared into his eyes like this.

And then the thought slams into me that *he* is *not* the only person who's stared into *my* eyes, and a darkness, a blackness, washes over me, pressing down on me.

I break the eye contact, but not before I see shock flash across Sonny's face.

His watch timer goes off.

Matilda breathes out one word: '*Yes!*'

And Sonny and I glance at each other and away again. I feel oddly shivery and then I think it dawns on us both at the same time that Archie and Matilda are snogging each other senseless.

'You mean it?' I hear Archie whisper as they pull apart.

I turn to see Matilda staring at him, her eyes shining.

'What's going on?' I can't help but ask.

'Archie's asked me to marry him,' Matilda says in a voice thick with emotion. 'And I've said yes.'

Chapter 17

Condensation retreats from the glass like vapour trails fading behind an aeroplane in the sky, a ghostly mist that vanishes bit by bit to reveal the girls in the mirrored cabinets. The left-hand cabinet is slightly ajar, so two faces stare back at me, their green-golden eyes penetrating and accusatory.

'I should never have lowered my defences,' I say in a small voice. 'I thought he was safe. If he hadn't sworn himself off sex, there's no way I would have allowed us to get this close.'

The sound of the phone ringing interrupts my flow. I frown and hurry downstairs to the living room, picking up the one and only phone my uncle keeps in this house. I don't know why I bother: it's probably a telemarketer.

'Hello?'

'Hannah!'

'Hello!' I exclaim. Speak of the devil: it's Charles. 'Where are you?'

'Cape Town! We're here for two nights. I'm about to take

a cable car up to the top of Table Mountain, but I wanted to give you a quick call first. How are you, dear?'

'I'm fine. I want to hear about you. Where else have you been since your last email?' I take a seat on his sofa, tucking my feet up underneath myself.

'We've mostly been cruising the Atlantic Ocean, but we were in Namibia a couple of days ago. Walvis Bay. There's a lagoon that attracts hundreds of thousands of birds, including an awful lot of flamingos. It was fabulous!'

'And where are you off to next?' I ask with a smile at Bertie as she enters the room and flops down on the carpet.

'Hang on, let me get my itinerary. It's hard to keep track.'

As I wait, listening to the sound of a zipper followed by rustling papers, I pick up the photo frame from the side table. This picture was taken only a few years ago. Charles's grey-white hair has been combed back neatly from his forehead and his blue eyes are crinkled at the corners as he smiles. June, beside him, has a sort of wry look about her, her pale-green eyes surprisingly sharp. She never did like having her photo taken.

Charles comes back on the line. 'We're sticking to South Africa for a bit: Mossel Bay, Durban and Richards Bay, and then moving onto Maputo in Mozambique.'

'And are you still having a good time?'

'Truly, *truly*,' he replies emphatically. 'I've met some wonderful people. Of course, there are a few characters too, but they're all fascinating in their own way.'

'I hope you're not psychoanalysing everyone on board,' I tease.

He chuckles. 'You know me. And how are you?'

'I'm fine. Getting on with it. Bertie's great.' Her tail thumps against the carpet at the mention of her name. 'I cleaned up your old canoe the other day and took her into Cambridge.'

'Only the two of you?'

'Um, no, we went with friends.'

'Danielle?'

'No, I haven't seen her since I went to meet Calvin.'

'I'm sorry.'

'Don't be!' My cheeks burn at the arrival of his pity.

'Who, then?'

'New friends. Matilda who works next door to me, her fiancé Archie. And his friend Sonny,' I add.

He latches onto my reluctance to spill the beans. 'Sonny! What's he like, then?'

'He's nice.'

'Nice? That's a very bland word, Hannah.'

'Don't start.' I place his photo frame back on the side table with a little more force than I'd intended. It promptly falls over.

'I'm not starting! I simply want to know how you are.'

'I'm fine. I'm well! It's all going well. June's roses are looking beautiful.' I fumble around, trying to stand the frame upright.

'Don't change the subject, dear.'

'I'm not.'

'You are. Tell me about Sonny.'

'He's nice.'

I hear him sigh.

'Okay, no, he's not nice. He's got issues. I'm trying to be a friend to him.'

135

'Friends sounds good. Do you talk to him?' he asks after a moment's pause.

I hug my arms around my chest. 'I talk to him, yes. And I talk to Matilda.'

'That's good. Are you open with them?'

'As open as I'm capable of being.'

'So you're not open with them.'

'They're new friends, Charles!' I'm raising my voice now.

'I only want you to be happy.'

'I am happy.'

Silence extends between us.

'This phone call must be costing you a fortune,' I say eventually.

'Do you need to talk, dear?'

'No, Charles, I'm fine.'

'Are you talking to *her*?'

I swallow.

'Oh, Hannah.' He sounds desperately sad.

'Please, Charles. Leave it.'

It's a relief when I hear the tour operator telling him it's time to go up the mountain.

I don't make any attempt to move from the sofa. Instead, I sigh and put my feet up, muttering to Bertie, 'Your master is a pain in the butt,' and frowning at the internal door that leads to his one-time clinic.

It's a while before I'm able to push aside the niggling burden of Charles's concern, but eventually I allow my thoughts to spill out of my head.

'So, Archie and Matilda got engaged yesterday! That was weird. Well, I thought it was weird at first, but apparently

Archie has been talking marriage for a while. Matilda wanted to get her course out of the way and Archie said he'd wait until she was ready, but during the staring game they both somehow knew that the time was now.'

Bertie has lifted her head to look at me. I ignore her and edge down on the sofa until I'm flat on my back, staring up at the ceiling.

'Sonny and I were really happy for them. But I was also glad to have a diversion. I found it hard to look at Sonny when our five minutes were up. Luckily, I didn't have to. We put Archie and Matilda on the middle bench and paddled most of the way home with Sonny at the back and me at the front. Sonny and Archie carried the boat up to the cottage and the three of them shared a taxi home so he and I barely spoke.'

My mobile phone beeps to alert me to a new text. I sit up and reach for the device, checking the display. It's from an unknown number.

'Amsterdam flight 6.30pm Sat – can you get off work early?'

My stomach is immediately flooded with nerves. Sonny must've got my number from Matilda and Archie.

'Are we still doing this, then?' I murmur. 'I guess it would be weird not to, now, wouldn't it?'

I re-read his text.

An evening flight at that time would mean knocking off at four o'clock latest. We only work until five on Saturdays and rarely have clients coming by late in the day. I have a feeling Sonny wants to get the flights booked now, so I bite the bullet and give Umeko a quick call, apologising for bothering her on a Sunday. Not only does she have no problem with me leaving early, she also offers to look after Bertie for a couple of days.

I text Sonny back to say that the time works for me.

He replies to ask about a Monday evening return and when I agree, he tells me he'll book and asks me for my surname. I haven't had reason to share it before now.

'*Culshaw*,' I reply.

He reveals the price in a final text.

The exchange is brusque and businesslike, but I'm edgy at the thought of going alone to Amsterdam with him. I feel as though I'm losing control, if it's not already lost.

With my phone still in my hand, I type out a text message to Johann.

I can think of one way to regain some of that control.

Chapter 18

Five days later, I'm in the bathroom, putting the finishing touches to my make-up, when the doorbell rings.

'That'll be my Johann-shaped distraction,' I mutter, sweeping on my lip-gloss and hurrying downstairs.

'Oh. Hello,' I say.

'Hi,' Sonny replies, his gaze steadier on mine than it was when we last parted company. 'I was next door.'

Bertie barges past me.

'Are you leaving straight from work tomorrow?' he asks, getting to the point as he greets Bertie.

'I'll need to come back here to get my bag,' I reply apologetically. It'll be too heavy to carry to work if I'm walking.

'I've got the taxi coming to me at ten to four, so shall we swing by your work and pick you up? We can grab your bag on the way to the airport.'

'That sounds perfect.'

He gives me a quick once-over as he stands up. 'You heading out?'

'Er, yes.'

I sense he wants to say something else, but then Johann appears behind him.

'Hallo!' Johann calls, lifting his hand in a small wave as Bertie barks her usual five-bow-wow greeting.

Sonny spins around and watches him coming up the garden path.

The fact that this feels awkward is exactly why I'm doing it, I remind myself.

'Hi,' Johann says to Sonny with a friendly grin.

'Sonny, this is Johann. Johann, Sonny,' I introduce them cursorily, not offering up any more information as they shake hands.

Sonny has a small crease between his eyebrows when he turns back to me. 'See you tomorrow, then.'

I nod. 'See you.'

He sidesteps Johann and walks down the path. I watch him go with a pang before coming to my senses and opening the door wider.

'Come in.'

'What a cool little place,' Johann comments as he ducks under the doorframe and enters the chocolate-box cottage. He's so tall that his head almost bumps against the ceiling.

His chin-length strawberry-blond hair is wild and unruly, and a week's worth of stubble graces his square jaw. He's hot, but I feel strangely unaffected. I press on regardless, giving him a choice of a drink here or heading straight out to the pub. He opts for the pub.

'Perhaps we'll end up back here later,' he adds with a twinkle in his eye.

'Are you single?' I reply candidly, clipping Bertie's lead to her collar.

'Yes.' He grins down at me. 'Are you?'

'Always.' I smile and nod at the doorway.

'So who's Sonny?' he asks teasingly as he exits.

'A friend.'

I pull the door shut behind us.

We go to the Blue Ball and sit in one of the two cosy front rooms at a table lit by candlelight. Johann hasn't changed a bit. He's chatty, playful, flirty and easy to be around.

We fill each other in on what we've been doing over the last few years. Mostly he talks and I ask the questions, which is exactly the way I like it.

But Sonny is never far from my mind.

He's on my mind as we return to the cottage. He's on my mind when Johann tangles his fingers in my hair and pulls me towards him as we stand in the brightly lit hallway. And he's on my mind when Johann brings his mouth down to mine.

'Why did you leave without saying goodbye?' he asks against my lips in a hot whisper.

I shrug and he kisses me again, pressing himself up against me.

This could be so easy. All I have to do is take him upstairs.

But…

I gently but firmly push him away.

'I've got an early start.'

'So have I,' he replies, reluctant to let me go.

'Sorry.' I keep him at arm's length. 'But it was nice seeing you.'

He stares at me with mild disbelief. 'That's it?'

I nod.

'What's happened to you?' He's genuinely perplexed.

I walk over and open the door, and a moment later, he passes by me into the cool night, muttering what I'm almost certain are a few choice words in German.

I don't blame him. I'm mad at myself too.

Chapter 19

There's an odd atmosphere inside the car. We're almost at Luton and Sonny and I have barely spoken two words to each other.

He was wearing sunglasses when the taxi came to pick me up. He still is. It's not that he's doing anything wrong. In fact, he's been polite and well mannered. He got out of the car and opened the door for me when I came out of work, and he checked I'd remembered my passport after we'd gone via Charles's to collect my bag.

He's been tapping away at his phone for most of the journey, mumbling about needing to sort out some work stuff, and I've sat and stared out of the window.

I exhale heavily as we arrive at the airport and he glances across at me, slipping his phone into his pocket.

'Sorry about that,' he mutters.

'Everything okay?'

'Yep, all set.' He pulls out his wallet and waves off my attempt to retrieve my purse. 'Get the return.'

'Are you sure? I still owe you dinner too.'

He makes a dismissive-sounding noise and leans forward to pay the driver.

We've only got hand luggage and checked in online so we're able to go straight through to Departures.

'Are you working tomorrow?' I ask as the queue in front of us slowly dwindles.

Sonny nods, his mouth set in a line.

'And Monday?'

'Yeah.' He lets out a small sigh.

He's stressed about work.

The realisation makes me spontaneously reach up to squeeze his shoulder. He stiffens and then his features soften as he recognises compassion.

'It'll be okay,' I murmur.

He nods and proceeds through security.

We don't have much time on the other side and I want to buy a magazine, so we agree to go our separate ways and meet at the gate.

On the plane, he continues to be silent and I'm a bit lost for words myself. He hasn't mentioned Johann and neither have I. I don't know if he's even given him a second thought – his mood probably has nothing to do with my love life, or lack of it, as it stands. I'd sensed he was worried about returning to Amsterdam – it's part of the reason he asked me to come with him. A problem shared is a problem halved and all that. But he may as well be alone for all the good it's doing us.

After a while he asks if I'd mind him putting his headphones on and listening to music. I start to flick through my magazine, but it's hard to concentrate. I feel as though a chasm has opened up between us.

His eyes have closed and his arms are folded across his chest. He looks tired and drawn. Another wave of compassion sweeps through me.

By the time we reach his apartment, it's almost ten o'clock at night. I'm inexplicably shattered, but Nina is expecting me for a few drinks tonight, so I only intend to drop off my bag before going to hers. Sonny has told me it's about a ten-minute walk away.

He lives on the top – fourth – floor of a tall terraced black-brick building with white-framed windows. It's adjacent to a canal and the water is gleaming like an oil slick in the dark night, a couple of narrow houseboats moored at the banks. The cobbled streets are lit by old-fashioned street lamps and there's a warm glow coming from a nearby bar, the sound of music and chatter spilling out of its open door.

I feel a bubble of excitement at the thought of seeing our surroundings tomorrow in daylight.

Unlocking the front door and bypassing the mailboxes while muttering something about needing to sort out his post tomorrow, Sonny leads me up the stairs. There's no lift and I'm out of breath as he opens his front door. He flicks on lights and my eyes go round.

'Holy shit,' I breathe.

He lives in an open-plan loft apartment and, although small, it is *breathtakingly* cool. Apart from a lower, flat section near the front door, the ceiling mirrors the roof of the distinctly Dutch-style townhouse, curving up and over in a high arc. The old wooden parquet floors have been stripped and are bleached in

colour and the furniture is minimal, designer and undoubtedly expensive, from the pale-grey sofa to the modern yellow
chaise-longue and the giant orange Anglepoise floor lamp
bowing over a low coffee table. The kitchen on my left has an
industrial-looking island formed of what appears to be polished grey concrete, and there's nothing out on display apart
from a gleaming silver commercial-looking coffee machine
against the charcoal-coloured back wall. The far-right wall is
exposed brick hung with a series of photo frames containing
black-and-white prints that I will definitely be taking a closer
look at, but currently I'm finding it hard to tear my eyes away
from the enormous Crittall window overlooking the tree-
lined canal. My feet take me towards it in a daze. There are
no blinds or curtains obscuring the view, and when I finally
turn around, I see that the lower section of ceiling near the
door contains a high-level bedroom that is also open-plan.

'You don't favour privacy much,' I comment weakly,
wondering what the neighbours opposite have witnessed. I
shudder as my imagination goes into overdrive.

'Do you want a drink?' he offers as I go to take a closer look
at the images hanging on the wall. He has a workstation here
with a computer and printer. There are several large silver
cases piled up together on the floor along with umbrellas, a
lightbox and other photography equipment that he must use
for his shoots.

'No, I should probably get going,' I reply distractedly. 'Is
this your work?'

'Mm.'

The collection is a combination of abstract indistinguishable shapes and lines, and random shots of a bespectacled,

suited man striding past a brick wall, a sixties-style blonde model leaning against a classic car, and dark, moody images of architecture and landscapes. Each picture is distinctive, but they all fit together.

'They're incredible,' I murmur, a moment later recognising the curve of a woman's hip in one of the up-close abstract shots. Urgh.

'The bathroom is through here.' Sonny opens a door to reveal a brightly lit white-tiled room and goes in, returning with towels and linen. 'The cleaner's been, so the sheets on the bed are fresh,' he tells me.

'I'll sleep on the sofa, Sonny,' I protest.

I don't want to deprive him of his one and only bed.

'No, you won't,' he says firmly, dumping the sheets on the yellow chaise.

I have a feeling he won't be persuaded otherwise.

'Right, well,' I say with a sigh. 'Guess I should get going.'

'I'll walk you,' he states.

'Don't be silly. It's not far.'

'I know you're perfectly capable of looking after yourself,' he says a touch sardonically, handing me his spare key. 'But it would make me feel better.'

My insides are plagued with pesky winged creatures as we head downstairs together.

'How long have you lived here?' I ask.

'A couple of years.'

'Will it be hard to leave?' I can only dream of having a place like this.

He shrugs. 'In some ways, but there are more important things in life.'

'Are you all right?' I ask him outright as we reach the bottom of the stairs and exit the building. He still seems subdued. 'Is it this job and coming back here, or is something else bothering you?'

'I'm being a miserable git, aren't I? Sorry. I'll feel better once this weekend is out of the way.'

It's only after he changes the subject, telling me about the bar on the corner and how it does a great brunch, that I realise he didn't answer my question.

Nina and Aart, her boyfriend, live in an ordinary-looking apartment block, but it overlooks another pretty tree-lined canal and there's a wisteria vine climbing up the wall by the door, abundant with flowers.

Sonny sees me to the door.

'Come and say hi,' I urge, my finger hovering over the buzzer.

He's loosened up as we've walked, telling me about the local area and recommending places to visit tomorrow. I'm barely going to see him because he'll be working, and I'm not ready to say goodbye to him yet.

He hesitates before agreeing.

Seconds after I press the buzzer, Nina bursts out through a door on the ground floor.

'Hannah!' she squeals, almost knocking me over in her desperation to hug me.

I squeeze her back just as hard. It's been so long. *Too* long. Almost three years? That's crazy. She was one of my best friends at school.

She hasn't changed a bit. She still wears her chocolate-brown hair in a sleek chin-length bob and continues to rock the geek chic look with her tortoiseshell horn-rimmed glasses and quirky fashion sense. Tonight she's wearing a red and black tartan miniskirt with a clashing bright orange jumper. Very Velma from *Scooby Doo*.

She withdraws and stares with unchecked interest at Sonny, who's hanging back.

'Nina, this my friend, Sonny,' I say.

She goes straight in for a double cheek kiss and flashes me a wide-eyed look of pure glee.

I laugh because she's not even trying to hide her expression.

'You're coming in for a drink, right?' Nina asks him cheek-ily, taking his arm and frogmarching him towards her front door. 'Abagael!' she calls to the waif-like brunette who's sitting on one of two bright-red sofas in the navy-painted living room. Aart's sister, I presume. 'Abagael, I've brought company! She recently split up with her boyfriend,' she tells Sonny as an aside. 'She needs eye candy. You don't mind, do you?'

Abagael blushingly but good-naturedly stands up to be introduced. Sonny still seems uncertain about his agreeing to stay, but for now he's going along with it.

'Where's Aart?' I ask.

'Oh, he's in his office, *working*.' Nina pulls a face and then shouts, 'Aart! Get your butt out here now and have a drink with us!'

A frazzled-looking Aart emerges from a door off the living room.

He's a few inches taller than Nina and me at about five foot nine, and he's older – in his mid-thirties with heavy stubble and black hair.

'Hannah,' he says, coming over to kiss me hello while holding my upper arms affectionately. 'It's good to see you again.'

We've only met a couple of times, but he's so warm and personable that I feel as though I've known him a lot longer.

Nina turns the music up – a crazy-sounding Dutch pop song – and we take to the red sofas with some drinks. There are bold pops of colour in every direction, from the canary yellow moulded plastic coffee table to the bright green curtains and the purple-and-orange rug.

'You live in Amsterdam, Sonny?' Nina asks.

'Yeah, I've been here for almost ten years now.'

'What do you do?' Aart interjects.

'I'm a photographer.'

'What's your surname?'

'Denton.'

Aart's eyes widen. 'Sonny Denton?' he asks.

Sonny nods.

'We've got some of your work hanging in our shop!'

'That's so cool!' I say proudly, turning to look at Sonny beside me.

He seems unfazed and I realise he probably plays down how good he is.

'Which ones are Sonny's?' Nina asks Aart.

My friend and her boyfriend run a design shop that sells everything from quirky gifts to artwork. Nina handles the former, whereas Aart is more involved in the art side of things – he has the right name for it.

'The naked girls, neon lines, ultraviolet light.' He abbreviates his description, but it makes sense to Nina because she's regarding Sonny with admiration.

'That sounds titillating,' Abagael chips in.

She's not wrong, but the other emotions it evokes knock me for six.

I don't like the idea of Sonny photographing naked models. And I *hate* that I don't like it.

Suddenly I'm furious with myself for pushing Johann away last night. I had a perfect opportunity to distract myself from the confusion of whatever it is I'm feeling about the man sitting next to me and I cocked it up.

The conversation moves on and I try to stay upbeat, but it's a surprisingly exhausting act and when Sonny tells me he needs to make a move because he still has to prep for his shoot tomorrow, I fight the urge to tell him I'll join him.

Nina, Aart and Abagael have left us alone momentarily.

'Catch a taxi back,' Sonny urges.

I roll my eyes.

'Just because you're confident you can handle yourself, doesn't mean you actually can,' he says quietly, and when I look at him he holds my gaze until my heart begins to quicken.

He breaks the contact by standing up when Aart comes out of the kitchen, closely followed by Nina. They exchange a few final words while I sit on the sofa and yawn violently.

Abagael spies me as she comes through from the bathroom and laughs, following suit.

'I don't know about you, but I'm going to bed,' she says.

'Will you have another drink, Hannah, or are you heading off too?' Nina calls over to me.

I glance at Sonny to see his questioning look. He doesn't seem to have considered that I'd be willing to leave with him.

'Maybe I should come home with you,' I say.

He's surprised, but not unpleasantly so. 'Okay.'

He waits by the door as Nina and I make plans for tomorrow and then we say our goodbyes and leave.

'Are you okay to walk, or would you prefer to catch a taxi?' he asks as we set off.

'Walk,' I reply obstinately, which is bloody stupid, really, as a taxi would be blissful right now.

We set off in silence, but I notice he takes a slower pace than on the way here. I'm wearing my walking shoes, but my bones are weary.

'How did it happen?' he asks gently, his gaze dropping to my left leg. 'The car crash.'

I shake my head regretfully, feeling bad because I don't want to offend him.

'I don't like to talk about it. Sorry.'

'Fair enough,' he replies, staring straight ahead.

He definitely feels slighted, but it's not something I can help.

'Late night last night?' he asks drily as I yawn.

'Not really. I'm just tired.'

A few paces later, I realise he was asking about Johann.

I sense he has more to say, but is resisting. I'm not sure how I feel about that.

'Did you get up to anything?' I'm not exactly steering the conversation away. 'Oh, weren't you hoping to have the girls?'

'I was, but Rochelle said no. She wanted to stick to tonight for her date, so she roped her mum in to babysit instead. I caught up with Archie.'

I remember when he came to see me first on that Friday

night a few weeks ago, he told me that Archie was his fall-back option. Was that the case last night too? If Johann hadn't turned up, would he have suggested us doing something? I like that he likes my company.

I like it too much.

'So was that one of those no-strings-attached things?' he asks, and it thrills me that he's finally caved. He's trying to sound flippant, but it *did* bother him, seeing me with Johann. I wasn't at all sure before.

'Mm,' I reply noncommittally. 'Didn't quite turn out like that,' I add, unable to help myself.

He shoots me a look. 'Are you okay?'

I smile. 'You might not think I'm safe walking through the streets of Amsterdam late at night, but I *am* capable of fending off giant Germans.'

He laughs loudly, adding, with a butterfly-inducing grin: 'I'm glad to hear it.'

Fuck, I fancy him.

Chapter 20

It's the smell of fresh coffee that finally tempts me from what has to be one of the comfiest beds I've ever slept in. Pushing Sonny's soft downy duvet off my face, I'm instantly blinded by bright sunlight.

Ouch.

The unhindered view is lovely, but I'm not convinced it's worth sacrificing blinds for at this hour of the morning.

The display on my phone reveals that it's seven thirty. I've only had a few hours' sleep, if that. I found it hard to settle once we got back here.

Sitting up in bed, I crane my neck over the low safety rail to see Sonny down in his kitchen. He's wearing low-slung grey tracksuit pants and is shirtless, his lean back rippling with a surprising number of muscles as he works his coffee machine like a professional barista.

I flop backwards on the bed and stare up at the ceiling, feeling restless.

I can't even get this stupid crush out of my system by sleeping with him because of this goddamn promise he's made to himself. *And I made a promise too*, I remind myself.

I'll have to rustle up some other distraction. Maybe he'll do us both a favour and put me off him by being a complete knobhead while he's here in Amsterdam. Here's hoping.

'Morning,' I say as I traipse downstairs in pale pink pyjama bottoms and a white vest top. If he's still wearing what he slept in, I can too.

'Oh, hey,' he says over his shoulder.

'Aw, you're wearing your glasses,' I note. They really do suit him.

'Yep.' He looks amused, then apologetic. 'Sorry, did I wake you?'

'No, your sun did.' I nod at the window.

'It's the only downside.' He gives me a sweet smile.

His hair is squashed flat in several sections and there's day-old stubble on his jaw. He looks adorably sleepy and unkempt.

Adorable? Sweet? What is wrong with me? This is not good.

'Coffee?' he asks.

'Thanks.' I jerk my head towards the bathroom and he nods, getting back to prepping the drinks.

'Don't,' I whisper as I pass by the mirror. 'Just don't.'

When I return to the living room, Sonny is taking his sheets off the chaise longue and folding them up.

'Do you want me to strip the bed?' I offer.

'No.' He brushes me off with a frown, placing the bedding in a messy pile. 'You know you're welcome to stay here again tonight?'

'Oh. Thanks.' I'm touched. 'Are you sure?' It would be easier as Nina's at work tomorrow anyway.

'Of course I'm sure.' He walks towards me and it takes a scary amount of effort to tug my eyes away from his exposed skin. The way those pants cling to his narrow hips is *just... so...*

He nods at the concrete island where my coffee is waiting.

I turn around and pick it up, trying to collect my thoughts as he goes upstairs. I track his journey to the chest of drawers doubling as a bedside table and watch as he pulls a white T-shirt out and slips it over his head.

Sighing, I take my coffee to the sofa and try to lose myself in the view out of the enormous window. The leafy green treetops are shining in the dazzling early morning light.

Sonny brings his coffee over and sits down beside me.

'What are your plans—' he starts, glancing across at me and freezing.

'What is it?'

He doesn't answer, placing his coffee cup down on the table and striding across the room to where his silver cases are sitting on the floor. He opens one and extracts a camera.

I watch with confusion as he hastily fixes a lens and comes towards me, his eyes focused on my face.

'What are you doing?' I ask with alarm as he falls to his knees at my feet and brings the camera up to his eye. 'Wait! Sonny!' I lift my hand to block the viewfinder and he lowers the camera, an imploring look on his face.

'Hannah, please,' he begs desperately. 'Put your hand down.'

'No!' I feel a bit cross now. What does he think he's doing?

'Your eyes,' he beseeches. 'Please. I *have* to.'

I've never seen anything like it. I stare at him.

'Please,' he says again, making to lift the camera.

I very reluctantly let my hand fall to my lap and he clicks off a shot.

'Look towards the window,' he says. 'Please.'

I don't know what's got into me, but I follow his direction, inwardly flinching as he clicks off a couple more shots.

He checks the images in his viewfinder and makes an adjustment, then takes a few more pictures, repeating the process of checking, adjusting and photographing.

A sense of urgency is radiating from him and he's tense and full of purpose, but finally he relaxes and his limbs become looser as he sits back, scanning through the images on his display.

He looks up at me, dazed.

'Well, that was weird,' I say with a small laugh and his face breaks into a grin.

'You want to see?' he offers.

'I don't know. Do I?'

'Yes.'

He stands up and sits down so close to me on the sofa that we may as well be squashed together on Archie and Matilda's snuggler seat. We're hip-to-hip, leg-to-leg, and the instant heat of him pressing against me is making me feel heady. I try to concentrate as I peer at the camera's screen.

The shot is a close-up and the way he's captured the sunlight on the planes of my face is incredible. My cheekbones seem sharper and my lips look fuller, but my eyes are the stars of the show. There's a depth to them that I've never seen before: light filtering through pools of gold.

'You've made me look beautiful,' I murmur when I can find my voice.

'You *are* beautiful,' he replies with a frown, staring at me.

I am well and truly screwed.

The sound of a loud buzzer reverberating through the apartment makes us both jump. Sonny looks at the door and gets to his feet, placing the camera on the coffee table as he pads barefoot across the bleached parquet floor.

Still shaken, I watch him open the door to the most exquisite creature I have ever seen.

'Sonny,' she says breathlessly, practically hurling herself into his arms. 'I heard you were back.'

I watch with a sick sort of dread as his arms snake around her.

She has a thick accent that could be French and she's as tall as he is, but he's very broad in comparison to her stick-thin frame.

She spies me over his shoulder and pulls away from him, her green cat-like eyes flaring.

'You have company,' she states accusatorially, glaring at him and then at me.

He takes a small step away from her and waves his hand towards me. 'This is Hannah, a friend from the UK.'

'A friend?' She walks past him into the apartment, tossing her long chestnut hair.

I see him press his lips together with what appears to be mild annoyance as he closes the door behind her, but then I'm distracted by her making a beeline for me. I stand up, feeling horribly underdressed. Just before she reaches me, she clocks the sheets piled up at one end of the chaise longue, and her ensuing smile is brilliant.

'Katya,' she says, kissing my cheeks, one after the other.

Katya? Oh, this is getting better and better. Freaking *Katya*? Could she *have* a sexier-sounding name?

'Nice to meet you,' I say.

'How long are you here for?' she asks, her question directed at either or both of us.

'We leave tomorrow night,' Sonny replies.

'Oh.' She pouts prettily. 'Why so short a visit?'

'Do you want a coffee?' he asks instead of answering her.

'An espresso,' she replies, sashaying after him into the kitchen.

He looks over his shoulder at me and I point at the bedroom followed by the bathroom, indicating that I plan to get dressed. He nods at me, understanding.

When I come out of the bathroom, wearing a long skirt and an olive-green off-the-shoulder top, Sonny is over by his desk, doing something to his camera.

'Has Katya gone?' I ask with surprise.

'Yep,' he replies shortly.

'One of those no-strings-attached things?' I raise my eyebrow.

He glances at me and lets out a wry snort before returning his attention to his camera.

I was already feeling nauseous, but his non-answer makes me feel even worse. 'You're only human,' I force myself to add in the same indifferent tone.

'I'd rather spend a minute in your company than an hour in hers,' he replies in a low voice.

His words floor me.

He's too consumed by what he's doing to notice.

I steel myself.

'Listen, Sonny, thanks for the offer of staying here tonight, but I'm going to head to Nina's.'

It was a decision I came to in the bathroom.

'When are you leaving?' He carefully places his camera on the desk.

I can't tell if he's put out or not.

'As soon as I'm ready.'

'Do you want breakfast?'

'I think we'll go for brunch.'

He nods and turns away, leaning over his desk and pulling a folder out of a stack of papers.

Now walk away. Go upstairs. Pack your bag.

I feel as though I'm wading through mud, but I make my limbs do as I command, gathering together the few things I brought with me.

'What time does your shoot kick off?' I ask as I return downstairs, bag in hand.

'Eleven, but I've got a shedload of work to do before then.' He stares at my bag and then at me. 'Won't you come back tomorrow?'

'You're working then too, right?'

'Only for a couple of hours. I've got a meeting at ten, but I'll do most of my editing when I get to the UK.'

'What time will you finish tonight?'

He shrugs. 'Six, seven…'

'Have you got plans for afterwards?'

What are you doing?

He seems dejected. 'I should probably catch up with a few people.'

160

Now I'm worried about him. He didn't want to come here in the first place and now I'm deserting him. What sort of a friend am I?

'Actually,' I say, ignoring the voice in my head as I place my bag down at my feet. 'This is a bit stupid, isn't it? Nina's working tomorrow, so maybe I *should* come back here tonight. In fact, why don't you join us for dinner later? Aart will be there too, so it won't be three's a crowd, and I'm sure he'd like to chat to you some more.'

They hit it off last night with impassioned discussions about photography, art and architecture. I was talking to Nina and Abagael so only caught snippets of it.

He gives me a small smile. 'Thanks, Hannah, but it's probably time I faced my demons.'

'What does that mean?'

'Come back tonight, by all means. Maybe we can do something tomorrow if Nina's working?'

'Are you sure I won't be interrupting anything if I do return later?'

He knows what I'm asking and holds up three fingers in a Scout's promise, a smile playing about his lips.

I laugh and pick up my bag.

'I'll put it upstairs,' he offers, walking over to me. His fingers brush against mine as he takes it, sending a shock zipping up my arm.

'If you need me, you've got my number,' I say feebly, averting my gaze from his beautiful blues.

'I'll see you later,' he says quietly.

I nod and walk out of the door.

Chapter 21

'Right. Sonny,' Nina says determinedly. 'What's going on there, then? Spill the beans.'

Here we go…

'He's just a friend—'

'Bullshit!' she calls me out, grinning. 'The chemistry coming from you two could have sent the curtains up in flames – and they're fireproof, so that's saying something.'

I smirk and rest my chin in the palm of my hand.

We're at the coffee shop/bar that Sonny recommended on the corner of his street. It's cool: stripped-back walls plastered with gig posters, big windows letting in loads of light and shabby-chic furniture. I came here because I basically needed to get out of his apartment before I said or did anything that I wouldn't be able to take back. Nina wasn't supposed to meet me until ten, but she came as soon as I texted, bless her. It's only eight thirty.

'Sonny's complicated,' I say uneasily, picking up the stroop-wafel that arrived with my coffee and taking a bite.

She gives me a significant look. 'And you're not?'

I cock my head to one side and nod, acknowledging the truth of her comment. 'That makes it worse, not better,' I state with my mouth full.

'What's up with him, then?'

'When I met him, there was definitely chemistry.' We told them last night the story of how we met at my work, but left out the more noteworthy details. 'The way he looked at me... The attraction was mutual. He was due to collect his glasses the day before he returned to Amsterdam and I thought... Well, you know what I thought.'

She raises her eyebrows at me, understanding, but not approving. She knows I don't do long-term. She knows *why* I don't do long-term. I think she appreciates my reasons, but that's not to say she's happy about it. She only wants what's best for me, and for Nina, that means a loving relationship with someone who could be there for me for life.

That sort of scenario is not in my stars. It never has been.

'Anyway, when he came back in he was a changed man. He could barely look at me and he seemed broken.'

She frowns, perplexed and curious.

'Then I saw him coming out of Charles's consultation room next door. He'd been seeing Evelyn.'

'He's in therapy?' she asks apprehensively.

I nod.

'Do you know why?'

'Turns out we have something else in common. He doesn't do long-term relationships either.'

She flops back in her seat. 'Seriously? What's *his* problem?'

'He has several. He's never been in love. He bounces from

girl to girl. He got one of these girls pregnant ten years ago when he was only twenty-two and has had hardly anything to do with his daughters until recently.' I pause. 'They're twins.'

Her brows pull together. 'Identical?'

I nod. 'Nine years old.'

She takes a deep breath and lets it out slowly as I continue. 'You know he's a photographer, but most of his paid work is in fashion. He sleeps with a lot of the models he works with.' I have to force myself to say this, but if I can be totally straight with anyone, it's Nina. 'He implied that he'd been on a downward spiral for a long time. I don't know if it was drink or drugs or both, but one of his friends died back in April and Sonny said he could see himself in this friend. He felt as though he was heading the same way. He said he hadn't been *feeling* for a long time. His life had lost meaning. Maybe he was suffering from depression – I don't know – but he was a mess when he came into Umeko's that day, and it's taken him time to get better. He's still not right. Sometimes he seems optimistic, but other times it's as if he's hit a brick wall and feels hopeless. He's been trying to make changes. He wants a relationship with his daughters and has been working on that. It's been difficult with their mum, but he's determined to make a fresh start and put things right for the future. He doesn't know what he's going to do about work yet, but he doesn't enjoy the fashion side of things. I don't think it makes him feel good about himself. And he's stopped sleeping around,' I say finally, glancing at her in time to see her eyebrows jump up.

I've been mostly absorbed in stirring long-dissolved sugar into my coffee instead of meeting her gaze directly. I'm so desperate to get all of this out of my head and into words for the benefit of someone who can actually talk to me about it all.

I haven't felt as though I can speak to Matilda, Danielle has been otherwise engaged, and I am *not* getting started with Charles…

'He's basically celibate,' I continue, tapping the spoon against the edge of the cup and watching a drip of coffee run down the outside. 'He's sworn to himself that he won't sleep with anyone for at least six months. He believes it's the only way he'll learn how to develop relationships that will last and not fizzle out after sex.'

I'm trying to sound blasé, but when I dare to meet her eyes again, I wish I hadn't.

Her concern is palpable. 'Have you talked to him about you?' she asks gently, pointedly.

'No! Of course not!'

'Why not? Hannah, it sounds as though you two are close. This could be the lasting relationship you've *both* been looking for.'

'I am *not* looking for a lasting relationship,' I state.

'Okay, fine.' She holds her palms up in acquiescence. We sit in uncomfortable silence for a bit until she muses, 'I wonder what happened to him to make him behave like that.'

'His family is all very normal, apparently.' I'm thankful she's returned to the only subject I really want to explore, which is Sonny.

'But to never stay with someone long enough to develop real feelings for them… That's odd.'

'It is,' I agree. 'But if anyone can get to the bottom of it, Evelyn can.'

'That's true. She certainly helped me.' Evelyn was the counsellor Nina saw when she was going through her cancer treatment. 'And you, right?'

I shrug. Sometimes I think I'm beyond help. I down the last of my coffee. 'Come on, let's get going.'

Chapter 22

I'm so fatigued after a whole day exploring Amsterdam and catching up with Nina that I turn down going to a bar after dinner and head back to Sonny's. Yes, in a taxi.

Nina didn't mind. We saw more of each other today than we have in years. She's promised to try to make it over to the UK later in the summer to see her family, Danielle, baby Calvin and me.

It's a little after ten o'clock when I unlock Sonny's apartment door, fully expecting him to still be out. I'm surprised to see him at his desk, working.

'Oh, hey!' He jumps to his feet.

He's dressed in black jeans and a plain grey T-shirt. He's still wearing his glasses and his appearance is a combination of sexy-stylish and endearingly nerdy. 'I wasn't expecting you back for ages.'

He seems genuinely pleased to see me.

'It's been a long day,' I say with a small smile, freaked out by how glad I am to see him too. 'How was the shoot?'

'Fine. You want a drink or are you heading straight to bed? I can turn off the overhead lights so they don't bother you.'

'A drink would be nice.'

He smiles and pads into the kitchen.

He wants to know what Nina and I got up to, so I fill him in as he pours a glass of wine for me and tops up his water before nodding at the sofa.

Nina and I mostly wandered and took in the sights, but we also made it to two museums: the Rijksmuseum and Moco, the museum of modern art, which is one of Sonny's favourites.

'I've been meaning to check out that Banksy exhibition,' he says.

'You could go tomorrow. It might be gone when you next come back.'

His chest deflates. 'I have to return in a few weeks.'

'Really? Why?'

'I've agreed to do another job, but I also need to decide what I'm doing with this place.' He looks around the apartment.

'Do you own or rent?'

'Part-own,' he replies, getting up and heading into the kitchen. 'It's half Katya's.'

I'm taken aback. He gets the bottle of white wine out of the fridge and continues to talk as he brings it over and tops up my glass.

'She got a deal on it from this old developer guy she was seeing and asked if I wanted to come in on it. It was in a right state when we bought it, but I did all the work and she conceded to a lower rent rate. We'll make a good return on it if she agrees to sell.'

'Do you think she will?'

'Who knows with her? The mortgage isn't up for another year, so we'd have to take a hit on an early repayment charge if we sold.'

'You didn't ask her earlier?'

'No, she had to go to work.' He picks up his mobile from the coffee table. 'She's been texting, asking me to meet her and some friends at a bar.'

Over his shoulder I see a tiny red number hovering over his text icon.

'She's texted you five times?'

'Way more than that. Those are just the ones I haven't opened.'

There are a bunch of WhatsApps too. Is she a total mental-head?

'They're not all from her. Word is out,' he adds derisively, taking a sip of his water and discarding his phone on the sofa between us.

'All your friends know you're here?'

'Yep,' he replies bluntly. 'I'm not sure I'd call them friends, though. People I used to party with would be more apt.'

'I thought you were going to face your demons.'

Not that I want him to hang out with a group that might have contributed to his problems.

He glances across at me. 'I really can't be arsed.'

I giggle and he smiles, holding eye contact for a few lovely seconds. Almost unthinkingly, he reaches across and tucks a lock of hair behind my ear. 'Those shots I took of you...' His voice trails off. 'Can I do some more in the morning?' Although he doesn't sound as desperate or as beseeching as earlier, there are definitely undertones of begging.

Why? I can't compete with the likes of Katya. I don't want to be his subject, under scrutiny, but I can see how much he wants this, so I'm torn.

'I suppose so,' I mutter.

He smiles with relief.

'Have you photographed Imogen and Natalie much?' I ask as another text message comes in.

'Not a lot,' he replies, glancing down at his phone, but not attempting to read the display. 'I know that's bad.' He hesitates before continuing. 'I haven't felt like it.'

He's right. That's bad.

His Adam's apple bobs up and down. 'Before this summer, I never felt as though they were mine,' he admits.

I can tell he finds this difficult to say out loud, although I imagine he's discussed it with Evelyn. I give him what I hope is a suitably sympathetic look and wait patiently, trying not to judge.

'I was a shit of a dad when they were born and – this sounds awful – in the years that followed, I saw them because I felt I *had* to. I never connected with them. Not until now.' He smiles at me suddenly. 'They're so funny, *so* cute. And so *different* to each other. I feel as though I barely knew them before and I can't ever get those years back. I've missed out on so much.'

He roughly takes off his glasses and presses the heels of his palms to his eyes.

My hand is halfway to his back when the buzzer sounds.

He lifts his head and several emotions flicker across his face: first confusion, then horror and, finally, weary resignation as the buzzer sounds again.

'This could be messy,' he warns, putting his glasses on and getting to his feet. 'I'll try to get rid of them as quickly as I can.'

The buzzer goes again before he reaches the door, and he wrenches it open to the sound of high-pitched squeals and a few deeper-toned yells coming from outside in the corridor.

Five loud and obviously wasted people pile past him into the apartment – two men and three women, including Katya, who shoves Sonny's chest and proceeds to chew his ear off about not responding to her text messages. Within seconds she's laughing and hugging him, clearly preferring to party than argue.

'Guys, I'm not up for this,' I hear Sonny say despairingly, trying to hold Katya at bay.

'Hannah can join in too,' Katya brushes him off dismissively.

Even from this distance I can see how dilated her pupils are – it doesn't take a genius to work out that she's high.

The men come over to introduce themselves to me while the women peel off into the kitchen, helping themselves to glasses from the cupboards and drinks from the fridge as if they own the place. They're likely models: tall, skinny and stunning. One has draped herself over Sonny in the kitchen. He seems on edge, but he hasn't moved her away.

A hipster named Fabian plugs his iPhone into the stereo and club music begins pounding out into the room. Everyone is talking loudly and half in Dutch, so I have no idea what they're saying. Then the other man – I think he said his name was Erasmus – kneels at the coffee table and begins chopping lines of cocaine on the glass.

These people are something else.

'What the *fuck*?' Sonny's voice cuts through all the other noise and he strides towards Erasmus, his face furious. 'Pack that shit away!' he yells. 'All of you! I don't want this! I've told you I don't want this and you're not fucking listening!'

The club music is still belting out of the stereo and everyone is staring at Sonny, but no one seems particularly bothered – it's only me who's shocked. I've never seen him so angry.

Behind me in the kitchen, a girl begins to laugh, and then another starts up, but my eyes are on Erasmus and Sonny, who are staring each other down.

Sonny's hands are clamped into fists at his sides and his arm muscles are straining. Erasmus regards him with surprise, but doesn't make any attempt to do as he's been asked. At least he's stopped chopping.

Sonny stalks over to the stereo and unplugs Fabian's phone, holding it out to him. The laughter stops and the silence is deafening.

'Get out,' Sonny says, his eyes returning to Erasmus.

Erasmus shrugs as if he can't see what all the fuss is about and, without any sense of urgency, begins packing away his Class A drugs.

Katya breaks the silence. 'What the hell has happened to you?' she demands, swaying slightly. 'When did you become such a bore?'

The other women start chattering away to each other in Dutch, rolling their eyes and throwing mini-tantrums by slamming their wine glasses down on the countertop in annoyance. I half expect the glasses to shatter, but they don't.

They noisily exit the apartment and Sonny shuts the door after them.

He turns to look at me, his expression stricken.

'That went well.' I grin at him, trying to lighten the mood.

'I'm so sorry,' he says as he comes over to me. 'You would've been better off at Nina's.'

I smile and stand up, lifting my arms over my head and stretching. 'Could've been worse,' I say with a yawn. 'You told me what your life here was like.'

His shoulders slump and he scrubs his face with his hands, groaning.

I punch his arm and he looks at me bleakly. 'You got to face your demons after all.'

His face breaks into a weary smile. 'Yeah, I guess I did. Now the sooner I get out of here, the better.'

Chapter 23

I jolt awake. It's dark and for a moment I'm not sure where I am, then I remember I'm at Sonny's, and at the same time I hear footsteps on the stairs.

'Hello?' I ask aloud.

'Are you okay?' Sonny whispers, and in the light from the street lamps down by the canal, I see him crouch at my side. 'You were having a nightmare.'

'Was I?'

'You don't remember?' He sounds disturbed.

'No. I'm fine. Go back to bed.'

For a long moment, he doesn't move, but then he stands up, says 'okay' and heads downstairs.

I stare up at the shadowy ceiling, alarmed. *What the hell did I say?*

I'm too scared to go to sleep again afterwards, and my head continues to spin as the hours tick by.

When Sonny finally stirs at around seven, I'm lying in bed reading. I wonder if he's always been an early riser.

I wait until he's been to the bathroom and is at the coffee machine before venturing downstairs myself.

'Hi,' I say, my voice betraying what little sleep I've had. I sound hoarse.

'Hey,' he says, coming over and standing right in front of me. I think he thought to hug me but he doesn't follow through. 'How are you feeling?'

'Fine.'

'That was some dream.'

'Was it?' I ask with attempted amusement.

'You were calling out your name. Like, *screaming* it, really.'

I screw up my nose. 'Sorry about that. Did you get back to sleep okay?'

He frowns. 'Yeah, but—'

'How's that coffee coming along?' I interrupt, walking past him to the machine.

I hear him sigh, but he doesn't push it. 'I'll bring it over to you.'

I go upstairs to hunt out my sunglasses because it's bright as hell in here.

'Oi,' Sonny says when I return downstairs. 'Don't think you're getting out of it.'

'What? Oh no.' My heart sinks when I realise he's after another photo shoot.

'This is the only thing that has inspired me in I can't tell you how long. It would mean a lot to me.'

'Pressure, much?' I gripe, flopping down on the sofa.

'Sorry.' He smiles, passing me my coffee. 'But I can't take no for an answer.'

'You are so pushy.'

He nods, still smiling. 'I am.'

'Are you going to bring your camera equipment back with you?' I ask as he goes over to his desk where his camera is waiting.

'Some of it. I've been thinking about what you said – about Imogen and Natalie. Rochelle's birthday is coming up and—'

'That's a great idea!' I say, so enthusiastically that I've cut off the end of his sentence.

'I wondered if we could even do a photo shoot on the Cam in your canoe?'

'Of course!'

Smiling, he lifts up his camera and nods at my sunglasses.

'Urgh,' I mutter, reluctantly taking them off. 'I'm a mess. Shouldn't I get dressed at the very least?'

'No need: I'm doing close-ups.'

'But I haven't slept. There must be bags under my eyes the size of suitcases.'

'You're perfect.'

I narrow my eyes at him, knowing I'm anything but. 'I can see why women throw themselves at you.'

He snorts and clicks off a shot.

'They do, don't they?' I'm curious. 'Do you ever see someone you simply *have* to have and won't stop until you get them?'

'That's never happened,' he replies, checking the display.

'So it's usually the other way around? And you can't say no?'

He shrugs. 'I guess.'

'How many women have you slept with?'

'Too many.' He makes to lift the camera. 'Look towards the window.'

I do as he instructs. 'Don't you miss it?'

'Hmm?' He clicks off another couple of shots.

'Sex. Don't you miss it?'

'Weirdly, no,' he replies in a low voice. 'Bizarre, right?'

'What do you think would happen if you still lived here? Do you think you'd fall back into your old lifestyle?'

'Stop talking,' he orders.

I shut my mouth, frustrated.

As the minutes clock up, I go from feeling ill at ease to finding it strangely electrifying being his subject. It's intense, under his scrutiny, but I can't say I don't like it. He's extraordinarily focused and attentive, and when his face is not hidden by a camera, his fixed concentration is mesmerising.

'Christ, Hannah,' he murmurs, sounding awed as he studies the shots he's taken. 'Your eyes are insane.'

A shiver runs down my spine and I clear my throat, trying to sound unaffected.

'Does your sister cut your hair?' I remember him saying one of his sisters is a hairdresser and I've been wondering this as I've watched him. It always looks roughly the same sexy length – even when he was at his lowest point, it never seemed to get too long.

'Yeah,' he replies, his brow furrowing. 'Harriet.'

'Are the two of you close?'

He shrugs. 'Sometimes she treats me like her fourth child.' He shrugs again. 'Do you have any siblings?' he asks.

'No,' I reply bluntly. 'What's your other sister called again?'

'Jackie.'

'How much older is she?'

'Nine years older. Harriet is twelve.'

'Bet they loved having a baby brother. Did they dress you up and pretend you were a doll?'

He smirks. 'Jackie did. Harriet was practically a teenager when I was born.'

'So you cramped her style?'

He nods. 'She was always shouting at me.'

'Maybe she's making up for it now by looking out for you.' She set him up with Evelyn, after all.

He looks down. 'Maybe.'

A thought occurs to me. 'Did they have many boyfriends when you were growing up?' I'm wondering if he learned his promiscuous behaviour from his teenage sisters, if not from his strait-laced parents.

'Not really,' he replies, but the oddest expression passes over his face. He robotically stands up and crosses the room to his workstation.

'Are you okay?' I ask with confusion, watching him put his camera down.

'Yeah, fine,' he replies in a strange-sounding voice, his back still to me.

'Did I say something?' I get to my feet, concerned.

'No, not at all.' He spins around to hold his hand up, intending to halt my progress. 'Listen, I've got this meeting at ten. Are you going to visit Nina at the shop?'

'I told her I'd drop in.' I've come to a standstill in the middle of the room, but I'm still trying to make sense of his behaviour.

'We should leave for the airport at six-ish, but we could do something this afternoon?' He's back to normal, or at least trying to seem as such.

'Sure.'

'Thanks again for this,' he adds, reaching behind himself to tap the top of his desk. He's aiming for a casual gesture, but there's something off about it, something off about him.

'Sonny,' I say worriedly, continuing towards him.

His expression grows wary and then he turns around and rests his hands on his desk.

'Did something happen when—'

'Don't!' he cuts me off before I can speak. 'Change the subject,' he commands. 'You're good at that.' He turns and glares at me. 'What, you think I don't notice? Even a simple question about whether you have any siblings shuts you down.'

I swallow and fight the impulse to walk away, but the urge to get to the bottom of what's going on with him is stronger.

'Have you confided in Evelyn?' I ask tentatively.

He doesn't move, but his jaw has clenched, there's a tic above his left eyebrow and his body is rigid with tension. He reaches for his camera, unscrewing the lens. His hands are shaking.

Nina's words from yesterday are ringing around my head: *I wonder what happened to him to make him behave like that.*

What was it I said that set him off? His sisters... No, his sisters' *boyfriends*.

And then understanding comes crashing down around me.

'Did someone hurt you?' I ask in a tiny, appalled voice.

He slams his camera down on the desk, causing me to leap back. His hands are scrunched into fists and he looks like he wants to punch something, murder someone, hit out, *hurt*.

My head tells me to keep my distance, but my heart pushes me forward.

'It's okay,' I whisper, bringing my hands up to cup his furious face. 'It's okay.'

His eyes meet mine and a jolt ricochets through me at the sight of his pain. He looks lost, overwhelmed, and his whole body is trembling. He raises his hands and for a moment I think he's going to fling me away from him.

He does the opposite.

It all happens too fast and I'm so taken aback that for a moment I barely register what's going on. His hands have knocked mine away from his face and he's taken hold of my face instead. He brings our lips together – pulling me up towards him and closing his mouth over mine – and for a moment, I'm powerless to do anything other than kiss him back. Shockwaves pulse through my entire body as his tongue frantically collides with mine. I'm barely aware of him walking me backwards until I hit the wall and then I feel him pressing against me through the thin fabric of my pyjama bottoms – and he is *so turned on*.

And oh, so am I…

But then a thought crashes into my head: *If we have sex, I'll lose him.*

And I'm not ready to lose him.

With every ounce of the willpower I retain, I force my hands between our locked bodies.

He stumbles backwards as I push him away. His blue eyes are almost black and his lips are swollen, his chest heaving.

But his skin is ashen and his expression haunted.

I feel dazed and confused and for a moment nothing makes sense.

I *wanted* it. I *still* want sex with him. I don't understand how or why I stopped it.

Because I promised him that I would? No, that doesn't feel important right now.

Something occurs to me.

'Do you use sex as a distraction technique?' I ask breathlessly, trying to focus.

He winces and steps backwards, breaking eye contact.

'Please don't walk away,' I beg.

He roughly drags his hand through his hair and stares at the floor. 'I'm sorry,' he says. 'I shouldn't have done that.'

'Please talk to me.'

He shakes his head. 'I need to get ready for this meeting.'

'Sonny,' I whisper. 'Does sex help you to forget?'

He hesitates, his gaze still cast on the floor. It's a long while before he says anything and when he does, he speaks so quietly that I strain to hear him. 'I'm not entirely sure *what* I remember.'

'Come and sit down?' I ask softly, stepping forward to tentatively take his arm.

He allows himself to be led to the sofa, where he sits hunched forward with his elbows resting on his knees and his head in his hands.

I rub his back, patiently waiting for him to speak.

'Harriet was working at a hairdresser in town,' he says and it's hard to remember to breathe, I'm so on edge. 'I was about ten. She was still living at home.' Every word is laboured, every sentence broken by seconds of silence. 'She was seeing this guy.' He clears his throat. 'He was a few years older than her, but he had a lot of time for me. He used to want me to join them occasionally – at the park, café, once we even went to the zoo. My parents would get all gooey-eyed about how good he was with kids.'

I nestle closer, my heart contracting at the bitterness in his voice.

'He and I once played a staring game where we weren't allowed to blink,' he continues. 'I'd forgotten, but it came back to me when we were on the canoe.' His eyes flick to me and away again, and I remember our five minutes coming to an end. I had assumed it was something in *my* expression that had shocked him, not a recollection of his own.

'Harriet wasn't around – we were at the park so maybe she'd gone to the café – and after he won, he told me that he liked me. He told me that he liked me *even more than Harriet*.' He shudders. 'I felt guilty and bad for her, but I was also kind of thrilled.'

He looks sickened suddenly. Then he bolts to his feet and rushes towards the bathroom, locking the door behind him.

I stay where I am, my heart breaking.

Chapter 24

Sonny refused to pick up where we'd left off when he finally emerged from the bathroom looking freshly showered, but shattered.

'I can't talk about this now, Hannah,' he warned, putting his hand up to keep me at bay. 'I've got to go to this meeting.'

I'd hoped he'd cancel it, but he made it clear that the idea was out of the question.

Later, he texted to say that his meeting was overrunning and he couldn't meet up after all.

I went to see Nina and somehow managed to stay upbeat so I wouldn't risk giving his secret away.

When he finally returned home, he could barely look at me.

'I can't talk about this now,' he kept saying as he packed up his things, fending off my concern.

I tried to respect that, but the tension on the return journey was horrendous.

'Please don't tell anyone,' he mumbled when the taxi pulled up outside the cottage.

I wasn't due to collect Bertie until the following day.

'I would never do that!' I hiss-whispered, hating that he'd even consider I might betray his confidence.

I reached for his hand to reassure him, but he gave me a cursory squeeze and disengaged himself.

That was four days ago. Since then, Sonny Denton has consumed most of my waking thoughts – and plenty of my sleeping ones too. I have no idea how I've managed to function at work.

I texted him on Tuesday to ask how he was and he waited until that afternoon to reply, *Fine. I'm with the kids.*

Rochelle has agreed to him taking over the childminder's afternoon school run, looking after the girls from Tuesday through Thursday until she gets back from work.

Don't forget to book in your canoe photo shoot, I messaged back, trying to keep things light.

I won't, he replied.

On Wednesday morning, I bumped into Matilda coming into work and she asked if I was up for another *Stranger Things* session that evening. I absolutely was, but later that afternoon, she popped her head around the door of Umeko's to let me know that Sonny couldn't make it. She offered to still have me over, but I opted to postpone.

Trying to find a balance between hounding him and being supportive, I waited until Thursday to text him again, and once more he replied that he was fine.

A minute later, he sent me another text: *Seeing Evelyn tomorrow.*

That's good! I enthused.

He didn't respond.

Now it's Friday and I've arrived home from work to find a bike locked up out the back – I think it's his, although I don't really remember what it looks like, only that it's blue.

I know I need to let him be – if he wants to see me, he'll call for me afterwards – but keeping my distance is hard.

I sit at the kitchen table and stare out the window, but as ten minutes turns into twenty, my resolve crumbles.

'I can't do this.' I get up and impulsively hunt out June's old gardening gloves from under the kitchen sink. I'll be more in his face if I'm out the back, so I'll go out the front and consider it a compromise. At least he has the option of cycling straight past me if he wants.

It's another half an hour before Evelyn's door opens and the sound of her gentle farewell carries on the breeze.

When I hear Sonny's footsteps heading around the back, followed by a pause as he unlocks his bike, and then the crunch of his wheels on gravel, my heart feels as heavy as a rock. I'm on my knees in front of the rose bushes, fighting the urge to flag him down, but he appears around the side of the building and clocks me anyway.

Bertie's tail thumps against the ground, but she doesn't go to the effort of standing.

'Hey,' he says, coming to a slow stop.

'Hi.' I smile at him.

His face is blotchy, and even though he's wearing sun-glasses, he can't hold my gaze. I suspect if he were to remove the shades, his eyes would be horribly bloodshot.

'Have you got to head straight off?' I ask.

He nods.

'Okay.'

He puts his foot back on his pedal and launches himself out onto the street.

As I watch him leave, I'm hit with an overwhelming urge to cry.

'Hannah.'

I turn to see a stout female figure in a sky-blue tunic and matching pants standing at the side of the cottage. Evelyn.

'Hello,' I reply in a husky voice, trying to contain my tears. My trembling lips give me away.

'How about a cup of tea?' she asks softly, her hazel eyes warm and kind as she nods at my front door. 'I haven't caught up with you in a while.'

I want to say no, but I'm too weak to resist so I nod and get unsteadily to my feet.

She begins with pleasantries, asking after Charles and how I'm enjoying my summer, but she soon gets to her reason for coming.

'I'm in a bit of a difficult position,' she says in her soothing, motherly fashion. 'You and Sonny are both patients of mine.'

He's told her what happened in Amsterdam, then. She won't have forgotten me flagging her down to ask about him, either.

'I haven't seen you in a long time.' I don't mean to sound as defensive as I have.

'No, but I still have a duty of care towards you.' She regards me with compassion and for a moment I'm back in the past, open and exposed with nowhere to run or hide.

'I was hoping to speak to you, to find out how you're feeling.'

'I…' My voice trails off. 'I'm worried about him.'

She nods, encouraging me to go on.

'I've come to care about him,' I admit. 'We're friends.'

'Is that all?' she asks.

I take a sip of my tea. I can't escape from this woman. It's futile to even try.

'Can we talk about what happened in Amsterdam?'

I feel my face heat up. 'He was trying to distract himself from the memory of abuse he suffered as a child. At least, that's what I believe. Has he confided in you about that?'

She's regretful. 'I can't go into detail. But will you tell me what happened from your perspective? I think it would be helpful. For both of you,' she adds.

Steeling myself, I start from the beginning, talking her through the photo shoot, the mention of Sonny's sisters and their boyfriends, and everything that went on afterwards.

'Let me take a backwards step here,' she says softly. 'You pushed him away?'

I nod.

'Would you mind if I asked why?'

'Because I sensed he was using sex as a coping mechanism.' As the words come off my tongue, I realise I'm parroting her phrase back to her.

And then I know why she wanted to have this conversation: The Hannah *she* treated would have *never* pushed a man away.

The Hannah *she* treated used sex as a coping mechanism too.

I was only seventeen when Charles first arranged for me to go and see Evelyn at her practice in town and I'd already had sex with three boys. I desperately craved comfort and closeness, but only on a physical, fleeting level. Charles and June were concerned, but this was the one thing I couldn't confide in them about.

My eyes begin to sting. I squeeze them shut and bring my knees up on the sofa, hugging them to myself. I'm fighting the urge to curl up into a ball.

Evelyn's voice cuts through the fog of pain. 'It's okay, Hannah. Take your time.'

As the seconds dissolve into minutes, she repeats this phrase again and again: 'take your time'.

Eventually I'm able to speak.

'I wasn't ready to let him go,' I mumble against my knees.

'You thought that, if you had sex, it would be the end of your friendship,' she clarifies.

I nod. I know she'll be disappointed to hear that, after all these years, I still haven't moved on.

Something inside me snaps. 'But it's not just me, you know!' I can't help raising my voice. 'He wouldn't have wanted anything to do with me afterwards, either. That's his thing: he uses women for sex and then runs a mile.'

I'm still reeling from the fact that I was almost another notch on his poor battered belt.

She's contemplative. 'Do you believe he would have done that with you?'

A chill goes through me as I realise what she's worried about: she thinks *I'm* going to break *his* heart.

She lets out a small sigh. 'This promise that you made…' She's not talking about my promise to Sonny. 'You were only a child.'

I start shaking my head fervently. *Don't go there.*

'Have you considered confiding in him?' she asks.

'No.' My reply is abrupt and final.

For a fleeting moment, Evelyn looks as though she has the weight of the world on her shoulders.

Chapter 25

A week later, I come to in the early hours of the morning feeling hot, shivery and flustered. I was having a sexy dream about Sonny and I didn't want to wake up.

For a moment, the memory of our kiss and the feeling of his body pressed against mine plays over in my mind. And then guilt consumes me and I drag myself from bed.

On my way to turn on the shower, I catch sight of my flushed reflections in the mirrored cabinets: twice the amount of evidence of my reprehensible behaviour.

'What sort of a person would reduce a man to a sexual fantasy when he's going through what he's going through?' I whisper aloud.

It's not the first time it's happened, either.

I press my hands to my hot cheeks.

'What's wrong with me?'

My face is burning, but shame is responsible for colouring it now, not desire.

I haven't seen Sonny since last week when he was leaving Evelyn's. Matilda has asked after him too – he turned down another *Stranger Things* evening on Wednesday, but he promised he'd be up for it next week.

Matilda invited me to the pub last weekend, which would have been a good distraction if I'd wanted a fun night out – I didn't – and Danielle called a few nights ago, asking me to go to her place for an early dinner. When I went, all she wanted to talk about was Sonny – Nina had filled her in.

But I had only told Nina everything up to the point of our kiss. I wasn't in the mood for speculating about why Sonny is complicated – I know the answer to that question now and can't reveal it.

My friends want me to settle down and be like them: normal.

But I'll never be normal.

I tear my eyes away from the mirrored cabinets and get ready for work.

It's Friday and I have a day packed full of appointments. At around three o'clock in the afternoon, I'm in the middle of fitting a client with glasses when Sonny walks through the door.

My heart leaps. 'Hello!' I exclaim.

'Hi,' he replies, flashing me an awkward smile.

'Oh, you're Sonny, aren't you?' Abbey remembers. 'What can we do for you?'

'I was wondering if I could have a moment with Hannah,' he asks tentatively, half addressing her, half addressing me. 'I'm happy to wait.'

'I won't be long,' I call across to him. My insides have expanded tenfold. 'Take a seat.'

I return to dealing with my client – a middle-aged man with smoker's breath – but even his rancid exhalations can't quell my feeling of joy.

'Would you like a coffee?' Abbey calls across to Sonny.

'No, I'm fine,' he replies. 'Thanks.'

He's uncomfortable about being here. He doesn't want to be any trouble.

'How's my sister's place working out for you?' Abbey asks, and I'm grateful to her for making light conversation while I finish up as quickly as possible.

She was surprised and more than a bit gleeful to hear that Sonny and I had been socialising outside of work.

'*Get in there*,' were the words she used.

I don't think the phrase, 'we're just friends' has ever been said more often about two people.

Abbey takes over from me as soon as she can, inviting the client to the till to pay.

I turn to Sonny with an expectant smile and he gets to his feet, nodding at the door.

'Don't forget Mrs Simmons is coming in at three fifteen!' Abbey calls after us.

My face must betray my frustration.

'I only need a minute,' Sonny reassures us both.

'I'm sorry,' I say as we walk around the side of the building, out of view of inquisitive eyes.

'No, it's okay.' He leans against the wall, folding his arms across his chest. 'I only wanted to say that I'm going to Evelyn's later, but I won't call on you afterwards.'

'Oh.' I swallow. 'Okay.'

He's come to see me to tell me that he doesn't want to see me? It's hard not to mask my dismay.

'It's just that...' He looks at me and then away. 'These sessions are taking it out of me a bit and...' Once more his eyes meet mine for only a second before returning to the ground at his feet. '...I need time to work through things afterwards.'

Now I want to wrap him up in my arms and never let him go.

'I wondered if you were free tomorrow, though,' he continues. 'After work? I wanted to show you the shots I took in Amsterdam, and there's something else I want to run by you. Will you come over to mine?'

'Of course!' My emotions are up and down like a yo-yo. 'Yes! I'd love to!' I try to contain my reaction, but it's impossible.

He smiles sweetly. 'Okay.' He nods and pushes off from the building. 'I'll let you get back to work.'

'Cool.' I beam at him.

Now he's amused. 'See you.'

'Bye.'

It's all I can do to stop myself from standing there like a giddy idiot on the pavement, watching him until he disappears from sight.

Sonny lives only a short walk from work so the following day, after getting changed, retouching my make-up and going via the off licence – only to stand there dithering about whether or not I should buy a bottle of wine because I don't want to seem presumptuous – I arrive at Cecily's converted garage.

It's five twenty-five, so I hope he's okay with me coming this early. He might've thought I'd need to take Bertie home first, but Robert and Umeko offered to have her overnight to save me the trouble. They've been so kind and accommodating.

The garage is at the front left of a large detached Victorian house. Abbey has already told me, slightly acerbically, that her older sister married a surgeon who is 'loaded'. But neither he nor her sister drives so they considered the garage a waste of space. Cecily, who's a stay-at-home mum, wanted a hobby so came up with the idea of doing Airbnb.

'*It's all right for some,*' was the way Abbey summed up the situation.

The garage door has been replaced with an opaque glass brick wall and a warm glow is emitting from within. It's hammering down with rain and I'm not sure my mini-umbrella will withstand the onslaught for much longer, so I hurry to the front door and knock.

'What happened to summer?' Sonny exclaims when the door whooshes open. 'Quick, come inside.'

I shake off a cascade of raindrops before closing the door and propping my umbrella up on the floor.

'Where's Bertie?' he asks.

'Robert and Umeko offered to keep her overnight.'

'That was nice of them.' He steps forward to give me a quick kiss on my cheek before turning and waving his hand at the room.

This simple contact alone brings on a blush, so I walk past him, hoping he won't notice.

'This is cool,' I say.

'Not quite my apartment in Amsterdam, but I like it,' he replies as the heat on my face thankfully begins to recede.

The space is compact but functional, with a living area looking out onto a private courtyard at the back, accessed by glass sliding doors. The bathroom is on the left and the kitchen is at the front on the right. There's no dining table, but I spy three stools tucked underneath the central island unit.

Two large roof lights overhead mean that the place would be flooded with sunlight on a sunny day, but right now the sky is dark and stormy and the sound of heavy rain is thundering through the room.

'Where do you sleep?' I ask, spying Sonny's photography cases beside a desk. He had to go to the trouble of arranging and paying for more luggage on our return journey from Amsterdam, a hassle he couldn't have been less in the mood for.

'Sofabed,' he replies.

'Aha!'

'Drink?' he offers over his shoulder, going to open a fridge under the kitchen counter. 'I've got Prosecco.'

'Ooh, yes please.' I wonder if this means we're settling in for the night. 'I brought this too,' I add, bringing out a bottle of red from my oversized handbag.

'Thanks! Would you prefer red?'

'No, I'll go with the Prosecco. Thanks.'

I look for glasses.

'In the cupboard under the island,' he directs me, unwrapping the silver foil top on the bottle. 'I'll have one too.'

As he pours, I notice a packet of artisan pasta out on the

counter by the hob and a loaf of crusty bread. There are also a couple of bowls of nuts and olives.

He passes me a glass and indicates that we should move to the living area, bringing the snack bowls and placing them on the coffee table in front of me as I sit at one end of the sofa.

'Are you hungry?' he asks.

'A little. Thanks.' I lean forward and pluck out an olive.

'No, I mean, I've got pasta. I can put it on whenever you like.'

'You're cooking?'

'Of course. You thought I'd ask you over and not feed you?' His entertained expression grows wary. 'Unless you've got other plans...'

'No!' I reply quickly. Too quickly.

He laughs awkwardly and I take a sip of my drink, trying to calm my nerves.

Frowning up at the roof lights, he walks back into the kitchen.

A Billie Eilish song is playing from a speaker on his desk. It's slow and sultry, and the low bass is vibrating through the glass.

He returns with a couple of posh candles and proceeds to light them.

'Sexy music... Candles... If I didn't know better, I'd think you were trying to woo me, Sonny Denton,' I say with a smirk.

He snorts. 'I've tried that. Didn't go down so well,' he adds as he sits at the other end of the sofa.

Even though we're bantering, his words make my insides dance.

'Harriet gave those to me as a moving-in present,' he says, nodding at the candles and getting out his phone. He offers it to me. 'You can put on something more upbeat, if you like. I was listening to this while I was working.'

'No, I like it.'

I turn to face him. He knocks back a mouthful of Prosecco and I realise he's nervous too.

'How are you feeling?'

'I'm all right.' He lifts one shoulder and keeps his gaze averted. 'I'm not thinking about it much outside of my sessions with Evelyn. They're kind of harrowing,' he adds with an uneasy laugh. 'I'm remembering some things I'd tried to forget.'

I give him a sympathetic look. 'She has a way of getting it out of you, doesn't she?'

He glances at me sharply. 'You see her?'

'I went to her when I was younger,' I reluctantly admit, having unintentionally let that slip.

'Why?'

My eyes widen.

'Sorry, too direct.' His apology is genuine, but when I don't answer, he frowns and adds cuttingly, 'I'm the only one who gets to spill deep dark secrets around here.'

I feel ill as he gets to his feet and puts his glass down on the table, crossing the room to the desk against the far wall.

But then he looks over his shoulder and says, 'Sorry. That was a shitty thing to say.'

'It's okay.' I shake my head dismissively.

He returns to the sofa and hands me some large 8×10 prints. They're close-ups of my eyes and they're... *stunning*.

The colours sing out, and there are so many: from gold and amber to brown, green and hazel.

'I've had an idea,' Sonny says as I study the pictures, awe-struck. 'Has Mel come to see you yet?'

I have to think for a moment, then realise that he means the homeless girl who was knocked over by a cyclist.

'I'm afraid not.'

'You know what we were talking about with Archie and Matilda, how tricky it is for homeless people to get free eye care?'

I nod.

'There's a charity that specialises in it. It's called Vision Care for Homeless People. It's true what Mel said: the majority of homeless people aren't getting financial benefits so they're not eligible for NHS eye examinations or the vouchers that can be put towards buying glasses. The voucher often doesn't even cover the price of glasses, but this charity provides everything for free. They don't have a clinic in Cambridge yet, but maybe with more funding that will happen one day.'

I'm impressed with his research. 'What are you thinking?'

'I'm thinking about taking some more photographs.' He nods at the images I'm holding.

Sonny's idea involves photographing the eyes of people living on the streets and putting on an exhibition to raise money and awareness for eye care for the homeless.

'I'm talking *huge* close-ups,' he says animatedly, drawing a large square in the air. 'Only one eye and possibly just the iris, so the depth and colour would be more impactful. The images would be inescapable – there would be no looking away, not like we normally do when walking past homeless people. Perhaps the exhibition could be called "Now We See You", or something like that.' He shrugs self-consciously. 'I don't know. But I reckon Archie would get on board to do the graphics for the poster. If not, I could.'

He studied graphic design at university, of course.

'Sonny, this is a brilliant idea! But how will you get homeless people to agree to be photographed?' I'm not sure how I'd feel about having my photo taken under their circumstances.

'I've been in contact with a couple of the local shelters and they think some of their guests will be keen to take part. I've also offered to do some volunteer work at Jimmy's.' That's one of the more well-known shelters in town. 'It's something I should be doing anyway while I have time on my hands, and it may help if I'm a familiar face rather than some wanky random photographer.'

I'm blown away. Not only has he come up with this idea, he's actually executing it. He knows it won't solve the bigger problem of homelessness, but it's *something*, and anything that improves the lives of homeless people has value.

'You said you wanted to do something meaningful.'

He nods. 'I need a purpose. I love spending time with my daughters, but I can't depend on them to make me happy. That's expecting too much from a couple of nine-year-olds.'

'I can't believe you've been doing all of this when you've had so much else going on.'

His expression briefly sobers. 'It's taken my mind off things, to be honest. It's been a good distraction.' He gets to his feet. 'Are you hungry? Shall I put on the pasta? I only have shop-bought pesto, but it's fresh.'

'That sounds perfect.' I get to my feet and follow him into the kitchen, pulling up a stool.

The thought of walking around his exhibition fills me with an enormous sense of pride.

And then something occurs to me.

'When are you hoping to put on the exhibition?'

He shrugs. 'I haven't got that far ahead. I guess I'd need three or four months to do it properly, with publicity and everything.' Something in my expression makes him falter. 'Won't you be here?'

'Charles gets back in less than three months,' I remind him.

He sighs heavily and pulls up a stool, staring at me despondently.

I return his stare equally as miserably. I don't want to miss this.

'Why do you have to leave?' he asks quietly.

'I just do. I can't live with Charles.' I stayed with him for a few weeks before he went away and I'm not keen to repeat the experience anytime soon.

'Why not?' He doesn't wait for my answer before saying, 'So get another place. Don't leave. Stay.'

'It's only early July now. Can't we aim for the end of September? I'll help in any way I can. If you need an assistant… Someone to stick up posters around Cambridge… Optical volunteers… I'll do anything.'

'We *could* aim for the end of September,' he says. 'But why do you have to go when Charles gets back?'

'I need to see my parents. I haven't visited in almost two years.'

'They're in Australia?'

'Yes.'

'How long will you stay with them?'

'A couple of weeks. I'd probably throw myself in the river if it were much longer. They live on a houseboat,' I remind him.

He nods, remembering. 'And after you've seen them? What will you do?'

'I'll travel for a while.'

'Why?' He's perplexed. 'I mean, obviously I get why you want to see the world, but you already seem to have done a lot of that. Wouldn't you like to stay in one place for a bit?'

'I *have* stayed in one place for a bit. This is the longest I've been in the UK for ages.'

'You don't like it here in Cambridge?'

'It's not that.'

'Whatever it is you feel you can't tell me, does anyone else know?'

I nod, staring down at my hands. 'Charles. Danielle. Nina. Evelyn. And my parents.'

Suddenly I feel weary to my bones. It's exhausting, carrying my past around with me. It's wearing me down. *He's* wearing me down.

He sighs, then, after a long pause, says: 'I'm going to tell my sister Harriet about the abuse.'

I look up at him.

'I need to know who he was,' he explains. 'I remember his first name, but not his surname. I want to find out what happened to him.'

'What will you do when you find out?'

'I don't know,' he admits. He swallows, hesitating, and then: 'Are you and your parents close?'

Is he telling me things so I'll confide in return? I suspect this is the case, but I find myself responding.

'It's hard to be close to people who live on the other side of the world. They don't even have a telephone.'

'But is your relationship with them generally good?'

'It's okay,' I reply slowly. I sigh. 'Something happened when I was younger, which we haven't ever really got over.'

'The accident?'

I wince.

'One of them caused it?'

I shake my head quickly. I've already said more than I ever intended to.

'When will you tell Harriet?' I steer the topic of conversation back to him.

'I'm seeing her tomorrow.'

'Will you tell your parents too?'

He's horrified. 'No.'

'Why not?'

'I couldn't bear it.'

'What about Rochelle?'

'No way!'

If I thought he looked disturbed before, it's nothing compared to how he looks now.

'But maybe it would help her to understand why you were the way you were.'

'Do you know how many paedophiles were abused as children?' he asks. 'If she thought there was any chance, any chance at all that I might...' He jumps to his feet, agitated. 'If anyone hurt our kids, I'd kill them,' he says passionately. 'I would never... I would never...'

'Of course you wouldn't!' I'm indignant on his behalf. 'Rochelle must know you're incapable of hurting them.'

'I can't take that risk. I will *never* take that risk.' He's so distressed.

I slide off my stool and slip my arms around his waist.

For a moment, he's rigid, and then he hugs me back.

It's bliss. He's so warm and solid. I can feel his heart beating – it's resonating through my ribcage.

'I wish you could talk to me the way that I talk to you,' he mumbles against my hair. 'Don't you trust me?'

'It's not that.' Now I'm twitchy.

'No, you're right not to. The last time you hugged me, I tried to get into your knickers.'

I laugh against his chest, loving him for lightening the mood.

'Well done for keeping your promise, by the way,' he says in an oddly buoyant tone. 'I am sorry for kissing you,' he adds in a whisper.

'Forget it,' I brush him off, pulling back to look at him.

I'm surprised to see that his expression is serious.

'I can't,' he replies with a small, helpless smile.

Then he lets me go and picks up the packet of pasta.

'Right. How much of this do you think I should do?'

Chapter 26

Sonny comes to collect me on Tuesday night. We're heading over to Archie and Matilda's to get stuck in to a proper *Stranger Things* marathon after Archie warned Sonny that he and Matilda were on the verge of cracking on without us.

He was joking. From what Matilda has told me, Archie has been worried about Sonny. He has no idea why his friend has taken another downturn.

'Good evening,' Sonny says when I open the door to him. He peers past me, cocking his ear to the wall. 'Is someone here?'

'No, only me and Bertie.' I awkwardly hop back, trying to avoid trampling on the post scattered at my feet for the second time that day.

Sonny swoops down to pick it up.

'Oh, thanks.' I hold my hands out. 'The phone was ringing when I got home so I rushed in.'

It was Charles, touching base from the Maldives, lucky sod.

'Hannah C?' Sonny asks, studying a letter with familiar handwritten scrawl on the front. 'Who can't be bothered to write your surname?'

'That'll be my mother.' I waggle my hands at him.

He frowns at what is almost certainly a bill and passes the whole pile over. 'Charles's surname is Culshaw too? I thought he was your mum's brother?'

'Mm? Oh yeah, he is.'

'So—'

'How are you?' I interrupt. 'Did you want to fill me in before we head out?'

He cocks an eyebrow at me, letting me know that he's onto me, before going along with my change of subject.

'Shall we go through to the living room?'

The living room is cosy, but it hasn't been touched in years with its grubby cream walls, worn pale-green carpet and antique furniture. It's not that Charles can't afford to do it up – he just doesn't see the point. He likes the familiarity of his surroundings.

Sonny walks over to the door that joins to Evelyn's clinic and presses his ear to the wall.

'Soundproof,' I tell him, sitting down on the sofa. 'I used to try to listen in as a teenager.'

'Naughty,' he murmurs with a smile, taking a seat on the armchair.

Sonny caught up with Harriet on Sunday. I've checked up on him via text, but he said he'd bring me up to date in person.

'She knew something was wrong because I'd asked in advance if Dave could take the kids out. That's her husband,' he explains.

He tries to recount the meeting to me succinctly and matter-of-factly so he doesn't have to relive the experience, but it sounds traumatic even at this surface level. He didn't go into detail with her about what happened – I don't know myself – but she was distraught: in floods of tears and reeling from shock.

She remembers the boyfriend in question, of course. The worst thing is, she claims she wasn't even that into him.

Sonny blinks rapidly. 'She said she stayed with him partly because he was so good with me. She thought he was a *keeper*.'

I flinch at his bitter, sarcastic words.

'It's okay.' He raises a hand to discourage me from going to him. 'It's better if I just get it out, if you don't mind. I think I'm still in shock myself, but I'll no doubt process it on Friday when Evelyn gets her claws into me.'

'So Harriet told you his name?'

He nods. 'I looked him up on the internet yesterday. He's dead,' he adds with a shrug.

'Oh God.'

'Yeah.' He drags his hand across his mouth. 'I don't know how to feel about it,' he mutters.

Neither do I. On the one hand, I'm glad that the bastard is no longer walking the earth. On the other, he's stolen every chance Sonny might've had of getting justice.

'Do you know what happened to him?' I ask.

'He was hit by a train about ten years ago. It was in the papers.'

'Shit! Suicide?'

He swallows and shrugs again. 'I don't know. Maybe somebody pushed him. I wish it had been me.'

'I really want to hug you,' I whisper.

He stands up. 'It's better that you don't. Come on, let's go. I need to show you my new car.'

'You've got a new car?' I ask brightly, trying to force cheer while inwardly swallowing the lump in my throat.

'Yep, finally given my poor dad his wheels back.'

It's a second-hand sporty Seat Leon, ideal for doing the school run and taking the girls out on excursions. It's another sign that Sonny is committing to making the UK his permanent residence.

'How are things with Rochelle these days?' I ask on the way to Archie and Matilda's.

'Not bad,' he replies with a nod. 'We're getting there.'

'Is she still seeing that guy?'

'Yep. She seems happy.'

We continue to chat and before I know it, he's pulling up on Archie and Matilda's road.

Archie answers the door to us.

'At long bloody last!' he yells, ruffling Sonny's hair and giving him a hug. 'You all right, mate?' he asks kindly.

'Yeah, fine,' Sonny replies, moving past him.

Archie slaps his back and then gives me a hug. 'Thank God you're here,' he growls in my ear. 'Matilda needs someone to talk weddings to. There's only so much I can hear.'

'There's only so much you're *allowed* to hear, you mean,' Matilda calls out to us. She grins at me as I follow Archie into the kitchen. 'Wedding dresses,' she says significantly, pointing at a stack of magazines on the island unit.

'Ooh, have you found something you like?'

'I've only had a quick flick through, but I'd love to show you a couple.'

I eagerly pick up the stack and follow her through to the dining room.

Later, when we're ready to resume our television watching, Matilda is insistent on taking the snuggler seat.

'No, no,' she says, shaking her head adamantly as she settles herself. 'Archie and I can squeeze onto this. You guys have the sofa.'

She thinks she's doing us a favour by giving us more room, but from the quick look Sonny casts me as he sits down, I don't think I'm alone in my disappointment.

I'm curled up on my side, leaning against the armrest. We're about three quarters of the way through Episode Two and I am scared out of my mind. Winona Ryder is screaming, light bulbs are flickering and The Clash's 'Should I Stay or Should I Go' is blaring out of a speaker.

That last one might not sound terrifying, but trust me, in this context, it is. I will never listen to that song the same way again.

Sonny reaches over and pulls my feet closer. I look at him, but his eyes are trained on the television.

Is he trying to still my racing heart? If so, it's not working. The warmth of his hand is making me feel skittish and his thumb drawing circles on the bare skin of my ankle is incredibly distracting. A monster seems certain to appear imminently on the screen, but my attention has zeroed in on his touch.

I've been craving intimacy with him ever since Saturday night when we stood in his kitchen and held each other. This is still not close enough.

I sit up and he draws back, perhaps wondering if he's crossed a line, but then I swivel and lie the other way so my head is resting on his lap.

His hand slowly collects together the loose strands of my hair and pulls them back from the nape of my neck, and then his thumb brushes my jaw, his fingers gently stroking my neck.

The pace has changed onscreen – the danger has passed for now – but I'm so jittery, I can barely breathe.

What is this that I'm feeling? I've never experienced it before. It's been so long since I've had any sort of intimacy with anyone. The last person, honestly, was Danielle. And I don't mean intimacy on a sexual level – it wasn't like that between us at all – but we were *so* close. Like, legs entangled, holding hands, tickling backs close.

Nina and I were never like that, nor Nina and Danielle. Nina didn't seem to crave touch the way that Danielle and I did.

But as soon as things got serious between Danielle and Brett, she put walls up. I know she's uncomfortable about how familiar we were. It's a big reason for why we're a bit awkward now.

A sigh escapes my lips as these thoughts run through my head.

It's all very confusing.

Chapter 27

On Sunday morning, almost two weeks later, I get a text from Sonny: *Are you in? Are you free?*

I reply immediately – *Yes!* – and race around getting ready.

He's been in Amsterdam this past week and had the girls for their first sleepover last night. I have no idea know how they managed to squeeze into his tiny converted studio, but I bet they had fun.

When the doorbell goes, I decide I'm not going to even try to disguise how happy I am to see him. I've missed him.

'Hello!' I cry as I yank the door open. My face falls.

There's not one person on the doorstep, but three. Sonny has brought his daughters.

'Hey!' he says, but his expression is instantly wary at the sight of my reaction.

I quickly rearrange my features. 'Hello, girls! Don't mind Bertie, she won't bite.' She's pushed past me, wagging her tail and thankfully forgoing her usual barky greeting. Imogen and

Natalie are all over her in a flash. I remember Sonny saying they'd love a dog.

'Sorry,' Sonny murmurs over the noise of their chatter. 'I thought we might go out in the canoe, but I should have called.'

'Of course you can go out in the canoe. Do you want to come around the back? I'll get the paddles.'

'I was hoping you'd come with us,' he says.

'Oh, I…'

His eyebrows pull together. 'You've got other plans?'

'No.' I've already told him I'm free.

I look past him to his daughters and he turns to see them on their knees, going doolally over the dog. When he meets my eyes again, his smile fades.

'Sorry, I don't know why I thought you'd be up for it.'

He thinks I have a problem with spending the day with his children.

But he doesn't understand at all.

'I am,' I decide impulsively, bracing myself. 'I am up for it.'

'Really?' Now he seems unsure.

'Yes. We won't bring Bertie, but I'll come.'

He looks relieved. 'I was hoping to take some pictures – Rochelle's birthday is on Wednesday; I could use a little help.'

'Sure. Sounds great.' I feel bad that I've made it necessary to reassure him. 'Shall we take a picnic?'

'I haven't brought anything, but thought we could go to the Orchard afterwards?'

'Perfect. Let me grab a few fun bits for on the boat too. Come in.'

We file inside, Imogen and Natalie still fawning over Bertie.

Sonny hesitates. 'Actually, can I grab my camera from the car first? I'll be back in a sec.'

I watch from the kitchen window as he stalks down the footpath, nerves creeping into my stomach at the realisation that I'm alone with his daughters.

'Can we bring her on the boat?' Natalie asks eagerly, patting Bertie's stomach – the old madam has put it on full display.

'I'm afraid not,' I reply regretfully. 'The last time she came on the boat, she jumped in.'

Both of the girls' faces light up with identical looks of glee.

'We could rescue her!'

'Dad said we could go swimming!'

'We could jump in too!'

These little voices come at me in quick succession. My stomach tightens.

'But she could capsize the boat and your dad's photography equipment would be ruined.'

Not to mention how dangerous that could be for them. The thought of them getting caught up in the reeds... I shudder.

'But we can come back and get her before lunch,' I promise over the sound of their protests. 'You can take her for a walk around the orchard, if you like.'

'Can I hold the lead?'

'Can I?'

'You can take turns,' I interrupt. 'We'll flip a coin to see who goes first.'

Sonny comes back in at this point, looking from me to his daughters on the floor. 'All right?'

'Yep. Let me grab those bits.' I turn around and busy myself in the pantry, trying to take a few calming breaths.

Sonny pulls the canoe along on wheels while I carry his camera, the girls obediently tucking in between the boat and me.

Every time a car goes past I tense. What if they step out onto the road? What if a driver misjudges the corner?

It's a relief to get to the Meadows. Natalie and Imogen run across the grass, giggling.

'No cricket today,' I comment, trying to take my mind off the rollercoaster of emotions I'm experiencing.

'Archie has asked me to play next weekend,' Sonny divulges. 'A few of the guys are on holiday.'

'Are you going to?'

'I thought I might.'

'I'll come and watch if you do.'

'Will you?'

'Faith was there last time,' I say casually. 'We had a good chat.'

Now he seems disconcerted.

'She was nice,' I add.

He switches over the hands he's using to pull the boat. The canoe is heavier than it looks – his arm muscles are straining.

'It's not going to put you off playing, is it?' I was only making conversation, but I shouldn't have mentioned it. 'It's not like there are any hard feelings between you, are there?'

'No.' He sounds hesitant. 'But I still wish I hadn't gone there.'

'Try not to have regrets, Sonny,' I say gently. 'You've got

enough crap to sort through without that too. And from what I heard, no one was complaining. Well, except for Nessa. But that was only because she wanted more than you were willing to give, right?' I add with a giggle.

'What have you all been saying to each other?' He's perturbed.

I laugh outright. He throws me a wary smile before his expression grows serious.

'I don't want to be that guy any more.'

I nod. 'I know.' I look straight ahead, but out of the corner of my eye, I see him glancing at me occasionally as we walk across the large green expanse.

'Girls, don't go near the river!' he shouts suddenly.

'I'll catch up with them.' I pick up my pace.

Imogen is standing near the water's edge, pointing at some reeds.

'Look! There are those blue butterflies again,' I hear her saying.

'They're damselflies,' I tell her as I come to a stop. 'Those bright blue ones are called Beautiful Demoiselles. The "beautiful" bit is actually part of their scientific name, but it's a good description too, don't you think?'

Both girls nod in agreement and then Imogen turns to me with a frown. 'What's a damselfly?'

'They're very closely related to a dragonfly, but they're slightly different. 'There's a dragonfly.' I point. 'See how his eyes wrap right around from the side to the front of his face? Damselfly eyes are smaller. And dragonflies have bulkier, thicker bodies, whereas damselflies are stick-thin. Their wings are different too,' I add as Sonny joins us.

'Dad, that's a—' Imogen starts to say before looking at me with confusion.

'A damselfly,' I tell her.

'A beautiful damsel,' Natalie adds seriously.

'A Beautiful Demoiselle,' I lightly correct, smiling at Sonny.

'Dragonflies have bigger eyes,' Imogen tells her father in a grown-up-sounding voice.

'They also have different wings,' Natalie adds, expectantly awaiting my explanation.

'Yes, right, well,' I say, hastily, trying to get the lesson out of the way so we can crack on with this photo shoot. 'They both have two sets of wings, but a dragonfly's hind wings – that's their wings at the back – are broader at the base. Damselfly wings are the same size. But it's the way they look when they're not flying that sets them apart. Dragonfly wings go out like this, like an aeroplane.' I mimic the movement. 'Whereas damselflies fold their wings up so they follow the line of their bodies, going straight down their backs. Come on, let's get in the boat and see if we can find some that are sitting down so I can show you what I mean.'

'How do you know all this?' Sonny asks as I help him carry the boat to the launch platform – it's more of a rotten piece of wood, really.

'I grew up in the fens,' I reply with a shrug.

'What is Thefens?' Natalie asks, rolling the two words into one.

'It's a flat, watery landscape not far from here. Have you ever been to Wicken Fen?'

They shrug, unsure.

'You should ask your dad to take you. It's National Trust,'

I tell Sonny. 'Great for a daytrip, and they have a dragonfly centre there too.'

Both girls turn to their dad. 'Can we go?'

The sound of their question asked in unison tugs at my heartstrings.

'Sure,' Sonny replies, getting the gear out of the boat and laying the paddles on the grass. 'Maybe when the school holidays start.'

'Can you come?' Natalie asks me.

'Oh…' I'm aware of Sonny regarding me in that way again, the way that makes me think he's misunderstanding my hesitance to spend time with his daughters.

'We'll see.' He cuts off any response I might've given, throwing the girls their life jackets. 'Pop those on.'

Sonny sits at the back, I take the front and the girls go in the middle, facing forward for now. We plan to travel upriver, where it's quieter, but once we've found our spot, the girls will turn around so Sonny can photograph them.

We spot plenty of dragonflies and damselflies on the way and Imogen and Natalie soon get the hang of telling them apart.

I point out an orange-red male Common Darter and also a male Southern Hawker with bright apple-green and powder-blue markings.

'Who taught you all this?' Sonny asks me when I indicate a female Black-tailed Skimmer, which is yellowy-brown with two black stripes running the length of its body.

'My parents,' I reply, smiling at him over my shoulder. The girls are looking away from each other and their high blond ponytails almost obscure his face. 'We had a very outdoorsy lifestyle,' I add, returning my gaze to the front.

'Part of the joys of homeschooling?' he asks.

'I guess so.'

'I think here is good.' He drags his paddle through the water to bring us to a stop. 'Ready to have your pics taken, girls?'

They're eager. Sonny has told them that they're doing this for their mum's birthday present. He's sworn them to secrecy, but only time will tell if they'll be able to keep it a surprise.

Sonny clutches the bank so I can cautiously disembark, and then I help to hold the boat steady while Imogen and Natalie move to my seat at the back, facing their dad.

Sitting on the bank under the shade of a weeping willow, I'm able to watch Sonny at work. He's far more relaxed around his daughters than he was with me: there's smiling and cajoling rather than fixed intense concentration.

He gets them to tell him what they've learned about drag-onflies and damselflies, asking them to point out which is which, and all the while he's click-click-clicking off shots. They hold out their hands to the Beautiful Demoiselles dancing in the rushes, hoping to encourage one to land on an outstretched finger. At one point a Common Blue dam-selfly comes close and both girls squeal and giggle, all of which Sonny captures on camera. The whole thing is both heartwarming and heart-wrenching to watch, for entirely different reasons.

'You all right?' Sonny asks while his daughters are dis-tracted with a passing duck.

'Yeah, I'm good.' I unfold my arms from where I'd crossed them over my chest, realising I must look uptight. 'That seemed to go well?'

'I think so,' he replies. 'Might take a few more at the Orchard. You still up for that?'

'Absolutely. Do the girls want a chocolate biscuit before we go?'

Silly question. Sonny paddles over and passes me my bag. While I'm rooting around inside, I hear a click. I look up to see his lens pointed in my direction.

'Sneaky,' I chide as he clicks off another shot.

He lowers his camera and grins at me. My insides warm and I almost forget what I'm doing, but Imogen soon reminds me.

As promised, we return to the cottage to collect Bertie and drop off the canoe before going to the Orchard. Natalie wins the coin toss, to Imogen's desperate disappointment.

Sonny is firm with her.

'If you cry and ruin the experience for Natalie, I'll let her have a longer turn. That means she'll be the one walking Bertie around the orchard once you get there,' he warns.

Imogen stops crying immediately, and soon afterwards, her bottom lip retracts.

Even in the few weeks since I last saw him with his daughters, he seems to have become more comfortable, more in control, more *Dad*-like.

I comment on this when we're sitting at a table under the shade of an apple tree. The girls are taking Bertie for a walk around the inner perimeter of the garden and occasionally we catch glimpses of them through the trees. It's a large space, but there are plenty of people around so it feels safe to let them wander. Sunday is one of the busiest days of the week. I waited in line for ages to be served. It was that or look after Imogen and Natalie while Sonny went. I opted to queue.

'You seem to have really got into the swing of the whole dad thing,' I say as Sonny pours apple juice from a large bottle into four glasses.

'Do you think so?'

'Yeah. You're more confident.'

'I'm getting used to putting my foot down. Rochelle said I was being too soft. I needed to stamp my authority on them or they'd wrap me round their little fingers, apparently.'

'You're good with them,' I say. 'They obviously adore you.'

'They're getting there.'

'How did the photos come out?'

'You want to see?'

'Yes please.'

He passes the camera across the table to me. He must've been taking photos while I was in the queue because the first few shots are of the girls here in the gardens with Bertie.

'Those are for me, not Rochelle,' he says.

I come to one of me under the willow tree and turn the display towards him, raising my eyebrow.

'Those too.' He smiles.

I continue to scroll through the pictures – they're beautiful. The girls' blond hair shimmers gold in the sunlight and their blue eyes sparkle. I especially like one shot of them laughing as they look at each other with dancing damselflies glinting blue in the background.

'This is my favourite,' I say, showing him.

Sonny nods. 'I like that one too.'

'Rochelle is going to go mad for them,' I state with certainty, passing him his camera.

'Thank you for coming with us,' he says.

'I'm sure you could have managed on your own.'

'If all I'd wanted was help, I would've asked Archie,' he points out.

I reach forward and pick up the pager from the table, turning it over in my hand. We've ordered jacket potatoes – the device will buzz when they're ready for collection.

'Katya's agreed to sell the apartment,' he says, taking a sip of his apple juice.

'Really?'

He nods. 'She wants me to take the hit on the early repayment fee for the mortgage, but that won't be much in the grand scheme of things. I've appointed an estate agent, so they can start showing buyers around immediately.'

'That's… exciting?' I try tentatively, uncertain how he feels about it.

He nods. 'Yeah. It'll be good to move on. Now I need to look for something permanent around here.'

'What will you go for?'

'Probably a two-bed apartment in town – somewhere the girls can easily come to stay – but I'm open to moving further out and getting some more space for them. Although, they have got that with Rochelle, so maybe it'd be nice to live more centrally.'

'Nice for you too, to be somewhere lively. I'm not sure I can imagine you being out in the sticks on your own.'

'No, me neither,' he admits, and I'm struck with a vision of him picking up a woman at a bar and taking her home with him.

I feel queasy.

'So you saw Katya when you were in Amsterdam last week? How was that?'

He shrugs. 'Fine. She didn't bring anyone over, so that was an improvement on last time.'

'How do you know each other?'

'She modelled for one of my very first shoots when I moved to Amsterdam.'

'Have you and she…?'

He nods once, his eyes resting on me for a long moment.

My queasiness swells.

'Afterwards, our paths kept crossing – work, social life. She was part of a large group of mutual *acquaintances*.' He sounds cynical. 'She was the one who introduced me to Scott. They dated on and off for a couple of years. Broke up the year before he died. He was a mess. She didn't give a shit. No one did. No one cared enough. *I* didn't care enough.' He looks upset as he says this, adding, 'He went to a dark place and went downhill from there.'

'I'm sorry.'

'I'm glad to be out of that group. They weren't good people to be around. Now *you*, on the other hand,' he says with a smile as he leans forward and swipes the pager from my hands. 'Are *much* nicer. And Archie and Matilda,' he adds.

I beam at him. 'I'm glad you think so. You're not so bad yourself.'

'Not likeable enough to entice you to stick around past the end of September, though. Or…?'

'I've booked my ticket to Australia.'

His shoulders slump. 'When do you go?'

'Fourth of October.'

He flops back in his deckchair. 'Wow. You're not beating around the bush, are you.'

I avert my gaze, trying to find Natalie and Imogen through the trees.

'They're behind you,' Sonny says, nodding past my right shoulder.

I crane my neck to watch them happily trotting along after Bertie, letting her pull them wherever she wants to go.

'They would love a dog, wouldn't they?' I turn back to Sonny. 'Do you think you'll get one?'

'No, I'll be away too much.'

'Where will you be going?' I ask with a frown.

'Wherever work takes me.'

'Fashion photography?'

He nods.

'I thought you didn't like it anymore?'

'I don't. But anything else is just a hobby at the moment. It'll take time to kick things off and I can't afford to not work.'

'But you've needed time to heal,' I say, defending his reasons for taking a break. 'You and Evelyn still have a lot to sort through, right?'

'Yeah, but I'll have to put some of our sessions on hold going forward. I've taken a job in New York this week.'

'When?'

'I fly out Tuesday and return Saturday morning.'

'Oh. What's Rochelle doing about childcare?'

'She still has a flexible arrangement with the childminder, and she's taking her birthday off on Wednesday anyway.'

'When are you planning to fit in your photo shoots at the shelters?'

'I'll start the week after next,' he replies. 'I'll have to miss a couple of my volunteer sessions, which I feel bad about, but I hope not to mess them around too much.' He's been helping out on reception at Jimmy's, one of the shelters in town.

The pager goes off.

'I'll get it,' he says.

I'm struggling with the thought of him going to New York. He'll be so far removed from all of us here. What's to stop him from slipping back into his old ways?

My eyes track his journey away from me, watching him duck under a low-hanging branch and step around fallen fruit on the grass until he reaches the gravel pathway. It's only when he arrives at the café serving hatch that I realise there are two trays to carry. I jump to my feet.

'I'll bring the other one,' I say as we pass at the halfway point.

'Thanks. I'll round up the girls.'

I guess that's the end of our conversation for now.

Chapter 28

Archie and Matilda's friends have taken over the outdoor room at the rear of the Blue Ball Inn's beer garden. I hear them the moment I step outside.

'HANNAH! BERTIE!' Matilda shouts, spying us. She gets to her feet and bumps against the wooden table, sending the contents of a couple of recently filled pint glasses sloshing over the top. No one else notices.

As she gleefully edges out along the length of the rectangular table, trying to avoid the balloons that someone has attached to the ceiling in honour of Archie's birthday, I do a quick scan of the other people here.

There's Faith and Cameron, Kev and Warren and a couple of other cricketers I recognise from the match a few weeks ago, plus two girls I haven't met before. The birthday boy himself is missing, as is Sonny. I didn't see either of them at the bar.

Sonny only flew in from New York this morning. Has he already been and gone? I hope not.

'I'm so glad you could make it!' Matilda squeals, leaping about a mile in the air as another bunch of balloons breaks free from the ceiling and bounces down on her head. 'Shit, that scared me!' she gasps, batting them away before giving me a hug.

She had the day off today to hang out with Archie. I'm figuring they've spent a large chunk of it here.

'Where's your fiancé?' I ask with a grin, brandishing a card and present.

'Ooh, that sounds weird,' she replies, her lightly freckled nose wrinkling prettily. 'I haven't got used to calling him that yet.' She looks around before answering my question. 'He must've gone to the loo.'

Archie comes out of the pub doors at that very moment and genially throws his arm around my shoulders, introducing me to those I haven't met before. Some of his mates are standing up, but there are three girls around the table, including Faith who gives me a friendly wave. The other two girls smile and say brusque hellos before returning to whatever it was they were discussing. One of them, I have just discovered with a nasty little kick to the stomach, is Nessa, another of Matilda's friends who has slept with Sonny.

She's attractive – a slim brunette with long, slightly bushy hair and blood-red lipstick that she's recently reapplied, judging by the amount smeared onto the rim of her glass.

'Prosecco?' Matilda offers as Nessa throws her head back and cackles loudly.

I think she's been here most of the afternoon too, from the way her eyes are lolling.

Matilda reaches for the bottle in the ice bucket on the table.

'I'll get another one,' I insist immediately, spying from here that it's almost empty. 'Do you mind looking after Bertie for me?'

She all too gladly relieves me of the lead.

'This is for you,' I say to Archie before I go, handing him the paper bag with his present inside.

I picked up a bottle of fancy gin from the Cambridge Distillery in Grantchester. I hope he likes it.

'Aah, thank you!' he exclaims.

I wait while he unwraps his gift and makes all the right noises as he reads aloud from the label.

Nessa is now shouting over Faith and the other girl, Keri.

'Is Sonny coming?' I ask Archie, wondering if the present company could be the reason for his absence.

'I think so,' he replies with a frown, checking his watch. 'He said he'd aim to get here around five.'

That was an hour ago.

'I'm going to nip to the bar. What are you drinking?' I ask.

'Let me go!'

'No, no! I'd rather get a bottle in early so I can chill for a bit. Drink?' I prompt again.

'I'm good, thanks,' he replies, picking up one of the now not-quite-full-thanks-to-Matilda pint glasses from the table.

'Back in a tick,' I say with a smile, checking the whereabouts of Bertie. Matilda has taken her over to see Kev and Warren.

I pull out my phone while I wait at the bar, but there's no message. I resisted texting Sonny earlier, but now I type out a quick message to ask if he's still coming.

It's a warm night and the air is scented by red geraniums in pots dotted around the beer garden.

The outdoor room is basically a wooden cabin without a door and it's the perfect place for a party. Even without the balloons, it looks festive, with fairy lights, colourful paper decorations and bunting hanging from the ceiling. Spaced around the walls are framed photographs of the Grantchester cricket team, past and present.

Faith calls for me to sit down with her at the table. Matilda overhears and brings Bertie, pulling out a couple of chairs for us both while I get down to the serious business of filling glasses.

I need something to take the edge off Nessa's presence – and, if I'm being honest, Sonny's absence.

'What do you do, Hannah?' the third girl at the table, Keri, asks.

'I'm a dispensing optician,' I reply.

'Oh right! What's the difference between a dispensing optician and a plain old optician, then?'

Nessa appears bored out of her brain while I tell Keri as succinctly as possible, aware that it's not the most stimulating of explanations.

'What about you?' I ask, relieved to turn the question around on them.

'I'm a project manager and—' Keri starts to say before Nessa cuts her off.

'I'm a graphic designer. I work with Archie,' she adds, smug in the knowledge that she does a cool creative job, something she deems worthy of boasting about to strangers. 'Oh, I meant to tell you…' She turns back to Keri and starts filling her in on something her boss did, not making any attempt to include the rest of us.

I reach for my drink and take a large sip. Faith excuses herself to go to the bathroom.

'Still coming to watch the cricket tomorrow?' Matilda asks me.

'That's the plan.'

'I need to come your way in the morning, actually.'

'Why?' I'm glad the others are talking amongst themselves – it's nice to have her to myself for a bit.

'I'm going to church,' she replies.

'Are you? I didn't know you were religious?'

'I'm not,' she whispers. 'Don't tell the vicar.'

'Why are you going to church then?'

'I'd quite like us to get married at St Andrew and St Mary.' That's the name of the one in Grantchester. 'I know that's naughty. It should be about God and stuff, but it's just such a gorgeous church, isn't it?'

'It is.' I remember from when I used to attend the occasional service with Charles and June.

'Is Archie going with you?'

'Nah. He's *really* not religious. He thinks I'm crazy, but I always imagined...' Her voice trails off and her eyes take on a distant, faraway look. 'Never mind,' she says abruptly, reaching for her glass. 'Yeah, maybe it's not the best idea.'

'I'm confused. You *don't* want to go to church tomorrow? Or you don't want to get married in one?'

'No, I do. But I don't. I don't know what I want.' Her eyes become clouded. 'Oh dear, silly me,' she mumbles, turning her back on the table and leaning down to pat Bertie.

I do the same so we're in easy earshot. 'You okay?'

'Yep. Let's talk some other time.'

'Why don't you come over in the morning?' I suggest. 'Before or after church, whatever suits.'

'Don't suppose you fancy coming with me?' she asks hopefully.

'To the service?' I shrug and nod, sensing she needs this. 'Of course I can do that. But come over for a cuppa too.'

'Okay.' She smiles gratefully.

'Oh great,' I hear Nessa say sarcastically. 'Look what the cat dragged in.'

I bolt upright quickly and expectantly and, sure enough, Sonny is crossing the garden. Even Nessa's sarky comment can't prevent my heart from flipping.

He looks no different to how I've seen him in the past – light-grey shorts and a white T-shirt – but something about the sight of him tonight has my pulse racing that little bit faster.

He makes a beeline for Archie and I tear my eyes away from their endearingly joyful greeting to hear Nessa grumbling, 'Wonder whose pants he'll try to get into tonight, then. Be careful,' she warns Keri. 'He's already screwed Faith so you're next in line.'

'Ew,' Keri says.

Nessa looks pleased at this reaction. Faith hasn't come back from the bathroom yet so can't stand up for herself, but if Nessa is trying to put Keri off Sonny, she's doing a decent job.

Nessa looks at me directly. 'Has he tried it on with you yet?'

I want to crawl under the table.

'Sonny and Hannah are good friends, actually,' Matilda says.

Nessa scoffs and grabs the bottle out of the ice bucket.

'He's different from how he was,' Matilda insists in a lovely,

229

earnest way as Nessa pours herself a glass of fizz. 'Archie and I have spent a lot of time with him recently and he's a changed man.'

I'm surprised and pleased to hear her defending him. She even sounds faintly sober.

But Nessa, who has been shaking her head with disbelief, now barks out a laugh.

'Whatever you say.' She passes the bottle to Keri, not going to the trouble of filling her friend's glass herself. 'Well, hello!' she says brashly and unpleasantly, eyeing someone over the top of my head.

I twist around to see that Sonny has made his way over.

'Hi,' he says, briefly placing his hand on my shoulder. His eyes flit from me to Nessa, Keri and Matilda.

Matilda gets up to give him a hug and I want to do the same, but Nessa has made me feel grossly uncomfortable so I stay where I am.

'Anyone want a drink?' Sonny offers and I can tell he's keen to escape.

'I'll have a bottle of Prosecco!' Nessa shouts rudely.

I see him clock the glasses on the table and he nods, coming to the conclusion that we're all drinking the same thing.

'Back in a bit.'

'Thanks,' I call, watching him go with a pang.

Matilda gives Nessa a dirty look.

'Buying a bottle of booze is the *least* he can do,' Nessa snaps at her dismissively.

'I might take Bertie for a quick toilet break,' I say to Matilda, pushing my chair out from the table.

She nods, understanding.

I go straight to the bar.

Sonny is already ordering. I wait for him to finish and for the bartender to move away before running my forefinger down his taut back.

He jumps and looks over his shoulder at me with alarm.

I laugh and his expression relaxes. 'You're on edge tonight.'

'I was half expecting it to be Nessa with a knife,' he admits sheepishly, turning to face me.

'She's a fun one, isn't she?'

'Mm.'

He gives me a wry smile. The moment stretches on with neither of us speaking nor looking away. My nerviness ramps up a notch.

'Thanks for your text,' he says at last. 'It woke me up.'

'Is that why you were late?'

'Fell asleep on the sofa,' he explains.

'Bed,' I correct him.

'Sofabed,' he corrects in turn, grinning. 'All-night flights suck.'

'How was New York?' I ask, pulling Bertie back from the fireplace. It's not lit, but I don't think she should be rummaging her snout around in it.

'Fine.'

The bartender places his fourth and last pint down and Sonny turns around to settle up. 'I need more hands,' he murmurs, shoving his wallet back in his pocket while eyeing the number of drinks on the bar top.

'I can carry a glass if Bertie behaves.' I'm not really taking her outside. I was only using it as an excuse to get away. 'And I guess I could also manage the bottle of Prosecco.'

'Don't sound so enthusiastic. I thought you were drinking it?'

'I am. But I'd rather not go back to that table.'

'She scares you too?' He's amused.

I nod. 'For a while there I didn't think you were going to show up.'

He frowns. 'I wouldn't have missed Archie's birthday. Not on Nessa's account.'

'How does Matilda even know her?' I'm baffled as to how they could be friends.

'She's actually a pal of Archie's sister,' Sonny responds, reaching for one of the drinks lined up. He necks about a third of the pint and places it back on the bar. 'I needed that.'

'I didn't know Archie had a sister.'

Neither of us is making any attempt to return to the others.

He nods, brushing the froth away from his upper lip. 'Ursula.'

I narrow my eyes at him.

'No,' he states adamantly, knowing exactly the direction my mind was taking me. 'There are lines I draw. Anyway, she has a long-term boyfriend.'

I roll my eyes and wrap Bertie's lead around my wrist to make her more secure as Sonny continues.

'Ursula's boyfriend Sean used to go to university here in Cambridge, so Nessa and Ursula would come up from London to visit. And Archie lived here too, of course. According to Matilda, Nessa once had the hots for Archie so I don't think she was too happy when Nessa sweet-talked Archie's boss into giving her a job after university.' He begins to gather three pint glasses together, leaving the one he's been drinking on the bar.

'You seem to know a lot about her,' I mutter as I grab the bottle of Prosecco with the hand that's also holding Bertie's lead, picking up his pint glass with my free hand.

'I do usually tend to talk to people before I sleep with them,' he replies, and although it's an irreverent comment designed to entertain, I find I've lost my sense of humour.

I lead the way back through the pub and into the beer garden, plonking the bottle of Prosecco in the ice bucket and making Nessa and Keri jump before swiping my glass from the table.

'Cheers,' I mutter to Matilda, knocking back a mouthful. I presume it was she who refilled it. I hand Sonny his own glass once he's distributed the others and choose to ignore the odd, quizzical look he gives me before turning my back on him. 'I might go and chat to Faith,' I tell Matilda. She's now on the other side of the cabin with Cameron and Kev.

'I'll join you in a bit,' she promises.

Chapter 29

The more I drink, the less I care about Nessa and Sonny. I can still hear Nessa cackling and shouting over Keri and the other two girls from Archie's work who have now turned up, but I'm kinda content here on my side of the cabin. All I need to remember is that Bertie is right behind me and I must not step on her. She's sprawled out with her back against the wall and is clearly exhausted. I regret not leaving her at home, poor old girl.

Archie's cricket pals and Faith are making me laugh and now Matilda has joined us too, having swiped the bottle of Prosecco to refill our glasses.

'She's fine when she's had *a couple* of drinks,' she's saying, still on a mission to defend Nessa. 'She's kind of bitchy but funny with it, you know?'

'She's deplorable,' Faith states, deadpan.

Matilda giggles and raises her palms to the ceiling. 'I give up.'

One of Archie's mates – a cute twenty-something with the curliest blond hair I've ever seen on a guy – reels backwards at something Kev has said.

'Careful!' I put my hands on his waist to stop him from stumbling over Bertie.

He swivels around to look at me, his eyebrows jumping up.

I point at Bertie, who's blissfully ignorant and quite likely snoring.

'Oh, sorry!' he exclaims, turning to face me. 'Is she yours?'

'I'm her bodyguard,' I tell him, mock-seriously.

He grins and holds out his hand. 'Keane,' he says.

'Keen as in, you're keen? Or is Keane your name?'

'Keane's my name, but I'm pretty keen too, to be honest.'

I can't help but laugh at his brazen flirtatiousness.

'And you are?' he asks with a self-assured grin.

'Hannah,' I reply, indulging him.

'How do you know Archie?'

'Through Matilda. You?'

'We used to work together.'

'You live in Cambridge?'

'No, York. I'm down for the weekend. Haven't seen Arch in a while.'

As we chat, I become aware that we have Sonny's attention. I can see him out of the corner of my eye, surrounded by Archie's cricketing pals, and he keeps looking over.

I don't know what my motivation is – I'm too drunk to think about it – but I have a horrible urge to make him jealous. And I suspect that me getting chatted up by another guy will do exactly that.

'Are you local?' Keane asks.

'Yep. I live up the road.'

He arches one eyebrow. 'That's convenient.'

'Isn't it?'

He grins. 'I'm supposed to be kipping on Mal's sofa.'

'Who's Mal?'

He leans his head close to mine and points at a tall skinny guy standing outside the cabin.

We've long since spilled out into the rest of the beer garden. Archie has a *lot* of friends. Not that I'm surprised. He's that kind of guy.

After a while, Faith interrupts us to say goodbye. She and Cameron are going on holiday to Mauritius first thing in the morning so won't be at the cricket match tomorrow.

'See you soon,' she says, but as she leans in to give me a hug, Cameron accidentally steps on Bertie's tail, causing her to yelp and leap to her feet.

Cameron clearly feels awful, and although Bertie is almost immediately wagging her tail again, I've got a serious case of the guilts. I should take her home. She settles back on her haunches, not daring to sprawl out again. I distractedly stroke her head while trying to concentrate on what Keane is saying.

Sonny materialises at my side.

'Do you want me to run her home?' he asks, his gaze steady on mine.

It's a lovely, genuine offer and it makes me feel terrible for trying to hurt him.

'I was thinking about doing that,' I reply.

'It'll take me two minutes,' he insists, underestimating or perhaps under-exaggerating the distance – he'll be at least five-to-ten.

'Are you sure?' We both know it'll take me substantially longer in my sandals.

'Yep. Keys?'

I go and get them from my bag, which I left over by the table. When I return, Keane has moved outside to join his friend.

Sonny follows the line of my sight. 'I might've frightened him off, sorry.'

He doesn't sound in the least bit apologetic.

'How did you manage that?' I ask drily.

'I think he accidentally assumed we're living together.' He pulls a face, pursing his lips in a comical 'whoops' kind of gesture.

His phrasing was quite clever, now that I think about it, offering to run Bertie 'home'. That could have easily meant 'our' home.

'It's a shame,' he adds with an insincere frown. 'I reckon you could've been in there.'

'The night is young,' I say saccharinely, pressing Bertie's lead into his hand. 'And he's only here for one night.'

'Perfect. No strings attached.' His nonchalance is unquestionably fake. 'If you like the whole Justin Timberlake-in-the-late-nineties-poodle-hair thing,' he adds disdainfully.

'I *knew* he reminded me of someone!' I play-punch his arm.

His lips tilt upwards, just a little, but the crease on his brow remains. And then his smile fades until he's simply staring at me with dark unfathomable eyes, seemingly trying to work me out.

'Are you taking her home or what?' I mumble.

He nods and shakes himself, breaking the eye contact. 'Come on, girl.'

Bertie dutifully follows him out of the cabin.

'Is he running Bertie home?' Matilda asks, tracking their journey across the beer garden.

'Yeah.'

'That's nice of him.'

I nod because I can't speak. I feel as though I've swallowed a stone.

Why, why, *why* am I trying to hurt him? He's been nothing but kind to me. I'm too tipsy to understand. Too confused.

I look over at the table and catch Nessa and Keri's eye. They're huddled together, and I assume they're bitching from the way they're smirking at each other.

I feel like the only thing that makes sense right now is to have another drink.

Last orders have been and gone and everyone is outside on the pavement, deciding what to do next. Some people are talking about heading into town to go to a club, but I'm simply trying to stay upright.

'You carrying on?' Sonny asks me.

It's the first time he's spoken to me in almost two hours. He returned my keys to me when he got back, but barely looked at me, then proceeded to talk to Archie's cricket mates for the rest of the evening.

'No. I've had too much to drink. I need to go home. You?'

He nods, his lips drawn into a thin line. 'Same.'

'You don't look pissed to me,' I say. 'Neither of you do.'

He glances to his left with a frown then meets my eyes again. 'Are you seeing double?'

I giggle, delighted at my joke.

'Oh Hannah, you are so drunk.' He shakes his head at me woefully.

'I'm completely and utterly shitfaced,' I reply.

'I'll walk you home.'

'You don't need to.'

'I know I don't. You've already told me you're capable of fending off giant Germans and no doubt Justin Timberlake lookalikes too. What happened to that idiot anyway? I didn't see you talking to him again.'

'No, my heart wasn't in it.'

He looks at me with surprise. I'm a bit surprised myself at my honesty.

'Turns out I wasn't so keen on Keane after all,' I whisper gravely, trying to keep a straight face.

We say goodbye to Archie and Matilda, who conspiratorially admit to us that they're desperate to head home, but they're dealing with a hefty amount of peer pressure.

'Are you still on for tomorrow?' Matilda asks me.

'Yes.' I nod purposefully. 'What time?'

'The service is at ten thirty.'

'Eesh.' I pull a face.

'I'm being mental, aren't I? We're going to be so hungover,' she laments.

'Nah, let's do it,' I urge. 'Swing by mine at ten? We can have our cuppa afterwards.'

'Done. See you then.'

Nessa's mouth falls open at the sight of Sonny and me leaving together. She turns to say something to Keri.

I am *that* close to giving them the finger.

We set off along the pavement and I'm grossly aware of the hole being bored into the back of my head by Superbitch and her sidekick.

'Are you okay?' Sonny asks after a while, noticing that my limp is more pronounced than usual.

'I've been standing up for too long,' I reply, brushing him off. 'Wasn't loving the company at the table.'

'Ah.'

'I can understand Faith, but Nessa?' I erupt. 'What were you thinking?'

He exhales on a rush of breath. 'Yeah,' is all he says in a heavy, resigned sort of way.

We walk the rest of the way in brilliantly drunk, contemplative silence.

When we reach my front door, I spend a significant amount of time fumbling around in my bag for my keys. Where are they? Oh, here. Why are there so many?

Sonny extricates the bunch from me and deftly unlocks the door.

'Clever,' I murmur, staggering into the hallway.

'Want me to make you some tea and toast?' he asks, waiting on the doorstep.

I spin around to look at him. 'God, you're adorable.'

'I'm adorable?' He grins.

'A-DOR-A-BLE,' I repeat, stressing each syllable.

'Not a word that's often used to describe me.'

'It's true.' I turn and walk towards the kitchen, dumping

my bag on the hallway floor as I go. I expect him to follow so I'm glad he does, pushing the front door closed behind him with a click.

I pull a chair out noisily from under the kitchen table and slump onto it, then drag another chair over so I can put my foot up.

Bertie's asleep in her basket in front of the Aga, too knackered to even look up, let alone wag her tail.

'Where do you keep your bread?' Sonny asks, searching kitchen cupboards.

I point at the pantry door.

He finds everything else he needs. I track his movements around the kitchen slowly and deliberately.

After what seems like either a very short time or an eternity, he places buttered toast and a cup of tea on the table in front of me and pulls up a chair for himself.

'How are you so perky?' I mutter, picking up a slice and tucking in.

'I slept all afternoon,' he reminds me.

'Oh yeah. So how was New York? Did you sleep with any models?'

'No!' He recoils, then when he's recovered, asks with a frown, 'Did you think that I would?'

I shrug. 'Dunno.'

'The only time I've come close to breaking my vow was with you.'

A shiver goes down my spine. Alcohol dulled the sensation, but I definitely felt it.

'Can I ask *you* a question?' he asks after a minute or so.

'Depends what it is.'

'Were you trying to make me jealous earlier?'

'Yes,' I reply without a second thought.

He lets out a snort of amusement.

'Did it work?' I ask boldly.

'Yes,' he admits, resting his chin on the palm of his hand and staring at me.

'Really?' I'm thrilled.

'Why were you trying to do that?' He seems puzzled.

'I would've thought that's obvious,' I reply.

'I'd like some clarification.'

'Why do *you* think I did it?'

He regards me for such a long moment that dozy butterflies start to awake in my stomach. I realise I've stopped eating.

'Probably for the same reason that I got jealous,' he murmurs.

'I *really* fancy you,' I say suddenly, dropping the last mouthful of toast down on the plate and leaning back in my seat, eyeing him recklessly.

He's caught off guard, surprised.

'Are you one hundred per cent committed to your vow?' I continue without waiting for a response. 'Because I'm thinking that maybe we should just do it and get it out of our systems.'

His eyes widen. 'Should I take everything you're saying tonight with a pinch of salt?' he asks after a long moment.

'Definitely not. I speak the most truth when I'm drunk.'

'Is that right? I'm going to struggle not to take advantage of that.'

A memory from university assaults me and I cringe.

'I'm joking,' he reassures me, his brow furrowing as I stand up.

'Whoa.' The room is spinning.

'Are you okay?'

'I think I'm going to be sick.'

He's on his feet in an instant. 'Bathroom?'

'Upstairs.'

I stumble, but he catches me, lifting me into his arms and somehow managing to navigate the steep, narrow cottage staircase without cracking my head against a wall. The bathroom is straight ahead – he switches on the light and gently places me on my feet, only for me to drop to my knees in front of the toilet. Everything is swimming, from the contents of my gut to the thoughts whirling around my head.

Sonny gathers my hair together as I retch, vomiting the quantity of approximately two bottles of Prosecco into the toilet bowl, plus the toast I've just consumed. When I'm finally done, I grab some toilet paper and wipe my mouth before flushing the loo.

'Yuck,' I say. 'Sorry about that.'

'It's all right.' He carefully unravels my hair from where he'd wound it around his fist.

I shakily stand and hunt out my toothbrush from the left-hand mirrored cabinet, squirting out some toothpaste. I still feel wretched, but less spinny from having expelled some of the booze.

Sonny is waiting with his back resting against the wall and his arms folded. He's staring at the floor.

'Do you want me to stay?' he asks, lifting his head to look at me.

I balk at him.

'Not like that!' he says gruffly. 'Just to make sure you're okay.'

'Oh. All right then.' I nod.

I put the toothbrush and paste away, but leave the cabinet ajar in its usual position.

On the way out of the bathroom, he reaches over and closes it.

I frown and take a step backwards, opening it back up again so two reflections are once more visible in the angle of the mirrors.

He cocks his head to one side, baffled, but doesn't question my actions.

I walk out of the bathroom.

Chapter 30

Sonny is gone when I wake up in the early hours of the morning with a dry throat and a pounding headache. He's left a glass of water and two paracetamol on the bedside table with a note to say he decided to head home – he'll see me at the cricket match. I swallow the pills and down the water before endeavouring to get back to sleep.

My memory is hazy, but a few things begin clicking into place and soon the likelihood of me being able to fall back asleep goes from slim to non-existent.

I groan and cover my face with my hands.

Downstairs I can hear Bertie's claws clipping over the kitchen tiles. There's nothing wrong with her hearing. She lopes up the stairs and appears at the bedroom door, her tail moving leisurely from side to side.

I pat the bed, having long since given up keeping her off it.

She climbs into her place at my side and I edge closer, needing to feel the heat and warmth of another being.

'I'll take you for a walk in an hour or so,' I promise in a whisper.

Her tail thumps twice against the duvet and she rests her chin on her paws.

I close my eyes and let the events from the previous night play out in my mind.

'I *do* fancy him,' I whisper when I've exhausted racking my brain for information. 'But I also like him. I like being with him and I like talking to him. It scares me how much.'

Bertie's tail thumps half-heartedly.

I sigh and nestle closer to her, but I can't escape the feeling of being unbearably alone.

Matilda is late. She arrives wearing sunglasses.

There's no time to waste if we're going to make this service.

'I've never seen you looking so rough,' she has the audacity to say when I've pulled the front door shut behind me.

I laugh then regret it because it hurts my poor dehydrated brain. 'Speak for yourself!'

'I feel so shit,' she admits, opening the garden gate. 'Can't actually believe we're going through with this. Shall we go for Sunday lunch instead?'

'It's ten twenty in the morning,' I point out, turning left towards the church.

'Doesn't the Red Lion serve food all day?'

'They won't serve *lunch* until *lunch*time. Clue is in the name.'

'Guess we'd better stick to the plan then.'

We're already a third of the way there. The church is literally a hundred metres away on the other side of the road.

'So you got roped into going clubbing?' I ask.

She nods slowly and painfully. 'What's your excuse?'

'Too much alcohol and not enough sleep.'

'Why didn't you sleep? You must've been home by eleven thirty. Wait!' she gasps. 'Did you and Sonny—'

'No!'

'Nessa was convinced you were going home to shag.'

'Urgh, she's unbearable. I don't know how you can be friends with her.' I glance at her. 'Too honest?'

She smirks. 'No, you're right, she can be awful. She's more Archie's sister's friend than mine. Or at least, she was. Their friendship seems to have fizzled out. She was on the boat the day Archie and I met. I thought she was his girlfriend from the way she was shooting daggers at me, but he soon put me right. She used to fancy him too.'

'You can't blame her,' I say flippantly, and she sniggers.

Neither of us says anything as we cross the road – too much concentration involved.

'Anyway, she got over it when she started dating someone from work,' Matilda continues, nodding politely at a couple of elderly lady parishioners, dressed in their Sunday best.

We are looking very worse for wear in comparison.

'We hung out for a while as a four, but they broke up and it was a bit messy until her ex left and got another job. Nessa is a woman who doesn't like to be scorned.'

'You don't say.' I feel an unanticipated pang of sympathy towards Sonny for having to bear the brunt of her fury.

I don't think Matilda would mind that Sonny has already told me some of what she's revealed, but I don't have the energy to repeat our conversation.

We've now reached the church entryway so we stop

speaking as we walk inside, nodding and smiling at anyone in the vicinity and trying to pretend we're not two desperately hung-over heathens.

'It really is the church from *Grantchester*, isn't it?' Matilda says in amazement as she looks around. It's true: they do film scenes for the television series inside as well as out. 'I haven't been here in years,' she adds.

I catch sight of the prayer board and falter. Matilda has also seen it. She wanders over and begins to read some of the messages that parishioners have pinned up.

I'm about to suggest that we sit down when I hear her murmur, 'Oh,' and I see that her eyes have filled with tears.

'That's so sad,' she mumbles, and grief momentarily engulfs me at the memory of some of the messages I've penned myself over the years on the rare occasions I've come.

Matilda reaches for a piece of paper and grapples with a pen, sniffing as she scrawls out a message. I avert my gaze from the tears rolling down her cheeks, unsure why she's so upset and too consumed with swallowing the lump in my own throat to ask.

She pins up the message: *For my dad, Peter Walker. I still miss you so much and hope you're at peace, wherever you are.*

Okay, now I'm crying too. What must we look like? First we walked in, a couple of hung-over heathens, and now we're blubbing by the prayer board. Maybe we're not heathens, after all, if we're taking it this seriously. However we are definitely hung-over, overtired and emotional. A fair sign that alcohol is the devil's work.

'Are you not going to write one?' Matilda whispers in a choked voice. The service is about to start.

I take the pen from her, scribbling out a message: *Please look after Charles on his travels and keep June safe at the end of her journey.*

'That's lovely,' Matilda mumbles.

As she blows her nose and goes to sit down, I surreptitiously pen another message: *For Anna. May you never walk alone.*

Chapter 31

'What did you think?' I ask Matilda.

We're on our way back to mine for our long overdue cuppa. Matilda is still banging on about a Sunday roast, but that will have to wait until after the match – Archie has begged her not to go to the pub without him. My friend, who is definitely at least *part*-heathen, was texting him during Holy Communion.

To be fair, we're running short of time anyway. The match is supposed to start in an hour.

'Once I got over the fact that the vicar is a lovely woman and not James Norton or Tom Brittney from *Grantchester*, it was fine. This is such a gorgeous cottage,' she says, looking around as we walk up the garden path. 'I was feeling too sick earlier to take it in.'

It's the first time she's been to Charles's.

We go into the kitchen and I make us tea and toast, the whole time remembering Sonny doing the same thing last night. Matilda is also unusually quiet.

'You okay?' I ask, wondering if her sombre mood is entirely alcohol-related.

She swallows and hesitates before answering in a shaky voice, 'I'm feeling a bit emotional.'

And then she begins to cry.

'I still miss my dad so much,' she tells me when she's recovered a little. 'Ever since I was a girl, I've dreamed about walking down the aisle of a church like St Andrew and St Mary with Dad at my side. The thought of walking down an aisle without him hurts so much. Archie doesn't even *want* to get married in a church. He'd do it for me, but if he saw me like this, he'd give me hell. I've already turned down one marriage proposal from him on account of my dad,' she admits to my surprise. 'Archie proposed to me a year ago, but it still felt too raw. Plus, I was at uni and I wanted to get my course out of the way. But mostly it was because of Dad. Archie said he'd wait until I was ready, until it wouldn't hurt as much, but I can't imagine getting married and it *not* hurting. How is that ever going to be the happiest day of my life?' She grabs another tissue. 'Are you close to your dad?' she asks.

'I mean, obviously I love him, but Charles was as much of a father figure to me.'

She knows that I lived here from the age of thirteen.

'Who would walk you down the aisle?'

I'm never getting married, but she doesn't need to know that, so I claim I haven't really thought about it.

She's taken aback. 'Not even when you were a little girl?'

'Nope.'

'I was always daydreaming about my wedding. When I was a teenager, my parents fought like cats and dogs, but even then

I never stopped believing in the fairy tale, the big princess-style wedding with flowers hanging from every pew. It's actually quite embarrassing, now that I think about it. We couldn't afford a wedding like that. Not even close.' She purses her lips, deep in thought, then seems to shake herself out of it. 'I should probably get myself sorted before the game.' She checks her watch. 'Argh, it starts in ten minutes! Can I use your loo?'

'It's upstairs, straight ahead.'

She jumps up and I sit there for a moment, toying with my bracelet with my name engraved on the inside – two capital *H*s flanking a lowercase *anna*. And I wonder what it might've been like to grow up in a normal household where weddings were something someone could daydream about as a matter of course.

Our boys are already playing by the time we arrive – the other team are batting. Archie clocks us and waves. I spy Sonny on the other side of the field, closer to the river, and nerves jangle around the walls of my stomach. I wonder if he's hung-over – he's too far away to tell. Archie is definitely looking off colour.

We lay our picnic blanket out under the shade of the trees up by the Orchard – it's too hot today to sit out in the sun, but I keep my floppy straw hat and sunglasses on to further muffle the light. There are a few other spectators watching nearby, and although a couple of people wave at Matilda, they don't come over. I'm quite glad not to have to make small talk. Matilda and I sit and watch the first half without saying much, both lost in our own thoughts and headaches.

At half time, I become fidgety as the men start coming off

the pitch. Archie reaches Matilda quickly and gives her a hug and a kiss, before breaking away to say hi to me.

For the first time, the sight of their easy, loving relationship makes me feel envious. I overhear them exchanging a few words about the church service, but get the feeling Matilda will go into more detail about it later when they're alone.

'Hello,' Sonny says when he's a few feet away.

I feel seasick as I smile up at him. It's probably more of a grimace, to be fair. 'Hi.'

'Nice hat.'

'Thanks.'

He drops to his side on the rug next to me and a tiny acrobat gets to work in my stomach, back-flipping this way and that and throwing in a couple of cartwheels while she's at it.

Sonny gazes out across the meadow.

We haven't kissed hello.

'How are you feeling?' he asks, twiddling a blade of grass between his thumb and forefinger.

'Rough. You?'

'Same.'

If that's true, it's impossible to tell, with his sun-kissed skin and brilliant blue eyes. Cricket whites *really* suit him. The way his biceps swell to fill out the capped sleeves of his polo shirt...

Someone pass me a fan.

'Did you get back to sleep when you went home?' I ask.

'No.' He's still staring towards the river.

'Thanks for looking out for me,' I force myself to say.

He turns to face me, his expression oddly serious.

'Water?' Archie offers, making him jolt.

'Thanks,' Sonny grunts, sitting up and holding his hand out to catch a bottle.

When the boys have returned to the pitch, Matilda snaps. 'What on earth is going on with you and Sonny? The tension between you two is *insane*! You like him, don't you? He *definitely* likes you. I know I warned you off him, but I won't give you hell if something has happened.'

'Nothing's happened,' I reiterate when she pauses for breath.

'Really? What is it, then? You do like him, don't you? Don't tell me that you don't.'

'I do,' I confess.

She lets out a loud breath. 'So what's stopping you both? Is he still sworn off sex?'

'I'm afraid so.'

'Talk about sweet torture. Aren't you heading to Australia before his six months are up?'

'Yep.'

'*Surely* he'll crack before then!'

I'm starting to think I'll explode if he doesn't.

The match is over and we've relocated to the riverside because the need to cool off has become even more critical than Archie and Matilda's determination to consume a pub lunch. Some of the men have left, but others are swimming. Every time someone jumps in, I welcome the resulting splash.

Matilda is cross with me for 'forgetting' my swimming costume again, even though she reminded me before we left the cottage. She's in the water, her arms looped around Archie's slippery neck and her fingers tangled in his sodden hair.

I'm sitting on the bank with my feet dangling off the edge. The ground is rock hard beneath my bum – we haven't had rain in ages and the earth has dried to a concrete-like consistency.

Sonny is nowhere to be seen. I watched him set off down-river, unable to pull my eyes away from his back and arm muscles rippling and flexing as he did a slow forward crawl.

I'm feeling hot and restless and annoyed. I hate that I can't get into a swimming costume and I'm toying with the idea of going home and sulking there instead.

I should leave soon anyway. Bertie will be lonely. I didn't dare bring her out in this heat.

Sonny reappears, eyeing me for a long moment before swimming over and pushing himself out on lean forearms. I watch, fixated, as water streams down his body, hugging the grooves of his muscles.

The temperature soars.

'You not going in?' he asks me, swooping down to pick up his white shirt and using it to haphazardly dry himself off. He's wearing navy-blue swimming trunks.

'No.'

Reaching into a rucksack, he pulls out a pale-blue T-shirt. His chest disappears beneath it. He looks at me, pushing his hand through his hair and setting it back off his forehead, before cocking his head towards the next field.

I accept the invitation, because I think that's what it is, and get to my feet, following him to a patch of shade under a tree where we're out of sight from the others.

He lies back and folds one arm behind his head.

'Still feeling rough?' he asks.

'A bit. You?'

'Mostly just tired.'

He gazes up at the leaves above our heads and the blue sky beyond. A moment later, his eyes close and he sighs.

His hair looks so soft and I wonder what it would be like to run my hand through it. His eyelashes are long and dark and they're creating tiny fan-shapes where they fall closed against his cheeks. I want to trace a line along the edge of his nose and press my fingertip to the indent of his lips.

I want to lie down beside him. I want to feel his arm around my shoulders. I want to rest my hand on his stomach, underneath his T-shirt.

I *want* him.

'What are you thinking?' he murmurs, and now cobalt blue glints from a crack between his lashes.

I shrug dismissively and take off my hat, throwing it a few feet away and twirling my hair up into a bun to give myself some respite from the heat of it around my neck. I don't have a hair tie with me, which is extremely vexing.

'I'm thinking I'm hot and bothered,' I mutter, letting my locks fall over my left shoulder.

Wordlessly, Sonny reaches up and takes off my sunglasses.

I jerk away slightly, but let him do it, squinting at him as he folds up the arms and places them on the grass beside his hip.

'What are *you* thinking?' I ask.

It's a while before he answers. 'I'm thinking about what you said to me last night.'

A flutter of panic goes through me. 'Which part?' I ask uneasily.

'The bit about us "doing it".'

My mouth forms an oh-shape, but no sound comes out.

'I was very drunk,' I say as insouciantly as I can once my vocal cords have obliged me. 'You should probably forget it.'

'You say that like it's possible.'

I bite my lip, staring down at him, taking in his day-old stubble. 'It'll have to be if we're going to stay friends.'

He rolls his eyes. 'We're *not* friends,' he states darkly.

Eh? 'Aren't we?'

'I don't spend half of my waking minutes thinking about fucking my friends.'

I stiffen with shock. At the same time, goosebumps erupt all over my body, making each and every one of my hair follicles stand on end.

'Sorry,' he mutters, scrubbing his hand over his face. 'Crude choice of words, but I can't say the others without feeling like I'm going to throw up.'

'What? Sex?' I ask in a small, stunned voice.

He shakes his head, his lips pencil-thin. 'Make—' He waves his hand in the air.

'Make love?' I'm squirming.

He nods tautly. 'Those were the words Glen used.'

Now I'm cold all over. That's the name of the man who abused him?

He squeezes his eyes shut, inhaling deeply and exhaling heavily.

I am clueless as to which of these very big topics I should tackle first.

A bug lands in his hair, momentarily distracting me, and I instinctively reach forward and attempt to pincer it between my thumb and forefinger. His hand snags my wrist and his eyes spring open.

'There's a bug in your hair,' I quickly explain, sounding idiotic, and he releases me, leaving searing heat circling my wrist as I finish what I started, plucking a greenfly from a caramel-blond strand.

He sighs again, lighter this time. 'That feels nice,' he murmurs.

I hesitate and then push my fingers through the roots of his hair. I was right with my assumption earlier: it *is* soft.

He makes a sound deep in his throat and I have an overwhelming urge to seek out the place where the sound came from and kiss it. The thought causes my fingers to stall and his eyes to open.

'Are you okay?' My head is still reeling from the two bombshells he's dropped.

He reaches up and twirls a lock of my hair around his finger.

'Last night you used the phrase "get it out of our systems".'

I tense.

'Is that what you want?' he asks. 'To have sex and move on, put this behind you?' He lets go of my hair to indicate the two of us. His eye contact is steady on mine.

'You know I don't do relationships,' I say awkwardly, turning away and pulling up a handful of grass.

'We are *in* a relationship,' he snaps, making me jump. He sits up with frustration and plants his palms on the ground behind him. 'You know that, don't you? This is the closest thing to a relationship I've ever had. The only thing that's missing is the sex,' he adds with exasperation.

I have no idea how my fuzzy head is expected to process all of this.

'And you want to rectify that?' I ask slowly. 'You want us to have sex?'

'Of *course* I do!' He rakes his hand through his hair, agitatedly. 'But I also *don't*! There's so much shit I still need to sort through. I'm scared of using you to dull the shame because then I might associate sex with you with sex with *him*. And then there's *you*. And all of *your* shit to deal with that you refuse to talk about. And the thought that you could just fuck and forget and disappear and that I might never see you again... I'm not sure I've ever hated the idea of anything more.'

His eyes are blazing and I feel as though a tiny bomb has exploded in my core, detonating everything I thought I knew.

I stare at him breathlessly, wordlessly, and he sighs again and flops back down to the ground.

'When was the last time you talked to someone about whatever it is that happened to you?' he asks out of the blue. 'I don't mean Evelyn, I mean someone new.'

'A few years ago. When I was at university.'

'How did it go?'

'Badly.' My voice wavers. 'I lived to regret it.'

'That's why you won't confide in me?'

'We've only known each other a few months. I promised myself I'd get to know people for a lot longer – *years* – before trusting anyone again.'

'I trusted *you*,' he says simply. 'I'm not saying that to pressure you, but doesn't it count for something? You really think I'll let you down?'

I breathe in sharply, anguished.

'Oh, Hannah,' he whispers with what sounds a lot like despair. 'Come here.'

He pulls me down to his chest and folds his arms around me, holding me close. My heart skips and skitters, my mind racing. There's no way I'll be able to relax into the hug so I lift myself up onto my forearms instead, bracing myself on either side of his head. He stares up at me. Then he takes my face in his hands and waits a moment, his eyes dark and unreadable. I don't retreat – that's the last thing I want to do – and he must see this as he pulls me down to him.

His lips are soft yet unyielding and when they part, mine instinctively follow suit, moving and sliding against his. Where our kiss in Amsterdam was frenetic and chaotic, this kiss is slow and deep, causing shivers to ripple down the length of my body in waves, crashing and waning, over and over. His tongue brushes against mine and I feel the action echo right down deep in my solar plexus and *oh God… Have I ever wanted anyone more?*

His hands are still clamped to my face so when he breaks our kiss there's nothing I can do about it. His breath is hot against my mouth. He's panting and out of control, yet somehow in control because he's no longer kissing me.

'*Sonny…*' I will him to continue.

And then Matilda's laughter carries across to us from the direction of the next field and he releases me completely. I scramble to a sitting position in time to see her round the corner with Archie, both fully dressed and ready to go.

'You guys coming to the pub?' Archie calls as Sonny abruptly stands up, the tips of his ears burning as he gathers his things together.

'I've got to head off,' he replies, passing me my sunglasses without looking at me.

My heart is still beating so fast I can feel it right up at the base of my throat. I take them from him shakily, my chest contracting as I put them on.

'I should get back to Bertie,' I manage to say, and then it occurs to me that maybe he intends to come to the cottage with me to finish what we started.

I hope I'm right.

But I'm wrong.

After a brusque goodbye to all three of us, he sets off at a stride towards Cambridge, not once looking back.

The next day, I open the door to Sonny and can tell immediately that he's come from Evelyn's. He looks both devastat*ed* and devastat*ing* with his now-*two*-day-old stubble and hair that's craving to be mussed up. Resisting the urge to touch him, I step back, inviting him in.

He shakes his head and puts one hand up against the doorframe, resting his cheek against his knuckles. 'I can't stay,' he murmurs. 'I just wanted to say…' His voice trails off and his jaw clenches, his resolve seeming to harden as his eyes cut away. 'I'm not going to be around much over the coming weeks. School holidays kick off on Wednesday and I'll be helping out with the kids more. I've got to get cracking with the charity shoots and I don't have a lot of headspace right now – even less after yesterday,' he adds grimly.

As he lists his excuses, my stomach sinks further and further until finally he gets to the crux of it: 'I think we could do with a bit of space from each other.'

He meets my eyes and pain ghosts his features at the look on my face. When he next speaks, he's gentler.

'Obviously I'll still see you around Archie and Matilda, but if you need me for anything else, if you want to *talk*,' he adds with meaning, 'call me.'

The message is clear: until I'm willing to roll up my shutters and let him in, he's pulling his down.

Chapter 32

'*I don't spend half of my waking minutes thinking about fucking my friends.*'

Sonny's words keep coming back to haunt me.

'*This is the closest thing to a relationship I've ever had.*'

This is the closest thing to a relationship *I've* ever had too. That is blindingly obvious to me now.

And: '*The thought that you could just fuck and forget and disappear and that I might never see you again… I'm not sure I've ever hated the idea of anything more.*'

That's the one that keeps repeating on an endless loop, more than any of the others.

Then there's the kiss. Kiss*es*. Plural. They're even harder to forget.

At night they play over and over in my head, jolting me from sleep and keeping me awake for hours. I'm a mess at work, constantly struggling to concentrate. I keep wondering what Sonny is doing and where his head is at.

The days stretch into a week with no sign of him, and then a second week begins to tick by and it dawns on me that he's probably moved his sessions with Evelyn to avoid us crossing paths.

Archie and Matilda are on holiday in the South of France and it's almost August with eight weeks to go until Charles returns. The thought makes me feel panicky and unhinged.

More than anything, I *miss* him. I can appreciate exactly what he meant when he said we were already in a relationship because I feel like he's broken up with me.

There's another one of his statements that I can't get out of my mind, and on Friday, over a week and a half since we last saw each other, I'm sitting at the kitchen table and pondering it while unenthusiastically poking my fork around the plate of my sad little dinner-for-one.

'*I'm scared of using you to dull the shame because then I might associate sex with you with sex with him.*'

A paedophile assaulted him when he was ten. I understand there must be a multitude of conflicting emotions abuse victims face, but why is he still feeling shame after all of these years? Hasn't Evelyn helped him to see that it's not his fault? It was *never* his fault?

I want to talk to him and ask him and be there for him, but he's shut me out.

It is acutely frustrating and upsetting.

And then it occurs to me that this is what I've been doing to him all along: shutting him out.

I hear a car door slam out the back and jump to my feet, hurrying outside to catch Evelyn as she rolls down the driveway. She stops and puts the window down, looking troubled at the sight of me.

'Are you okay?'

'I'm confused,' I blurt. 'Tell me what to do.'

She regards me with compassion, I'm sure, but I register it as pity because I *am* pitiful.

'Would you like to make an appointment?' Her voice is gentle. 'I might have a window for next week.'

'Will you tell me what to do if I do?' I ask desperately.

She smiles. 'You know it doesn't work like that.'

So I come right out and say it: 'Sonny wants me to confide in him.'

A spark of something flashes across her face. 'And what do you think about that?' she asks carefully.

'I don't know,' I mumble, losing my nerve. It's late. I feel bad. I should let her get home.

'What does Anna think?' she asks, pulling the rug out from beneath me.

Ooh, that was a low blow...

'I don't know what she thinks!' I snap. 'Nothing's clear. Everything's cloudy.'

She stares at me for a long moment, her mind ticking over. 'You really want to know what I think?' she asks at last.

This is unprecedented.

'Yes.' I nod determinedly.

'Anna would not want you to be lonely.'

Lonely, not sad. Sadness is not something I can control.

But loneliness is.

It's close to ten p.m. by the time I've collected myself together. My stomach is writhing with nerves as I press dial on Sonny's number.

He answers on the third ring.

'Hello?' He sounds wary.

'It's Hannah.'

'So says Caller ID. Are you okay?'

'Oh, I'm a little…' I'm trying for breezy, but I can't even get the words out. My eyes are stinging and now they refill with tears. So much for getting my act together before calling him.

'Hey,' he says gently as I swallow and swallow and swallow the lump down. 'Hannah.'

This is ridiculous. *I* called *him*. Now I can't even speak.

'I miss you,' he says quietly.

'I miss you too,' I manage to get out.

'I did another photo shoot today,' he says, and I appreciate him trying to distract me from whatever it is that's distressing me.

'Did you?' I encourage him to go on.

'It was my third one so far. It was with Mel.'

'No way?'

'Yeah. I found her on the corner of Green Street and Sidney Street. She took some persuading, I can tell you, but she came around. I was processing the pics when you called – they've come out well, I think.'

'That's amazing. Have you got a gallery space lined up for the exhibition yet?' I ask tearfully.

'Funny you should ask, I got something agreed today. It's all coming together. Archie's finishing the posters when he gets back next week, so soon you'll see them plastered all over the railings in Cambridge.'

'I can put some up for you,' I offer.

'Thanks,' he replies softly. 'That would be great.'

'How are the girls?'

'They're good. We went camping a few days ago. Natalie had a freak out when an owl started up outside the tent, but other than that, it was uneventful.'

'Have you taken them to Wicken Fen yet?'

'No, we were thinking about going on Monday.'

'Do you... Do you think... Could I come with you?' I ask hesitantly, dragging a fresh tissue across my nose.

He pauses. 'You want to come with me, Imogen and Natalie?' He sounds doubtful and I'm reminded of the look on his face when he realised I was reluctant to spend the day with all three of them.

'I'd like to see them,' I insist, but it comes out sounding false.

He sighs. 'You don't have to—'

'No, you don't understand,' I cut him off. 'I *do* find it difficult to be around them, but not for the reasons you're thinking.'

'What, then?' He's confused.

'It's... It's all part of it.'

'All part of what you're not telling me?'

'All part of what I'd *like* to tell you,' I reply bravely. 'I grew up near Wicken Fen. I thought perhaps I could take you there.'

There's silence at the other end of the line.

'Do you want me to come over?' he asks after an age, and oh God, I *do*. I'm *aching* to touch him, to have him hold me.

'I think I need a couple of days to compose myself,' I force myself to reply.

'I could take you to Wicken Fen another time. We don't have to go with the girls.'

'No, despite what I've just said, I think it will help to have them there. They'll keep things light-hearted.'

'Okay, if you're sure.'

'I am.'

I don't think either of us is entirely convinced.

Chapter 33

Sonny comes to collect me at ten thirty on Monday morning after texting me to say he's getting his daughters first. He pulls up on the driveway and I watch from the kitchen window as the back doors of his car fly open and the girls spill out.

I try to take a calming breath as I walk into the hall, but I can't stop breathing up into my ribcage. I'm wracked with anxiety.

Bertie barks and pushes past me as I open the door and Imogen and Natalie fawn all over her, their eagerness to get to the door explained.

Their father appears behind them and my breathing becomes shallower still.

'Hi,' he says. His mouth has formed a soft smile, but his eyes have a touch of trepidation about them.

'Hi.'

He sidesteps the wriggling bundle of limbs at his feet and comes to give me a hug.

As soon as our bodies connect, my butterflies burst into a frenzy, the feeling of his chest pressed against mine and his steady hand on my back doing funny things to my heart.

His arms slacken after a quick squeeze and I dutifully begin to withdraw, but then he brings me back in for another hug. It's fierce and all-encompassing, but still over too soon.

'Can Bertie come too?' Natalie asks me, her blue eyes pleading and her hands clasped together in prayer.

'It's up to you,' I say to Sonny. 'Otherwise, Evelyn will take her out at lunchtime.'

'Please, Daddy, please?' Natalie implores.

'Are dogs allowed at Wicken Fen?' Sonny asks me.

'On a lead, yes, but we wouldn't be able to do the boat ride.'

'Boat ride?' Imogen's eyes have gone round.

'They have a motorboat there that takes you on cruises around the waterways, but no dogs are allowed and we can't leave Bertie in the car. I'm afraid it's one or the other: boat or Bertie.' I feel mean for putting nine-year-olds in this position.

'Can we go on your canoe again another day?' Imogen asks me.

'Of course we can.'

She looks at Natalie and they both nod, a mirror of each other, before turning to me and saying simultaneously: 'Bertie.'

Every time they do that it's like a knife through my heart.

'Sounds like we have a plan.' I reach for Bertie's lead from behind the door.

Oblivious to my pain, Sonny ruffles his daughters' hair and goes to ready the car boot for our fifth passenger.

It's about a half-hour drive to the nature reserve and we

keep conversation light on the way. I spend most of the time swivelled around in my seat chatting to Imogen and Natalie. Imogen wants to tell me all about her latest Minecraft world in great detail, while Natalie is more interested in regaling me with story ideas, reading out one of her creations when she can get a word in edgeways from a notepad she's brought with her.

Soon we're driving through wide-open fields full of crops, past rows of pebble-dashed houses and under towering power lines resembling tall metallic trees.

This area has an end-of-the-world kind of feel about it – the sort of landscape you'd see in zombie movies. Natalie points out a scarecrow and Imogen notes that the higgledy-piggledy gravestones belonging to the old church are on both sides of the car – the road carves straight through the graveyard.

I'm quiet as we drive into Wicken, lost in my memories of the journeys I took to come back here as a teenager when I was older and wiser and starting to make sense of my unusual upbringing. I used to think that this little village with its restored windmill that produces flour was a bustling metropolis, but that was because I'd grown up in a landscape of fields and skies, one tiny cottage and not much else.

Cambridgeshire is known for its vast skies because there are so few hills, but here in the fens they're even bigger, arcing right up and over the flat wetlands that stretch out in every direction.

The landscape today is a wash of pale greens, blues, whites and greys, with clouds punctuating the heavens above.

Every so often, the sun breaks through before disappearing

behind forbidding formations that look as though they could offload at any second. The weather forecast claimed the rain would hold off. I hope we weren't wrong to trust it.

'This was the first nature reserve owned by the National Trust,' Sonny reads aloud from the guide as we set off on a trail around the ancient Sedge Fen – a remnant of un-drained fenland. 'It used to be two acres in 1899 and now it's almost two thousand. *Nine thousand* species of plants, animals, birds and insects live here,' he tells the girls.

They're nonplussed. The only creature they care about right now is Bertie.

Imogen won the coin toss.

'Can we go to the windmill?' she asks her dad breathlessly, pointing up ahead at the old black weatherboarded wind pump with its dominant white sails.

'Sure.' He nods and they set off at a run, their trainer-encased feet pounding the recycled plastic boardwalk.

We follow at a slower pace.

On our right is a field containing two ponies, one a rich chocolate brown and the other tawny, his cream underbelly contrasting with his grey socks, mane and swishing tail. He reminds me of Finnegan, the pony we used to have.

It's so quiet. It may be the school holidays, but it's a Monday and there aren't many people here. Occasionally we hear far-off chatter, but mostly the clean air is filled with the sound of tall reeds rustling and shivering in the breeze. They sound like waves at the seaside or a seashell when you press it to your ear.

Or whispers.

'You okay?' Sonny asks as I shiver.

'I'm nervous,' I reply unevenly.

'Why?'

'I want to tell you. I want to tell you everything. But I... It's hard for me to say it.'

A gust of wind causes the reeds to bend and lift, a rippling Mexican wave that begins on our left and carries on towards the windmill. I can hear the girls laughing.

'You don't have to do this now, you know,' he says gently. 'We can talk later, drop the girls home and go back to yours.'

'No, I need to get it out. Make it quick, like pulling off a plaster.'

Despite me saying that, we walk on in silence.

'Do you want to start with the accident?' he prompts.

I wince at the lie, then tell him the truth. 'It wasn't an accident.'

This makes him pause for thought. 'But you were in a car crash?'

'No. It was easier to say that. But I need you to know,' I add hastily, 'that it's not because I'm ashamed. That's not why I find this so hard to talk about. I'm *not* ashamed.'

'Okay.' His voice is measured, but there are worry lines etched onto his brow.

I swallow down hard and force out the words. 'I had a sister.'

He's listening intently.

'Anna. She was my twin. My *identical* twin. I lost her when we were seven.'

'Oh, Hannah,' he murmurs with shock and sympathy, and I'm sure he understands now why I find it so hard to be around his daughters.

He snags one of my horribly clammy hands and pulls me to a stop, but I place my palms on his chest and hold him at bay. He wants to console me, but there's more that I need to say and how he reacts to this next part will be crucial. It could change everything. It *will* change everything. It will go one way or the other and I feel sick to my guts, but I need to know.

He's regarding me with concern and confusion, waiting for an explanation. I release his chest and take a step away from him, meeting his eyes directly.

'We weren't just twins.' I jut my chin out defiantly and tell him: 'We were conjoined.'

He visibly pales.

A stinging sensation starts up at the back of my eyes. He takes a step towards me, but again, I put my hands up and he stops.

'We were joined at the hip. Literally.' I touch my hand to my left-hand side. 'We were fused together at our pelvises.'

He looks shaken, but to my relief, he doesn't seem repulsed. Not as far as I can tell.

'When we were born, doctors wanted to separate us, but our parents wouldn't let them. Later, Anna pushed for it. But she died soon after the operation.'

An operation to separate conjoined twins is never simple, but ours should have been a fairly straightforward procedure – even more so had we been separated as babies. We didn't share any internal organs and we had two full sets of limbs, although Anna was slightly smaller – a feature that impacted on the early growth of my left leg.

As seven-year-olds the operation was more complicated,

but there was still relatively little risk involved. What actually caused Anna's demise was an infection post-op and her death devastated everyone who had known her.

I was destroyed beyond repair. I'm still reeling from her loss.

She was a part of me then and she's a part of me now. I still carry her name within mine – our parents made it that way, named us so we could never truly be parted, even if we one day chose to be physically so. The inside of the bracelet they gave me weeks before the operation is engraved with my name: *HannaH*.

Anna had a near-identical one: *hANNAh*.

My throat closes up.

And then I'm in Sonny's arms and he's holding me tightly, crushing me against his chest, his hand cradling the back of my head and his breath warm against my hair.

The weight I've been carrying slides from my shoulders and it is such a relief, such a blessed, blessed relief that I could burst into tears.

Before I can entertain doing any such thing, I pull away, knowing that I can't – *don't want to* – lose it. I look up at his face to see that his dark eyelashes are spiked with tears.

'I'm so sorry,' he whispers, caressing my face with the back of his hand.

I swallow, nodding fervently, then turn to walk towards the windmill. He swipes my hand, squeezes it hard, and barely lets it go for the rest of the walk.

By the time we drive further north towards the home where I grew up, the clouds have grown even blacker and a golden light is spearing through the cracks. It's the sort of weather that could lead to rainbows and it's gratifyingly dramatic.

I direct Sonny down a narrow country road. It's in good shape now, but it used to be a dirt track, overgrown with grass and riddled with potholes. Whoever is living here has had it fixed up.

That's if the cottage even still stands. It's been a few years since I've been back.

The road winds around to the left and I'm on tenterhooks as we drive past the final copse of trees, then, there it is: a small whitewashed building with a low wonky red-tiled roof, crooked walls, lopsided windows and a tall fat central chimney.

My heart squeezes. 'Stop,' I whisper.

Sonny pulls over on the verge and waits patiently for instructions.

'That's where I used to live, kids,' I say, doing my utmost to keep my voice light as I point out the front window.

Natalie and Imogen lean forward.

'Aw, it's so cute!' Natalie cries.

'It looks like where Goldilocks would live!' Imogen pipes up.

'Where the three bears would live, you mean,' Natalie corrects her.

They continue to squabble as I stare, trying to absorb the scene before me, a lump in my throat.

There's no smoke spiralling out of the chimney. We almost always had a fire going. Not only because we had no central heating, but because my parents cooked directly over the flames in a cast-iron cauldron, everything from soups to casseroles. I feel a pang at the memory of larder cupboard shelves lined with homemade preserves that glittered red and orange when you held them up to the light.

'They still have a vegetable garden.' I point at the bean trellis off to the side of the house. Further back, behind a garden bursting with summer flowers, it's possible to make out large leafy vegetables – cabbages, I think.

'I wonder if they still have chickens. We used to keep them in the pen over there. And there's the pond. We had ducks too.'

'Do you want to get out and take a closer look?' Sonny asks. 'It doesn't appear that there's anyone in, but I'm sure they wouldn't mind you knocking on their door anyway, especially if you told them you used to live here.'

'No, I'm good. You should never go back. It won't be the same. They've done it up. I want to remember it how I remember it.'

With its bowing ceilings, low beams, peeling paint and exposed floorboards.

I blink back tears and smile at him. 'But thank you for bringing me. We can go now.'

'Are you sure?' he asks hesitantly.

I nod. 'I'm sure.'

He puts on music for the return journey and I sit and stare out of the window, lost in my thoughts. At one point he reaches across and takes my hand in his. The feeling of his steady warmth brings comfort to my aching heart.

I feel a deep relief at having told him about Anna, but it doesn't quell the pain. Nothing ever will. And there's still so much I haven't explained. I'm sure he has questions.

'I'll take the girls home first, okay?' he checks with me in a low voice. 'Shall we pick up a bite to eat on the way back to yours?'

I nod, unable to ignore the churning in my stomach.

He *definitely* has questions.

Rochelle comes outside to say hello – I'd stayed in the car, but when I see her approaching, I open up the door and climb out, dangling my arms over the side. It would feel rude to speak to her through an open window, but I sense this is going to be a quick conversation.

'Thank you for the book,' she says with a reserved, slightly uncomfortable smile.

I bought the girls a book about dragonflies in the gift shop at Wicken Fen. Couldn't resist.

'I hope they like it,' I say as warmly as I can, maintaining eye contact with her even as Sonny joins us. He's said good-bye to the girls – they're already inside the house. 'How are you?' I ask politely.

'Good, thanks. You? Nice day?' she asks in turn.

'Lovely.'

It's an awkward exchange, but it's something. She's trying and I'm grateful.

I haven't fully comprehended why she's trying or why I'm grateful, but I decide to bury that one and examine it later.

'Okay, then. Well, see you soon.' She backs up the drive.

'Bye.'

Sonny raises his eyebrows at me over the car roof and climbs in the car.

He's introspective as we tuck into our Chinese takeaway at the kitchen table.

'I'm dying to know what you're thinking, but I've been too scared to ask,' I say at last.

The Minute I Saw You

He places his chopsticks together on his plate and looks at me. He hasn't finished his stir fry.

'Do you want to talk?' I ask.

'Is that okay?'

'Let's go through to the living room.'

I sound calmer than I feel.

Chapter 34

I sit down on the sofa and Sonny eyes the space next to me, followed by the single armchair. He's pondering his options and I'm secretly pleased when he chooses to settle at the other end of the sofa. I turn to face him, bringing my bare feet up and resting against the arm. Over his head, the cuckoo clock begins to go off.

He looks up, watching the little wooden bird pop back in behind its shutters and then checks his watch. 'It's ten minutes early,' he says.

'It always ran early, no matter how often Charles changed the time. I've given up on it, but I still like hearing it go off.'

'Why did you come to live here?' he asks, *and...*

We're off...

That's the first of his questions, but it won't be the last.

'You know I was homeschooled.' I'm steeling myself, wanting to get through this as painlessly as possible. 'Mum and Dad lived way off the grid. You've seen our house now, I'm sure you can imagine how far removed from society we were. That was the way my parents liked it. They didn't know we were conjoined until we were born. They avoided traditional medicine, rarely went to the doctors – Mum didn't even have a scan when she was pregnant and probably would have had Dad deliver us at home if she hadn't suspected something was off. It was her first pregnancy and she was in her forties – she ended up in an ambulance and having a C-section. Can you imagine how shocked the doctors who delivered us must've been? How staggering it was for my parents? It was in the news – Charles will still have clippings somewhere.' I look around the living room, as if pondering where he keeps them, before returning to what I was saying. I'm finding it easier not to look at Sonny too much – his attention is fixed on my face, but I'm staring at the flowers on my skirt, tracing my fingers down the stems. 'Surgeons wanted to separate us,' I continue. 'But Mum and Dad were having none of it. It's not that they were particularly religious, but they still had this sense that nature had created us that way and it wasn't up to people to tear us apart. In their eyes we were a miracle.'

Approximately half of conjoined twins are stillborn, and an additional third die within twenty-four hours, so the fact that we'd survived and were doing well made us even more special.

'So we went home and Mum and Dad were determined to protect us from the outside world, hence the homeschooling. They kept us pretty much hidden – they were very worried about our privacy after the initial interest from the press, so for years it was just Anna and me.' My eyes prick with tears. 'I was the talker, she was the quiet one.' My throat has begun to swell. 'I'm sorry, I haven't even answered your question yet,' I mumble, meeting Sonny's eyes.

He looks upset – not tearful, but sad. He reaches across with one hand and laces our fingers together.

'You can tell me whatever you want, whenever you want,' he reassures me.

I take a deep breath. 'I think we were happy.'

My eyes well up. I take another deep breath, my bottom lip wobbling uncontrollably. Sonny squeezes my hand and waits patiently.

'We were very close.' He knows I'm not talking about our obvious physical closeness – Anna and I were close on a transcendent level. We finished each other's sentences, even read each other's minds sometimes. We would lie in bed, talking and whispering until our parents rustled up threats big enough to convince us to shut up – usually it involved banning us from playing with some kind of farm animal, whether that was a litter of kittens or day-old chicks.

'But Anna was very shy, even around Mum and Dad,' I say. 'Only in my company, when we were alone, would she come out of her shell. There was still a lot of interest in us from the medical world. Mum and Dad refused to take us to London to see specialists, so the specialists would come to us – that was the one thing our parents consented to, but I know they hated the intrusion. Anna didn't like it either. I felt very protective of her, partly because she was a little smaller than me – that's why I have a limp,' I explain. 'But mainly because she was so shy. She would whisper in my ear and I'd speak for her. I didn't mind doctors visiting. In fact, I liked it. New people were exciting to me and I was a bit of a show-off.'

Sonny's mouth curves into a smile. Compassion radiates from him, but I feel something deeper than that too. He *cares*.

'I remember several different doctors and psychiatrists, but there was one in particular that Anna and I *both* liked. She was beautiful with this gorgeous, glossy mane of red hair and a big smile. She totally charmed our parents too. With the other doctors, I did most of the talking, but with Colleen – that was her name – Anna would also talk. I think Colleen started coming to see us when we were four or five, but it was general stuff: what games we liked to play, what were our favourite stories, how did we help out on the farm. Later she moved on to talking about our futures and what we wanted to be when we grew up. We hadn't really thought about it, so she told us about a bunch of different jobs we could do. Anna became very invested in the idea of working in a library, surrounded by books and peace and quiet, whereas I liked the idea of being a schoolteacher, because that was one of my favourite games, to line up our teddies and teach them. Then Colleen said…' My voice wavers and I have to take a moment to compose myself. 'She said that we would have to choose *one* job. That, effectively, only *one* of us could be happy. The other would have to forfeit because we were joined together. It was the first time she'd come close to bringing up separation and I still remember the sick feeling in my gut that it brought on. And she didn't stop there. Over time, she mentioned marriage and children and explained how complicated our lives would be. But if we chose to have an operation, we could have it all. She soon sensed we weren't ready to hear any of this and backed off, but Anna and I had already begun to dread her visits. At night we would whisper to each other that we

The Minute I Saw You

There's honestly nothing I'd like more right now.

I nod, hoping it's clear which way my head is moving – I'm still tucked under his chin.

'Okay,' he whispers.

Chapter 35

Dawn has barely broken when I wake, but I can make out Sonny in the shadows. He's lying on his back, his face turned towards me.

I inch closer to him, craving his heat, but feeling deceptive, like a thief. I have always longed to feel the warm solidness of another body beside mine, someone to fill the gap that Anna left. It used to freak Danielle out. Not at first – it took her a while to realise that me squeezing next to her on the sofa was an attempt to claw back some of the comfort I was missing from my twin. This understanding came at around the same time Nina was diagnosed with a brain tumour. Soon afterwards, Danielle started dating Brett. Going out with Josh helped take away the sting of Danielle's sudden aloofness, but I didn't dare trust my new boyfriend with the truth of my past. I had told him the car crash lie, but I didn't feel confident it would hold up under scrutiny so I couldn't let him get too close to me or my scars. I have only ever had sex with most of my clothes on.

Years earlier, Charles had persuaded me to open up to Danielle and Nina about Anna, knowing how isolated I would feel if I had to go through my teenage years carrying such a hefty secret. But I was terrified that others would find out and treat me differently. Perhaps I should have had more faith in my classmates, but my only other foray into traditional schooling – primary school the year after Anna had passed away – didn't go well. I was surrounded by children for the first time in my life and I'd never felt more alone.

To be fair, I *was* different. Even without Anna, my hippie parents and homeschooled start to life set me apart. I was also used to making what I later discovered to be an uncomfortable amount of eye contact. I had spent incalculable hours staring unguardedly into Anna's eyes, and it was only later, when I went to live with Charles and June, that they gently explained to me that this level of eye contact wasn't normal. It was no surprise that they went on to actively encourage a career in optometry, hoping to find a positive outcome from what I had learned to consider a flaw.

But what distinguished me most from the other kids at primary school was the fact that I didn't try to hide losing Anna. I was suffering so acutely with the pain of her loss that I retreated from everyone and everything.

Really, it had been far too soon to send me to school at all, but the psychiatrists had thought it might help. They wanted me to have hope, to make friends, to find comfort in other children and to look towards the future, but I was too broken to see the light at the end of the tunnel. My parents pulled me out within a year, desperately worried about my mental health.

Sonny turns on his side towards me, but I don't move away in time to make room for him so his legs knock against mine. He jerks back and his eyes flutter open.

We stare at each other in the grey light.

'Hi,' he whispers.

'Hi.' I pause. 'Are you freaked out?'

'About what?'

'Me. Everything.'

He pulls a face. 'I thought you'd have more faith in me than that. How would you feel if I asked you that question?'

'I'd be deeply insulted.'

'Exactly.'

He smiles and makes to slide his arm around my shoulders so I lift my head and shuffle towards him, letting him pull me into his embrace.

Something that feels a lot like a balloon expands within my chest as the seconds tick by.

'What happened when you were at university?' he asks.

'I trusted a couple of people I shouldn't have: my flatmates, a guy and a girl. I'd only ever lived with family, so I was apprehensive about sharing my space with strangers, but we all got along brilliantly at first. I actually felt relatively normal those first few months, even though I was a few years older than them – I was a year behind at school and I'd also had some time off before uni. We hosted house parties and got drunk a lot and generally acted like the students we were. Then I ended up confiding in them. We were all tipsy and they made a big show of being understanding and supportive and accepting. I was *so* relieved, but it was a farce. They were both much more freaked out than they'd let on. I'd walk into a room and catch them whispering, and then they told a few other people too. It all came to a head when a guy I had the hots for tried to chat me up. Luckily I sensed something was off so it didn't go anywhere, but it later got back to me that he'd wanted to see me naked so he could tell his mates about it.' I shudder, feeling sick at the memory.

'Fucking hell,' Sonny mutters menacingly.

'Yeah, he was a dick. They were young and stupid. But I was very upset at the time. I wanted to run away, drop out, leave that place and never go back. Charles persuaded me not to quit my course, but I did move out. Rented a room in an old lady's house for the rest of my time at uni, but I never trusted anyone enough to make friends. When one of my course tutors helped me to secure a twelve-month work placement at an optician in Bradford city centre, I felt obliged to take it, but I didn't enjoy it much. My boss, Karl, was the complete opposite of Umeko: domineering, unsupportive and short-tempered, and my only other colleagues were a lot older and on different wavelengths. Charles would have liked me to move back to Cambridge, but I'd saved up some money and I used it to go travelling. I felt like I needed a bit of time and distance to decide what I wanted to do with my life.' I roll over onto my stomach so I can look at him. 'Charles and June were the ones who encouraged me to seek a career in optics. I wasn't at all convinced it was for me.'

'I think it suits you,' Sonny murmurs. Then he smirks. 'You rock that uniform.'

I giggle.

'No, seriously, I do think it suits you. You're good at your job and you're great with people.' He says this earnestly, but now his lips twitch. 'And also, you're lovely to get up close and personal with.'

I slap his chest and he laughs.

'I've enjoyed these last few months more than I thought I would,' I admit. 'I was sure I'd miss the grittier work that I did in India. That was hard, but so varied and interesting. I'd like to line up some charity work here too at some point.'

'That'd be good.'

'But I do like my job. How could I not when it led me to you?'

He smiles warmly and kisses my forehead.

'And Archie and Matilda,' I add, snuggling back into the crook of his arm.

'You could trust them too, you know,' he says quietly.

I sigh. 'The truth complicates things. I don't want them to look at me differently. Surely you, of all people, understand that.'

His grip on me tightens. I think it's an involuntary reflex because it only lasts a second.

'Have you told anyone other than Harriet about what happened?' I ask him tentatively.

'No.'

'How is she?'

'Really struggling with it. Evelyn wants to see us both together on Friday.'

'How do you feel about that?' I move to rest my chin on his chest again so I can look at him.

'Not great. She's traumatised. She was sobbing down the phone to me on Saturday. It's hard enough dealing with my own shit; I don't know how to handle hers as well.'

'Would it not be better for her to see Evelyn on her own?'

'I think she'll do that after this session, but Evelyn asked for us to both come together for the first one.'

'Will you call in afterwards and let me know how it goes?'

He hesitates a moment before nodding. 'I'll try.'

My brow furrows. 'Sonny, what you said... About using sex to dull the shame... What did you mean? Why do you feel shame for what he did to you?'

He exhales heavily and reaches for my unused pillow, using it to prop himself up in bed. I sit up to give him some space. 'Do we have time for this?' he asks miserably, grabbing his phone from the bedside table and checking the display. 'Six thirty-five,' he reads aloud.

'Yes.' I place my hand on his chest, hoping it grounds him in the same way that his contact grounds me.

His hand closes over mine and he takes another deep breath. 'Glen...' He shudders, looking nauseated. 'He was grooming me from the start. I've already told you he made me feel special to him, that he said he liked me more than Harriet.'

I nod, rhythmically stroking his stomach with my thumb.

'He built on that. Mum had gone back to work and Jackie was having a gap year before university. Jackie was supposed to pick me up from school every day, but she had a boyfriend and a life to lead and really couldn't be arsed with the responsibility. Harriet was employed at a hairdresser's in town, but Glen worked flexible hours at a supermarket, so he offered to help us out. I loved it,' he confesses grimly. 'We'd play computer games, chase each other around the house with toy guns, watch telly together. He'd ruffle my hair and hug me and tell me that he loved me *so much*. And he'd ask me if I loved him. I did.' He takes a quivering breath. 'Then he decided to show me what people who loved each other did to each other.'

I feel so sick I could throw up. And he's nowhere near finished.

'It had to be our "*special secret*", he said. I couldn't tell anyone else because Harriet would be "*so sad*" if she knew he loved me more than her and my parents would be "*furious*" at us for hurting her. I felt guilty, but I enjoyed being the centre of his attention too much to do anything other than go along with it. And that's the thing that I find the hardest to deal with.' His jaw clenches, his teeth gritted, disgust and revulsion riddled across his face as he continues. 'I went along with it. I wanted it. I *liked* it.'

His grip on my hand is so crushing that I feel as though he's bending my bones.

'Sorry.' He realises all at once that he's hurting me. He releases me and edges back in bed so he's sitting fully upright, resting against the wall. He's broken all contact between us and I think it's on purpose – I'm not sure he wants to be touched.

'This went on for months. I'm not exactly sure of the timeline, but I never spoke a word about it to anyone. I didn't *want* to. I *liked* that we had a secret. I didn't feel like I was being molested, I felt like I was being loved. I was absolutely devastated when Harriet broke up with him. It was as though she'd ripped my heart in half and I was so angry at her, at Mum and Dad, at everyone. I only saw him one more time after that and I remember bawling my eyes out, begging him to still come over and see me. He was crying too and he said he'd never forget me, that he'd always love me, but that I had to let him go. He basically broke up with me. It was fucking awful. I felt like he'd died. And then, later that same year, we did sex ed at school.' He folds his arms across his chest, hugging himself as he stares straight ahead – he's barely looking at me as he's talking. 'That was very confusing. Over time, I came to understand that I had been abused, and I felt so fucked up. What confused me more than anything else – what I was so ashamed about and why I never could bring myself to tell a single soul – was that I had *let* him touch me. And I had touched him. He hadn't forced me to – I had been *glad* to do it. I hadn't been sexually aroused – not really, not like him – but then came puberty and that was a total head-fuck. My mates were into girls and porn – Glen had already shown me some porn and I remember feeling a little weird about it, but once I hit puberty it affected me on a whole other level. Sex turned me on. Sex with girls, I mean – I was never into guys. After I realised that Glen was a paedophile, I tried to bury what had happened down deep. I just wanted to forget it. But then, when I was sixteen, I got a girlfriend who was in the year above me. She'd already had sex with a previous boyfriend, and the first time we did it, I was flooded with memories. It made me feel dirty and tainted the whole experience, but it's not like I hadn't also enjoyed it. I was so confused, I behaved like a total arsehole afterwards. She tolerated me for a little while but soon broke up with me and labelled me a bastard. Fuck knows why, but that seemed to attract more girls. Sex made me feel better about what Glen had done to me. But

lap, bringing my body flush to his. He holds me tightly and I hope I'm helping to eliminate a gap now.

I only wish he could fill the void Anna left, but I know that no one will ever be able to do that.

Chapter 36

'What are your plans for today?' I ask Sonny as he drives Bertie and me to Umeko's.

After our very heavy chat we managed to have a surprisingly ordinary breakfast. Sonny's only qualm was the absence of bacon because he felt like a fry-up, but he settled for a cheese and chive omelette, preparing it while I got ready for work.

'I've got a photo shoot at a shelter with a homeless man called Derek,' he tells me, answering my question.

'I'd love to come to one of these photo shoots,' I say.

'You can, if you like.'

'What time are you doing today's?'

'Eleven, so probably no good for you, but I might be able to arrange one for Monday next week?'

'That would be great!'

His phone buzzes. I glance down instinctively and see a message has flashed up from Archie.

'What does it say?' Sonny asks me casually.

'It's from Archie. I didn't see what it said.' The phone's screen has gone black again.

'Four two seven four,' he prompts, and it takes me a moment to realise he's told me his phone's security code.

I pick up his phone and tap in the code, reading aloud: '*Stranger Things tonight? M's asking H.*'

He looks at me. 'I'm in if you are?'

'You're not sick of me?'

'Are you sick of me?' he asks with a frown.

'Absolutely not!' I reply indignantly.

He laughs and nods at his phone. 'Do you want to reply?'

'Happy to. What shall I say?'

'*Sounds good. H is with me. We're in.*'

'You want to tell him we're together at this time of the morning? Isn't that going to bring on a barrage of questions?'

'Oh, sure. Okay. Just say "sounds good" then.'

By the time I've done that, he's pulled up outside Umeko's. He cuts the ignition and gets out of the car, meeting me round at the back. He holds Bertie's collar in place while I attach her lead.

'Thanks.' I don't know why, but suddenly I feel shy.

'So I'll see you tonight?' he asks, his eyes searching mine.

I nod, having no idea how to say goodbye to him after what we've been through. I tug Bertie and she dutifully hops out of the car.

He cups the back of my head and briefly touches his cheek to mine before withdrawing. 'Bye,' he says quietly, slamming the boot shut and turning to get into his car.

I listen to the car drive away as I walk to Robert and

Umeko's front door. Before my finger can make contact with the doorbell, the sound of someone shouting 'Oi!' makes me spin on my heel.

Matilda is striding towards me, her jaw on the pavement.

'What the hell have you two been getting up to while we've been in France?' she hisses when she's close enough for me to hear.

I laugh. So much for no questions.

'Don't get excited,' I say. 'He's still very much committed to his six-month thing.'

'But things have moved on, right?'

'Um… Kind of. I don't know. Listen, argh, I'm late for work, but I'm coming to yours later.'

'We will talk on the way there,' she replies ever-so-slightly threateningly.

'Okay!' I manically agree.

Needless to say, I'm a little flustered when I walk through the door of Umeko's, so I don't realise Abbey is looking like the cat that got the cream until I'm sitting at my desk. She's staring at me, her face stretched into the biggest, most excited grin. She looks fit to burst.

'What on earth is it?' I ask with a giggle.

'Guess who's just made an appointment!' she cries.

I shrug. 'Who?'

'No, you have to guess.'

'Don't be ridiculous, it could be anyone.'

'They're famous.'

I laugh. 'Still could be any number of people.'

'Have a go,' she urges.

I indulge her. 'Someone from *Grantchester*?'

'*Way* more famous than that! Oh, and they live locally!'

I frown at her. Stephen Hawking is, alas, no longer with us. Who else? Obviously there's Joe and Alice Strike but there's no way— Or is there?

'Joseph Strike?' I ask, cringing with one eye closed because I'm expecting her to laugh at me.

She slams her hands down on the table, looking like she's going to spontaneously combust. 'HIS KIDS!' she scream-whispers.

My eyebrows jump up. 'Really?'

'YES!'

'Surely Joseph won't bring them in himself,' I say with a frown.

She jiggles in her seat. 'He might do! Or maybe it will be Alice! But it could also be the nanny,' she acknowledges. 'Either way, we still get to meet the kids!' she cries excitedly. 'It'll be the best day ever!'

Okay, even *I* am a little excited about this and I rarely go gooey over celebrities.

Joseph Strike is an actor – we're talking Hollywood block-busters, Oscars, Baftas, the works. Alice was his first love, but they lost contact before he became famous only to later find each other again. They now have two kids: Jack, who Abbey informs me is five and a half, and Rebecca, who is three.

Umeko has told Abbey to book in a quadruple appointment so there won't be a crossover of clients. The appointment is in three weeks and we'll shut up shop for the duration of the visit – apparently they'll compensate for potential loss of sales.

'Why don't they have someone go to their house to do eye tests?' I wonder.

'I've heard they try to live as normal a life as possible, although they do have bodyguards. One will be accompanying them. How weird is that?'

'Weird but cool,' I say.

'I can't wait!' she erupts, clapping her hands like a child.

The rest of the day passes by uneventfully. I haven't heard from Sonny. I know he's busy with his photo shoot, but I can't help wondering how he's feeling after last night and this morning. It was so full on. I'm glad I told him about Anna, but even though he reacted better than I could have hoped, I don't know how he'll feel once he processes everything.

It's true what he said: we both have so much from our pasts to deal with. What if it's all too much for the other person to handle?

Something that Charles once said comes back to me. It was when he was trying to convince me to confide in Nina and Danielle. He told me that I could always depend on him, that he was family and he would always be there for me, but my friends would be the ones to take me through life, guiding and supporting me.

'One person alone can't cope with another person's emotional baggage,' he said. 'If I vented to June about everything that vexed me, she'd feel put-upon and anxious – and vice versa. We need to offload onto others, share the burden. That's what friends are for, helping to carry the load.'

I wonder… If I were brave enough to tell Matilda about my past, would Sonny consider confiding in Archie?

*

Earlier Matilda persuaded me to go straight to hers from work and bring Bertie. I'd prefer to change out of my uniform, but I'm too tired to walk home so I decide to put the journey off until later.

She's ready to leave work when I am so we set off together.

'How was your holiday?' I ask.

'Bugger that, tell me what's going on with you and Sonny.'

I hate that my life is so complicated. It would be so much easier if Matilda knew everything.

There are a few reasons why I don't talk about Anna.

One: It hurts. That's the main reason. It's agonising to talk about what happened so I prefer not to put myself through the trauma.

Two: I was brought up guarded, shielded from the public eye, taught to value my privacy. That, in itself, is hard to get past. I was scared to death the day I confided in Danielle and Nina; as it turned out, they were lovely. But later Danielle pushed back and made me feel, I don't know, icky. I never trusted easily anyway and lowering my defences at university turned out to be a huge mistake.

Three: Although I'm not ashamed of Anna, I still don't want to be regarded as different. As a child, I felt normal. Being attached to Anna was my everyday reality. We didn't mix with other children, so we didn't know how unusual we were. That realisation came later.

At primary school, I had a hard enough time trying to fit in. And in the years that followed, I came to understand how much the idea of conjoined twins freaks most people out. People struggle to see past the idea of two humans being joined together by flesh and bone. I knew that, once their brains had conjured up that image, they'd never look at me the same way again.

When I was a teenager, I considered telling people that I'd had a twin sister who'd died, omitting the fact that we were conjoined. But that seemed disloyal to Anna. It would also have likely raised questions about how she died, and I couldn't have brought myself to lie about that. I already feel dirty every time I tell someone I've been in a car crash – a story Charles and June helped me to construct when I went to live with them because it was simple and relatable. I've stuck to it for years, but unfortunately it sometimes dredges up more questions and I have to say I don't want to talk about it rather than build on the lie. I've learned that this sidestepping of the question only makes people more curious, and it would have been the same if I'd told them I'd lost my twin. As I couldn't fabricate details about Anna's death, it was easier not to talk about her at all. Not easier exactly, but more straightforward.

So how do I explain to Matilda that Sonny stayed over last night because I needed him on an emotional level?

Suddenly I'm sick of the secrets, the burden. I like Matilda so much – she feels as though she could be a lifetime friend, someone I'll always know. I was touched when she opened up to me about her dad and the fears she has about getting married. Our friendship has moved past being superficial and I'm glad of it.

I might've promised myself that I would never again confide in people I hardly knew, but I feel as though I *do* know Matilda. If I listen to my heart, I believe that I can trust her.

'He stayed over last night,' I admit shakily, going with my gut feeling.

She gasps and looks at me.

'Not like that. It was because I was a bit of a mess. He was comforting me.'

Her face falls. 'What's wrong?'

'It's a long story.' My apologetic tone belies how much of a big deal this is to me.

'Okay,' she replies slowly. 'Archie won't be home for another hour or so... Do you want to talk about it when we get to mine?'

'Maybe, but...' I try to swallow the panic that is creeping up my throat. 'I find it difficult to open up to people.'

'Hey,' she says gently, and stops walking.

I turn to her and see that her green eyes are brimming with concern.

'I'm not just "people",' she chides softly. 'I'm your friend.' She shifts her gaze to the footpath. 'I'm probably going to sound like a bit of Norman No Mates now,' she mumbles self-consciously. 'But to be honest, Hannah, in the short time we've known each other, you've become one of, if not *the*, closest friend I've got. I haven't really bonded with anyone else since I moved up here, but it's not like I had loads of mates back in London, either. I like Faith, but I'm not particularly close to her.'

'I feel the same about you,' I confess, casting her a small smile.

She grins at me. 'Phew. Well, I'm here to stay, all right? Whatever it is, I'll be here for you.'

'Thank you,' I whisper, my eyes pricking with tears as we arrive at her front door.

I don't go into all of the details that I shared with Sonny,

but I do tell Matilda about Anna, about how we were conjoined and how she died after the operation to separate us. I
also try to explain why I prefer not to talk about her.

She falls silent, deep in thought, and I give her time and
space to formulate what she wants to say, even though I'm
nervous about her reaction.

'I get what you're saying,' she begins at last. 'And I
believe you when you say you're not ashamed,' she adds as
I fixate on my wine glass. 'You're right when you say that
people will see you differently, but that's not a bad thing.
Far from it. Maybe when you were a teenager and you
wanted to fit in like everyone else, but not now, not with
your *friends*.' She reaches across the table and presses her
hand to mine. 'I completely understand how you might
not want to make it common knowledge, but friends –
we – should know you. Your differences are what make
you unique. They're what make you *you*. By not telling
us about Anna, we'd never really know the real you. Your
differences are your truth.'

I nod, my bottom lip quivering.

She ducks down to catch my eye. 'I do see you differently
now, I'll be honest. Sonny will too, and so will Archie when
you tell him – and I hope you will, or that you'll allow me to.'

I nod again, giving her permission.

'I see you differently, and I like you even more,' she adds
with a tearful laugh, squeezing my hand and ensuring I maintain eye contact. 'What you've been through… How strong
you are… Fucking hell, Hannah, you're amazing.'

She starts to laugh and, against all the odds, I do too.

*

Archie and Sonny arrive together, having been via his to talk about the poster design. They're still talking about it as they walk into the kitchen.

'Hello!' Archie says when he spies me sitting with Matilda at the dining room table. I get to my feet to give him a hug. 'You came straight from work?' he asks.

'No, this is my clubbing outfit,' I reply, giving him a half-curtsey.

He laughs and goes to kiss Matilda, leaving me to face Sonny.

'Hey,' he says, leaning down to press his cheek to mine, his hand touching the small of my back. 'You all right?' he asks as he withdraws.

No, I want a better hug.

I nod. 'I'm good. You? How was today?'

He waggles his head from side to side. 'Derek was fidgety. Tricky when you're working with a macro lens, but I think we got there in the end.'

'The photos are crazy,' Archie interrupts, getting a couple of cans of beer out of the fridge. 'They're *extreme* close-ups. The detail is unbelievable. It's actually quite uncomfortable to look at some of them, but at the same time, you can't look away.'

'That's the point,' Sonny says as he takes one of the beers from Archie and cracks it open.

Archie slaps Sonny's stomach. 'Mate, you should've brought some over. They're so freaky,' he tells us. 'You don't think of the human eye as being like that. They look like alien planets or something. Mad.'

'It's probably no different to what you see through a biomicroscope,' Sonny says to me, taking a sip of his beer.

'That's more Umeko's bag than mine,' I point out. 'I've seen eyes up close, but I've never taken the time to properly appreciate what they look like. I'd love to see your shots.'

He shrugs. 'I still have a few more photo shoots to do.'

'Are you blowing me off?' I ask, mock-affronted.

'I'll show you when you next come over,' he promises with a small smile that sends a shiver rippling down my spine.

I tear my eyes away and turn to Archie and Matilda, smiling brightly. 'How was your holiday?'

After an hour of chit-chat, we crack on with our reason for coming.

Archie hangs back in the kitchen to call and place our take-away Thai order, but Sonny barges past Matilda on her way to the living room and crashes over the side of the snuggler seat.

'What the—' she starts to say.

'Our turn!' he cuts her off gleefully, swinging his legs into a sitting position.

I laugh at the sight of him – his two beers have loosened him up. I also feel more relaxed than an hour ago.

Matilda is disbelieving. 'You say it like you *want* to squeeze onto that thing,' she says.

'I do,' Sonny replies with a shrug, his grin sparking a flame inside me as he pats the space beside him.

Matilda laughs and goes back into the kitchen.

I waste no time sliding into place, the left-hand side of my body pressing firmly against his right.

Sonny turns to look at me, a smile still playing about his lips.

'I told Matilda,' I whisper. I've been dying to let him know all evening. 'About Anna.'

His eyes widen. 'When?'

'Before you guys arrived.'

'You're okay?'

I nod. 'Surprisingly.'

'Wow, well done.'

'Thanks.'

'You coming in?' he asks, making to extend his arm behind my shoulders.

'Absolutely.' I snuggle against his chest, soaking up the feeling of tiny bubbles going off in my stomach.

'Are you guys okay there?' Archie asks with a frown as he walks into the room.

'They *wanted* to sit there,' Matilda tells him significantly.

Archie looks bemused and flops onto the sofa, stretching his long legs out.

'For two people who don't do relationships, you guys are sure looking cosy,' Matilda adds cheekily, settling on the sofa beside her fiancé.

Sonny flips her off and the three of them laugh, but his smile falters when he sees my face.

I'm afraid my happy bubbles have fizzled out.

Chapter 37

Sonny walks me home afterwards. I don't argue. I want to spend more time with him, even though I sense another heart-to-heart is coming.

'Sooo…' he says, speaking in quiet tones as we walk past dark houses with possibly sleeping inhabitants inside.

Here it comes…

'Relationships.'

There we go.

'What about them?' I ask.

'Your expression when Matilda cracked that comment earlier.'

'Mmmhmm.'

'You know where I stand, right?' He casts me a sidelong look in the light from the street lamps. 'Do you remember what I said to you that day at the river?'

'Yes,' I reply. 'This is the closest I've ever come to being in a relationship too.'

'Okay.' He sounds uncertain, as though that hasn't exactly answered his question, but we walk on in silence, leaving the city behind as we reach the green space of Grantchester Meadows.

The air is filled with the scent of wet grass and cowpats. I hope we don't stumble into a herd at this time of night. Above our heads, a full moon is shining brightly, lighting our way, so we should be okay. We don't even need the torchlight from our phones.

'Right,' Sonny says a few minutes later. 'Why don't you do relationships?' he asks directly.

'I never have,' I reply, but I'm holding back. I'm not there yet. 'I love nights like this,' I muse, looking up. 'The stars are so bright. It reminds me of being out in the fens, the wide-open fields and star-gazing.'

He sighs quietly, then: 'I got the all-clear from an STD clinic today.'

'Oh? I didn't know you'd gone for a test.'

'I went a few weeks ago. Thought it was something I should do. I've always been safe, but you know, accidents happen.'

'That's… great.' My reply comes out sounding awkward, even though it shouldn't.

'Yeah, I was pleased.' He chuckles at our polite to-and-fros. 'Have you ever been?'

'I went in April, actually. All fine,' I feel compelled to add. 'I haven't had sex since.'

Luckily you can't see blushes by moonlight.

Hang on. I turn to look at him. 'Are you doing your usual thing of telling me something personal so I open up to you in turn?'

'Does that work?' he asks hopefully.

'Kind of,' I reply with a smirk.

'So, back to relationships,' he prompts.

I groan.

'Quid pro quo, Clarice,' he says in his best Anthony Hopkins *Silence of the Lambs* impression.

I burst out laughing, the sound carrying across the Meadows.

'Tell me about your first boyfriend,' he says, and I can hear the smile in his voice. 'The one you had when you were sixteen.'

'You remember me mentioning Joshua?' I ask with surprise. That was ages ago.

He nods. 'You didn't tell me his name, but you said you broke up with him after it got physical.'

'That's right.' I exhale on a rush of air. 'I liked him, but I didn't trust him enough to tell him about Anna.'

I explain about Danielle and the closeness I used to crave. It's not a comfortable conversation because it's not something I like to remember. I hate how I made her feel squeamish and how it got awkward. I tell him how she put distance between us after she got together with Brett.

'Josh was Brett's friend,' I explain. 'Perhaps if Nina hadn't been in hospital so much that year, I wouldn't have gone out with him, but at the time I just wanted to be normal, like Danielle. I didn't love him, though. I didn't feel close enough to confide in him. There was no way I was ever going to let him see me naked. No one ever has. You won't even get me in a swimming costume.'

'Jesus, Hannah!' Sonny interrupts, shocked. 'You really go through life without getting your clothes off?'

I laugh gloomily. 'It's surprisingly easy, if you don't do long-term relationships.'

'But—' He sounds exasperated. 'Surely that's not your reason for avoiding relationships. *Is it?*' He's incredulous. 'It's that simple?'

'I don't want anyone looking at my scars or treating me like I'm something out of a freak show,' I mutter.

'Anyone who loved you wouldn't make you feel like that. *I* wouldn't make you feel like that,' he adds.

'There's no way you're *ever* seeing me naked!' I squawk, horrified at the thought. 'You photograph models, for Christ's sake. I can't think of anything worse than showing you my imperfections.'

Turns out he has nothing to say about that.

There's a tension radiating from him as we walk on. I replay our conversation over in my head until I come to, 'Anyone who loved you wouldn't make you feel like that. *I* wouldn't make you feel like that.'

Did he just imply that he…? Surely not.

'You coming in?' I ask nervily as we approach the cottage.

'You want me to?'

I nod. Despite the inquisition, I do.

'Drink?' I ask as we walk into the kitchen.

'Just water, thanks,' he replies as Bertie goes straight to her bed and conks out.

I get myself a glass too, all the time wondering what's next. He nods towards the living room.

Seems we're not done talking for the night. Awesome.

He sits at one end of the sofa; I take the other, facing him.

'What are you thinking?' Do I want to know?

He's looking at me strangely. 'Sorry, but I'm calling bullshit.'
Goddammit!

'I don't believe that's it,' he continues. 'You're not that superficial. I'm sorry, but you're not,' he insists, putting his hand up to stop me from denying it. 'I'm sure it's part of it, and I get that you'd feel uncomfortable and wouldn't bother with the hassle of explaining to one-night stands, but there's something else you're not telling me.'

'Fuck's sake,' I mutter.

'Come on, Culshaw, hit me with it.'

'I'm not a Culshaw.' He's unwittingly provided me with a way to derail the conversation. 'I mean, I am, but I changed my name by deed poll. I was actually born a Cooper. I took Charles and June's name when I came to live here. Charles's idea of how to stay under the radar.'

I explain about the press attention surrounding us, particularly after Anna died. It would have been very easy for any of my new classmates to type my real name into an internet search and read all about Anna and me.

'Charles wanted to protect me, and my parents went along with it – although my mum still can't bring herself to write Culshaw on my address. To her, I'll always be a Cooper.'

'That's why she wrote *Hannah C* on your letter?' He remembers the envelope that came for me.

'Exactly.' I nod.

He opens up his arms to me. As we hug, my conscience pricks me. I didn't mean to be manipulative, but I feel as if I've dodged a bullet.

'Will you stay with me again?' I lift my head from his shoulder to look into his eyes.

He stares back at me, his expression thoughtful. 'If that's what you'd like?'

'It is.'

When we go upstairs, the bathroom is straight ahead, the door open to reveal the mirrored cabinets on the wall. Sonny comes to a stop and stares at them, then he steps forward and studies what he sees while I hang back, my pulse suddenly racing ten to the dozen. The angle of the mirrors means that there are two faces staring back at him.

He turns to look at me, one more question in his eyes.

'You still talk to her,' he says, already reaching for and grasping the answer. 'Anna. You still talk to her.'

I crumble. 'All the time.'

Chapter 38

I was always the talker and Anna was the listener. It was the same when she was alive and it continued after she died. I talked and she listened.

I never wanted to be separated from Anna – that was *her* choice. But we were *both* happy until the outside world intervened.

Colleen, our psychiatrist, had already started to sow the seed, the idea that we should be separated. But Anna and I had resolved that we would face the future together and never be parted.

Then one day we wandered too far across the fields and came across a gang of teenage boys. The way they looked at us… The shock and disgust and incredulity on their faces… They told us we were different, not just in their words but through their expressions and actions. They made us feel dirty.

We ran all the way home, stumbling and falling.

Afterwards, Anna was in bits. She retreated into herself,

somewhere where I couldn't reach her. She wouldn't hear reason. She couldn't put it to one side and forget. It plagued her, the reaction from those boys. They made her feel like a freak. And she hated it.

The next time we saw Colleen, Anna talked. She talked more than I'd ever heard her talk to any of the specialists who came to see us. She asked questions. I wanted to shut her up, to silence her. I was so scared. I didn't want what she wanted, what she was considering. I begged her to stop.

But she wouldn't.

Our parents, who had always said that Mother Nature had made us the way we were and that we were a miracle, started to listen to the specialists. They started to listen to Anna.

I fought it. I argued. I begged Anna to stop talking about it. But instead, she stopped talking to me. She didn't want to be joined to me. She wanted to be her own person, free to do whatever she wanted.

Our parents made the decision to separate us. I was devastated. Anna was optimistic. I cried the whole way to the hospital. I wanted to turn away from her, but our pelvises were fused in a way that leant us towards each other instead of away. I had always loved that, loved how I could look into my sister's eyes when we spoke, loved how I could see her face and know what she was thinking. Our eye contact used to mean the world to me.

But that day, at the hospital, I wanted to look away.

Anna was excited, but when I refused to meet her gaze, she grew upset. She wanted me to be happy with the decision she'd helped our parents to make, but I believed it was a huge mistake.

One day she was there and the next she was gone.

When I woke up without her beside me, I cried and cried. She was on a twin bed in the same hospital room, but I couldn't reach her. She felt so far away.

I still remember those first few days after the surgery, how buoyant and positive she seemed. We were in so much pain, but she giggled with the doctors and nurses and was in high spirits.

I just wanted to sob. I felt so alone. But that was nothing compared to how I felt when Anna fell unconscious.

They brought me closer so that I could hold her hand and talk to her as she lay there, unmoving. My parents had a constant stream of tears coursing down their faces.

Colleen was there too. Colleen, who had been so jubilant and who, only days earlier, had tried to gee me up with excitement about my future and the possibilities it held, was stunned into silence. I still remember how pale her face was when Anna slipped away from us.

No one could believe it.

But I could.

I hated everyone for taking her away from me. I resented my sister for wanting to leave me. I was broken.

I lost the capacity to formulate sentences. I refused to see Colleen or any of the specialists who I had been so fond of. My parents respected that and kept them away.

But Charles, I would tolerate. He spent a lot of time with me.

'Do you talk to her?' he asked me months after Anna's passing.

I shook my head. I didn't talk to anyone.

'She's still with you.'

I knew he wanted to believe that. He wanted *me* to believe it. He wanted me to have faith, to feel that she was with me somewhere, somehow.

His words sparked something. I did start to speak aloud to her. I remember the first time: I was at home in the garden. The chicks had hatched and, despite my grief, I found happiness with them. They were so small and soft. I liked the way they'd hop onto my hands with their scratchy feet and hop off again, cheeping and flapping their little wings.

'What do you think, Anna?' I whispered. 'What shall we call them?'

We named them. *I* named them, but I felt as though she was there with me.

In the ensuing months, she was with me as I picked the cherry tomatoes from the vines. She was there when I fed the ducks. She was there when I read stories aloud. She was there when I lay on my back in bed, staring at the ceiling.

It was a long time before I lay on my side to sleep.

I know Anna is not with me now. In my heart I believe that when she died, she went for good. When I talk to her, it's not because I think she's still beside me. It's because it brings me comfort to imagine her listening.

I'm aware it makes me seem crazy. That was what actually freaked out my university flatmates: they heard me chatting and, when I was drunk one night, I blurted the truth.

Charles worries – Evelyn too. They fear that while I have Anna, I will never let anyone else in. They're right. I can't have a relationship because no one would tolerate me talking to my dead sister. And I can't imagine ever stopping. Anna is a part of me. She will always be a part of me.

'When I thought you were talking to Bertie…' Sonny whispers.

'Anna,' I say. 'Sometimes it was Bertie, but it was most likely Anna.'

'You talk to her…'

'Every day.'

'Only in the mirror?'

'No, anywhere. Morning and night, and I know you think I'm insane and I don't blame you—'

'No, I don't,' he interrupts. 'I understand it makes you feel better.'

I exhale heavily. 'Charles stresses about it. That's why I can't stay here once he returns.'

'He wants you to stop talking to her?'

I nod. 'He overheard me a few times in the weeks before he went away. He wouldn't let it go.'

'Why?'

'Because it's crazy.'

'I don't think it's crazy.'

I stare at Sonny, lying there on the pillow beside me, and I don't know what to say.

'I don't think you should stop if it brings you comfort,' he says.

'You… don't?'

'Of course not. Why should you? What harm is it doing anyone?'

'You don't think I'm psychotic?'

'I know you're not. Is this why you've never allowed yourself to have a relationship? Because you've thought boyfriends wouldn't be able to handle that you still talk to her?'

I nod. 'Evelyn believes it's because Anna and I promised each other that we'd never get married, that we'd only ever depend on each other and never be separated. She thinks that I still hold firm to that vow. A small part of me does, but mostly it's because I know that three would be a crowd. And if it comes to choosing between a man and choosing Anna, I choose Anna. No man could ever stop me from speaking to her.'

'No man who loves you would ever try.'

My eyes fill with tears.

'Hannah,' Sonny whispers in an anguished voice, folding me in his arms and bringing me close. 'Do you know how much I care about you?'

'Not really,' I mumble. 'But I care about you too.'

He holds me tight and eventually our breathing slows us to sleep.

Chapter 39

That night I dream of Anna, as I often do. She's reading aloud to me and I'm brushing her hair.

Then Colleen is there and Anna wants to go to her and I want to stay away. We're one being, pulling and tugging. I'm stronger, but she is my weakness. I go because she cries, but I don't want to. I feel like a ghost; vacant and empty as I let her lead the way.

I'm sulky on the sofa. Anna is doing the talking and Colleen is eager to listen. She keeps trying to prompt me to open up, but my jaw is clamped shut.

Anna wants to go across the room to get a book. I want to stay where I am. She tugs at me, pulls from me, raises her voice with frustration at me, so I contemplate doing as she bids.

But then she tugs one last time and tears herself from me. The shock on her face and the shock I feel is so severe that I scream.

'Hey, hey!' Sonny soothes, gathering me in his arms.

A cold flush has come over me and for a moment, I'm disorientated.

'You were calling her name,' Sonny whispers.

I hug him tighter, knowing it's probably dawning on him now that it was her name I called out in Amsterdam, not my own.

He makes me breakfast again while I get ready for work. The last two nights he's slept in a T-shirt and the one he's wearing this morning is crumpled and white. It looks like an old favourite.

I walk up to him from behind as he stands over the Aga and press a kiss to his back, right between his shoulder blades. The fabric of his T-shirt is soft and worn.

He spins around.

'I like seeing you in this kitchen,' I whisper, breathing him in as he pulls me into his arms. His aftershave ran out ages ago and he still hasn't replaced it, but I've come to appreciate the everyday smell of him: the grapefruit shower gel he uses, his deodorant, his warm bare skin.

'Did you just sniff my neck again?' he asks with amusement.

'Might've done,' I mumble, pushing my body firmly against his.

'Er,' he mutters, and before he edges me away, I feel him harden, an involuntary kick against my stomach.

Desire bolts through me.

'Sorry about that,' he says under his breath, adjusting his chinos as he turns back to the hob.

I have an overwhelming urge to touch him. It's so power-ful that I'm shaking a little.

He finishes flipping the eggs and glances over his shoulder at me, his face gratifyingly flushed.

'You all right?' he asks in a low deep voice that turns my insides molten.

'Um...' I waver. 'Not entirely.'

He looks apprehensive.

'I am enormously sexually frustrated,' I admit.

'You are *not* helping me,' he chides, trying to keep things light.

'Are you seriously going to last six months?' I ask.

'I was originally thinking a whole year,' he reminds me as the muffins in the toaster pop up.

'I think I would die.' I start to butter them.

He emits a small laugh and waits on hand with two fried eggs, using a spatula to slide them onto the muffins. Beneath his outwardly amused exterior I sense a certain amount of trepidation.

I feel like the worst human.

'I'm sorry,' I say as I pull a chair out from underneath the table and sit down. 'I'm being selfish.'

'No, you're not,' he says as if to be kind, tucking into his breakfast. 'Have you thought any more about what your plans are?' he asks between mouthfuls. 'After Australia?'

He wants to know if I'm coming back. I've been thinking of going travelling – that was my plan – but the bug hasn't caught me yet. I don't know what I want to do or where I want to go. It occurs to me that my heart isn't in it.

'Not yet,' I admit. 'Why? Are you thinking of luring me back with sex?' I raise an eyebrow.

He freezes, his egg muffin halfway to his mouth. 'Would

that work?' he asks, again in that low deep voice, his eyes dark and full of meaning.

'Mmmhmm,' I manage to say because my mind has conjured up an image of us doing it right here and now on the kitchen table and that's taken up most of my mental headspace.

He chuckles and devours the last of his breakfast and I want to attack his sexy mouth, suck his bottom lip and slip my tongue inside—

'You're thinking dirty thoughts about me, aren't you?'

'Do you have to sound so smug about it?' I reply in a small breathless voice.

'If you knew what was going through my mind half the time, you'd be the one feeling smug. Eat your breakfast.'

'Bossy,' I mutter, goosebumps shivering into place all over my body.

He leans back in his chair, his eyes watchful as I bite, chew and swallow.

I glower at him. 'Stop looking at me like that.'

'Like what?'

'Like you're still hungry.'

He laughs. 'Anything I say at this point is going to sound like a bad chat-up line, so I'll quit while I'm ahead.'

He gets up and clears our plates, taking them to the sink.

'I think I'll come back after Australia,' I say.

He spins around and stares at me. 'Really?'

I nod.

His face breaks out into the biggest, loveliest grin and the next thing I know I'm being hauled to my feet and engulfed in his arms.

I want to soak up this feeling forever.

He pulls away and looks at me, his eyes sparkling, and then he kisses me, right on the mouth. Just once. And all of the hairs on my body stand on end.

'How much longer...' I'm struggling to inhale.

'It's supposed to be November.' He knows exactly what I'm talking about. 'But I'll cut it short if you come back after Australia.'

'You will?'

He nods.

'That's still a couple of months away,' I realise.

'Call it foreplay,' he says with a cocky grin.

I let my head fall against his shoulder and bang it against him a few times.

His chest shakes as he lets out a silent laugh. He moves his hands to my hips, his thumb tracing a line across my left hip.

I lift my head to look at him, and now it's me who's full of trepidation.

'I'm going to want you naked,' he whispers.

A tremor goes through me.

'If we're doing this, I don't want anything between us,' he says seriously. 'No barriers.'

I begin to shake my head, but his hands come up to still my face.

'It's all going to be new for me too,' he reminds me. 'I haven't connected with anyone else before, not like this. You *know* me. You know what I've been through. That's terrifying to me. At the same time, I believe it could be beautiful. I'm going to stop there because I'm sounding like a wanker.'

I giggle and he smiles.

'On the contrary, you're being very persuasive,' I tell him. But I know what he means. I'm scared too.

'When you got your test, was it only STDs that you were concerned about?' I ask as he walks me to work.

Last night's starry sky has been enveloped by thick grey clouds, the sort that make you feel as though you won't see the sun for weeks.

'You want to know if I did drugs? Yeah,' he replies heavily, confirming my suspicions. 'I never used needles, if that's what you're thinking, but I sometimes wonder if I was headed that way.' He swallows. 'Scott overdosed on heroin.'

'Oh, shit.'

'Yeah.' He looks troubled. 'He was very fucked up at the end.'

'Do you know what led him down that path?'

He clears his throat, hesitating before speaking. 'We never spoke about it properly, but once, when he was high, he implied that something had happened to him when he was a kid. I think he might've been abused.'

I breathe in sharply.

'I'll never forgive myself for not trying harder with him,' he continues, sounding wretched. 'I wish I'd had the guts to talk about what had happened to me. It might've helped.'

'I'm so sorry.'

No wonder he fell into such a dark hole after Scott died. He said he could see himself in his friend, but I understand now that there was so much more to it.

I reach over and take his hand, wishing I could absorb some of the burden he's carrying.

Remembering Charles's advice about friends, I realise that I already am, just by being here.

Still, I wish I could absorb more.

'Do you think I should confide in Archie and Matilda?' he asks out of the blue.

'I do.' I try to keep my voice sounding neutral. 'But what do you think?'

'I'm considering it,' he replies. 'I'll get this session out of the way with Harriet and Evelyn first though.'

'How are you feeling about it?'

He shudders. 'Awful. Harriet called me yesterday when I was on my way to the shelter. Wants me to tell Mum and Dad – and Jackie. They keep asking her what's wrong because she's been in such a state over it. They think she's going through marital problems or having some sort of breakdown. She wants to tell them the truth so they stop worrying about her.'

'And worry about you instead,' I say.

'Exactly. I'm not sure I'm ready to handle that... Their anxiety... Their guilt... It's going to be a total head-fuck.'

I squeeze his hand and he squeezes mine back.

We walk the rest of the way in silence.

'What are you doing tonight?' I ask when we arrive at Umeko and Robert's.

'I've got the girls,' he replies, scuffing his shoe on the pavement. 'Thought I'd take them to Wagamama in town.' He lifts his gaze from the ground. 'Would you like to join us?'

'Do you think they'd be okay with that?'

'Yes, they like you.'

'Won't they want their dad to themselves?'

'I really don't think they'd mind one way or the other. Anyway, they see enough of me on my own.'

'Okay, then.'

'Yeah?' He smiles, seeming cheered. 'Pick you up at six?'

'Sounds great.' That'll give me enough time to take Bertie home and get changed.

'See you later, then.' He raises his hand to cup the back of my head as he did yesterday, but this time I turn my face towards him so his lips brush the corner of mine.

He withdraws to stare at me. He's mere inches away. He closes the gap between us, pressing a soft, lingering kiss on my mouth.

My breath catches, my lips inadvertently parting.

He growls and begins to retreat, but I lean into him and the next thing I know he's pulling me in for a full, deep, toe-curlingly sexy kiss.

Shivers are rippling up and down my body and I'm so turned on I could cry.

Oh hell, he is too. When my hands pull him against me, he gasps into my mouth.

Then Bertie whimpers and we jolt apart.

As my giddiness subsides and our surroundings come back into focus, I remember we're in broad daylight, standing right outside my uncle's friend's house, next door to my work.

Talk about inappropriate.

Bertie's tail is bashing against our legs. Sonny is still standing close to me.

'Right then,' I try to sound breezy. 'Guess I'd better get this little madam inside.' I nod at the door.

He shakes his head quickly, his expression strained. 'Don't press the doorbell yet.'

I frown at him and his eyes dart downwards, his implication becoming clear. 'I need a minute.'

I lean against the wall and smirk at him.

'All right, no need to be smug,' he mutters, breathing in raggedly and keeping his back to the street in case anyone walks past.

Knowing our luck, it'll be Matilda.

'Take my mind off it,' he implores.

'What are you doing today?' I ask, pandering to him, because there's a very real possibility of Robert coming downstairs and opening the door.

'After I've been home to jerk myself off—'

'What?!' I interrupt, outraged. 'How is that fair?'

'Who said life was fair?' he asks.

'Are you still allowed to do that?'

This is news.

'I'm abstinent, not a saint,' he replies, and now he's the one looking self-satisfied and superior.

I reach up and press the doorbell, intending to wipe the smirk off his face.

'Hannah!' he hisses, whitening as he hurriedly adjusts his crotch and backs away into the street. 'You're going to get me into so much trouble,' he whispers loudly, shooting a look left and right before jogging across the road.

I clutch my hand to my chest and laugh, trying to keep the sound in as I hear Robert come down the stairs.

The next couple of months are going to be interesting.

Chapter 40

'Our mummy wants to know if you're daddy's girlfriend,' Imogen tells me breathlessly as Sonny climbs back into the driver's seat.

'Does she?'

'What's this?' Sonny asks offhandedly as he buckles his seat belt.

'Rochelle wants to know if I'm your girlfriend,' I tell him, my eyes widening expressively.

'Is that right?' He looks over his shoulder at his giggling daughters. 'I'll talk to Mum, all right?' he promises, putting the car into gear and pulling out of the driveway.

Later, when we're safely ensconced at a bench table in Wagamama, the girls diligently working their way through the activity sheets given to them by a friendly waiter with brilliant blue hair, Sonny catches my eye across the table.

'What are you thinking? Or is that not safe to ask in present company?' he adds in a murmur that I can only just hear over the hubbub of the restaurant around us.

'I'm wondering what you're going to tell—' I cut my eyes to the left where his daughters are sitting.

Natalie is beside me. Imogen is across the table, next to Sonny. They're both too busy competing with each other to find all the words in the word search to pay us any attention.

'Hmm,' he says, a half-smile gracing his lips, but his eyes serious. 'I've been thinking about that too.'

'And?' I shift on my seat. 'What will you say?'

He stares at me for a couple of seconds before replying: 'Yes?'

It's a question.

Yes, I *am* his girlfriend?

I like the sound of that.

I nod.

His smile grows.

A plate of gyoza arrives at the table.

All conversation stops.

I go back to Sonny's after we drop the girls home. I won't stay because of Bertie, but I've been dying to see the photographs he showed Archie.

He leads the way inside, switching on lights as he goes.

The studio flat is not as tidy as it was the last time I came over. It looks more lived-in. There are a couple of dirty plates still on the counter and the sofa is laid out in its bed position, the sheets looking rumpled and slept in and the pillow still featuring an indent from where Sonny's head last lay. That must've been three days ago.

'Haven't been home much,' he apologises, gathering the bedding together.

'Don't bother doing that,' I say, presuming he's going to return the bed to its sofa configuration. 'You'll be sleeping in it soon. Unless you're coming back to mine again?' I'd like him to.

He gives me a rueful look. 'Can't tonight. I'm off to London early in the morning.'

'Why are you going to London?' I'm slightly unsettled that this is the first I've heard of it.

Not that he has any obligation to tell me when he's disappearing to different cities. Or even different countries, for that matter.

Except that I am now his girlfriend. He said so.

'I've got a meeting with a picture editor at a magazine,' he explains.

'Fashion magazine?'

He nods.

Urgh.

'That *face*!' he chides, grinning as he crosses the room to where I'm standing by the island. 'You know you never have to worry about me, right?' He dodges left so he's in my line of sight. I look away so he moves his head again. 'Those days are behind me,' he promises.

I allow him to hold eye contact.

His smile fades. 'I never felt good about anyone I slept with,' he says soberly. 'And I never felt good about myself. I'm so much happier these days.' He places his hands on my hips. I close my hands over them.

'What you said...' His voice trails off and his brow creases.

'I hate the idea of you feeling… I don't know. Like I'd compare you or something.'

'I wouldn't blame you,' I say with a grimace, removing his hands from my hips.

He places one hand over my heart. 'You are more beautiful to me than anyone else has ever been or ever will be. I need you to know that.'

My heart thumps against his palm.

'Anyway,' he says with a roll of his eyes. 'How do I know you won't compare me to one of your no-strings-attached blokes. Giant Germans and all that.'

I can't help but laugh, but he's finding his comment surprisingly unfunny.

'Johann has got nothing on you.'

He winces. 'I don't want to hear you say his name.'

I try to suppress a smile. 'Are you jealous?' I ask.

'Wildly,' he states flatly, then seems to shake himself. 'Let me show you these pictures before I make a total fool of myself.'

The photographs he's done so far are incredible.

'It was a challenge to capture them in the light without getting reflections of eyelashes and stuff,' Sonny tells me, leaning over my shoulder as I sit at his desk and click through the images on his computer screen.

The detail of the eyes is astonishing up this close. I can see what Archie meant when he said that a few were uncomfortable to look at. Some are beautiful, but others are bordering on grotesque.

I think I like the blue eyes the most. The threads spanning outwards from the central black pupil are clearer, more wispy and less of a solid mass. This one looks like a waterfall in reverse, as though the water is crashing outwards instead of falling into what looks like a deep central hole.

Another has feathery white patches like clouds or vapour trails in a blue sky.

And the threads on another remind me of a jellyfish, its stingers radiant in the watery blue.

This green eye has a wavy ring of creamy yellow threads circling the pupil, but as each thread spreads out they thin into a series of almost luminescent wiggly green lines. They look like underwater seagrass. I feel as if I could plunge my hands in, part the grass, and swim through the green depths.

Another green and amber eye reminds me of a flower, although the petals are indistinguishable from each other. It's the way that it fans out from a central circle, like a sunflower.

And this one looks like something in space, a rim of fire circling the pupil and brightly lit fibres streaming outwards as though they're stars seen through light-speed.

Others have very little variation in colour. Like this one: it's orangey-brown, like Mars, and it has lumps and bumps around the rim of the pupil, bringing to mind sand slipping into a black hole.

Some have patches of colour. This one looks like someone has spilt tea on a blue tablecloth.

And this one is tan-coloured and puckered and unappealing.

They are all so different.

I've been making comments and murmurs of approval as I've looked at the photographs because I'm genuinely stunned by the work he's created. I'm in awe of how many shoots he has pulled off in the space of a few weeks.

'How many more do you plan to do?' I turn around to look at him.

'I'd like to have twenty in the series,' he replies, backing up to perch on the end of the sofabed.

'So, what, you're about halfway there?'

He nods.

'Is Archie using a single image for the poster?'

'Yeah, I thought we'd go with this one.' He gets up and takes the mouse, clicking through the shots until he comes to the eye that looks like a flower.

'Whose is that?' I ask.

'Mel's.'

'No way?'

'Yeah.'

He's already told me that most of his subjects don't suffer with bad eyesight. That would have been too limiting. But they are all homeless and they all agreed to do it for charity.

A flood of warmth engulfs my stomach. 'You're so clever and talented.' I beam at him. 'I'm ridiculously proud of you.'

He kisses the top of my head. 'Thank you,' he says simply. 'I'm proud of you too.'

I stand up and loop my arms around his waist, pressing a kiss to his chest.

He sighs. 'I wish I didn't have to go to London tomorrow.'

'Yeah, I guess I should probably go home and let you get some sleep.'

'That's not what I was saying.' He nods at his computer screen. 'That's the sort of photography I'd like to be doing. It's hard to make a living out of it, though.'

'Especially when you're doing it for free,' I add with a small smile.

He returns my smile. 'But I've felt good about it. Much better than I've ever felt about fashion shoots.'

'You'll find your way,' I say, believing it.

He dips his head down and kisses me.

Chapter 41

The next time I see Sonny is on Friday night after his session with Evelyn and Harriet. I'm in the kitchen when an unfamiliar car rolls down the driveway to the road. Harriet leaving, I presume.

Shortly afterwards, Sonny passes by the kitchen window, his head hanging low, his shoulders hunched.

I open the door seconds after he's pressed the doorbell.

'That was quick,' he comments, coming in and closing the door behind him.

'Saw you from the window.'

He looks awful. His eyes are bloodshot and the colour seems to have drained out of his usually golden skin.

I step forward and he folds me into his embrace, holding me for a very long time.

I hate that he has to go through this. I hate it so much. My heart has swelled so fiercely, so protectively, that I feel like I'm going to burst. I barely think it before I'm saying it.

'I love you.'

He lifts his head and stares at me, wonder lighting his formerly bleak expression.

'I love you too. But that's been evident for a while, I think.'

It's Sunday morning and we're on our way to Archie and Matilda's. It wasn't prearranged – Sonny texted Archie this morning to ask if we could pop over for a cuppa.

He's decided to tell them. My heart is flipping out for him – he's so nervous.

I'd thought he might opt to speak to Archie alone first, but I think he wants to get it out of the way all at once. He asked me to come with him.

Archie opens the door. 'All right, guys?' he asks chirpily, patting Sonny on the back. 'This is a nice surprise. Come in.'

Sonny moves off into the kitchen to greet Matilda, leaving Archie free to say hello to me.

His hug is a little longer, a little stronger than normal.

'Matilda told me about Anna,' he says when he pulls away, his brown eyes brimming with concern. 'I'm so sorry.'

I'm taken aback – with everything that's been going on with Sonny this week, I'd almost forgotten Matilda was planning to share my own revelation.

'Thank you,' I say, emotion clogging my throat. At the same time, there's a warmth in my belly because I can see how sincere he is, how much he cares.

He leads the way through to the kitchen. 'Cuppa? Coffee?'

We sit at the dining room table with the doors flung open. It's one of those airless muggy days that have the added insult of rain thrown in. And not even proper rain, but stupid barely there drizzle.

Sonny cradles his cup, his shoulders crowded together. Underneath the table, I place my hand on his knee.

'So… guys…' he starts, looking as though he'd quite like the Demogorgon from *Stranger Things* to appear right now and suck him into another dimension. 'There's something I thought I should… Something I wanted to tell you.'

Archie and Matilda are all ears, switched on, their full attention fixed on the wounded man in their midst.

How I love these people.

This is all going to be okay.

Something alters that week. There's a shift in the fabric of our friendship.

On Tuesday I get a text from an unknown number and discover that Archie himself is checking up on me.

Matilda and I have lunch three days in a row, and Sonny joins us on one of those days. It's heartwarming to see the change in their friendship, the mutual care and consideration they're showing each other. It's surreal to recall how down Matilda was on Sonny earlier this year – she is so different with him now.

I still can't get the image out of my head of the way she hugged him after he confided in them, his hand extended behind him, still firmly entwined with mine as Matilda squeezed him hard.

All of these things lift my spirits in ways I could have never imagined.

The weather has finally come good again and the weekend is supposed to be hot and sunny. We make a plan to meet at the Blue Ball, just the four of us, and choose to sit at a round table out at the front of the pub in direct sunshine.

Sonny is telling us about his latest photo shoot yesterday.

On Monday, as promised, he allowed me to accompany him to one of the homeless shelters. His subject was a tall lanky middle-aged man called Leonard, who was extremely uncomfortable, while at the same time claiming he was happy to be there.

'Makes a change from the norm,' was how he kept putting it.

I loved seeing the interactions between him and Sonny. They chatted the whole time. Leonard wanted to tell Sonny his story and Sonny let him talk, but he also asked him other questions, trying to get to the bottom of what he was like as a person, what made him tick.

It made me fall even more deeply in love with him than I was already.

I've loved him for a while, I've realised. It's been creeping up on me slowly, but now that I've admitted it to myself, it's all-encompassing. I think it's the same for him. He looks at me with a new brightness in his eyes.

The oddest thing is that I'm hardly talking to Anna at all. It's Sonny who I want to talk to.

I've moved from being addicted to his aftershave to being well and truly addicted to him. He's spent every night at mine this week and somehow we've managed to keep our romantic entanglements at a PG level.

Okay, sometimes they go up to a 12A, and there might've been a couple of 15 moments, but we're saving 18 X Rated for when I get back from Australia.

And I *am* coming back. I'm certain of it. I've even told Charles I'll be sticking around in Cambridge for a while. He was ecstatic – it made his week, he said, when he called me from the port in Ho Chi Minh City, Vietnam.

Umeko was delighted. My trip to Australia is going to cause a bit of a headache because she's not sure how she'll get temporary cover for me, but she says they'll find a way around it.

Abbey has offered to take up some of the slack. In fact, she's asked if she can be trained up as an optical assistant so she can handle preliminary tests and glasses fittings sometimes. I've never seen Umeko look so pleased. This will also give me time to do volunteer work, something which I hope will be another piece in the puzzle that helps me to feel more complete.

'How are things going with wedding planning?' I ask Matilda when we've exhausted the photo shoot topic.

Matilda groans and even poor Archie looks disheartened.

'Did I say something wrong?' I ask.

'I still don't know what I want to do,' Matilda admits, glancing at Archie across the table. She turns to Sonny and explains. 'I've always imagined I'd get married in a church, but I thought my dad would be walking me up the aisle. It's something that I've found hard to get past over the last couple of years.'

Sonny's brow furrows. 'I'm sorry to hear that.'

Archie is staring into his pint.

'Arch just wants to get married.'

'I'd marry you tomorrow if you'd let me,' he mutters, his lips pulled into a straight line. He takes a gulp of his pint.

'It's been a bit of a tough few weeks,' Matilda confesses in the spirit of us being friends who don't hold back from each other any more.

'Matilda grew up picturing a fairy tale wedding,' I tell Sonny. 'It's something she's dreamed about for years. But then her dad passed away…'

'So your wedding has gone from what you've always thought would be the happiest day of your life to a day that's going to make you feel desperately sad,' Sonny muses.

'Hit the nail on the head,' Archie says.

Matilda stares at him disconsolately before speaking. 'The stupid thing is, I know that the day is supposed to be all about us, not my dad. I'm trying to recalibrate my thinking so I don't feel sad all the time. I can't even pick a wedding dress.'

'Do you have a date set yet?' Sonny asks.

'Nothing firm,' Archie replies. 'Sometime around Easter next year.'

'Which you are definitely going to be around for,' Matilda says with a smile at me.

'Definitely.' I meet Sonny's eyes across the table.

'People put so much pressure on weddings,' Sonny muses. 'I still remember how stressed Jackie and Harriet were. And Christ, my mum… You would've thought she'd learn from the stress she felt with Harriet when it came to Jackie's turn, but she was as bad, if not worse. When I get married, I want it to be as simple as possible, completely intimate, just my very favourite people.'

'Amen,' I say in my best American preacher impersonation.

Sonny grins at me.

I still remember all those weeks ago, right here in the Blue

Ball, when I asked if Rochelle was Sonny's wife. Archie made some wisecrack about Sonny and marriage being too much of a stretch for his imagination. No one mocks him now.

Poor Archie is still looking miserable. 'That sounds like my idea of heaven,' he says, tracing his finger across the grain of the wooden table.

'Maybe I need to tear up the fairy tale,' Matilda starts. 'It's not going to be a fairy tale anyway without my dad, right?'

Archie looks at her, a spark of hope in his eyes.

'How about if you imagine it as a big party, like, a joint birthday – your fortieth or something,' Sonny suggests. 'What would you do?'

'Probably hire out a pub,' Matilda replies.

'Like this one,' Archie adds.

'God, yeah, can you imagine the beer garden all lit up with fairy lights?' Matilda asks. 'We could have a sausage sizzle or something. And halloumi burgers.' She grins at me. 'And ice buckets full of Prosecco.'

'And walk home,' Archie says.

'No, *canoe* home,' Sonny chips in. 'Hannah and I could canoe you. In fact!' he says, getting into the idea. 'You could get married at a register office in Cambridge, then we could canoe you back up here, have some fizz on the boat, chill out a bit just the four of us, and the rest of your congregation could take the bus, or even walk, I don't know. They'd be waiting with shedloads of confetti for when you enter the beer garden.'

'I'm loving this idea,' Matilda says dreamily, leaning forward and propping her chin on her hand.

Archie stares at her. 'You are?'

'Aren't you?'

'Christ, yeah.'

'You could buy your flowers from the market,' I interject. 'I could get them for you even. We could arrange them on all the tables, get drunk and put together a playlist of your favourite songs to blare out of the pub's speakers. We could have candles everywhere.'

Matilda has a far-off look in her eyes. She nods. 'And I could just go and buy a pretty dress off a hanger somewhere.'

'Do we really have to wait until spring?' Archie asks.

She grins at him. 'How long do we need to organise this?'

'Make it soon so the river doesn't flood,' Sonny says.

'How about this October when Hannah gets back?' Matilda asks.

We all look at her. I don't think any of us has truly believed this is anything other than whimsical speculation until this very moment.

'I'm serious,' she says.

'Are you?' Archie asks distrustfully.

'I am *actually* serious. I'm sick of feeling so torn up about this. I want to marry you, Arch.' She reaches across the table and takes his hand in hers. 'I want to spend the rest of my life with you. If we did something like this, something I'd never dreamed of, it'll be ours, just ours, a day that doesn't come with any expectations. Just you and me, saying I do.'

Sonny raises his eyebrows at me. He's smiling. I beam at him, my eyes pricking with tears.

'I'm going to ask if we can book the beer garden out in October,' Archie says, jumping to his feet.

'I'll come!' Matilda chirps, sliding out from the table.

We watch them go, laughing.

'Wow,' I say. 'I wonder if this will happen?'

'I bet they pull it off.'

While we have the table to ourselves, Sonny reaches across and laces my fingers through his, brushing his thumb over the back of my hand.

Archie pops his head around the pub door. 'You guys want a drink while we're up at the bar?'

'Sure,' Sonny says, lifting up his almost drained pint glass.

'Same again?' he asks us both.

'Yes please,' I reply as Sonny nods.

We go back to smiling at each other like lovesick fools.

'I like those sunglasses,' I say. 'I still remember the day you turned up at Umeko's. I saw you standing outside on the pavement. You were talking to someone on your phone.'

'Was I?'

'You don't remember?'

He frowns, casting his mind back. 'Oh,' he says, nodding. 'Rochelle, I expect.'

'How are things going with her?'

'Much better,' he replies. 'She's really happy with Phil, her boyfriend, so that helps.'

'Have you met him? What's he like?'

He nods. 'He's a good guy. The girls like him, which is the most important thing. I'm glad Rochelle and I have finally called a truce after all these years.'

'Did you ever tell her about us?'

He nods and smirks, downing the last of his beer.

'What?' I ask with a grin.

'She was fine. She claimed to not be surprised in the least.'

Archie and Matilda return to the table, Archie with beers, Matilda with gin and tonics.

Sonny lets go of my hand and, at the same time, I realise we have company.

'Well, well, well,' a nasty all-too-familiar voice says.

I look up to see that Nessa has come up the steps. 'So you've succumbed, have you?' she asks me.

Right, that's it.

'Back off, Nessa,' Matilda snaps, beating me to whatever retort I was going to make. 'Sonny's in love with Hannah, she's in love with him, get over it. And quit being a bitch. It's unbecoming.'

Shock blasts the smile from Nessa's face and the insults from her lips. Her mouth drops open like a goldfish and, without another word, she spins on her heel and stalks into the pub.

I stare at Matilda with awe. 'You're amazing.' I lean in and kiss her cheek.

'Oh, stop.' She waves me away.

And then Sonny does the same thing to her other cheek.

She laughs as he grins past her at me. Her face has brightened. 'Sorry, Arch,' she says with belated regret. 'I hope that doesn't make things difficult for you at work.'

He's smiling and shaking his head at her, and then he shoves his chair out and leans over the table to give her a full kiss on the mouth.

'The next thing we know she'll be accusing the four of us of swinging,' Matilda jokes as he sits down again and we fall about in hysterics.

*

I don't know whose idea it was, because we are all very drunk, but we seem to be stumbling down a hill towards the river.

Someone had the crazy notion of going for a dip – the weather is balmy and the Cam's water is famously temperate, plus night-swimming is something Archie and Matilda have always wanted to do.

Tonight they seem intent on taking the plunge in more ways than one.

So here we are.

Matilda grabs my hand and sets off at a run. I clap my other hand over my mouth to stop myself from squealing.

Above our heads, the sky is glittering with starlight.

The boys catch up with us, Sonny grabbing me round my waist and spinning me in a circle. I'm laughing, unable to keep the sound in.

'Shh!' Matilda hisses. 'We don't want anyone breaking up our party.'

In the moonlight, I see Archie tug his T-shirt over his head.

Through my drunken haze, I feel a pang of nerves.

Sonny turns me to face him, his hands clasping my face. 'You're coming in, right?'

'Undecided,' I whisper.

'It's dark,' he points out.

I hesitate and then nod uncertainly. 'Okay.'

It's now or never, I guess.

Somewhere nearby, Matilda is giggling as she tries to unbutton her dress.

'Whip it off over your head,' Archie urges in a whisper. We hear him slip into the water and simultaneously gasp.

'Is it cold?' Matilda asks worriedly.

'It's fine,' he replies. He is totally lying.

Sonny, two feet away from me, is watching me intently as he removes his T-shirt, only breaking eye contact when the fabric passes over his face. His bare chest gleams in the dim light. I want to put my hands on him. I take a step forward, but he raises his palms.

'Quid pro quo, Clarice,' he says in a low, deeply sexy voice.

I crack up laughing. 'You can't make me fancy you when you're doing a serial-killing cannibal impression – that's wrong on so many levels.'

'Fuck me, it's cold!' Matilda hisses.

I giggle and look over at her before realising Sonny is still waiting for me to take my top off.

'Are you guys coming in or what?' Matilda asks.

'Getting there,' Sonny calls back, and there's something in his tone that carries a warning.

My friend hears it. 'Let's swim to warm up a bit,' she suggests to Archie, setting off downriver.

Surprisingly perceptive for one so alcohol-ridden.

I take a deep breath and lift my top off over my head.

Sonny smiles and unbuttons his shorts, sliding them down his long legs.

I wriggle out of my skirt.

I would never be this brave sober. Or would I?

He takes off his shoes.

I kick off mine.

He peels off his socks and nods at my bra. 'Leave that on, please. No way I want Archie to catch a glimpse of your tits when I haven't even.'

I laugh and he takes my hand, leading me to the water.

'Run and jump?'

'Is it deep enough?'

'There it is.' He points, familiar with this part of the river.

'Okay.' I nod determinedly. 'Let's do it.'

'Three, two, one…'

He doesn't let go of my hand.

I come up gasping. It's so cold! Sonny laughs and tugs me against his hard body, his arms lifting me and holding me tight. I soak up his heat and wrap my legs around his waist as his mouth finds mine in the darkness. Our kiss is hot, slippery and wet, just like our bodies, our tongues entwining as our limbs are.

I feel a familiar kick against my stomach and my breath hitches.

'How is that possible?' Sonny mutters. 'I'm freezing my nuts off.'

I giggle against his lips.

He kisses me again, slower, more languidly, and withdraws. I stare at him in the starlight and hesitantly take his hand from around my waist and slide it down to my left hip.

I shiver as his fingers find my hipbone, the distinctive angle of it, the sharpness that isn't mirrored on my other side. He presses his hand firmly against my skin, steadying me, centring me, telling me that he loves me, every single part of me, his eyes locked on mine.

'I'm sorry if you're having a moment,' Matilda calls, breaking the silence. 'But we've done night-swimming now and it wasn't all it was cracked up to be.'

We laugh and clamber out of the water, cold, wet, drunk, muddy and, above all, happy.

Chapter 42

Every time a car goes by outside the window, Abbey and I jump. And then a big black SUV with tinted windows drives past and she lets out a squeal. A minute later this same car pulls up at the kerb, presumably after going around the block, and a tall broad man in a well-fitting black suit gets out of the front passenger seat and comes inside. He looks like something out of a film himself with his square jaw and heavy brow. Think *Terminator*. Machine-like. Inhuman.

'Can we help you?' Abbey asks, slightly manically.

'Vince Howley,' he replies. 'Strike Security. I need to check the place is secure.'

'Sure! Of course!' Abbey stands up. 'Would you like me to show you around?'

'Please.'

I daren't look at her as she walks past me – this is one of those moments I definitely intend to keep my cool.

Abbey has forgotten to put the Closed sign on the door

so I do that myself. A short while later, Vince and Abbey return and Vince goes straight outside to open the back door of the SUV.

'*Joseph*, *Alice*, *nanny*,' Abbey is murmuring. 'Alice!' she squeals.

'Shh!' I hiss, trying to stifle a giggle myself as Alice unfolds herself from the car and steps out onto the pavement. She's wearing a black-and-white shift-dress and looks absolutely stunning with dark, almost ebony, hair that falls halfway down her back.

She turns around and bends over, reaching into the car and bringing out a little girl with dark chin-length hair. Vince, meanwhile, has emerged from the other side of the car with a tousle-haired boy in his arms. He's actually smiling like a proper human.

Alice leads the way inside, holding her daughter's hand.

'Hello,' she says, warmly but softly, smiling at Abbey first and then at me before turning to Vince. 'You can leave us now, thanks, Vince.'

He nods and heads out the front door, closing it behind him and then proceeding to stand right in the doorway.

'I'm so sorry about this fuss,' Alice apologises, shaking Abbey's hand. 'I'm Alice.'

'Abbey. Practice manager,' Abbey says, trying to sound professional.

I come out from my desk. 'Hannah.'

She has small hands, but a firm handshake.

Her skin is creamy and flawless and her eyes are green and almond-shaped – she's beautiful.

I hear Umeko's door open and our boss emerges, greeting

Alice as I crouch down and smile at the children. 'Hello,' I say. 'And what are *your* names?'

'Jack,' the boy replies in a shy, husky voice, his big brown eyes staring at me. He has very long eyelashes. 'And this is my little sister Becca.'

My God, he's adorable.

'We getting an eye test!' Becca tells me eagerly.

'Yes, you are,' I say with a smile. 'Are you excited?'

She nods determinedly. 'I wanna see the bawooons.'

'You want to see the balloons?' I ask, presuming she's talking about the autorefraction test that shows a hot air balloon coming in and out of focus.

She beams and nods.

Someone has told her what to expect, from the sounds of it.

I giggle and look up at Alice and Umeko.

Alice is smiling at me as I stand back up.

The Strikes' PA had the forms filled out in advance so we can crack on. I feel Abbey's eyes on us as we go. She's gutted to be missing out.

'I'll leave you in Hannah's very capable hands and will see you shortly,' Umeko says to Alice, Jack and Becca. My boss smiles at me as she heads into her treatment room.

The children are a delight and Alice is warm and friendly, making casual conversation with me throughout the appointment.

No problems present themselves so I do a quick handover with Umeko and return to my desk, only to catch sight of Matilda walking past the window, her mouth agog.

She texts me: *What the hell?*

Tell you later.

She disappears from sight, probably after being eye-balled by Vince.

Umeko's door opens and she leads Alice and the kids out to the shop front. She smiles at me and nods once, so I gather the kids' eyesight is fine.

Alice and Joseph are bosses for starting them with optometrist visits nice and early.

'Ooh, have you seen this?' Umeko asks casually, nodding at the poster of Sonny's exhibition that she allowed me to put up on the wall behind my desk. 'Hannah's boyfriend Sonny is a photographer,' she tells Alice as my heart skips a beat. 'His exhibition is in aid of vision care for the homeless. He has photographed the eyes of many of Cambridge's homeless community.'

'How remarkable,' Alice says, stepping up close. 'Is that a human eye?'

'Yes,' I reply. 'Taken with a macro lens. You should see the others – they're all so varied and different.'

The background of the poster is black with the iris – just the iris – taking up the middle of the design. The exhibition is entitled, *Don't Look Away*, and underneath the iris are the date and details of the show.

'I don't suppose you have a spare one of these?' Alice asks me.

'I can easily get one,' I tell her hastily. 'Please take this in the meantime.'

'Are you sure?' she asks as I waste no time carefully unsticking the poster from my wall.

'Absolutely.'

I roll it up and hand it to her, my hand shaking slightly.

'Thanks. I'll speak to Joe.'

Behind her back, Abbey and Umeko give me a double thumbs up.

I decide not to tell Sonny because I don't want to get his hopes up. But I do tell Matilda. She gets me a replacement poster direct from Archie and is barely able to contain her excitement. After that, I try to put it out of my mind. Alice was probably only being nice. The likelihood of her – and Joseph – turning up seems incredibly slim.

But you never know.

Nina comes over from Amsterdam for the Bank Holiday weekend at the end of August. Danielle leaves Calvin at home with Brett and joins us for Movies on the Meadows, Grantchester's outdoor cinema event, which takes place every year as part of the Cambridge Film Festival.

Archie, Matilda and Sonny are meeting us there, but I'm having time with my oldest friends first. We grab an early bite to eat on the sunny balcony of the Rupert Brooke pub. We have so much to catch up on, and naturally they want to know the latest on my love life.

There's no point in playing it down; I've never been so happy. My friends can't wipe the smiles from their faces.

A tiny part of me doesn't like that they're so keen for me to conform, fall in love and settle down, but I know that's unfair. All they have ever wanted, first and foremost, is for me to be happy. We may not be as close as we once were, and that might not ever change, but I'll forever be thankful for the lifeline they threw me when I started secondary school. They know me so well and we will always have history. I'm very glad I have them in my life.

'Have you told your parents about him?' Nina asks me.

'Nah. I'll tell them in person. Mum and Dad still don't have a phone and it's too much to go into in a letter. Anyway, I'd probably arrive before it did – they're so slack about going to the post office to pick up their mail. Nothing's ever urgent to them.'

Sonny's ears must've been burning, because later that night, lying in bed, he asks about them.

'You never talk about your parents,' he says. 'Is that because there's nothing to say or because there's everything to say?'

I roll over onto my stomach and look at him. 'The things you come out with sometimes... You should be a counsellor,' I add with a smile.

He folds his pillow over to prop himself up a bit. 'Do you blame them for what happened to Anna?' His question is asked very gently.

I look past his right shoulder to a spot on the wall. 'Not really. I understand their reasons. For a long time I felt guilty for leaving them and coming here to live with Charles and June. Sometimes I feel frustrated with the choices they made, their determination to live on the outskirts of society, the choice they forced *me* to make because for them it was one or the other. If they'd been different, we could have all moved to another part of the country together to have the fresh start that I so desperately needed. But they chose to let Charles and June take me in instead.' I sigh and rest my chin on his chest. 'Sometimes I think that it was so painful for them to look at me, to look at me and see the absence of Anna, that they let me go to spare themselves.'

'I'm sure that's not true,' Sonny murmurs, running his fingers through my hair. 'They probably did what they thought was best for you. They would have seen what Charles and June could offer you. And if your mum still refuses to write Culshaw on an envelope, that's proof in itself that she loves you and struggled to let you go.'

My nose begins to prickle. 'I don't usually get upset about this,' I mumble, blinking back tears and giving up as they spill over.

Sonny brushes them from my cheeks.

'I also kind of resent them for emigrating to Australia,' I admit tearfully, propping myself up. 'They couldn't move out of their beloved cottage for me, but when my dad's mum fell ill, they flew to the other side of the world to look after her. Then she died and they bought a frigging houseboat and never came back. I was left to sort out the cottage and the animals. Luckily I was taking a year out after my A levels, and Charles and June helped out a lot, but that year ended up stretching into two because I spent so much time dealing with the house sale. Charles was furious.'

'I love that he's now got you house- and dog-sitting for *him*,' Sonny chips in mildly.

'I know. The irony, hey?'

'Not that I'm not grateful to him,' he adds, brushing the pad of his thumb over my lower lip.

I kiss his thumb.

'About your parents...' he starts. 'I can't imagine how hard it must've been to stay in that cottage after you'd left. Maybe they needed a fresh start too?'

I think back to some of the times I visited, how empty and

dark the rooms seemed, even with Mum and Dad pottering around. Suddenly I'm not sure what kept them there for so long. I couldn't wait to get away again after each brief stay, back to Charles and June and their normality. Could my parents sense that urgency in me, that reticence to visit? That must've hurt.

At least when I went back to sell the house and find homes for the animals, I often had June with me. Sometimes Charles too. They brought their normality with them and the task kept us focused, but it wasn't easy. It was anything but. Everywhere I turned, there were memories and all of them hurt.

Yes, maybe my parents *did* need a fresh start. Maybe they'd needed one for years, but it took Dad's mum falling ill to give them a nudge. Do I really hold that against them?

On reflection, I'm not sure that I do.

That Sunday is Sonny's thirty-third birthday and his parents have invited us over for a big family lunch.

Sonny is kind of dreading it, but he's glad I've agreed to go with him.

Everyone is going to be there: Harriet, Jackie, their husbands, kids, plus Natalie and Imogen.

'Do your parents have much to do with the girls?' I ask on the drive to collect them.

'Not as much as they have to do with my sisters' kids. Their five keep them busy. I'm sure they'd do more if I asked, though. They do know Rochelle. She used to make a point of taking Imogen and Natalie over for the occasional cup of tea, but she was doing it out of duty so the kids would know their grandparents. It was hard work for her, I think. My parents bore her senseless. I love them, but they *are* incredibly boring.'

I splutter out a laugh, taken aback by his bluntness.

'You'll see for yourself in a bit,' he adds.

Actually, they are *lovely*.

Sonny's parents are short and cuddly. His dad, in particular, is ridiculously cute, with a white moustache and eyebrows that seem to have a life of their own, they're so animated.

Sonny still hasn't told his parents what happened to him, but I know he's trying to psyche himself up. Harriet's counselling sessions have helped her. She's been less inclined to ring Sonny up and is trying to work through her guilt with Evelyn instead. I know he finds that a huge relief.

I hate that he's going to have to go through a similar thing again with his parents and Jackie.

But today is a celebration and I'm happy to be a part of it.

Because Sonny had Imogen and Natalie at such a young age compared to when Harriet and Jackie began their families, there's not much of an age gap between the seven children. It's lovely seeing them playing and interacting. It hurts my heart a little for reasons I don't want to think about then and there, but the pain is not acute. It's wistfulness more than anything.

Jackie is quick and funny and reminds me of Sonny in small ways. She has the same quirky half-smile and blue eyes. Harriet is more reserved, her smile a tad pinched, her eyes warier. I don't know what I was expecting when Sonny spoke of her, but for some reason I'd pictured her to be a bit matronly, perhaps because of their age gap. In actuality, she's slim and glamorous, with false eyelashes and a feathery blond hairstyle that swishes when she moves.

When we leave, she gives me a hard squeeze, her eyes betraying her misery as she withdraws.

'Take good care of him,' she says in my ear, gripping my forearm with a cool slender hand.

I pull her back in for another quick embrace and whisper, 'I will. I promise you that I will.'

I have a feeling we'll get to know each other better with time.

Chapter 43

Charles arrives home on the day of Sonny's exhibition, unfortunate timing that no one had any control over thanks to a storm in the Atlantic Ocean on the cruise ship's approach to New York. He was supposed to be home yesterday.

I had promised to collect him from the airport and I stick to that plan, but I'm inwardly stressing about not being able to help Sonny set up at the gallery. He claimed to have it all under control and sounded as cool as a cucumber. The only thing he says he's nervous about is meeting Charles.

'Look at you!' I cry as my uncle comes out of the sliding doors at Arrivals. His shock of grey-white hair is wild and unruly – there were hairdressers on the boat, but he clearly didn't bother using them – and his skin is more deeply tanned than I've ever seen it. He's tall and slim and looks fit and healthy, every bit the intrepid traveller of the seven seas.

For the first time, like, *ever*, he reminds me of his sister.

'Hannah, my darling girl!' he cries, rocking me this way and that before holding me at arm's length as I beam from ear to ear. 'It is so good to see you again!'

'It's *so* good to see you too,' I reply, clasping his dear old face in my hands.

He pulls me in for another hug.

We talk the whole way home and, for once, we match each other word for word. When I first went to live with my aunt and uncle, it took a lot of coaxing to get me to open up, while Charles could've talked the hind legs off a donkey. June was quieter, more willing to embrace the silence. I feel a pang, missing her – she was very comfortable to be around, a soothing, calming soul who always made me feel safe. But it was Charles who challenged me, who encouraged me out of my shell and who helped me to rediscover my voice and the confidence I'd had when my sister was beside me.

I might've sometimes found him to be exhausting, but I'll forever be thankful for his eternal resilience. He never came close to giving up on me.

I reach across and squeeze his hand.

Bertie is damn well beside herself at the sight of her beloved master. She jumps right up, her paws on his chest and her tail crashing against the hallway wall as she madly licks Charles's face. She drops down, yelping and barking until my equally delirious uncle chases her through to the living room. I find them sprawled out on the floor, hugging like a couple of humans.

'I think we can safely say that she missed you.' I'm laughing at the sight of them.

'I missed her too,' he replies affectionately, rolling her onto her back so he can pat her tummy.

I leave them to their love-in and go and get ready.

The exhibition is being held at a church, which has a large café attached, in the centre of Cambridge. Sonny is talking to the manager when we walk through the door, an hour before official opening time.

My breath catches at the sight of him. He's wearing a slim-fitting dark-blue suit over a white shirt, unbuttoned at the top to reveal a patch of bronzed skin. His sun-lightened hair has been swept back from his face in its usual retro style. I ache to run my hands through it.

He looks our way and smiles, excusing himself from the manager and coming over, his hand extended to Charles.

'It's really good to meet you,' Sonny says as Charles clasps his hand with both of his, giving him a warm double-handed shake.

'It's very good to meet you too,' Charles replies sincerely.

Sonny gives me a quick peck on the lips as Charles turns to look around.

'Gosh,' Charles says. 'This is really something.'

I hold Sonny's hand as we walk from picture to picture, getting our own personal preview before the public arrives.

The photographs have been blown up to giant size. A central coloured iris is set on a square white background, and tiny words run around the rim of the iris in a circle, telling us about the subject: who they are and what they'd like people to know about them.

Sometimes the subjects recount how they became

homeless: Derek lost his job while caring for his sick mother, while Samantha, who suffered with depression, fell out with her family and sofa-surfed at friends' houses until they gave up on her.

Some people talk about their mental or physical health problems and how they had very little access to treatment or support. Others admit to having issues with drug or alcohol use. Many had traumatic experiences as children: they were the victims of sexual or physical abuse, or they suffered from lack of stability, being moved around between foster homes or divorced parents. These experiences often led to them becoming dependent on drugs or alcohol while still in their teens.

Some try to convey how it feels to be living on the streets, like Mel who can't sleep for more than thirty minutes at a time because she's scared of being raped or mugged. As a woman, I can't imagine how terrifying it must feel to be in her position. And in Mel's case, her situation has been made even more horrifying because she hasn't been able to see very well. She must have felt unbearably vulnerable.

Most ask to be treated as people, to not be made to feel like they're less than nothing, less than human. They just want to be seen.

Some are being seen now – Sonny extended an open invitation and a few who took part in the photo shoots have come along.

Right now I'm looking at Leonard, who's standing proudly by his photo, talking to Archie and Matilda.

'It made a change from the norm,' I hear him say buoyantly.

I've just gone to say hello to Nina and Aart, who flew over for the exhibition, when Abbey comes over and screeches into my ear: 'They're here!'

I cut my eyes to the door and see Vince surveying the joint.

Squeaking something incomprehensible to my friends, I hurry off to find Sonny. He's deep in conversation with a silver-haired man sporting a fantastic handlebar moustache.

'Excuse me, I'm so sorry,' I say, apologising to the man. 'Can I borrow Sonny for a moment?'

'Sure, sure.' He backs away.

'What is it?' Sonny asks me, perplexed.

'Joseph and Alice Strike!' I whisper.

He stares at me, not comprehending.

'The movie star and his wife!'

'Yes, I know who they are. What about them?'

'They're here! They've come to the exhibition!'

I wish I had a camera to snap the look on his face. He shoots his head towards the door as Vince re-enters, closely followed by Alice and her tall, dark-haired, instantly recognisable husband.

A frisson of excitement ripples through the crowd.

I take Sonny's hand and lead him in a daze towards them, making eye contact with Alice as we approach. She lifts her hand in a small wave.

'Hello!' I say when we're in their midst, Vince standing close by. 'I'm so glad you could come! This is Sonny Denton, the photographer.'

'And your boyfriend,' Alice says with a smile. 'Hello, I'm Alice.' She shakes Sonny's hand and Joseph steps forward, holding his hand out. 'Joe.'

He and Sonny shake hands and then Joseph turns to me. I try not to faint as his firm hand grips mine, his warm brown eyes crinkling at the corners as he smiles.

'Would you like to wander? Or perhaps Sonny could give you a bit of a tour?' I ask.

'A tour would be great, if you've got time?' Joseph asks. 'The project sounds interesting.'

'Absolutely,' Sonny replies. 'Let's start with Derek.'

He gives me a wide-eyed look of bewilderment as soon as their attention is diverted. I thought I'd leave him to it, but he grasps my hand. 'You're sticking with me,' he murmurs.

I don't need to be told twice. I'll be telling this story to my grandchildren.

Maybe even *our* grandchildren.

Focus, Hannah, focus. And whatever you do, don't look at Abbey.

The call comes the following morning when I'm at work.

'If I swing by in fifteen minutes, will you have time to talk?' Sonny asks me.

'Sure! What's up?'

'Tell you when I see you.'

A quarter of an hour later, I look up to see him standing on the pavement outside the bay window opposite my desk. He's wearing his sunglasses and a half-smile as he talks on the phone, scuffing the pavement with his shoes.

My heart flips over and, at the same time, I experience an odd feeling of déjà vu. It's surreal. So much has happened since he first appeared outside my window all those months ago.

Sonny peers in through the window and pauses, making eye contact with me. His smile widens. Then he ends the call and I stand up, meeting him in the doorway.

'Back in a bit,' I tell Abbey.

'Okay,' she calls after us.

'What's all this about?' I ask with a smile as Sonny leads me around the side of the building.

'Joseph Strike called me twenty minutes ago,' he says in a low excited voice. 'Joe – not his PA, *him*.'

I bounce on the spot giddily.

'He's bought the whole collection!'

I clap my hand over my mouth. 'What?' I ask through my fingers, wide-eyed with astonishment.

'Paid way, *way* over the odds,' he says. 'He's donating the collection to homeless shelters, but he wants it to tour the country first to help raise awareness for Vision Care for Homeless People.'

'Oh Sonny, that's incredible!' I squeal.

'Shh! I don't want to jinx it by telling anyone else. I didn't even dare tell my mum just then.'

I presume that's who he was on the phone with. She and his dad have been calling him daily since he confided in them about Glen, but they've been handling it in a more bearable way than Harriet did. His parents' phone calls are brief, but caring. They're letting him know that they love him and are there for him, without breaking down in tears and requiring him to comfort them. They've made their own appointments to see a therapist.

I'm awestruck. 'He won't back down on it, especially not if he called you personally. Oh my God!'

Chapter 44

The next few days fly by. Joseph Strike's people put out a press release about the exhibition and the news makes the national papers, a photograph of Alice, Joe and Sonny flanking Mel, wearing her brand-new glasses, taking centre stage.

Sonny convinced Mel to come in for an eye test before the exhibition and Umeko kindly covered all costs. My boss has agreed to commit to voluntary work too.

Obviously the first priority is to help homeless people get off the streets, but Mel's increased confidence, now that she's able to see properly, is proof that vision care matters. Ultimately, benefits need to be more accessible, but until the government make some changes, *every* charity for the homeless needs all the help it can get.

Sonny has been upbeat, but on the day he drives me to the airport for my flight to Australia, he's subdued, lost in his own thoughts.

'I can't imagine how shit I'd be feeling if I didn't know you were coming back,' he comments with a humourless laugh as he waits with me at the check-in queue.

'Two weeks,' I remind him reassuringly, resting my head against his shoulder.

'I'll come and collect you,' he promises. 'It's mad that Matilda and Archie are getting married that same week.'

'I know!'

They got the whole thing organised so quickly in the end. I went with Matilda to London to go wedding-dress shopping. That was a fun day. There's a lot to be said for buying a dress off a rack at a twentieth of the cost of a couture gown.

'Hey, I hope you have a good time,' he says softly.

'Thank you.' I swivel in his arms and press a kiss to his lips. 'I wish you could come with me.'

'Next time?' he asks with a raised eyebrow.

'Definitely.'

The man behind us clears his throat. Sonny picks up my battered old backpack and moves forward in the queue.

'No one could accuse you of not knowing how to pack lightly.'

'That's about all I own,' I reply. 'Surely you've seen me wear the same seven skirts enough now to know that.'

'I love your seven skirts,' he says with a lopsided smile.

'I love *you*.'

A little over twenty-four hours later, I'm on a bus heading along a long straight dusty road somewhere in South Australia. The landscape on either side of the bus is as flat as Cambridgeshire, but it's a palette of oranges, reds and creamy yellows instead of the vibrant greens of England.

The Minute I Saw You

Mum and Dad don't have a car, but they've given me directions on where to meet them. I only hope they come good on the plan, because I imagine it'll be a fair old hassle to track them down via river radio or whatever they call it.

I've come off two crazy long flights, got to a bus station in Adelaide, caught a bus to Murray Bridge and swapped to another to take me to my final destination, and I am dead on my feet.

Wearily slinging my backpack over my shoulder, I traipse through the tiny town of Mannum, dragging my stinging eyes past shop window displays and inhaling the fried-food smells of delis, too tired to really take in anything. It's been over two years since I last came to Australia, but it's exactly as I remember it, bar the blue skies and skin-scorching sunshine of my last trip. Today it's cool and overcast, spring to England's autumn.

I find the Community Club and take the road alongside it that allegedly leads to the water. Sure enough, there it is: the wide brown Murray River, approximately fifty times fatter than the Cam.

Crossing the parking lot behind the Community Club, I look past the playground on my right to see a green stretch of parkland butting right up to the riverbank. That's where Mum and Dad said they'd moor up.

There's zero sign of them.

A spark of irritation ignites inside me.

My footsteps grow heavier as I walk into the park, taking a seat at a bench table underneath several soaring gum trees. Tree bark is peeling from the trunks in ghostly shreds, and the air is damp and heavy with the scent of eucalyptus and impending rain.

All of a sudden, in a great cacophony of noisy squawking, a flock of snow-white parrots with yellow crests flies over my head and lands on the branches of the gum trees. I look up at them, smiling, despite myself, before returning my eyes to the river.

And then I see the ramshackle two-storey houseboat with its top deck that holds more plants than standing space, and the small figures of my parents squeezed amongst the foliage and waving wildly. My relief snuffs out my annoyance and I get to my feet, walking down to the grassy bank.

Who's captaining the boat? I wonder, and then Dad stops waving and the boat very slowly begins to turn towards me. I remember now that there's a second wheel on the top deck so he can sit out in the open air and steer.

'We were moored across the river!' Mum shouts to me as they approach at smooth snail-speed. 'We forgot you're not allowed to pull up here for long!'

The boat makes a horrendous noise as it comes into the bank, spluttering and groaning and chugging up water at the back as Dad tries to slow it down before it hits land.

Mum is now down at ground level, pushing out a ramp for me to board.

'Can you jump?' she asks, breathless and giddy, her long wispy hair streaming freely down her back.

I carefully swing my backpack on ahead and take a leap of faith. My mum grabs my arms and gathers me in a crushing hug. She's my height, but thinner – and, paradoxically, stronger – there's steel in her bones and I feel it in her embrace.

My eyes are stinging, but now it's more from emotion than lack of sleep.

The boat is making the same chugging noise as Dad reverses away from the bank.

'Let's go upstairs,' Mum urges, her greeny-gold eyes shining. 'He's dying to see you.'

I help her pull the drawbridge back in and then she slings my backpack over her shoulder, reminding me of the hippie traveller I've seen in photos. She leads the way around the deck to the outdoor stairs, hurling my bag through an open doorway to the living room as we pass.

No worries, Mum, no valuables inside.

She grins over her shoulder at me, looking ten years younger than her late sixties in her tiny shorts and minuscule vest top. I laugh and experience an unexpected swell of affection.

'Take over, Ellen!' Dad bellows, letting go of the wheel well before she reaches it and winding his way through the jungle of the top deck until he's got me in his arms and is lifting me from my feet.

'You're here!' he cries, his soft beard brushing against my cheek as he kisses me.

I didn't realise how much I'd missed my parents. It's clear from their welcome that they've missed me too.

Dad's hair is a lighter shade of brown than Mum's and comes almost to his shoulders. He's ten years younger, but roughly the same amount of grey streaks their hair.

'Aren't you cold?' I ask, shivering slightly as the sight of his baggy T-shirt and shorts.

'You must be exhausted.' Mum glances over her shoulder at me from the captain's chair. We're moving forward again, still at snail-speed, but very smoothly.

'I'm absolutely knackered,' I admit.

'Cuppa or do you want to rest?' Dad asks.

'What sort of tea is it?' I query dubiously, remembering my parents' home brews of years past, bits of ginger bobbing around on the surface and whatnot.

'I bought some builders brew, just for you,' Mum chips in.

'Go on, then.'

Something she's never quite forgiven Charles and June for: getting me addicted to Yorkshire Tea.

The top deck has changed since I was last here. There are several small trees in terracotta pots that have shot up a couple of feet: the lemon, orange and grapefruit trees are laden with fruit. And there are dozens of pots and troughs containing a myriad of plants. I spy carrot tops and potato plants, and above ground are artichokes, asparagus, broad beans, broccoli, spring onions, lettuce, cabbage and peas. Strawberries are coming into season, I see, as are kumquats, and there are herbs galore, from fragrant leafy basil, mint and sage to rosemary, thyme and oregano.

All this leaves little standing space, but there are three chairs up on deck: two deckchairs and the captain's chair, which Dad takes over while Mum goes downstairs.

She returns with a tray and familiar brightly coloured material slung over her shoulder. Putting the tray down on an empty plant pot, she tosses me the hand-crocheted blanket that once belonged to Anna and me as babies.

'Keep you warm,' she says, and if she's aware of the twang-ing of my heartstrings, she doesn't show it.

I drape the blanket over my knees. It's as soft as I remember and smells of wood smoke. I spy a cast-iron fire pit nearby that contains charcoaled logs from its last few uses.

I'm too tired to get onto the subject of Sonny so instead we talk about Charles. He sent them the occasional letter from the cruise ship, but they're keen for more details so I regale them with second-hand stories until my cup is empty and my eyes are drooping.

'Don't let me sleep for too long,' I beg Mum as she sees me to my bedroom.

There are two rooms at the back of the boat, both with small en-suites, but mine is also the study and, from the looks of it, the dumping ground. I'm pretty sure my parents will have tidied up so I dread to think what it looked like before. There are boxes and containers piled up on top of cupboards and chests of drawers, and two bookshelves crammed full of books, three deep in some places. There's barely enough room to fit a sofa in the remaining space, let alone one that's been extended into a bed. It's impossible to walk round to the side so I climb on from the end, the springs boinging beneath me as I clamber into place, making me think of Sonny and his bouncy sofabed back in Cambridge. No wonder he's spent so much time in my bed of late.

Or maybe that's not the only reason.

'How long would you like?' Mum asks from the doorway. She looks so pleased to have me here that I feel momentarily guilty for depriving her of my presence.

'Two hours max, thanks, or I won't sleep tonight.'

'Done.'

She smiles and slides the wobbly concertina door across. I waste no time falling into a deep dreamless sleep, the crocheted blanket clutched to my chest.

*

I am a ship on an ocean in a storm when my mother carefully crawls across the bed, cooing my name.

I groan.

'You've had two hours. Time to get up or you won't sleep tonight.' She has cunningly used my own words against me.

'So tired,' I grumble.

'Do you want me to tickle you awake?'

God, she hasn't done that in *years*...

Before I can answer, she's beneath the covers and tucking me under her arm.

It doesn't take me long to relax as she soothingly strokes my back and hair. This is a version of my mum that rarely makes an appearance and I wasn't expecting to see her so soon.

I'm not complaining; I'm just a little taken aback, that's all.

Dad appears at the doorway, smiling at the sight of us.

I lift my head blearily to look at him. 'Who's manning the boat?'

'Oh, we're all moored up for the night. Want to come upstairs and check out the sunset?'

Logs are crackling in the pit on the deck, but the sky is the most spectacular fire of the night, the clouds dark smoke against a backdrop of flame red, blazing orange and twilight blue.

Dad passes me a glass of red wine. They don't drink much so I'm figuring this is considered a special occasion.

We raise our glasses in a toast.

'To you,' my mum says. 'Here's to a great holiday.'

'I'll drink to that.' I lean forward and chink their glasses.

I realise, as I take a sip, that I feel completely at ease in their company. Last time I visited, it took a few days for us all to warm up, but the mood this time has been better from the start.

'So what else is new in your life?' Dad asks.

'I've met someone,' I admit, feeling compelled to open up.

'Ooh!' Mum cries. 'Boy or girl?'

'Boy,' I reply, and she claps with excitement, a reaction that I don't doubt would have been the same whatever answer I'd given.

'What's his name?' Dad asks.

'Sonny,' I reply. 'Sonny Denton. His real name is James, but he was nicknamed Jimmy as a little boy, then his grandfather called him Sonny Jim and Sonny ended up sticking. It suits him.'

Mum and Dad share a delighted look.

They want to know *everything*. I indulge them with the details of *some* things, telling them about his latest project and how it came about. They have no idea who Joe or Alice Strike are – they might as well live on Mars, my parents – but they're very impressed with the charitable aspect.

'What's that light over there?' I ask.

It looks like giant yellow torchlight being shone through the silhouetted trunks of the eucalyptus trees on the bank.

'The moon,' Dad replies casually.

'You are kidding me.' I get to my feet.

It's absolutely enormous, the biggest I've ever seen.

'I wish Sonny was here with his camera,' I say out loud.

Once again, Mum and Dad share that same look of delight.

'Do I sound like I'm in love?' I ask them with a bashful smile. 'Because I am.'

Mum squeezes my knee. 'We're so happy for you. I hope next time you'll bring him.'

He could probably cope with a short stint of being in close quarters with my parents, but the way that sofabed squeaks when you so much as kneel on it...

A shiver goes through me at the reminder that he's calling time on his abstinence when I return from Australia.

The anticipation is killing me.

I wake up to the sound of sulphur-crested cockatoos, which is the real name for the parrots I saw in the gum trees in Mannum, I've remembered. They are the noisiest birds I've ever heard, but as alarm clocks go, there are worse ways to wake up.

Wait a sec... That *smell*! Maybe *that* was my alarm clock.

Mum is in the kitchen, taking a loaf of crusty bread out of the oven.

'Yum!' I exclaim at the sight of this home-baked piece of heaven.

'Breakfast,' she replies with a smile. 'With apricot jam.' She places a jar on the counter in front of me. 'One of our neighbours at our Mannum mooring has a daughter with apricot trees. They always have millions going spare.'

Although they don't pay much attention to the outside world, to say that they are removed from society is no longer the right way to describe my parents. Over the last few years, they've become part of a friendly group of river dwellers. They spend most of the year moored up at Mannum, socialising – and goods-swapping, from the sounds of it. This trip up the Murray is more for my benefit, a houseboat holiday with a moving landscape.

Speaking of the landscape, I can finally see where my parents stopped last night. On the other side of the river, tall ochre-coloured cliffs, brightly lit in the early morning sunshine, jut out of the water's edge and soar high into a cornflower-blue sky. Tiny holes carved into the rock host gazillions of cockatoos, probably nesting.

'Where's Dad?'

'Oh, he's upstairs, birdwatching.'

As if to illustrate her point, a black swan glides by outside the window, its legs no doubt kicking ten to the dozen under the surface of the brown water, and nearby, three white pelicans are perched on a dead tree trunk protruding from the cool still water.

'Do you want to go and call him down for breakfast?' Mum asks.

Over the next few days, my suspicions are confirmed. My parents are definitely more relaxed and content than the last time I saw them.

Or maybe I'm the one who's changed. A couple of years ago, I was intent on travelling aimlessly, turning my nose up at the idea of staying in one place or committing to anyone or anything for any length of time. I was unhappy, unsettled in more ways than one, and still trying to come to terms with the wreckage of my past. I can't have been easy to be around.

Most likely, we have *all* changed. They definitely seem happier and more at peace. I know I am.

'Sonny has children,' I tell them one morning when we're setting off on a walk, making the most of our limited chances to stretch our legs.

It's a beautiful morning, the sun low in the sky and blindingly bright as it reflects off the water. The light glimmers against blades of grass swaying in the breeze and filters down through the leaves of the gum trees overhead.

'Does he?' Mum asks.

I guess she's wondering why I've waited so long to mention it.

'Two daughters.' I swallow, kicking the soft sand out of my flip-flops as we wander along the track. 'Twins,' I add. 'Identical.'

'Oh,' Mum says.

Dad looks troubled. 'How old?' he asks.

'Nine. Imogen and Natalie.'

No one says anything for a while. I concentrate on trying not to step on black ants the length of my big toenail.

We come to a lake. The shore is patchy with unusual-looking grasses and animal droppings. Kangaroos? Rabbits? Wombats, maybe, from the circumference size of the nearby burrows. The ground is coated with white – salt, I think. It looks like hoar frost and is crunchy under our feet. I say as much, but my parents do not seem to be in the mood to discuss the landscape.

'Hannah,' Mum says gently, coming to a stop so she can look at me.

I blink back tears.

Dad makes a noise of sympathy, rubbing my back. 'It must've been difficult for you to be around them at first,' he says gruffly.

'It still is a bit,' I reply, fidgeting with the bracelet on my left wrist.

'Does Sonny know about Anna?' Mum asks, gently taking my left hand. She and Dad are the guardians of Anna's bracelet.

I nod. 'I've told him everything. Spending time with Natalie and Imogen has actually helped in some ways,' I confide, glancing at her. Then I look away because her pain only makes this harder to talk about. She's aware of how closely I've guarded our secret since I left. 'It hurts to see their same smiles and hear their identical giggles. Sometimes they finish each other's sentences. Natalie sounds like Anna did when she sneezes, but Imogen doesn't, which is weird.'

My parents stand on either side of me, facing the lake, caught up in what I'm saying and lost in thoughts of their own. We've stopped walking.

'There was one occasion recently, at Sonny's birthday lunch with his entire family, when Imogen was playing on the PlayStation in a nearby room with her cousin, Benji.' Harriet's youngest. 'And Natalie was sitting on the floor of the living room doing a jigsaw puzzle with Sonny's sister Jackie's two girls. I could hear Imogen chattering away to Benji in the next room, cracking up in a fit of giggles as she did something cheeky that won her the game. Meanwhile, Natalie was sitting right in front of me on the carpet, content as could be.'

Mum hugs her arms to her chest and my dad hangs his head low.

'I know that's what you wanted for Anna and me, a chance to be able to live our lives and do as we pleased without constantly having to compromise.'

'Our biggest regret,' Dad begins huskily. 'Our biggest regret, the thing that we've always struggled to get past, is that we didn't allow the doctors to separate you as babies when the operation would have been simpler.' He swallows rapidly.

'But Anna still could have contracted an infection,' I point out. 'Or I could have. We might've grown up not knowing each other at all. No one was to blame for what happened. It was a tragedy, nothing less.' I take a moment to gather myself together. 'If you'd separated us as babies, we never would have experienced the wonder of what we were, what we were born to be. I wouldn't have wanted to miss out on that. Nor would Anna. Those memories are so precious to me. I'm glad you didn't deny us.'

They move at the same time, uncannily in sync with each other as they step closer to my side and slip their arms around my waist.

'We love you, Hannah,' Mum murmurs.

'I love you guys too.' I incline my head and rest it first on her shoulder, and then on Dad's, before raising my chin to the sky.

Chapter 45

Our conversation by the lake isn't the only heart-to-heart I have with my parents while I'm in Australia: We talk about their agreement to let me go to live with Charles and June, and their decision to wave goodbye to the UK.

Sonny was right. In the first instance, they thought they were doing what was best for me, even though it caused them immeasurable pain, and in the second, they chose to do what was right for themselves.

They hadn't intended to move to Australia permanently, but once they were away from our little cottage in the Fens, their relief felt colossal. The thought of going back suddenly seemed impossible. They had a chance to start again, and after all they had been through, who could blame them for wanting to take it?

We also talk about Anna. Until now, it has always felt too painful to speak about her, but in avoiding the bad times, we've neglected the good.

We laugh and cry and share countless memories. At one point, Dad has us in stitches with tears streaming down our cheeks as he recalls my efforts to persuade Anna to create a snail garden. She was incredibly reluctant, but ended up getting so into it that she convinced me to sneak the snails inside one evening in a mixing bowl. Naturally they escaped.

My parents nearly fall off their deckchairs in hysterics as they remember the look on the face of a visiting doctor at the sight of a snail crawling across his perfectly polished shoe.

Those snails left behind countless silvery trails that my parents could never bring themselves to scrub off.

At the end of my two weeks, I feel closer to my parents than I have in years, possibly ever. This trip has been incredibly therapeutic – for all of us, I hope.

'How about we come and see you in Cambridge next spring?' Mum asks when I promise not to leave it as long between visits.

'I would love that,' I reply, hugging her and Dad goodbye, and trying to gear myself up for my return journey.

I'm almost at the end of that journey now, full of nervous excitement and anticipation at seeing Sonny again. I've told Charles I'll catch up with him tomorrow. Tonight I'm staying with my boyfriend…

Sonny is there waiting as I come out of Arrivals, standing behind the barrier, motionless, with his hands in his pockets and wearing an oddly pensive expression. Then he sees me and his face lights up.

It feels incredible to be back in his arms. I clutch him to

me, my hands fisting in his T-shirt in my attempts to bring him closer.

'I've missed you so much,' he growls in my ear.

But on the car drive back to his place, it becomes clear that the expression I caught on his face when I came through the doors into the Arrival hall was not a one-off. When we fall silent, which is fairly regularly because I'm shattered, he seems peculiarly contemplative and brooding.

'Are you okay?' I ask at last.

'Yes! Of course! I'm fine!' he responds suspiciously readily.

By the time we reach Cambridge's outskirts, I'm feeling deeply disconcerted.

'Do you want to take me to Charles's?' I ask warily.

He casts me a perturbed look. 'No. Do you want to go to Charles's?'

'I didn't, but you're acting a bit oddly. I'm not sure you want me at yours.'

He reaches across and grasps my hand tightly. 'Hannah, of course I want you at mine. I've been desperate to see you. I've missed the fuck out of you. Don't say you want to go to Charles's.'

A wave of relief surges through me. 'So why are you being so off?' I ask, turning to look at his side profile in time to see his Adam's apple bob up and down.

'I'm not.'

'You are,' I maintain.

He releases my hand to flick on his indicator and then places it on the wheel. We're almost at his place so I decide to give it a rest until we're inside.

He seems tense as he shuts the door behind us. I'm tense

myself. I thought our reunion would be better than this. I'd
built it up in my head and it's falling well short.

'Has something happened while I've been away?' I ask,
unable to keep the anxiety out of my voice as he puts his keys
down on the island, his shoulders taut under his shirt.

He spins around to look at me. 'No!'

'I'd rather you were honest with me.'

He sucks in a sharp breath and then exhales heavily, dragging his hand over his face. 'I feel like a twat,' he mutters.

'What? Why?'

I take a step closer to him and he slowly reaches out and
gently pulls me flush to his body. He sighs, burying his face
in my hair.

'I'm nervous,' he whispers.

Against his shoulder, I frown. 'Why?' I whisper in turn,
allowing him to remain hidden from my scrutiny.

'I'm nervous about what happens next.'

This is not an admission he feels comfortable making, that
much is clear.

What's not clear is exactly what he's talking about. And
then I get it, all at once.

'You're worried about us having sex?' I lift my head to stare
at him because I can't not.

His cheeks brighten as he nods.

'Oh,' I say, surprised.

'We've waited so long. I've missed you intently. I'm scared
it's not going to live up to expectations.'

'Is that all?' I ask with relief.

His blue eyes meet mine apprehensively and he nods again,
just once.

'We don't have to tonight,' I tell him, placing my palms flat on his chest.

'I *want* to,' he says, his hands resting lightly on my hips. He gently bumps me against him, bringing me closer again. 'But after all this time, I don't want it to go wrong.'

'Come and sit on the sofa,' I urge, wanting to take his worries away. 'There's no rush,' I insist, propping myself up at one end so I can look at him. 'I'm knackered anyway. I'd be happy with you just holding me tonight.' Like he did almost every night in the weeks leading up to me going to Australia.

He reaches out and pulls my feet onto his lap. 'What if I think of *him*?' he asks in a tortured voice. 'I might not be able to…'

'Then we press pause,' I reassure him softly. 'I'm not going anywhere, Sonny. I love you. We've got all the time in the world. You were originally going to hold out longer anyway, so if it doesn't happen this week, or next month, or next year even, then we give it another go whenever you feel ready. I have learned to be patient when it comes to you.' I smile and reach across to take his hand.

'Sorry,' he mumbles.

'Don't you dare apologise for this,' I say sharply. Then instinct takes over and the need to hug him overcomes everything else. I move to straddle his lap.

He gives me a half-smile and I kiss away his worry lines before bringing my mouth down to his.

Our kiss is soft, slow and full of love. We break apart after a few moments and rest our foreheads together as he wraps his arms around my waist, holding me tightly. I can feel his chest expanding every time he inhales.

'I love you,' I whisper.

'I love you too,' he replies, pulling me in tighter still.

Desire pulses through me. I try to ignore it.

His hands come up to my face and, when I stare into his eyes again, his pupils have dilated.

Our next kiss is nothing like the last. This one is deep and passionate, our tongues locking and colliding, our mouths slipping and sliding. His lips find my neck and then he's lifting me in one fluid movement and laying me down on the sofa, the warm solid length of his body pressing me firmly into the cushions. I wrap my legs around him and pull him even closer.

Be okay if he stops, I remind myself sternly. *Show no disappointment.*

It's okay. I've got this. We're taking it slow.

Except that we're not. His lips are back on my neck and he breaks contact only to tug his T-shirt over his head.

He shakes his head at me, wide-eyed and startled at how ready he suddenly is.

I reach for the buttons on his shorts, but he takes over when my fingers fumble, so instead I whip off my own top and try my best to wriggle out of my skirt with him kneeling between my legs.

Seconds later he helps me rid myself of the cumbersome fabric and now we're in only our underwear and he's regarding me with awe as he moves back down to kiss me. The weight of his body is blissful and my skin is igniting with tiny electric shocks as his chest brushes against mine, soft skin, hard muscle. And then he's removing my bra and his mouth is on me and I can barely believe we're in broad daylight and I'm almost naked and *I'm okay with it*. Better than okay.

I gasp, arching my back as he draws away and brings his mouth back up to my lips.

'This might be very, very quick,' he warns me.

'That's okay. I'm fine with that,' I say in a delirious jumble of words, pushing my hands through the roots of his hair and tugging. He rocks against me.

'Holy shit,' I mumble, wanting him in me. Like, *yesterday*.

'We'll go slower next time,' he promises in an unsteady, spine-tinglingly sexy voice.

And then he's easing his boxer shorts down and I'm attacking my own underwear, my eyes devouring him as he takes over from me, putting himself back between my legs.

'Look at me,' he requests in a low deep voice.

I nod quickly. I wasn't planning on looking away, but I know what he's thinking. He's remembering that neither of us has made eye contact during sex before.

With our gazes locked only on each other, he slowly sinks into me.

And I am lost in sensation, light-headed with lust, giddy with love.

I can't catch my breath for a long time afterwards. Sonny's body is still covering mine, but every time he makes to retreat, concerned that he's crushing me, I hold him in place. I don't want to let him go yet.

Eventually I find my voice. 'That was...' I falter. 'Well, it surpassed all of *my* expectations.'

He lifts his head and gives me a small, sleepy smile, propping himself up on his elbows so he can better study me.

'How was it for you?' I inwardly chastise myself for not checking with him sooner.

His smile turns into a slightly cocky but endearing smirk. 'Worth the wait.' He gives me a soft kiss. 'Sorry it was a bit quick,' he adds in a quiet apology.

'No, it was fine,' I hurry to say. 'More than fine.' I've had much quicker and far less satisfying encounters. 'I promise I'll never have expectations, okay?' I reiterate lightly. 'Let's always agree to take each and every moment as it comes.'

'You're naked,' he realises abruptly, his expression marvelling. He skates his hand down to my hipbone.

I laugh and cover his hand with mine, not even flinching, not in the slightest. 'Have you only just noticed?'

'There's daylight and you're naked and I love you,' he announces.

My insides melt. 'I know you do. I love you too, Sonny Jim Jimmy James Denton. You have no idea how much.'

Chapter 46

'You may kiss the bride.'

The congregation – only their very nearest and dearest – erupts into applause. There could be three times the amount of people here for all the noise we make.

Archie and Matilda are finally married, and no one could be happier for them.

Matilda cracks open a bottle of Champagne. She and Archie might be squeezed together in an even smaller space than the snuggler seat, but they are ecstatically happy.

'Pull over and have a toast with us,' she urges as Archie pours chilled fizz into flutes.

Sonny and I navigate the canoe out of the way of passing punters and I carefully turn around in the front seat so I can see everyone better. Archie passes out glasses, first to his new wife, then to me, followed by Sonny, retaining one for himself.

'To a lifetime of love and happiness,' I declare, raising my glass.

'For all of us,' Archie adds pointedly, and then we almost capsize the boat trying to chink glasses.

Matilda looks so beautiful in her floor-skimming flutter-sleeve white dress. Her long dark hair has been left down and is perfectly tousled into gorgeous glossy waves, and she's wearing a crown of tiny white roses. She's glowing.

Archie himself is heartbreakingly handsome, his broad shoulders encased in a slim-fitting black suit and skinny black tie, and his sandy blond hair as messily dishevelled as ever.

'Thank you so much, guys,' Archie says sincerely, his brown eyes shining. 'If it weren't for you two, I don't think this would be happening.'

'It *would* have happened,' Matilda scoffs. 'But yeah.' She grins at us. 'Thank you for helping it to happen sooner rather than later and in such a bloody brilliant manner. This is incredible!' she squeals, reaching her hand into the water and flicking some up in the air.

I laugh and flick some back towards her.

'I'm so happy,' she says, grinning at Archie.

Sonny and I smile at each other over their heads.

He looks hot as hell in a suit that is very similar to Archie's, on Archie's request. Sonny is his best man and, to my amazement and joy, Matilda asked me to be her one and only bridesmaid. Sonny and I were witnesses, signing the register. I have never felt more honoured or flattered.

I'm wearing a floor-skimming dress of my own in emerald silk, also chosen on our London shopping trip. My hair is down and wavy, but pinned back at the sides with costume jewellery emerald-studded golden combs that Matilda gave to me as a bridesmaid thank you gift.

Sonny gets out his camera and clicks off a few shots. He offered to do the photos so Matilda and Archie wouldn't have to stress about finding a wedding photographer at short notice.

I'm not sure this outcome is stress-free for Sonny, but he's chilled. He only wants the best for the people he loves.

'Hannah,' he calls.

I look his way and he clicks off a shot.

I'm getting more used to him photographing me now. I'd wondered if he might ask to do macro shots of *my* eyes, seeing as he was so invested in them in Amsterdam, but he admitted he didn't want to look at me under a microscope; he wanted to take me as he saw me.

There was something quite lovely about that, I thought.

The rest of the evening flies by in a whirlwind of bubbly, confetti and dancing. Archie's cricket pals are here, and Faith too. She and I have a laugh and a bit of a boogie and she drunkenly confesses that she's thrilled Nessa wasn't invited. Archie told us that she's applied for a job in London where her family lives. Can't say I'll miss her if she moves away.

Archie and Matilda are having so much fun that they're in no hurry to call time on the evening. Because Sonny and I are canoeing them home, we decide we'd better cut back on drinking as the night wears on.

It's a sound plan, but we're nevertheless pretty damn tipsy when the four of us stumble down to the river. It's everything we can do to hold the boat steady for our newly-weds to climb in.

Luckily the return journey is downriver so less strenuous

than the trip up. The tide helps carry us home and we're drunk anyway so our strength is superhuman. We talk and laugh until we reach the point in the river where we've agreed we can safely moor up. Sonny and I will return in the morning and paddle back to Charles's, but now we're heading to his.

I feel a thrill at what the rest of the night has in store. The last few days have seen us making up for lost time and it has honestly been so far beyond expectation that it's unfunny.

Archie and Matilda are off on a mini-break tomorrow to Amsterdam. Sonny is putting them up in his apartment, a last farewell before his sale goes through. He's planning on buying a place here in Cambridge and has asked me to help him look. He wants me to move in with him, and while I know we're undoubtedly jumping ahead fast, it doesn't *feel* like it – we've been practically living together for the last couple of months anyway, and let's not forget that we were in a relationship well before I even knew it.

My heart has already said yes to him.

Archie, Matilda, Sonny and I exchange emotional farewells on the muddy banks of the River Cam, no doubt made even more intense by the amount of alcohol we've all consumed. There are lots of 'I love yous' and 'you're the best friends ever' and '*Stranger Things* when we get back, yeahs?'

We make a date for Tuesday and I'm already looking forward to it. We can fight over the snuggler seat when we get there.

Sonny and I walk the rest of the way, hand in hand, falling into his sofabed at the end of our journey – and nearly bouncing off again.

I can't wait to get a proper bed.

*

The next morning, we gingerly paddle back upriver to Grantchester, hung-over but happy. Yesterday couldn't have gone better for our friends and we are elated for them.

Charles and Bertie give us the warmest of welcomes when we arrive at the cottage, Bertie even leaping up on my chest the way she did with my uncle on his return. Charles puts on the kettle and makes us a cuppa and we sit at the kitchen table and tell him about yesterday. He also wants to hear more about my trip to Australia. I had to go straight back to work when I returned, so we've barely seen each other.

'I really must make Australia my next big holiday. Ellen is forever asking me to visit. I won't go for a while, though,' he says, scratching Bertie behind her ears, a fond smile on his face. 'This old girl isn't going to be with me for much longer, sadly.'

'I would always be happy to look after her, I hope you know that,' I say sincerely.

'Oh, I do, dear. I'll keep it in mind if I ever need an excuse to drag you home again.'

I gawp at him.

He winks at me.

'Did you use emotional blackmail to get me to stay put in the UK for a while?'

'It worked, didn't it?' He smiles at Sonny.

'I had no idea you were so manipulative,' I say with amusement.

'I simply wanted you to settle in one place for a bit, my dear, to give you a chance to make proper friends instead of fleeting flirtations with fellow travellers.'

Sonny and I grin at each other. My uncle is a cad.

I use the bathroom before we leave. Charles has closed the left-hand cabinet, as he always did when I lived here. Out of habit, I reach forward and open it a touch until two faces stare back at me.

I am smiling, smiling at life, smiling at Anna.

'It's all going pretty well now, Sis,' I say quietly, looking at her face in the mirror. 'I've found a man who loves me as much as I love him, and I've even come to love his two little girls who remind me so much of you and me. I'll watch them grow over the years and I know I'll never stop thinking about what you and I could have had, what we could have been. I'm so sorry you're not here with me. I'm so sorry I haven't got to watch you grow and find love and happiness. But you *will* always be with me, Anna. I carry you in my name and in my heart. And although I might not talk to you as much as I used to, I'll always love you. Do you know that? I love you.' I take a deep shaky breath, letting the seconds tick by as I stare into her greeny-gold eyes. 'But for now, I'm saying goodbye.'

I reach up and gently push the mirrored cabinet closed.

And I am still smiling as I walk downstairs.

Acknowledgements

My first thanks go to *you*, lovely reader! Whether you've been with me since *Lucy in the Sky* or are new to my books, I can't thank you enough for choosing to read *this* book. I adored writing Hannah and Sonny's story and I hope you enjoyed reading it just as much.

I'm going to be doing a series of auctions to win signed copies in aid of charities related to this book, so if you're interested in bidding for one, please keep an eye on my social media channels and sign up to #TheHiddenPaige at www.paigetoon.com.

Thank you to every book reviewer, blogger, Booktuber, Bookstagrammer and anyone who has ever taken the time to write a few kind words about one of my stories – I read all your reviews and appreciate every single word, so please keep them coming!

Huge thanks to the talented team at Simon & Schuster UK, but especially Rebecca Farrell, Jessica Barratt, Sara Jade Virtue, Pip Watkins, Gill Richardson, Dominic Brendon, Hayley McMullan, Richard Vlietstra, Joe Roche, Amy Fulwood, Rachel Bazan, Maddie Allan, Francesca Sironi, Judith Long, Amy Fletcher, Anne O'Brien and, above all, Suzanne Baboneau, who has been there for me at every stage of this book-writing adventure – I hope you know how much I appreciate you!

Thank you to all of my friends who continue to indulge me when I'm wittering on about people who don't exist, but in particular this lovely lot who read early drafts of *The Minute I Saw You* and gave me some fantastically helpful feedback: Jane Hampton, Katherine Reid, Femke Cole, Rebecca Banks, Dani Atkins and last but not least, Kimberly Atkins, who continues to go above and beyond – thank you!

Also, heartfelt thanks to Ali Watts for her spot-on advice and the team at Penguin Random House ANZ for everything that they continue to do for my books Down Under. Ditto to Carla Grosch and the team at S. Fischer Verlage who have published my books in Germany for the past fourteen years and are long overdue a HUGE DANKE!

I am also very grateful to the following people for their help with my research: Hannah Burgess, Sophie Burgess, Russ and the team at David Clulow Opticians in Cambridge, Barry Griffiths at Jimmy's Cambridge, Will Pearce from Vision Care for Homeless People, Emma at Cambridge Cyrenians, Will Hill from the School of Art at Anglia Ruskin and Dr Lewis Barnes, Georgie Barnes and their dog Berry, who in no small way inspired a certain black Labrador in this book.

Please note that the character of Evelyn is dedicated to Debbie McGreevy in memory of her late mother.

Finally, thank you, always, to my family: my parents Vern and Jen Schuppan and my parents-in-law Ian and Helga Toon. And above all, my husband, Greg (who does so much behind the scenes for my books but hates me gushing about him in my acknowledgements), and my kids, Indy and Idha. Thank you all for putting up with my madness when I'm on deadline – I love you to bits xxx

Please turn over to read

An Unusual Valentine's,

a short story I shared on The Hidden Paige

Introduction

The Minute I Saw You is actually a spin-off of the short story below, which first introduced Archie and Matilda to readers. I wrote this story a few years ago for a local Cambridge magazine and have since shared it in #TheHiddenPaige (my free newsletter – sign up at paigetoon.com if you haven't already). Many of you asked for an update on Archie and Matilda afterwards so I hope *The Minute I Saw You* delivered!

I live in Cambridge and it's been a joy to write about the city I'm now so familiar with. Readers of *One Perfect Summer* and *One Perfect Christmas* will know that I've written about Cambridge before – we actually moved to the city at the same time as I was writing about the heroine, Alice, moving here, so I felt like I was getting to know Cambridge along with Alice herself. I hope these readers enjoyed the Alice and Joe cameo in this book!

But back to Archie and Matilda and the story of how they met... Enjoy!

An Unusual Valentine's

I was seven, the first time my dad took me punting. I'd gone to stay with him after the divorce, and I remember looking up at him, and my heart hurting because he was no longer an everyday part of my life.

Now he's no longer a part of my life at all.

My eyes sting with tears as I lift the pole clear of the water, steeling myself as freezing-cold droplets run up the insides of my coat sleeves. I let the pole slip back through my fingers until it hits the riverbed, and propel the punt along.

It's Valentine's Day and the Cam is full of loved-up couples. I studiously ignore a man kissing a woman under the Bridge of Sighs. Mark and I may have broken up months ago, but right now everything feels raw. I don't actually know why I'm doing this to myself.

Dad would have been sixty-eight today if cancer hadn't got the better of him. Only my father, the least romantic man in the world, according to my mum, could have been born on the most romantic day of the year. He was nothing if not contrary.

Tucking a lock of dark hair behind my ear, I let the pole drift up to the surface, using it as a rudder to correct the boat's position as I navigate a bend in the river. Up ahead, a group of punting novices are creating havoc outside the Wren library. Students, probably – two couples. Their laughter carries across the water as the guy charged with pole duty tries desperately to straighten up the boat while his mate madly paddles an oar at the other end. They're currently straddling half of the river with a packed tour boat bearing down on them. I really don't have the energy for this, I think with a sigh. And then the professional punter on the tour collides with their boat, sending it sluicing through the water towards the bank as his dozen passengers overexcitedly cry out.

Good. Now I can nip up the outside while the rookies are drifting.

My plan is sound, until the pillock with the pole gets it stuck in the mud.

'No!' he shouts, hanging on for dear life while his friends roar with laughter.

'Let go or you'll fall in,' I command, words spilling out of my mouth of their own volition.

He obeys immediately and his punt coasts away from the embedded pole. His hair is dark blond and a dishevelled mess, but his eyes are warm and brown, and right now they're staring imploringly at me.

'Help,' he beseeches with a crooked, lovely smile.

That'll teach me for interfering. 'Hang on,' I mutter as I

go to retrieve his pole, yanking hard until it comes loose. His friends cheer.

'How do you do it?' he asks hopelessly as I return to his side. He's gorgeous: tall, broad and older than I initially suspected. Late-twenties, at a guess – about my age.

'Practice,' I reply with an amused shrug, handing over the pole. His fingers accidentally overlap mine, making me jolt. I quickly let go, but I can feel his gaze on me as I blush and look away, inadvertently locking eyes with one of his female passengers – his girlfriend, judging by the poisonous look she's giving me.

'You're useless, Archie, let me have a turn,' she snaps as she wobbles to her feet.

'Easy, Nessa,' he scolds her, trying to steady the boat.

Time to go...

'Good luck,' I call as I set off.

'Wait!' he replies, compelling me to glance over my shoulder at him. To my surprise, he appears oddly torn. 'Thank you.'

'You're welcome,' I reply.

I'm still feeling unsettled about my run-in with a total stranger when I relinquish my punt to the boatyard a short while later. I've barely thought about Dad, which was what I'd intended this little jaunt to be about: doing something symbolic on his birthday. I'm also here to sort out his house – a task I've been putting off for weeks. I've always loved coming up to Cambridge, but his cosy home feels cold and empty without him. I should go and get started, but I can't quite get my feet to move off this bridge. I stare in a daze at the water tumbling over the weir below.

Happy birthday, Dad. I miss you so much.

As I brush away my tears, I see him – Archie – heading towards The Mill. His eyes widen and his footsteps falter as he catches my eye, and then he calls after his friends and they continue into the pub without him.

'Hello again,' he says with a smile as he approaches.

'Hi,' I reply, butterflies filling my stomach despite myself. His girlfriend is not going to like this. 'You made it back alive, then.'

'Yeah.' He shrugs. 'My sister's friend was a natural.' *Sister's friend?* His smile fades. 'Hey, are you okay?' he asks with concern.

'I'm fine.' I dig around in my bag for a tissue. How embarrassing.

'Want me to beat him up for you?' he offers affably in an attempt to cheer me up.

I laugh and shake my head. 'I'm not crying about a boy. My dad passed away recently.'

'Oh.' He immediately looks crestfallen. 'I'm sorry. When?'

'Just before Christmas. It's his birthday today.' I pause. 'I don't know why I'm telling you this.'

He smiles a small smile and holds out his hand. 'I'm Archie.'

'I know.' My palm tingles inexplicably as our skin connects.

'Are you going to tell me your name?' he asks with amusement.

'Matilda,' I reply, belatedly extracting my hand.

He shifts on his feet. 'Um, do you think… Could I buy you lunch? I owe you for saving me from falling in the river.' He seems nervous, although I can't imagine why.

I glance towards the pub where his friends are. 'Shouldn't

you be getting back to your friends?' *More specifically, your girlfriend?*

'Nah, I've seen enough of them for today. They can entertain themselves.' He leans against the bridge wall and folds his arms. 'Anyway, they're not strictly *my* friends.'

'Whose friends are they, then?' I'm confused.

'My sister's. Her boyfriend's at Cambridge. She and her pal are visiting.'

'Nessa is not your girlfriend?'

'Christ, no.' He looks horrified. 'No, I'm single.'

My butterflies go haywire.

Fifteen minutes later, we're sitting at a packed bench table in Fitzbillies, near the window. It's not very private, but the atmosphere is buzzing.

'Do you live nearby?' Archie asks as he takes a sip of his raspberry lemonade.

'No, London,' I reply. 'I'm just here for the weekend to sort out Dad's house.'

He raises one eyebrow. 'You're doing that in one weekend?'

'Not likely, when I'm sitting here with you.' I smile at the look on his face. 'I'll have to come back. I was supposed to arrive on Wednesday night, but my boss decided she was too busy for me to take two days off.'

'What do you do?' he asks.

'Bookkeeping.' Snore. 'You?'

'I'm a graphic designer.'

'Wow.' How cool! 'Do you live in Cambridge?'

'Yeah, I've got a flat on the other side of town. Where's your dad's place?'

'In Newnham, a few minutes' walk from here.'

'Newnham?' He looks impressed. 'You'll have no trouble selling it, then.'

'I know. Numerous estate agents keep telling me. They've been hounding me for weeks,' I explain with a wry smile.

'Bloodsuckers,' he commiserates. 'Is that the plan, then? To put it on the market?'

I stare down at my fingernails and nod. 'I have to pay inheritance tax, but I hate letting it go.'

He reaches across the table and squeezes my hand, and then the waitress appears with our food, forcing us to break apart. We tuck into our cheese toasties, but I seem to have lost my appetite. There's not much spare room in my stomach with all of the winged creatures flying around.

'If you live in Cambridge, how come you can't punt?' I ask, trying to make casual conversation.

He laughs. 'It's not a requirement by law. How did you learn?'

'Dad taught me. It's one of the things we did together when I came to visit.'

We sit there talking about our respective families and jobs for almost an hour, but at the back of my mind is the constant, pressing reminder that I have work to do.

'I guess I should be going,' I say reluctantly as we stand on the pavement outside the café and pull on our coats.

'Do you really have to?' he asks with disappointment, checking his watch. 'We could go for a walk or something.'

'I'd love to hang out, but I have so much to do.'

'Then let me help,' he proposes. 'Two hands are better than one.' He waggles them in front of my face to demonstrate his point.

'Four hands are better than two, don't you mean?' I correct him good-naturedly, while reeling from his offer.

'You're an excellent bookkeeper,' he comments seriously.

'I can actually count up to a hundred,' I reply.

'Stop boasting.' He nudges my arm and his face breaks out into a grin. 'Come on, Matilda. Just say yes. I've got nothing better to do.'

'Are you sure?' I ask hopefully. I'd love to spend more time with him, even in these sad circumstances.

'I'm sure,' he replies.

By the time the evening comes around, I'm shattered, both emotionally and physically. I keep reminding Archie that he can leave at any time, and he keeps insisting that he wants to be here. This task would have been a hell of a lot harder if it weren't for the hottie standing before me. I can't believe fate has come up trumps for once.

'Thank you,' I say with sincerity, meeting Archie's beautiful brown eyes over a pile of boxes. We've talked non-stop all day. I've told him things that I haven't told anyone – about my life, my loves, my ambitions… I feel like I know him – *really* know him – yet we haven't even kissed. It's bizarre. 'Are you hungry?' I ask. 'We could order in a pizza?'

'Sounds good.'

As I go to get my phone out of my bag, he grabs my hand and tugs me towards him, making me gasp with surprise. My heart hammers against my ribcage as he stares at me intently.

'I think I've made a mistake,' he says quietly. My stomach flips. What sort of mistake? What does he mean? 'Once this house is packed up, you won't need to come back.' He sounds despondent.

I smile with relief and squeeze his hands. 'I'll still have to return. There's loads to do.'

'Why don't you quit your job and move up here permanently?' he asks.

'I can't just do that.'

'Matilda, of course you can,' he states resolutely. 'You hate your job. You despise your boss. Your flatmate is a nutter. Once you sell this house and pay the tax, you'll still have more than enough to buy something smaller, mortgage free. And you'll have plenty spare to go back to university and retrain to do anything you want to do.'

My head swims with possibilities. Is he right? Could I move here permanently, have a fresh start in a city that I adore? *Will* I still adore being here, when Dad is not?

Looking up at Archie's face, I have a funny feeling that I will…

My dad might not have been a romantic who believed in fate, but he did advocate making the most of the opportunities we're given.

And right then and there, I resolve to make the most of this one.

'Do you think I can kiss you now?' Archie asks softly, cupping my face with his hands.

'Please do,' I reply with a smile.

Q&A with Paige Toon

After over a decade of being able to expect a new book from me every May, something went a little wrong this year, didn't it?! Because of Covid-19, we had to push back the paperback release of *The Minute I Saw You* to August, so to make it extra special, we decided to include some additional content. As well as the short story featuring Archie and Matilda, we also invited readers of the eBook edition (which came out in May) to take part in an exclusive Q&A. Thank you so much to everyone who sent in questions – my inbox was flooded and I had a hard time choosing between them! In the case of people asking something similar, I went with the reader who asked it first.

I really hope you enjoy this extra insight into the book and what goes on behind the scenes. I loved writing this one!

Paige x

Bryony Hughes asks: What inspired you to write this book?
There are two parts to my inspiration. A friend got the giggles during an eye test with a young, hot optician – I thought that would be a fun way to start a novel, but that idea alone wasn't enough to drive me to write it. It wasn't until Hannah's backstory emerged that the two ideas came together. I watched a film on a flight to Australia last Easter – *The Children Act*, which was based on the book by Ian McEwan. There's a small reference at the beginning of the film to a conjoined twins court case ruling. For religious reasons, the parents want their children to remain joined, even though neither child will survive. If they are separated, one would have a good chance of survival. The judge has to make that decision. I jolted awake with jetlag at three in the morning and thought, what would it be like to be the surviving twin as an adult, knowing that, if a court of law hadn't intervened, your parents would have sacrificed you along with your sibling? How could you forgive them? Would you suffer survivor's guilt? The idea for Hannah grew from that, even though the circumstances around her separation ended up being very different.

Heidi Philpott asks: Have you ever had a 'minute I saw you' moment?
I once spotted a guy on the other side of a dancefloor at my university ball and drunkenly pointed at him and shouted to my friend, 'There's a good looking one, there!' I had just been lamenting to her about there not being any hot guys around. It was completely out of character for me to do that, even drunk – I used to be really shy about my feelings for boys – but luckily

I did because that guy laughingly came over to chat to me and he's now my husband!

Pernille Meldgaard Pedersen asks: How do you come up with your characters? Do they appear, complete, in your head, or do their personalities come as you write?

Hannah and Sonny were very strong by the time I sat down to write this book, even though they only came to me a few months before I began their story. Usually I've thought about characters for about a year, so they've had time to live and breathe inside my head, and when you throw in research and really get to know them and what they might have been through, their personalities grow even stronger. I've got a very clear idea of the three main characters for my next book, but there will always be elements that also develop as I'm writing.

Laura Cheetham asks: Whose character arc did you think up first, Hannah or Sonny's?

Hannah's. Sonny's character arc developed over time. I didn't initially know what had happened to him as a child – that fact unveiled itself to me as I was writing. I felt there was a reason for him being the way he was, but I didn't realise that it would be so dark. I think, in hindsight, I maybe did know deep down, but I resisted acknowledging it for a while because it was too upsetting.

Corinne Thomas asks: Did you have to take time away from writing because of how emotional the book is?

No. If anything, that emotion drove me to carry on – I felt so connected to these characters and wanted to see them right.

There were some very emotional scenes in this one – and I still can't read Hannah's last words to Anna at the end without tears in my eyes – but because their journey was ultimately uplifting and there was so much light mixed in with the dark, I found it more joyful than painful to write.

Gemma Barber asks: What is your favourite part of the book?
The scenes that come to mind are Amsterdam, when Hannah and Sonny kiss for the first time, and the revelation that comes after; the night when Hannah drunkenly admits she fancies Sonny, and the next day in Grantchester Meadows when he tells her they're not 'friends' and ends up kissing her. I think that last one is my overall favourite.

Kerry-Ann McDade asks: What was the hardest part to write?
I didn't struggle with this one much, to be honest. I probably found it hardest to write the scenes with Hannah's parents, but that was mostly because I wanted to get her back to Sonny and what I knew was finally going to happen between them… I've struggled more with other books. *Baby Be Mine*: that moment when Christian finds out Meg's secret – that was a killer as I was very fond of Christian and didn't want to hurt him. Probably even harder than that, though, was the final chapter of *Five Years From Now* when Nell pulls up outside the cottage after collecting Van from the airport – in writing time, they sat in that car for twenty-four hours because I just could not bring myself to reveal how life had unfolded. That book broke me.

Jen Elvy asks: Do you have a clear physical picture of the characters in your head as you write?

They're not crystal clear – sometimes I'll see their eyes or their hair or what they're wearing but, and this sounds weird, they're almost more of a feeling. I have an initial idea of what they'll look like – in fact, I saw a picture of a male model when I was trying to describe Sonny's hairstyle and was certainly inspired by him, but now when I think of Sonny he doesn't look like that guy. He doesn't look like anyone I know, which is why I find it so hard to say who I'd cast in a character's role if my books were ever made into films. I love hearing reader suggestions though!

Louise Potter asks: How did you come up with Sonny's name?

Names are strange. Usually it takes me a while to settle on one after throwing it around inside my mind for a while to see if it fits. 'Sonny' came to me out of the blue and I thought it worked for him because he was kind of cool, but then that cool vibe didn't tie in with his parents, hence the whole Sonny Jim bit. I've started books and changed names as I've written – I've even changed one right at the end because the new name tied into a title I liked: *Chasing Daisy*!

Roxy Butcher asks: What was your inspiration for Sonny's career as a photographer and the exhibition he organises?

I knew early on that Sonny would be a photographer because I wanted him to be inspired by Hannah's eyes and ask to pho-tograph them, thus prolonging their eye-to-eye contact. I also thought, as part of his therapy, he may feel compelled to give back and do something good. The idea of an exhibition to raise money for Vision Care for Homeless People came to me because there are so many homeless people on the streets of Cambridge. Once I started looking into it, I was disappointed to discover how hard it is to get free eyecare and was glad of the opportunity to highlight the issue.

Shannon Palmer asks: You've said on social media that Hannah and Sonny are two of your favourite characters – what makes them stand out above all the rest?

Perhaps it's because their journey is so intense. I've always had shades of light and dark in my stories, but the gap between light and dark here feels more extreme than in other books. I loved the chemistry between Hannah and Sonny and how they still made me smile and gave me butterflies, even though they were carrying around such heavy burdens. After everything they'd been through, I desperately wanted the best for them and felt very close to them by the end.

Sarah Hunt asks: What is Sonny's aftershave?!!

This question made me laugh. I don't know but I wish I did – I'd get some for my husband! I did think about sniffing a bunch of male aftershaves until I found one I loved, but decided to leave it to our imaginations.

Beth Kitchen asks: So many of your books are set in far-flung places. Why did you set this one so close to home? Did you enjoy it more or less than books where you'd be taking research trips?

I absolutely loved setting this one close to home. Perhaps this is also why I found it so easy to write, because I was already in tune with the characters and their settings. I adore writing about gorgeous places abroad, and I did that here with Amsterdam and the Murray River in South Australia, but going somewhere on holiday is very different to living and breathing a place. You definitely have to work harder when it comes to the writing process and usually there's more research involved online when you come home. I didn't have to do any research with my Cambridge and Grantchester settings, apart from popping to The Orchard for afternoon tea and going to a few pubs!

Chloe Shortall asks: Are there any characters who are still hovering around in your imagination and might reappear in a book soon?
Most of them hover, some more than others. I've been thinking a bit about Johnny, Meg and Jessie – lots of readers have written to me recently asking me to write another Jessie Jefferson novel. I can't imagine when I'll find the time, but I'm thinking on it! Angie and Alessandro from *If You Could Go Anywhere* are also in my mind as I said I'd write a short story for them. I had an idea for it, but then Covid-19 struck, and my idea has changed somewhat. I'd love to touch base with them to see how they're getting on during lockdown.

Faye Evans asks: I read that you listened to 'This Town' by Kygo a lot while writing the ending to *Five Years From Now* and it helped inspire the tone of the book. Is there a song that you listened to a lot while writing *The Minute I Saw You*?

Sufjan Stevens' 'Mystery of Love' and 'Visions of Gideon' from the *Call Me By Your Name* soundtrack are the songs that I kept coming back to. They channelled a lot of emotion in me, partly because of the film itself and the look in Timothée Chalamet's eyes at the end. I also listened to a lot of Yonaka, Billie Eilish and Catfish and the Bottlemen.

Anne Elizabeth asks: Would you ever write a full novel from a male POV?
Never say never, but my initial reaction is no. I like to be inside the female characters' heads, feeling what they're feeling and falling in love with gorgeous guys.

Maisy Harbert asks: Do you have a certain place where you find it easiest/most comfortable to write your book?
I have a small study which was initially created as a home-work station for our kids – it has no door, is right next to their bedrooms and is stiflingly hot in summer, so I only really use it in the autumn and winter months when the kids are at school. If I need peace and quiet, I go to the camper-van at the end of the garden. It's where I am now, actually. Readers of *The Last Piece of My Heart* would recognise it as Hermie, the campervan Bridget uses in the book. Sadly, Hermie had to be retired as he broke down one too many times, but as I'd always planned to build a garden office, I got to keep him!

Katherine Henderson asks: Looking back on the book, now that it's finished, would you change anything about the story if you could?

I don't think so, no. I'm at peace with all of my books, although I do recognise that *One Perfect Summer* felt unresolved. Many readers contacted me, asking for a sequel, and then my publisher suggested writing an ebook short story. It was the first one I'd written and I loved getting the chance to add more to the story after a pause to reflect.

Hayley Thorpe asks: Did you think readers might guess the plot to only half of the story – that Hannah was a twin, but not that she was conjoined – and was that your intention?

Yes, I thought they would probably guess that she was a twin – I'd left a trail of breadcrumbs – but I didn't think anyone would guess the conjoined part as it's quite unusual.

Britta Pescatore asks: How important is it for you to place your novels in 'real' landscapes? I imagine it would be easier to make up a town based on a real town?

I love writing about real places because it makes the stories feel even more real to me, and also readers can go to visit them – I'm often hearing from readers who do this! This does sometimes pose problems though. In the case of small towns, like, for example, Coober Pedy in *If You Could Go Anywhere*, I felt I needed to be careful not to include anything negative because I wouldn't want to offend anyone who lived there.

Tessa Stewart asks: What made you decide to link characters across books? I squealed when Alice and Joe made an appearance!

It's something that started with *Lucy in the Sky*. Writing that book was one of the happiest times of my life and, afterwards, I didn't want to let Lucy and Nathan go. I wanted to imagine them living on and having this whole other life outside of the book. Having read some of Marian Keyes' books and getting such a thrill at hearing about the Walsh sisters across various novels, I realised I could do something similar. During the editing process for *Lucy*, it occurred to me that one of the minor characters could become the main protagonist in my next book, *Johnny Be Good*, so I re-wrote my description of Lucy's stepbrother Tom's girlfriend to fit in with the character of Meg. Meg, the heroine in *Johnny Be Good*, was therefore able to ask after Lucy and Nathan. My readers loved the link and I've since found a way to include crossover characters in most of my novels.

Paige Blythe asks: Do you worry when you're writing new characters that people won't fall in love with them as much as you did?

Hello fellow Paige! No, I don't. Even after all these years, I still write for myself, and I've come to realise that my readers love the same things I love! I remember my publisher, Suzanne Baboneau, once saying to me: Write the book you're passionate about – it's our job to sell it. I really believe there's an audience out there for everyone, but you must stay true to yourself. I feel as though I have best job in the world, and that's because I'm doing what I love rather than what someone else is telling me to do. I hope that's always the case throughout my career. I do recognise, however, that I'm lucky in that the sort of books I want to write are also quite commercially successful!

Kirsty Oughton asks: I've heard it only takes you a couple of months to write a book – what is your schedule like during this time for other things?

It usually takes around three months. Although I often have the best intentions of starting earlier, I only really get into the swing of writing in September when the kids go back to school after the summer holidays. My deadline is the end of November. It always takes me a while to get going, but suddenly the characters will take off and develop lives of their own and there will be days when I can't write fast enough. I work better to tight deadlines – it was the same when I worked at weekly magazine, *Heat* – I'm more focused and in tune with what I'm doing. But during this time, I'm also a lot closer to my stress threshold! There's so little time to cram in everything else that needs doing, from housework to social media and my accounts, and I'm a mum, so I want to be on hand for the kids when they get home from school. As soon as the book is finished, I spend a long time playing catch up. I recently went through my Gmail account and realised I hadn't replied to anyone for six months!

Sophie Hodgetts asks: How do you think Hannah and Sonny would cope during lockdown?

I think they'd be pretty happy being holed up at home together, but I can imagine it would be more stressful for Sonny as he would want to see his girls, and Rochelle might not be happy about sharing custody at a time like this. I'm sure she'd relent, but there would be so much pressure on Sonny and Hannah to keep them very well protected. Sonny would probably struggle with Rochelle seeing her boyfriend as he doesn't live with her, but maybe the situation would speed up their relationship too – I'm sure that's the case with many in reality!

Tanja Capuana-Parisi asks: You write about so many difficult issues in this book – how do you manage to still keep the tone light?

I feel like the characters kept it light. From the moment they stepped onto the page they had strong personalities. Their flirty banter was great fun to write, and it seemed to fit with their personalities that they would be capable of dealing with darkness and not dwelling, so we were never too far away from lighter times. Sometimes it takes time to create the right tone for a character, but not these two.

Chloe Watt asks: Can we hope to see more of Hannah and Sonny?

Surely you know the answer to that one! I hate letting all my characters go and these may be my all-time favourites, so I'm sure they'll pop up in future books.

Amyleigh Christie asks: Have you got any ideas in mind for your next book?

I do! I'm researching it at the moment. It's the story of Leah, whose parents were foster carers. She grew up sharing her home with troubled teenagers, one of whom was George, who she developed a special bond with. Also in the picture is Theo, the son of a local landowner, who has issues of his own. It's a story about love and care and it's told in alternating chapters between Then, when the trio were teenagers, and Now, when they're in their early thirties. It's going to be emotional!

if you could go anywhere

**How do you find where you're going,
if you don't know where you're from...**

Angie has always wanted to travel. But at twenty-seven, she has
barely stepped outside the small mining town where she was
born. Instead, she discovers the world through stories told to
her by passing travellers, dreaming that one day she'll see it all
for herself.

When her grandmother passes away, leaving Angie with no
remaining family, she is ready to start her own adventures. Then
she finds a letter revealing the address of the father she never
knew, and realises instantly where her journey must begin: Italy.

As Angie sets out to find the truth – about her family, her past
and who she really is – will mysterious and reckless Italian
Alessandro help guide the way?

AVAILABLE NOW IN PAPERBACK AND EBOOK

**SIMON &
SCHUSTER**

one
perfect
christmas

and other
stories

One year after movie star Joseph Strike swept schoolteacher
Alice off her feet, they are spending Christmas together in
snowy Cambridge. But despite the romantic setting, Alice can't
help but question whether life in the spotlight is really what she
wants. Will a Christmas wedding provide some perspective? Or
will the life she'd be leaving behind be too much to lose?

In this irresistible collection, bestselling author Paige Toon
reunites a much-loved cast from across her fifteen novels,
including *Johnny Be Good, The One We Fell in Love With* and
Thirteen Weddings. Fall in love with nine witty and heartfelt
romantic stories, published in print for the very first time.

AVAILABLE NOW IN PAPERBACK AND EBOOK

**SIMON &
SCHUSTER**